Asia's Journey 2121

Safehouse

by

ai engels

Xpyr Press

Asia's Journey 2121 Safehouse, published by Xpyr Press, Los Angeles, CA

www.xpyrpress.com

Cover and text design by Xpyr Press
Printed and bound by Kindle Direct Publishing
Printed in the United States of America

ISBN: 978-1-7346514-4-7

BISAC: Fiction / Action & Adventure

Edited with Grammarly, and other AI tools.
Cover photo by Dall-E image generator.

Printed on recycled paper

dedicated to

Naielli Cobo

Climate Activist
Los Angeles

1. El Norte

It was 10 AM in Meiners Oaks, Los Padres forest. A diverse collection of forty women and children trudged through the arid mountains. To avoid capture, most of the females were dressed like men. Their clothes were stained with sweat and dust, and their lips chapped from dehydration. Younger children clung to their Mothers, their slight faces etched with anxiety and weariness.

Leaving the cooler Pacific Coast, the caravan traveled 30 miles Southeast for four days, trying to cross the mountains. The map promised a spring beyond the hills. It was an antiquated, tattered paper from when the 1.75 million-acre forest was greener. But after several massive wildfires, eighty-five percent of the trees were ash and dead stumps.

The leader, Asia, knew better than to trust fragments from a dead civilization. The once-flowing upwelling was likely a dry layer of dust and bones. Still, she had to check it out as the group was almost out of water.

She slowly treaded to the front of the convoy. Asia was 39, five feet four inches tall, and weighed 125 pounds. She spoke with a Southern California accent, and her drive belied her stature.

"You're doing great," Asia rasped at the weary figures behind her. "It'll start to cool off in a few hours." She was exhausted from the four-day march, but her courage was unshaken. She gazed into the distance, searching for moisture.

The Sun was like a heat lamp, and the cloudless sky offered no relief. It was 115 degrees Fahrenheit (46° Celsius) with 45 percent humidity. Asia was worried more about temperature than humidity.

Relative humidity of 60 percent or more hampered sweat evaporation and the body's cooling ability. It could lead to heat exhaustion, heat stroke, or worse. Humidity was an issue on the Coast, but it usually hovered below 50 percent in the woods and far less in the desert. It was hot but would get much hotter after they advanced out of the wooded area in a few days. To survive the heat, they needed to drink lots of water, and finding water was a daily challenge.

Asia knew they had no choice but to head North. Central California had become a climate graveyard with soaring temperatures, drought, and fires year-round. Food and water sources were scarce, and the coastal population had become desperate and violent.

The previous Summer, the region suffered from protracted heat waves and hot Santa Ana winds. Tens of thousands died from heat stroke. The Summer of 2121 would be hotter. And there were no cooling stations. After the collapse of civilization two decades ago, few public facilities remained.

The worn-out bodies staggered through the hills. It smelt strongly of burnt vegetation, a memento of the large wildfire that ravaged the timberland in January. "Keep your face covered," she cautioned. "It'll help from breathing in toxic ash."

Asia's mind raced. Where could she find water? She was becoming anxious and started to hyperventilate. She had to calm down. She took a deep breath and tried to focus on their route.

North was the only direction that offered relief. It had cooler weather and places where the Sun's wrath had not yet consumed the land. There, they might find water, shade, and safety. Coastal California was controlled by different gangs and militias, and no place was safe. It was especially hazardous for females and minorities.

The caravan had to travel East through the charred forest into the desert, then head North. They were stuck between coastal gangs, burnt forests, and interior desert. Asia chose the desert. They trudged forward, every step a battle against the undulating hills.

"Lower your voices, children." Lian, 26, warned. "There may be pedos lurking." The no-nonsense guard led the security team. She stood five feet six inches tall, weighed 120 pounds, and spoke with a Northern California accent. Lian was unofficially the second in charge, and the children in the middle of the convoy became quiet.

The female collective formed at the overcrowded Santa Barbara shelter on the Pacific Coast. At the sanctuary, european and latino gangs preyed upon females and kidnapped dozens of girls for the sex trade. The women were determined to save their daughters and opted to leave the unguarded asylum.

After abandoning the shelter, the caravan was stalked by gangs on Route 192, heading South along the Coast. Lian and the other guards repelled the assaults, but the girls remained vulnerable. On the third day, they trekked East into the sparsely populated forest and remained free from attacks for two days.

When civilization collapsed, gold and girls became the main currency between male militias. Pre-pubescent girls were the most sought-after commodity besides gold. But any female could be captured and traded. The only exception was older women, Crones, who had little value in the overwhelmingly racist and sexist post-apocalypse environment.

The collective took a break from the hilly terrain and sat in the shade of an overhanging pine tree. All around, millions of green trees were reduced to scorched wasteland. The two main guards, Lian and Xóchitl, scrutinized the area for trouble. Xóchitl was 24, five feet five inches tall, and weighed 125 pounds. She spoke with a Chicana accent.

Lisa, 11, glanced at Lian. "How far do we have to go?" Her speech faltered with the fatigue of days on the road. Lian shrugged.

Xóchitl rose slowly to her feet and met Lisa's gaze. "If we push ourselves and walk ten miles every day," she paused, letting the words sink in, "we have about

31 days until we reach the Safehouse at Cantua Creek. It's 200 miles from here, but we can do it."

The convoy resumed hiking. Asia led the line downhill after the Crones caught up. The cluster of Elders included Hehewuti, 74; Zaniya, 65; Mary, 61; Kuan-Yin, 60; and Zenobia, 58.

Lian hiked ahead to check for signs of pedophile hunters. The men worked with gangs and were known for preying on vulnerable girls. She saw nothing and motioned the others onward. The tattered figures advanced solemnly beneath the blazing Sun. The Crones and Mothers walked in the middle of the line, using umbrellas to shade the children.

Since leaving the shelter, the Crones' senses were keener. Their speech and movement were synchronized, almost like a ritual. They functioned closely with the rhythms of nature, the ultimate source of their allegiance. They called this force 'Gaia,' the Great Earth Goddess, and believed she guided and protected them on their journey.

Zaniya stopped for a benediction. The Crone was five feet six inches tall, weighed 110 pounds, and spoke with a California accent. She spread her arms broadly and entreated, "We stand like the mountains, unmovable, grounded, and eternally wise. Our spirit flows with the wind, and our strength is rooted in the Earth. May the Goddess be with us. Blessed be."

2. Thirst

It was 4 PM under a cloudless sky in the Southern Los Padres Forest. The climate evacuees, a group of 37 females and three boys, kept a steady pace in the 118°F (48°C) weather. Their leader, Asia, a woman of strong character and unwavering determination, was grateful.

The convoy traveled 15 miles South from Santa Barbara near Route 192, and two attacks left them shaken but unharmed. From the Coast, they turned left and trekked 15 miles East inland into the forest along Route 150. They were unprepared for the devastation they witnessed, mile after mile of dead stumps and silent hills. It was like the aftermath of a massive meteor strike, except the wiped-out vegetation was caused by man-made climate change.

After four days along Route 150, they finally headed North near Route 33. In the post-apocalypse, roads were no longer used as motorways. They were littered with potholes, covered in rockslides, and missing vast sections of asphalt. Besides, few vehicles remained operable.

They had another thirty miles to go in the once-verdant woods until they reached the barren Mohave desert. Their water supply was dangerously low, and they were in a desperate race against time.

Asia's gaze swept over the weary collection of females. The children, drained of energy, could barely climb the hilly terrain. Red-faced and silent, they clung to their Mothers and older siblings, too fatigued to even cry. Yet, their spirit in the face of such adversity was commendable.

The Mothers showed signs of their own malaise. Their steps faltered, and they struggled to keep pace. The two remaining canteens were circulated between the children. Each took a meager sip before passing it on to the next child.

The weight of her promise to the female collective of safety and a better future pressed heavily on Asia. As the day dragged on, her assurance seemed more like a far-off mirage. 'Was it a mistake going through the scarred forest?' she wondered.

Suddenly, Ma'at, 12, stumbled and collapsed into the ground. Her alarmed Mother, Simone, dropped to her knees to check on the child. Asia hurried over.

Ma'at was burning up. Her lips were chapped, and her body was limp. She tugged on her Mother's sleeve in anguish, "Mommy, I'm thirsty," she said. Her thin face was flushed from the relentless warmth.

The Mother used her umbrella to shade her child, fanning Ma'at's body with a piece of cardboard. "I know, baby. We'll find water soon." Simone, 40, crooned, trying to hide her exhaustion. She comforted her child with the only thing she had left, love.

Asia reached into her pack, pulling out the last of her water. It was barely a sip, but she handed it to Ma'at. The other children watched, longing for a drink, but said nothing. They knew their bitter reality.

"Mama, am I going to die?" Ma'at enquired weakly.

Simone swallowed hard. She forced a smile and fanned Ma'at's forehead. "No, sweetheart," she reassured. "We have to keep going, okay?"

Asia helped Ma'at to her feet, trying to mask her tiredness. "Come on, daughter." She wrapped her arm around the child. "I'll carry you." Simone nodded. Asia heaved Ma'at onto her hips and turned to the rest. "We keep moving. Until we find water."

The assembly pressed on, following Asia's lead. They all wore similar full-body, light-colored clothing with head and face coverings to block the Sun and ash. The women and Mothers wrapped their hair and wore loose-fitting pants and shirts similar to men. The scouts and girls shaved their heads and dressed to appear as boys. A few Crones wore wraps and shawls.

Every minute felt like an hour, with the hills and heat sapping their strength. But Asia pushed on. 'We need to find water fast,' she thought. She stared into the burnt hills, searching for any indication of relief. She had to find a way to keep them going, to prevent their motivation from unraveling.

"Only a little further," Asia called out. "There's a spring not far from here. Freshwater. We'll rest there." She had no idea if the fountain existed or had dried up like the others. It was a necessary lie, one of several she invented to keep them going. Stopping meant increasing their risk of attack since they were still close to the lawless Coast. Her strategic thinking was a demonstration of her cautious leadership.

The Sun was relentless, a fiery orb that radiated through space onto the hapless Earth. The atmosphere glimmered with heat, distorting the horizon into a mirage of false hope. Asia kept trotting forward, checking the landscape for any sign of water or shelter. The children's footsteps dragged. Their once lively chatter was replaced by the reticence of near collapse.

The climate evacuees trudged on, and the path shifted to a shaded valley. The hills were less suffocating, enough to spark a glimmer of optimism in the leader.

"Look." Asia pointed to a line of green in the distance. "We're almost there."

The limp bodies lifted their heads, tracing Asia's finger. Seeing something other than dead trees and blackened soil energized them, and their pace quickened.

When they drew closer, Asia's confidence began to waver. The green line was not an unburnt area of lush trees. It was a thick cacti wall of tangled, sharp branches like a spiked fortification. Asia hesitated for a moment, weighing the risks.

The grove was green, but it could be dangerous. Snakes, coyotes, cougars, or worse, might lurk within. But it could also be their salvation. The spiky trees were life saviors since the Crones could squeeze water droplets from their succulent limbs. And there might be a freshwater source hidden within the thicket.

"Come on," Asia urged, stepping into the embrace of the grove. "We'll stop here for a while."

The exhausted refugees tagged along, grateful for the rest. The temperature dropped inside the cacti stand, and their steps became lighter.

The caravan rested, and Asia allowed herself to breathe. She stretched out on the ground and covered her face, trying to unwind. But her thoughts stormed. They had eluded more gang attacks, but the real challenge was hydration. She had to find water.

She sat up and observed her community with pride. Mothers comforted the children with cacti drips, and the Crones squeezed enough liquid for dinner. After that, it was only thirst. 'I can't let them down,' she mused. 'I've brought them this far and have to keep them going.'

She needed to find a better source of water. Without it, the grove could be their final resting place. She took a deep breath and rose to her feet. She would explore the forest thoroughly and find the desperately needed liquid. Her day was not over. Not by far.

3. Asia's Childhood

Asia was born into a social milieu teetering on the edge of environmental ruin. She grew up on a ranch on the outskirts of Laughlin, on the tri-state border of California, Nevada, and Arizona. The eldest of three girls, her family had european heritage but maintained close relations with Indigenous Navajo and Latino communities.

Her grandmother loved Japanese culture and clothing. She had a lifelong desire to visit the East but knew it was nearly impossible. To fulfill her wish, she named her eldest granddaughter after the continent. Asia's father named her two sisters.

Her parents employed a dozen Navajo and Latino farm workers, and the ranch was profitable. However, the rain became unpredictable, and Lake Mohave slowly dried up. Irrigation supplies dwindled, and half the animals and crops perished. The crumbling state's response was slow and inadequate.

When she was sixteen, Asia witnessed the breakdown of social order in Laughlin firsthand. European and Latino landowners formed opposing camps, and ethnic clashes ensued for months. Males were killed, females were trafficked to Las Vegas, and it was unsafe to go anywhere.

To avoid getting drawn into the conflict, the Navajos abandoned their farms and moved to Indigenous reservations. Eventually, Arizona sent a powerful state militia that rounded up all the Latinos and enslaved them on european plantations in Texas.

Minorities in Phoenix and Tucson were also captured and enslaved.

With the ethnic conflict over, european ranchers began fighting among themselves. Her father was accused of collaborating with the enemy for hiding two Latino farmworkers. Their farm was torched, and her parents died trying to save two horses in the barn. Asia was left alone to provide for her sisters.

With the town in ruins and no safe place to stay, Asia led her siblings West as civilization went into freefall. She often went for days without food or sleep to ensure her Sisters' safety. They joined other displaced families and stayed in temporary settlements in Eastern California. In due course, they settled into a Buddhist community in Apple Valley and trained to become Buddhist nuns.

At the temple, Asia began to develop a strong sense of community. She had a knack for organizing people, rationing supplies, and making decisions that kept everyone alive. Her experience in Laughlin and the monastery convinced her that ethnicity was a trap, and she sought to build multi-ethnic alliances.

When she was 21, tragedy struck when her younger sister, Demeter, fell ill. Medical supplies were scarce, and despite the monks' best efforts, Demeter did not survive. The loss devastated her, but it also hardened her commitment. She could not save everyone but was determined to protect her last sibling.

Asia's second sister, Antheia, 13, remained by her side for two years. One day, the pair were out foraging, and Antheia went missing. Asia searched for weeks for her sibling without luck. Antheia was likely kidnapped and trafficked away by local gangs. Asia blamed herself for the separation and became severely depressed. Within a decade, she lost her entire family and community and was left alone.

Her training in Zen meditation slowly helped her to recover from utter despair. A decade later, she left the monastery and traveled West. In 2120, she arrived at a shelter in Santa Barbara, one of the last asylums on the Pacific Coast.

At the refuge, she met Hehewuti, Zenobia, Onawa, Marge, Gloria, and other women who formed the core of a female alliance. Asia initially hesitated to trust the others, but knew they were more effective together as women than divided into ethnic groups. Children were being kidnapped from inside the shelter, and Asia organized other women to fend off the assailants.

Gang attacks on the shelter multiplied. There were assailants from Santa Barbara Militia (SBM), West Coast White Power (WCWP), Sindicato de Cuchillos Brutales (SCB), Tijuana Cartel (TC), and others. It became clear to the Laughlin native that the girls had to leave the overrun asylum to be safe.

Asia carried the weight of the girls' survival on her shoulders. She saw in them the two Sisters she had lost. She placed their needs before hers and fiercely protected them from the gangs. In time, she convinced the Mothers to leave the shelter and travel North.

Asia's past was marked by tragedy and hardship. It was also defined by her unyielding tenacity to survive and her capacity to inspire courage in others. She was driven by the belief that there was a future worth fighting for and was willing to sacrifice herself to lead others to it.

One of the most perplexing problems was acquiring subsistence for her commune. Finding natural springs in the denuded forest was difficult. However, with keen observation and knowledge, scarce supplies could be located.

'I will not rest until I find water,' Asia reflected. 'The girls will become ill if they're not properly hydrated.'

She left the cactus grove in search of a spring. She knew hidden water sources existed and could be found when least expected.

4. Camp

It was 6 PM in the Los Padres Forest with a reading of 110°F (43°C). It should have been hotter, but the tall Western hills shaded the cacti grove from the Sun's fury. The forty climate evacuees sat inside the thicket, slowly rehydrating with drops of cactus juice.

Two hours earlier, Asia went lower into the valley, searching for a spring. To everyone's delight, she returned with four sacks of precious liquid.

Nzinga hugged her friend. "Why did you leave without me? And where did you find water?"

Asia beamed and pointed North. "I hiked downhill for an hour and discovered a creek. Tomorrow, you can go with me to restock our supplies."

"You're so awesome." Nzinga's excitement reflected the relief Asia brought to the collective.

"We all are." Asia beamed. "Now, let's gather to discuss a plan." She gestured with a subtle wave, her fingers curling inward, inviting the women closer. They assembled with the Crones sitting in front.

"Thank you all for hanging tough," Asia commenced. She sat confidently, with her head held high. The women's bravery was evident, but so was the toll their journey had taken on them. Nonetheless, their enduring positivity was a source of inspiration.

"It's been hard, especially on the children," Asia resumed. "But we're almost at the end of the forest. The next stage will be even more grueling as we go through the desert. And we're still a month away from the Safehouse."

The women nodded to show their support. They had persisted through the harsh conditions at the shelter, gang assaults on the route, and hiking the blackened forest. Each woman's role was crucial, and Asia recognized their contributions.

"As you know, there are several committees with different responsibilities," Asia continued. "The Crones oversee setting up camp." She glanced toward the Elders, smiling.

The Crones sparkled with approval and humility. Zaniya, 58, tilted her head slightly, her hands clasped in prayer. "Praise Gaia. May we rise with perseverance," she invoked. "Like peaks that weather storms, embodying grace, wisdom, and strength that will not fade. Blessed be." The other Crones echoed Zaniya's consecration, "Blessed be." Their spirituality and constant reverence were an enduring light for the cooperative.

"The security team watch over us." Asia resumed. She glowed at the guards, Lian, 26, Xóchitl, 24, and Nzinga, 40, conveying her trust. The three women straightened their backs and saluted their commander, ready to fulfill their duties.

"The Mothers manage the children," Asia pointed to the Mamas. "The girls are the reason we're here, and Moms have the most vital role in our clan." The Mothers: Simone, 40; Gloria, 35; Aisha, 26; and others, beamed. They worried over the children and were grateful for Asia's acknowledgment.

Asia returned the military salute. "The scouts assist security, search for shelter and food resources, and erase our tracks." Asia glanced at Riri, 19, Daria, 17, and Phoolan, 16. The young women grinned and waved.

"The nutrition team feeds and maintains us." Asia squinted at Frida and her two helpers. The cook nodded graciously. "The medic preserves our health." She waved at Emily, who curtsied.

"Logistics tracks supplies, tools, storage, and other tasks essential to staying alive." Asia glanced at Onawa, 41; Marge, 35; and other women. She bowed to the group and remained quiet, letting her words settle.

The women's faces reflected a range of emotions: grit, fatigue, and single-minded optimism that had carried them through the shelter and onward. Asia noticed the slight trembling of hands here and there, lined foreheads, and tightness around some mouths.

They showed signs of the strain everyone felt, but also willingness and spirit.

The silence that followed was soaked with unspoken understanding. It was a moment of shared purpose that transcended words. The adults were firmly committed to mutual aid and survival.

The leader gave a thumbs up. "Ladies, let's get to work." Xóchitl guarded the perimeter while Lian organized a watch schedule.

The Crones picked a shaded spot, and the teens took turns digging a shallow trench. Hehewuti, Zaniya, Kuan-Yin, Mary, and Zenobia began establishing camp in the dugout by spreading blankets on one end and building a fire hearth at the other. They hummed and chanted while they worked.

Nzinga and the scouts positioned traps and alarms. The sharp devices were made from simple, scavenged materials. They placed them below the camp's perimeter to deter intruders.

Daily, the women took turns at watch. The guards constantly inspected their surroundings for potential threats. Three scouts aided them. Two teen boys in the group, Stephen and Miller, were uncooperative, and the women rarely asked for their assistance. The unhelpful pair never sat for Cronetime and considered Zaniya's blessings stupid and nonsensical.

Two Mothers, Simone, 40, and Emily, 36, checked on the children, ensuring they were settled and comfortable. Marge, 35, gently rocked her son Elon to sleep on her lap. The Mothers' bond was growing. They frequently shared childcare and discussed their experiences, challenges with the children, and strategies for addressing them.

Lian, 26, and Xóchitl, 24, were positioned on the perimeter, vigilantly observing the vicinity. The Crones took turns sharing stories with the children. Their soft voices were a comforting murmur in the stillness of the evening.

Nzinga, 40, was the third guard. She also helped to organize supplies. The Mother was five feet ten inches tall, weighed 140 pounds, and spoke with a slight Southern, Cajun accent. She shifted from one cluster of women to another, ensuring everyone was comfortable.

Lian and Xóchitl sat at the Southern perimeter. Lian, usually a loner and skeptic, had developed a feeling of cautious optimism along the route. Despite the harsh conditions and uncertainty, the women remained in harmony. Each member performed their role, and their collective power was the convoy's greatest asset.

She grew more confident about their survival when she witnessed the women's close cooperation. She felt part of a caring collective for the first time in a long while. She desperately wanted to work with a female-centered community. Moreover, she and Xóchitl were becoming close.

Lian scoured the darkening scene. Xóchitl knelt beside her, carefully brushing sand from her clothing.

"Ola mi amor. Heard the one about the Enlightened Chicken, Bhikkhuni?" Xóchitl grinned at her companion. She loved telling Zen tales, but Lian was often a reluctant audience.

Xóchitl had explained to Lian that a Bhikkhuni was a female Buddhist monk who lived in female-only temples called a Sangha. The word means 'the one who begs.' A Samanerika was a student who was becoming a Buddhist nun.

Lian shrugged. The title was mildly interesting.

"A Samanerika," Xóchitl began calmly, "had spent decades seeking enlightenment. One day, she thought she had finally reached it. The student ran to the Bhikkhuni and blurted, 'I've achieved illumination.'" Xóchitl paused and grinned.

Lian snorted. "Have you?"

Xóchitl giggled and continued. "The Bhikkhuni looked at the nun curiously and said, 'Let's see.' She handed the apprentice a broom and said, 'Sweep the Sangha.' The Samanerika, slightly irritated, replied, 'But I'm enlightened now. Shouldn't I be beyond sweeping floors?' The Bhikkhuni smiled and said, 'An enlightened chicken still needs to scratch the ground.'"

"Ha," Lian smirked. "You're an enlightened liar."

5. Toast

It was 6:30 PM in Central California. The climate migrants were enjoying dinner and recovering near their campfire, North of Meiners Oaks. It was 105°F (41°C), but a cool breeze wafted in from the scorched forest. A flock of crows flew West to their nests. Zaniya called after them, and several corvids answered. The evening felt magical.

The women and children sat on mats in the trench eating a bowl of lentils and rice, a simple and cherished comfort. They ate peacefully, savoring the much-needed replenishment of the day's hardships.

Onawa, 41, the record-keeper, unfolded a cardboard map. On a crude drawing of the area, she carefully marked their daily progress using a piece of charred wood. She noted their current location, direction traveled, and distance covered.

"Another day down," Onawa commented. The Mother of Cha'Kwaina was five feet five inches tall and weighed 130 pounds. She belonged to the Hopi People of Arizona and spoke with a slight Indigenous accent.

The geographer displayed the board to the children, tracing the route they had traversed. It was like a community growth chart. The girls were keenly interested in their passage, and marking their daily progress became a nightly ritual that strengthened their bond.

On the outskirts, Lian and Xóchitl ate while guarding the area. The Latina shared some of her food with Lian, who was hungry. "¿Cómo estás? Wanna hear Everything is Best, Bhikkhuni?" She probed her companion, and Lian looked up from her meal with interest.

Xóchitl sipped her water and started. "A young nun came to the Bhikkhuni said to the teacher, 'I'm confused. Sometimes, you tell me to sit and meditate. Other times, you ask me to do work like washing dishes. Occasionally, you say nothing is needed, that I should simply be. So, which is it?'"

"Dishes," Lian answered. "I remember the Chicken must scratch story."

Xóchitl laughed and resumed. "The female Monk replied, 'Everything is best.' The nun was confused and asked, 'Which one is best right now?' The teacher shrugged and said, 'Maybe eating dinner.'"

Lian chuckled and continued eating.

Near the campfire, Hehewuti, 74, rose from the ground and addressed the women warmly. "Gaias, let's give thanks to our leader, Asia." She bowed and stared at Asia. "We wouldn't have left the shelter without you." She lifted her water bottle in a toast and shined. "And we haven't lost a single daughter in four days."

The women clinked canteens. Their wide smiles reflected shared triumph. They were relieved to be away from the dangerous shelter and empowered by their collective resilience.

Zaniya, 65, spread her shoulders and sparkled in an inclusive blessing. "Like rivers that carve through rock, Gaia's spirit shapes the Globe with patience and power. In Her embrace, rivers are born, winds find their song, and the sky touches the Earth. May the Goddess be with you. Blessed be." The women repeated "Blessed be."

Asia beamed. Radiating serene control, she raised her container. "May the Goddess be with all refugees."

The leader was a striking figure of toughness. Standing five feet four inches tall, her athletic build displayed decades of physical exertion and endurance. She appeared tough, yet exuded a gentleness, a nurturing inner self beneath her hardened exterior.

Her face was angular, and her high cheekbones gave her a distinguished look. Her skin was a deep, Sun-kissed tan, reflecting countless days spent under the unrelenting Star. A black birthmark rested in the center of her forehead, adding an element of mystery to her european features.

Her pupils were a rich, warm hazel. They often shifted in color depending on the light, from a deep amber in the Sun to a more subdued green in the shade. Her stare was intense, almost stinging. But there was also gentleness, especially when she looked at the children.

Asia rose from her seat and pointed to the cook in the back. "A toast to Frida, a true Goddess. Your food maintains our body and Spirit. Thank you for our health and happiness."

"You're welcome." Frida's face lit up, and the ladies lifted their flasks in unison, humming with appreciation. They had developed a strong bond with the cook and were filled with gratitude. They gestured thanks to the chef.

Asia pointed next to the nurse. "A toast to Emily, our healer. Your medical expertise, care and medicine keep us alive and well."

"We're here to help," Emily smiled modestly. "Me and my daughters. She pointed to her 14-year-old twins, Karol and Selina in the trench with their friends. The cooperative toasted the nurse. Her presence made them feel less vulnerable, and they showed her their deep-rooted appreciation.

Asia beamed. Her hair was a cascade of thin, oily strands that fell just past her ears. Its rich blackness was streaked with the beginnings of silver. She wore a cap and brushed her short hair daily to keep it unknotted.

Her arms and legs were muscular. They bore the scars of a life spent fighting for survival. A prominent scab ran diagonally across her right forearm, a souvenir from an encounter with a rapist with a sharp knife. Other scars showed the many battles she fought against unwelcome male suitors and kidnappers.

Notwithstanding the marks, her skin was smooth, with a subtle sheen of sweat always present. She stood upright and strode gracefully. The weight of her experiences did not slow her down. She had an intense yet serene presence.

Asia twinkled and raised her canteen. She turned respectfully to the composed Elders. "A toast to the Crones, our true leaders. Thank you, Hehewuti, Mary, Kuan-Yin, Zaniya, and Zenobia. You're the heart of our community."

The Crones beamed, absorbing Asia's recognition. Zaniya's shine met the leader. She bowed in salutation and spoke lyrically, "Gaia does not move against the mountains. She is the mountains, grounded, fierce, and forever at peace. May the Goddess be praised. Blessed be." The women echoed her gratitude.

Zaniya's soothing gaze hinted at a deep sense of fulfillment. Hehewuti bowed with hands on her chest. Kuan-Yin serenely savored the moment. Mary clasped her hands in quiet meditation, and Zenobia sparkled with goodwill.

The women gazed reverently at the Crones. They loved and honored the five Elders. The Crones were the heart of their female community, and the clan had profound respect to them.

Asia glowed, unconsciously rubbing down her pant legs. She had a practical approach to clothing. Like the other women, she wore loose garments to appear as a man. She preferred shorts and tight tops, but those would attract men's attention. She wore tan cargo pants with multiple pockets, a faded green long-sleeve shirt, and a grey bulletproof jacket.

Her shoes were sturdy combat boots. She modified them with additional straps for a tighter fit and reinforced the soles for durability. Her outfit reflected her readiness and resourcefulness to handle natural adversity and men's brutality.

Asia lifted her container proudly. "A toast to our security and scout teams. Thank you for keeping us safe and secure daily. To Lian, Xóchitl, Nzinga, Riri, Phoolan, and Daria."

The women responded joyfully, and their cheers brightened the cactus grove. The recipients beamed, delighted to serve as community protectors. Lian and Xóchitl were absent, and Asia planned to thank them later.

Her backpack was an extension of her practical personality, a medium-sized, weathered brown canvas bag. Tiny pieces of colored cloth hung across the back like Tibetan prayer flags. It was meticulously organized, with compartments for essential gear, a first-aid kit, and a cherished journal.

Asia sat down and finished eating while the collective spoke excitedly. Supper was the best time of the day, especially for the children.

Twilight approached, and the sky transformed into a mesmerizing multicolored canvas. A deep amber glow spread near the skyline, blending into streaks of subtle orange and nimble pink that rippled across the fading blue. Once white, a few patches of high clouds were tinged with gold and lavender. Their edges still shone brightly from the retreating Star.

6. Zenobia's Cronetime

It was 7:00 PM in Los Padres National Forest. The Stars began to appear in the twilight sky whilst the evacuees unwound in their improvised shelter. Ever vigilant, Lian and Xóchitl stood at the edge of the perimeter, guarding the convoy.

The day's heat had taken its toll, but the collective felt satisfied. They had survived four days' traveling since leaving the shelter. The campfire snapped occasionally, casting shimmering shadows on the loosened figures. The children mustered near Hehewuti in anticipation of Cronetime.

The eldest Crone was petite, standing five feet two inches tall and weighing 105 pounds, but she carried a powerful presence. She sat on a worn blanket spread out on the ground, and the children lounged in a semi-circle. She held up the community's treasured record of their journey, clapped, and announced, "It's Cronetime."

Hehewuti spread her arms, her stance open and inviting. "Listen carefully, daughters. Tonight, we're reading from *The Age of Sibyls*." With reverence, she glanced toward her left and continued, "And we are honored to have our Firekeeper read for us."

Zenobia, 58, sat cross-legged, dignified. She touched the book gently and paused. The small, hardcover text was originally hers but like most of the group's possessions, had become community property. The girls leaned eagerly when she opened the precious digest and rustled the pages, reading the contents intuitively.

"Da Age of Sibyls," she commenced rhythmically without reading. "It wuz da 'Golden Age' when we female foremothers wuz in charge ah things. Da Sibyls wuz women who coulda see far into da future. An folks even believe dey coulda predict when the messiah woulda come. Back then, we women held it down, leadin' dey people wid all kinda wisdom. Women wuz respected leaders, protectors, an saints."

The Crone noticed that her session had stirred the girls' imaginations and resumed with delight. "Back in da day, de Sibyls dem wuz deep, mystical ladies. Dey wuz mo than ah fortune-teller. Dey wuz seers an prophets, talkin' in riddles dat gats everybody listenin', from kings to every dey folks."

"That's so dope," Phoolan, 16, exclaimed. "Them some bad Queens with real power."

"Each Sibyl had she own sacred spot," the Firekeeper continued with certainty and reverence. "Like temples cut inna da mountains, secret caves out in da wild, or tucked away in da town's shadows. Folks wuz both scared ah dem an had mad respect fuh dem. Dey believin' dat Sibyls hada special blessin' from da Earth Goddess she-self."

"Girl, Sibyls be bussin," Sasha, 15, remarked. "We could use some now."

Zenobia paused to let her story sink in, then returned to her review of female spiritual icons. "Wan ah da most talked-about Sibyl wuz da Cumaean Sibyl.

She had she spot inna huge cave near da ole city of Cumae, in Italy."

The girls listened in hushed awe and the storyteller's eyes twinkled. "Da Sibyl's place wuz like a maze, with dez tight, twisty paths. Dey leadin' to dis big room where she be sittin' on ah stone throne. Da wall wuz covered inna symbols only she coulda understand. She sat dey with ah long line ah folks waitin' fuh see she, seekin' she advice."

The students' burning interest in the tutorial pleased the teacher, who continued in a hushed tone. "People woulda come from far an wide, bringin' da Cumaean Sibyl gifts like gold, wine, an incense. Dey hopin' to hear what she had fuh say."

The Firekeeper's hands waved dramatically, casting mystical shadows with the light of the flame. "When it wuz time fuh she speak, she woulda start shaking. She eyeballs rolled back, an den dis eerie voice, not only she own, woulda start spillin' out dey forecast."

The Crone's audience sat spellbound, and she centered her attention on her body for a moment.

"For real?" Ma'at was incredulous. "She could see the future?"

The humble educator smiled and enthusiastically went on with the lecture on female legacy. "Some time da Sibyl's words be like poetry, other time only bits an pieces. She prophecy wuz always deep an kinda scary. She be talkin' bout disasters, diseases, an wars yet to come."

The Crone grinned broadly, crinkling at the corners. "But she always had dis way ah sayin' dat da future was set, like a river. Yuh can't stop it." She paused briefly for effect. "But maybe yuh can figure out how fuh ride along."

"Fire," Cha'Kwaina, 14, blurted. "I'd like to be able to tell the future like them." The other girls shook their heads in agreement.

Zenobia gazed at her pupils with pride and resumed. "Time passed by in da ancient lands, an da Sibyls turned into legends. Dey voices wuz ah reminder dat when it come down to it, human plans ain't worth much against da will ah da Goddess."

"Yeet," Lisa cried out. "Female legends are cool."

"Some folks say da Sibyls wuz blessed wid holiness," the Elder picked up again. "Others feel dat dey wuz cursed, stuck wid seein' da future but nevah able to change or dodge it. But fuh dem who wuz scared of what tomorrow may bring, da Sibyls gave ah peek into da big mysteries of life."

"Girl, the well-to-do are always stressy," Daria, 17, commented dryly. "They're totes scared of dying."

Zenobia smiled and carried on. "One leader, right, wuz Sibyl of da Mountains." She tilted her head up, inviting her listeners to see the grandeur she described. "Dis Sibyl wuz truly great. She bring peace an good times to she land an da folks by wrappin' up da power of dem mountains."

"That Goddess slay," Karol, 14, exclaimed. "Where's she from?"

The Firekeeper shrugged. "She ole mo than recorded time. No wan kno' fuh sho'. But she wuz everywhere and powerful." Her arms spread wide to communicate the geographic extent and magnitude of the Sibyl of the Mountain's achievements. "She smarts mek sure da land wuz thrivin', an peace wuz da law fuh da land. She an she daughtas ruled for thousands ah years." The Crone ended with a sweeping motion, wrapping her story in a theatrical flourish.

With her reading over, Zenobia's gnarled fingers caressed the book's cover and closed it. "Remember y'all, da strength ah da Sibyls is hey wid yuh." She pointed to her chest. "Inside all ah yuh." She carefully placed the book on the mat beside her. "We movin' da gifts dey left fuh we. We movin' ahead wid every step we tek."

The Firekeeper's last words were filled with emotion. She stood up, bowed to the flames, and carefully packed away their precious knowledge, *The Age of Sibyls*.

Sitting nearby with her baby, Aisha had a wistful glow. She thoroughly enjoyed Zenobia's Cronetime. "Sibyl stories remind us of our potential," she gleefully commented to Onawa. "If our female ancestors achieved so much, we could find our way through this man-made dystopia."

Onawa smiled and said nothing. She was moved by her friend's inspiration and hope.

The girls glowed in the firelight. The Firekeeper's tales of powerful ancestors were uplifting, and they chatted enthusiastically about the golden age when females were leaders. They needed to prepare for sleep but were too thrilled to nap. The tales of female valor and wisdom created an astonishing sense of continuity and possibility.

The Sibyls were an incredible contrast to the society the young women lived in. They were amazed women were honored as rulers and prophets once upon a time. The knowledge was truly empowering.

Zaniya stretched her hands, palms downturned, to embrace the Earth. Reverent words flowed from her lips like a bubbling stream, cool and refreshing.

"Gaia's spirit is the dawn breaking over peaks. She illuminates the Earth with quiet strength and boundless compassion. May the Goddess be with us. Blessed be." Zaniya's fingers reached out to spread the divine blessings she evoked. The girls repeated "Blessed be."

Asia gazed fondly at the commune. She was proud of their psychic strength and ingenuity in adapting to the intensely racist and sexist post-apocalypse society. Amid their struggles, Cronetime offered a ray of light, a moment of solace that reminded the survivors of their shared chronicle and purpose.

The new Moon rose slowly, casting a faint radiance over the shadowy tree stumps. The clan was exhausted and drifted off into blissful sleep. They dreamed of an oasis, a safe shelter, a sandy beach, a positive future, and a safer place for females.

7. Zenobia

Zenobia's face bore the marks of fifty-eight years of hardship. Her once smooth skin was deeply lined with wrinkles. Her dark brown orbs shimmered with a sharp, attentive flash. Her hair, an amalgam of gray and silver, was short and wavy.

The Creole woman was born in a Southern coastal town. Her name comes from the Greek words *zeno,* or 'life,' and *bios,* meaning 'Zeus,' ruler of the gods. The most famous bearer of the name was the Queen of Palmyra in the 3rd century AD. She was a formidable leader who expanded her domain and challenged the Roman Empire.

The Firekeeper's parents were from the Islands of Jamaica and Haiti. The Gulf of Mexico was their lifeblood, providing food, trade, and connections to farmers far and wide. Her Caribbean heritage was not just a part of her; it was her essence.

Growing up, she learned to harvest salt, kelp, and seaweed, weave baskets, sculpt pottery, grow vegetables, cook, bake bread, and make herbal medicine. She also foraged for wild foods along the Southern coastlines and estuaries, like sea kale and marsh samphire, which she loved.

During her teens, the coastal ecosystem changed rapidly. The Gulf grew warmer, and the once-thriving region was frequently damaged by powerful tornadoes and hurricanes. Thousands were killed, starved, and infected with tropical diseases. Many residents migrated in search of better prospects. Zenobia remained, driven by a duty to care for those too aged or sick to leave. Her decision was an example of her loyalty and unwavering community spirit.

Then came the Great Storm, a cataclysmic hurricane that leveled her town and the entire county. The storm surge wiped out thousands of homes, leaving the land bare. She lost both parents, along with many friends and neighbors.

The young woman stayed with an aunt inland and weathered the storm. She became a healer, offering her services in exchange for food or shelter. She survived and could have thrived but encountered overwhelming hostility.

When national and state governments collapsed, cities and towns across the South were consumed by hatred, violence, and chaos. Racism became rampant, and light-colored militias reverted to the immoral practice of capturing and enslaving darker-colored individuals. Similar to the colonial period, millions of minorities were captured, chained, whipped, and forced to perform free labor on european plantations in Florida, Alabama, Louisiana, Mississippi, Texas, and Mid-Western states.

Enslavement and lynching were commonplace across the South. African American, Latino, Indigenous, and Asian men were often falsely accused and lynched for trivial offenses. Minority females were enslaved and trafficked into the sex trade. Several times, Zenobia narrowly avoided capture by european enslavers. When she was 18, she sailed with other Africans and escaped to Tamaulipas, Mexico. From there, she joined a migrant caravan headed North.

The racialized South deepened her understanding of people's selfishness and greed. In her 20s, she lived in a New Mexico county occupied by minorities and anti-racist europeans. The cooperative grew crops and offered protection to Southern escapees. She enjoyed developing a safe space for minorities and became a midwife.

However, minority men in the district became increasingly conservative and anti-female. She was abused by all her male partners and denied leadership roles in the group. She wanted to get pregnant but miscarried two times from beatings. Two decades later, she left the survivors' area and traveled West.

Upon arrival in California, she discovered a dystopian society where males openly preyed on females. Few women dared to venture outside, and the ones who did were likely to be abused and captured. Girls were caught like fish and traded in markets that dotted the Coast. To avoid seizure, she dressed like a male and tried to pass as a man.

Years later, she met Onawa, Asia, Mary, and others in the Santa Barbara shelter. She became known for her knowledge, calm demeanor, and ability to inspire optimism even in the darkest times. Her guidance, like that of a Sibyl, was sought after. Her positivity helped to fortify others, and she loved being the camp counselor.

8. Night Creatures

The Sun dipped below the horizon, casting a breathtaking spectacle over the Coastal mountains. The forest landscape was bathed in a palette of warm hues, transitioning from orange to purple, before the sky deepened into an inky black.

The temperature plummeted, marking the onset of a night filled with both beauty and peril. At 10 PM, three hours after Sunset, the thermometer dipped 30 notches to 78°F (26°C).

Animals lurked in the dim shadows, with their share of dangers. The haunting scene reminded Lian, the night guard, of the constant threat to their survival. Los Padres Forest was eerily quiet except for the occasional wind gust or the distant howl of a coyote. Her heart raced with each sound with her senses heightened by the darkness.

She kept her flashlight close but avoided shining it into the void. The unfamiliarity was unnerving, and her imagination conjured shadows that seemed to move on their own. 'This darkness could turn deadly in a second,' she reminded herself.

One of the most immediate threats was the presence of venomous creatures, like sidewinder rattlesnakes and scorpions, that prowled at night. The sidewinder, though elegant in its movement, was deadly if disturbed. Its bite could deliver a potent venom that would be difficult, if not impossible, to treat. The collective lacked transportation, and there were no hospitals to visit.

Scorpions were no less dangerous. A sting from one of the more venomous species could cause severe pain, swelling, and life-threatening complications. The evacuees had to remain vigilant. They carefully checked their bedding and gear each night to make sure no arachnid sought refuge in the warmth.

The night brought a different set of challenges. After the Sun's heat dissipated, the temperature plummeted. Without adequate shelter or clothing, they risked hypothermia, especially children more vulnerable to weather extremes. The drastic temperature change could sap their strength, making the next day's trek even more grueling.

Numerous predators roamed in the dark. Desert foxes, though small, could become a threat if driven by hunger or if they saw intruders in their territory. Larger predators, like coyotes and wild dogs, traversed the shadows with calculated stealth.

Although they usually avoided humans, hunger and desperation could drive cougars and mountain lions closer, drawn by the smell of food or the vulnerability of worn-out survivors. A sudden attack could scatter the tired commune and create chaos, making it difficult to regroup and defend themselves.

Hours passed, and exhaustion weighed heavily on Lian. She knew she could not nap, but her body begged for rest. To stay awake, she focused on the stars above, their brilliance undimmed by the New Moon. She traced constellations and remembered her parents' stories. They were comforting and kept her tired mind from spiraling into sleep.

While peaceful, the night's shadows carried a hidden danger, disorientation. Without landmarks, losing one's sense of direction in the dark was easy. The vastness of the forest could swallow a person whole and leave no trace if they stray too far from base. The cold, unyielding darkness made the land feel endless, and even a brief walk away from the campsite could turn into a fatal mistake.

Additionally, there was the ever-present risk of dehydration. The cool night air might mask their bodies' need for water, but the dryness continued to sap moisture while they slept. With water supplies continuously low, every drop was crucial. The fear of dying from thirst haunted everyone's dreams.

As the night wore on, the cold grew more intense. The campfire dwindled, and Lian huddled closer to the embers, wrapping herself in a jacket and scarf. Her fingers and toes grew numb, and she massaged her legs to keep the blood flowing. The wilderness was testing her, pushing her to the limits, but she refused to give in.

For the women and children, nighttime was a time to rest and be on guard. Each woman kept a weapon close, whether a sharpened stick, knife, or firearm, ready to defend against whatever might come. With all its beauty, the night was an unforgiving time where danger was never far away. The darkness amplified their vulnerability, turning every rustle, every distant howl, into a potential threat.

Despite the myriad dangers, Lian and the others persevered. With all its perils, the enigmatic night was merely another obstacle in their path. They faced the relentless Sun daily and the chilling darkness nightly, but their resistance remained unshaken.

Breathing was difficult in the smokey air. The almost two million acres of greenery in Los Padres Forest was gone. Large swaths of coniferous trees like Jeffrey pine, redwood, Douglas fir, and white fir were torched. Only sparse chaparral and ground cover remained.

The vast wooded area, formerly teeming with life, lay in ruins. Charred pines stood like blackened sentinels, their skeletal trunks clawing at the sky in silent agony. The scent of damp Earth and blooming flowers had been replaced by the acrid stench of burnt wood and smoldering dirt.

Where Moonlight previously danced through leafy canopies, an eerie haze clung to the air, swirling in the faint breeze. The ground, formerly a carpet of grass, bulbs, and native flowers, was a wasteland of gray ash. Lian stared at the brittle remnants of what had once been life. Her footsteps stirred up dust clouds, each puff a ghostly echo of what had burned away.

In the distance, a lone night bird called out, a survivor, searching for what no longer existed. The numerous streams and creeks had evaporated. The few remaining carried soot and fallen embers, their reflections distorted by the unfolding disaster.

In addition to the physical challenges, the trip took a heavy psychological toll on the survivors. The darkness amplified fears of attack and disorientation. In the mysterious blackness and ongoing emotional struggles, the collective was their only salvation.

The lead guard glanced at her companions in the trench with pride. 'My job is to ensure they survive another night in these backwoods,' she mused. She gritted her teeth in silent resolve, a determination as unyielding as the wilderness she faced. Nothing was going to prevent her from keeping her female companions safe.

9. How Long More?

It was 10 AM, and the Central California Sun was hours away from its peak. The temperature in Los Padres Forest reached 114°F (46°C) with 35 percent humidity. The morning mist had burned off, and the air was stifling.

The climate refugees continued their arduous trek North. Step by step, they marched through the hills next to Route 33 with unwavering will. A week away from the Pacific Coast, they had traversed over fifty miles, which felt like they were walking for months.

Greta, 13, staggered under the weight of her pack. Her face was flushed, and her body glistened with sweat. The orphan wiped her brow with the back of her hand for the tenth time. Her movements were sluggish and heavy. Her shirt clung to her drenched body, and she panted with labored breaths. "How long more?" she gasped, shaking. "I can't take another step."

Asia saw the teen struggling. "Stay hydrated," she advised. "We'll rest soon." She spun to lead the caravan onward.

Young and aged alike, the women and children tumbled on. The scenery around them was an unending expanse of arid, burnt trees, a stark warning of the severe drought gripping the West. The absence of water caused enormous wildfires that destroyed millions of trees. Ninety percent of the forest was gone.

On the Coast, there was mass famine and disease in urban areas. Private infrastructure crumbled into dust, and public facilities vanished. Only the harsh drought and the struggle to survive remained.

The relentless nuclear fusion Star cast heat and light from millions of miles away onto the survivors' heads and backs. Despite the early hour, the warmth on the third Planet was agonizing. Yet, they pressed on through the charred landscape.

The convoy reached their third break of the day, seeking refuge in the scant shade of a few dead pines. Sharp light bounced off the backdrop of blackened trunks and dead brush, stretching endlessly.

The weary figures unslung their packs and reclined into the warm soil. Nzinga distributed water and snacks, and they ate hungrily, trying to maintain energy and morale. The children bunched into small groups, some playing pleasantly while others napped.

The Crones held up a cloth screen to give the teens and women privacy to change their menstrual cloth pads. The red tent was a sacred space for the females. The girls shared concerns about their period, and the women offered advice and herbal treatments for severe cramps.

Outside the tent, Lisa, 11, sat near her Mother, Marge. Her tiny hands twisted her shirt nervously. Her chin shifted upward, and she hesitated before asking, "Why are the mens trying to capture us girls?"

Marge's face stiffened in anger. She was 35, five feet six inches tall, weighed 125 pounds, and spoke with a California accent. "They trade girls for food and goods." Her words were tinged with pain.

Lisa wrinkled her nose in confusion. "But why only girls?" She glanced jealously at her nine-year-old brother, Elon.

Marge pointed at the teen boys in their community, Stephen, 15, and Miller, 16. "They're stronger, but young boys are sometimes taken." She squinted at Elon. "We have to watch out for them too."

The teen boys burst into laughter while teasing Elon. "You'll get captured," Stephen baited the child. Elon's pupils welled up, and his lower lip quivered.

Lian watched the exchange with a scowl. "Not even close," she stated firmly to Marge. "One boy is taken for every hundred girls stolen." Her harsh tone betrayed her irritation. "Men prefer girls, and the younger, the better."

The Mother heaved a sigh and remained silent.

Asia checked her timer. "Alright," she announced. "That's our half-hour break. Let's get moving for another stretch." The women stirred, loaded their packs, and prepared to head back into the Sunlight.

Lian's attention lingered on the teen boys. 'Only a matter of time before they start harassing the girls,' she thought.

The convoy plodded on for a mile, then stopped to rest. Cha'Kwaina, 14, sat with her back against a boulder. She looked at Asia in agony. "How much further?" she gasped.

Asia's forehead creased. "We must push ourselves today," she said doggedly, pointing to the Northern horizon. "We've got hundreds of miles to go."

An assortment of emotions rippled through Cha'Kwaina, but she said nothing.

Asia addressed the group approvingly. "We've made good progress so far. If we keep up the pace, we can camp earlier."

Lian sat beside Cha'Kwaina and touched her arm. "Take it one minute at a time, Sister," she said affectionately. "Each klick, every mile we cover is a victory."

Cha'Kwaina's head slumped. "I wish it would rain. I'm black from dust and ash, like a zombie."

Lian met Cha'Kwaina's stare. "It feels that way," she admitted. "The land is dried out, but it has hidden oases. You can wash when we find one." The teen's mood brightened, and she searched for greenery.

Up ahead, Lian noticed a bright flash high in the Western sky. She became curious. "Is that a meteor?"

Asia looked up. A fireball streaked across the horizon and broke into four pieces. The fragments descended rapidly toward the forest. She recognized the danger immediately and ran to the nearest tree trunk. "Take cover now," she shouted. "It's a falling satellite."

The group scrambled to hide behind nearby trees. Moments later, several loud thuds rattled the forest and stirred up ash clouds. One piece fell really close and tossed metal shrapnel into the trees. However, everyone was shielded, and no one was hurt.

The women and children were shaken. They had never seen objects falling from the sky before.

Lian stared at Asia in surprise. "How did you know it wasn't a meteor?"

Asia shrugged. "It's path. Satellites don't fall straight down or sideways. They follow a curved path."

The women were impressed with Asia's knowledge and thanked her for warning them in time. The teens collected the sharp metal parts from the ground. They planned to fashion them into knives, tools, and traps.

Zaniya opened her palms, embracing the vastness before her, and spoke lyrically. "The Goddess is the keeper of ancient secrets, woven in the roots of every tree, echoed in every valley. Her knowledge is timeless, like the mountains She guards. All is Gaia. We are Gaia. Blessed be."

The women repeated her refrain, "Blessed be." They admired Zaniya's pleasant countenance, and their face mirrored the Crone's gratitude.

The wanderers resumed their grueling march through the dead forest. Depending on each member's perspective, the distance to camp seemed daunting or a potential goal. Regardless of the overwhelming odds against them, the climate wanderers held onto the chance of a better future where they could thrive and not just survive. Like a guiding light, their dream drove them on through the devastated landscape.

The detached hydrogen Star sustained its relentless assault. Still, the persistent women and children pushed on to the next stop, their optimism shining brighter than the scorching celestial body.

10. Sacred Land

It was 2 PM in the Southern Los Padres Forest. The thermometer hovered at 121°F (49°C), with little shade. The climate migrants staggered on, wilting under the blazing Star. Its abrasive light shone from across the inner Solar System to strike the Western side of the vast wilderness around them.

Asia walked alongside the Firekeeper. They both spent years wandering in California. The Creole woman took in the desolate vista, imagining the land the way it was before. "Dis area is going thru rough times," she began. "But it ain't always been like dis."

"How so?" Asia was not interested in delving into the past but felt socially obligated to act like she was.

"It wuz alive," the traditional healer exclaimed. "All ah dez lands. Nowadays, dey only dry an rough, but dey used to be bustin' wid life." She took a deep breath and continued, "Way back, Native folks lived an flourish here. Dey wuz Chumash, Luiseño, Gabrielino, Serrano, Cahuilla, Chemehuevi, Miwok, and Yokut peoples. It wuz all holy here. Da Earth wuz dark, fertile, an givin'."

She paused for a drink, then continued, "Even after dem pink folks came an took ova everythin', da land wuz abundant. It wuz covered wid dey crops, orchards an such, far as yuh can see." Her hand traced imaginary rows of harvests.

"Hard to believe," Asia murmured. She stared at the ruined forest, trying to picture the bountiful landscape the Crone described. But the acres of burnt trunks shimmering in the Sun limited her imagination. The draining monotony was occasionally broken by jagged hills, jutting out like defiant monuments to a lost, lush realm.

"Da almighty Sun took all ah dem farms away." Zenobia placed a hardened hand on her chest, feeling the loss personally. "Rivers wuz da first fuh go." Her stare fixed on the fractured riverbeds she imagined. "Drought turned rushin' streams into ah trickle, then ah drop, til dey only memory on da Earth's skin."

"Yes, the rivers here are long gone," Asia agreed. "The Kern River vanished. So has Santa Ana, Santa Clara, Cuyama, and Owens. Even the mighty Colorado no longer flows here." Her head was bent, weighed down by the dryness of the land.

The Southern native swept her hand over the panorama, tracing the scorched spaces where rivers and flora once flourished. "Da pink folks had big, big farms: miles ah vegetables, groves ah fruit trees, hills ah grape vines, fields ah almond trees. Dey all dried up," she sighed. "Year afta year, roots diggin' fuh water dat wasn't dey."

The Crone examined the hills, and her demeanor brightened. "But even today," she marveled, "dey is a weird kinda beauty to see." She pointed to the West. "Look at dem colors. Yuh see dat? Sky meltin' into land, blue mixin' wid tan an brown. Smooth an silky. Is like da wilderness holdin' on to da last bits of joy in She life."

Asia took in the blinding background. The sea of blackened trunks glowed with an inner light, catching rays and reflecting the colors of the rainbow. "It's beautiful," she agreed. "But it's so empty. There's little left to give us life. Only charcoal and thirst." She sighed, wiping sweat from her cheek.

"Da wilderness is ah Goddess of riddle," the Firekeeper said reverently. "It's ah place of life an death, full an empty, pretty an ugly, past an present." Her arms spread over the desolate terrain. "She mek yuh see wat is here, da real deal every instant. An we gats to face it, good an bad. Seeing life fuh da precious gift it is."

Asia nodded.

"Out hey, every drop ah water, every bit ah shade, every cool breeze is ah blessin' from Gaia." The Crone clasped her hands and bowed before resuming. "Dis is ah dangerous place, yet She keep we alive til now."

Asia was unconvinced. "It's a hard lesson that takes too much from us." She pointed North. "We're here so we can get to a place where we don't have to fight for every inch of life."

The Crone touched her leader's back. "An we gonna mek it," she reassured Asia. "Dez lands is big an merciless, but She ain't there forever. Dey is betta places ahead. Far up North, whey da Earth still kno' how fuh give, an how fuh keep folks alive. We gotta keep movin'."

She was calm and resolute. "We dun come out hey. We livin' hey now, so we gotta mek da best wid what we gats." She gestured expansively with one hand. "Means we gotta stay upbeat by takin' dis land for what She is, cruel an beautiful at da same time."

Asia smiled. She noticed a single green sapling stood defiantly, its fragile leaves trembling in the tainted air. It was a splinter of potential in a graveyard of trunks, reaching for the sky, promising that even in devastation, life would return. The forest had burned, but it was not dead. One day, it would rise again.

Asia felt the warmth of Zenobia's reflection. Their dialogue grounded her into the present, and she was grateful. As they lumbered up a steep hill, she sensed that the forest's haunting presence witnessed their bond and persistence.

11. Finding Water

It was 3 PM in Central California. The forty drifters snaked through the mountains next to Route 33. They completed 10 miles beside the winding road and were withered from climbing the steep terrain in 125°F (52°C) temperature. They were due for a break.

"I'm dying of thirst," Aisha, 26, lamented. The young Mother's face was flushed red and streaked with sweat. She squinted at the scorching Star, stiffening in irritation and fatigue. Shifting the weight of her child, she adjusted the shawl draped over them with a weary, practiced motion. Her upper back drooped under the weight of her infant, Ida.

Simone, 40, shook her head in sympathy. "We're all dehydrated." She inspected the smoldered forest for green plants, which may indicate moisture. "Please help us find water," she petitioned the sky. Her appeal went unanswered.

The convoy staggered on, and the uncompromising Sunshine sapped their strength with every step. The Elders shuffled at a snail's pace to conserve energy, their faces etched with exhaustion. In comparison, the young women kept a steady rhythm with drive surpassing their weariness. With parched throats and aching limbs, the women all searched desperately for signs of liquid.

Occasionally, natural springs can be found where groundwater leaches to the surface at the base of hills or cliffs. These founts are small and difficult to spot, often concealed by vegetation or rock formations. The women looked for signs of green plants or clusters of trees, like cotton woods or willows, which might indicate the presence of water nearby.

A desert oasis is a rare but vital water source where underground rivers or aquifers reach the surface. Oases are usually surrounded by palm trees and other lush vegetation that thrive in the presence of consistent water. They provide liquid, shade, and food sources like dates and other fruits.

Ephemeral streams can form during rare rains, carving out narrow geographic channels. These watercourses remain dry most of the year, but liquid can be trapped in deeper sections, particularly after recent rain. Even if the surface appears dry, digging into the ground at the lowest point of these beds can reveal damp soil or small pools of moisture.

Rock basins and potholes are natural depressions in stone that can collect and hold rainwater. These small pools could last weeks or months after a rainstorm, especially if shaded. The women usually checked these formations carefully. They knew rock basins could hold enough water to significantly improve their chances of survival.

Wadis or washes are dry riverbeds that could occasionally hold water beneath the surface. While the surface of a wadi may be arid, digging into the gravelly soil at the lowest point of the wadi could reveal moisture or even water seeping up from underground. Wadis often collected liquid from distant rain that filtered through the ground.

Though not a direct water source, collecting dew is one way to obtain modest amounts of water. When temperatures dropped at night, dew formed on plants, rocks, and objects. In the early morning, the Elders used cloths and absorbent materials to wipe the dew off surfaces and wrung them out to collect the moisture. While the amount accumulated was minimal, every drop counted in the wilderness.

Many cacti, like barrel cactus, store water in thick, fleshy bodies. By carefully cutting cactus pads, the wayfarers could access the moist interior pulp, which, while bitter, provided hydration in an urgent situation. However, it was essential to identify the correct type of cactus. Some, like the saguaro, contained alkaloids that could cause nausea or worse.

Remnants of old wells, cisterns, or water tanks from abandoned farms could hold water. When the collective stumbled upon such structures, they provided crucial fluid when not contaminated. Checking longstanding trails could lead to finding one of these life-saving relics.

Each potential source required careful searching and sometimes a bit of luck. The group's survival depended on their ability to find these hidden reserves. Even in the most desolate settings, nature often provided a way if one knew where to look.

The caravan snaked through the stark wilderness, searching for precious liquid. Sometimes, they encountered remnants of society before the collapse: damaged vehicles, crumbling buildings, piles of garbage, and abandoned infrastructures. Each sight was a ghostly reminder of what life once was.

They paused to rest under the scant shade of a few skeletal trunks. The women rehydrated and checked on each other. Their empathy and camaraderie, forged through shared hardship and struggle, helped to sustain them during the arduous expedition. They shared stories, laughter, and tears, forming a stronger bond than the harsh environment they found themselves in.

Nzinga approached Asia, grinning. "There's a trail ahead, on the left. It might lead to a settlement."

Asia's brows knotted. "That takes us back South," she replied. "And we don't know how long the trail is."

Nzinga's lips pressed into a thin line. "We really need some hope right now." Her words echoed the sentiment of the group, who clung to the possibility of aid. Asia relented.

The Sun was high in the sky when they started down the path. Asia turned to Nzinga. "We're in the third decade of a long-term drought," she panted. "And it may continue for much longer. Last summer, thousands of people and animals died on the coast."

She shook her head in pity. "This summer will be hotter, and thousands more will die." Her face sagged with the weight of their climate reality.

Nzinga nodded. "Chaos and violence will increase. So will sex trafficking and enslavement. We've got better odds at surviving out here." She glanced at her companion with gratitude. "That's why you made us leave, to give us a fighting chance." Her smile was the kind that lit up a room, even on the darkest days.

The women searched eagerly for a homestead or settlement. Two hours later, there was no hint of people or habitat. They made camp and settled into the trench for the night.

12. Asia's Beliefs

It was 8 PM in the Southern Los Padres Forest. A week away from the Coastal refuge in Santa Barbara, the climate escapees were 10 miles from the largest Central California desert.

The Mohave stretched from the state's Eastern border into the Central Valley to the Western Coast and Pacific Ocean. They had to hike North for a month through the desert Badlands to the Safehouse near Fresno, 200 miles away.

The temperature in the forest fluctuated from hot days to cooler nights. The mercury dropped to 80°F (27°C) from its daytime high. The nomads huddled in their blankets and tried to relax.

Asia, 39, lounged in the trench with her eyelids closed, listening to the faint murmurs of the collective drifting off to sleep: Mothers comforting their children, muted conversations between friends, and sporadic sighs of exhaustion. Her morbid thoughts were far from restful.

She reminded herself that the collective was advancing, one foot in front of the other. Earlier, they had backtracked two hours down a trail that led nowhere, but she was not upset. It raised the group's spirits for a few hours and was proof of their unwavering will to live. They were lucky, as many were no longer alive, like her parents and Sisters.

'Life and death.' The words echoed in her mind, unbidden. She had witnessed a great deal of violence and casualties over the past few months at the shelter. Too much. Before that, she and the others lost many loved ones and endured much anguish.

She thought of the Buddhist teachings she learned long ago in Apple Valley: 'Samsara, the cycle of birth, life, death, and rebirth.' Those who died will be reborn. Did her family reincarnate? And if so, what and where?

And how about those who lived during such forbidding times? Were they better off dead? Buddha attested that life was sorrowful but insisted that one could find a way to transcend it through meditation. She was unsure if she still believed that, but the thought offered slight comfort.

'Is suffering truly endless?' she wondered. 'Or is there a way to end the cycle of pain?' Her reality seemed like a relentless wheel of grief: heat, thirst, hunger, fear, repeat. Perhaps there were other situations beyond this dark sequence, something she could not yet see. But where?

She glanced at the women nearby, their faces mollified in sleep. Like her, they lost everything: homes, families, and previous lives. But they did not lose their will to live. Quitting was not an option for the Mothers. Their children needed them. The Crones, too, were not surrendering.

'Is resilience the key?' she mused. To keep going, even when everything screamed 'Stop' and 'Give up.'

Her thoughts drifted to impermanence or Anicca: 'Everything changes, and nothing remains the same.' Her lively social milieu at the monastery was gone, yet she loved her new community. Perhaps her destiny was learning to adjust to constant changes, a life-long journey of acceptance and adaptation.

'Death is not the end,' she considered. 'It's merely a transition, part of the cycle.' Were her parents and siblings at peace somewhere? Or were they trapped in endless misery in a post-apocalypse hellscape?

Asia inhaled and exhaled, focusing on the rhythm of her breath the way she was taught. Breath meant presence, and she lived as long as she continued breathing. 'My existence must have some hidden purpose in this man-made disorder. Why else was I alive?' Saving the girls and building a female commune were essential and consequential.

'The key is acceptance,' she reasoned. 'Being a part of what is, of reality, rather than clinging to what was or hoping for what can be.' Even amid all the suffering, she might find contentment if she could fully accept the unfolding turmoil. And if she can attain peace, perhaps she could help others to discover it, too.

Her awareness wandered to the route ahead. 'El Norte, where possibilities await.' Rumors of cooler climates where the Sun's fury had not fully exhausted the land. Hearsays about great Northern forests where they would find sustenance, safety, and most importantly, community. 'Were the gossips real, or were they another mirage, one more trick of hopium?'

She worried they were chasing shadows and would be late reaching the fertile land before it, too, turned to ash and desert. 'But what choice do we have?' Staying South was a death sentence, and her companions fled their homes due to extreme weather conditions.

'Buddha's Middle Path,' she recalled. Not clinging to expectations or succumbing to despair. She had to take each step as it unfolded and accept whatever lay ahead. There was little use in false hope or fantasizing about a return to the past. She had to stay on the path, regardless of the outcome.

She stared intently at the Milky Way's countless points of light. The Cosmos was beyond abundant and constantly changing. Yet, the Universe was totally detached and untouched by the immense sorrow unfolding on Earth.

'Stars don't suffer,' she reflected. They were just there, unassumingly shining through the darkness.

Perhaps that was their help, reminding her to simply exist and shine in whatever way she could. Even in the overwhelming darkness of post-civilization.

With that insight, her thoughts subsided. She accepted the delicate balance between life and death, optimism and despair, perseverance and resignation, and suffering and serenity. All her doubts and fears were merely thoughts, and her feelings depended on her perspective. Tomorrow would bring different challenges, and she would deal with them then.

Laying under the Milky Way, she was okay at that moment. She was part of the Cosmic web and content that she was shining some light in the darkness and helping other females. She accepted herself fully and drifted into blissful sleep.

13. Dinner

It was March 29th, eight days after they departed Santa Barbara. The climate caravan traversed the Coastal wilderness all day near Route 33 without incident. At 5 PM, they reached the border of the Western Mohave desert. They had traveled sixty miles from the shelter and were thirty miles East of the Pacific Ocean traveling North.

High clouds rolled in from Los Padres Forest, and the afternoon Sun lowered its intensity on the sparse drylands. The migrant community had become acclimatized to the strangling weather in the forest, but the desert was ten degrees hotter. Still, they survived over a week on their own, which felt good. And since turning East, they faced no further attacks.

Two scouts, Phoolan and Daria, returned to the line, tired but with a sense of accomplishment that shone in their eyes. Phoolan, with shaved head and dark skin, and Daria, with cropped hair and freckled face, carried four containers of water, straining under the weight. Their drenched clothes and muddy skin were proof of their exceptional efforts.

Phoolan met Asia's gleam. "We found a wadi going South." She dropped her two receptacles.

Asia beamed. "Great going, Phoolan. And what about a place to camp?"

The scout's focus shifted to the Southwest. "We're close to a shaded spot, about 15 minutes."

Asia turned to the convoy. "We'll set up camp soon." She placed a reassuring hand on Daria's back. "Thank you both. Eat and regain your strength."

The assembly found respite in the shadows of a rocky outcrop. They dug a narrow trench and established a camp inside. The mood was light since they had enough water for dinner and could restock the next day.

Lian and Xóchitl surveyed the perimeter for hazards. There was none. "Bueno, how about Zen Master's Secret, Bhikkhuni?" Xóchitl was relaxed as usual. Lian was bored and did not care either way. Even if she said no, she would hear the Zen tale anyway.

"A student came to the Bhikkhuni," Xóchitl started. "The curious disciple asked, 'Master, what is the greatest secret of Zen?' The female Monk sat quietly for a minute. 'It's a secret,' she replied. 'So, it cannot be said. It must be experienced.'"

The Latina grinned and continued. "The Samanerika was puzzled. 'Then, how can I experience it, Bhikkhuni?' The teacher smiled, 'By first enjoying a cup of tea and a good laugh. Sometimes, the secret is simply enjoying the moment.'" The pair snickered and continued their patrol.

The women and children gathered around the campfire, sitting on worn blankets. The Mothers chatted and helped their children get comfortable.

Frida was busy preparing a simple meal of lentils and rice, and the girls watched in awe. Their hungry bodies simmered in anticipation while they observed the familiar routine.

The cook quickly assembled a makeshift kitchen beside the fire. She carefully stoked the blaze, ensuring it was hot enough to thoroughly cook the meal but not so fiercely that it burned. She hummed a 1960s Beatles song whilst she prepared the main course.

First, she retrieved a large, dented pot from her bag, its exterior darkened from years of use. With a steady hand, she added a generous amount of water and placed the covered pot onto a metal grate above the flames to boil.

Next, she measured a portion of dried lentils from her supplies and rinsed them under a trickle of water from her canteen. The lentils were tiny red dots, and she carefully inserted them into the pot, followed by six handfuls of rice.

After the water returned to a boil, the lentils began to plump up and turn yellow. Their Earthy aroma mingled delightfully with the smoky scent of the fire, filling the camp with savory richness. The culinary fragrance caused everyone to salivate in anticipation.

Frida reached into her spice pouch and deftly retrieved pinches of dried herbs and seasonings: turmeric, cumin, coriander, and chili powder. She sprinkled these into the pot with practiced efficiency. The spices added a burst of color and aromatic complexity, and the pot gurgled with a soothing beat.

With the lentils and rice bubbling in the closed pot, she and her two helpers tossed diced roots and nuts into a salad bowl, and sliced cactus fruits for dessert. The meal was ready in less than half an hour.

"Who's ready to eat?" Frida called.

"Me," the children chorused with joy, anticipation evident in their bright eyes and eager smiles.

The chef ladled steaming heaps of colorful rice into each member's bowl. The main dish had a pastel, artsy look: yellow lentils tender and bright, mingled with white fluffy rice, and dotted with flecks of green herbs and red chili.

Frida's helpers added portions of salad and dessert to make a wholesome, balanced meal. The survivors' moods brightened at the sight of the nourishing food, and they savored the wonderful smells wafting up from their plates. The first bite was always accompanied by murmurs and moans of joy.

"This is bussin," Cha'Kwaina squealed.

The lentils were delicious, and the spices added a kick that enhanced their natural flavors. The fluffy rice was a perfect complement, soaking up the savory broth and providing carbs to replenish the group's energy.

"Pure fire," Sasha exclaimed. "I needs to learn me how to cook like this."

After devouring their food, the children smiled and thanked the chef and her assistants. The modest meal was the highlight of their day, a grand token of the community spirit they shared.

Nzinga was tranquilized by the food and approached Asia after scraping her bowl clean. They both took a moment to observe the reddening sunset. "Our cooperative is incredibly resilient," she declared. "Their courage inspires me to no end."

Asia met Nzinga's shine. "We've come a long way. I'm happy we left that horrible place." Her quiet confidence seemed to lift the air around them.

The twilight deepened, and the temperature began to drop. The women and children bunched for comfort near the fire. Hehewuti began Cronetime, a term derived from the ancient Greek word 'Kronos,' meaning time, and 'Crone,' which referred to wise Elder women.

A Crone represented the ability to perceive more than with one's eyes alone. It was to observe with the heart through the creative and animating force of the psyche. Cronetime was a period of storytelling and learning when the community gathered around the fire hearth to share knowledge and wisdom.

Hehewuti read a story from their precious book, "The Age of Sibyls." Her rhythmic reading created a soothing lullaby for her pupils. The girls listened intently. The tale of distant lands and brave sheroes provided a temporary escape from the Badlands, filling them with optimism.

Twilight settled across the sky in dark, muted hues. The fiery orange and pinks of sunset faded, leaving behind a pastel wash of lavender and dusty rose near the vanishing point. The beauty of the evening brought a sense of tranquility and peace to the survivors.

Directly above, the sky deepened into a dark blue, gradually giving way to the encroaching darkness. Thin wisps of clouds were bathed in faint purples, their edges glowing in the diminishing light. The once-vivid colors mellowed, blending into one another. Daylight relinquished its hold, and nightfall embraced the land with a serene, almost otherworldly glow.

14. Crones

Early dawn bathed the Western Mohave desert in orange rays. The sand dunes seemed like massive piles of gold dust in a vast storage room of an obscenely wealthy 21st-century broligarch. The yellow landscape was like a fairytale, except for the temperature of 110°F (43°C).

The climate evacuees emerged from the trench at 6 AM, squinting into the brilliant light. They skipped breakfast and prepared to trek early. Ten days and 60 miles from the Pacific Coast, they were 30 miles Northeast of Meiners Oaks.

Asia planned to travel parallel to Route 33 past Bakersfield, where the road ended near Coalinga, 135 miles away. Then, they would switch to Highway 5 and hike 35 miles to the Safehouse in Cantua Creek. She knew traversing 170 miles in the blazing desert was daunting, and the constant struggle to find water made their survival an even more gripping challenge.

Each day, the caravan felt more secure from gangs and pedophiles. As usual, Lian went ahead while Xóchitl took the rear, inspecting the scene for hazards. On point, Lian saw nothing but the relentless expanse of the Badlands. She signaled to the leader.

"We're clear," Asia called. "Let's get moving."

The migrants proceeded at a steady pace. The Mothers used umbrellas to shield their young from the Sun's radiation, and the others relied on hats for shade. The line was abuzz with Sibyl stories the girls heard the night before.

The Crones were acutely connected to nature. They walked together and moved in rhythm, like branches swaying in a gentle wind. The five Elders were in sync with the seasons and landscape, even the inhospitable desert. They viewed the Badlands as part of Gaia, like they were. Their wisdom and relationship to the Earth were a source of illumination for the entire group.

Kuan-Yin's deep-set orbs gazed outward, but she focused inward on her thoughts and breathing. "Let's embrace this new day," she entreated. The sixty-year-old's words were soothing like a bird song. "Let's honor life by being gentle to our body and mind." Her face was filled with gratitude as she clasped her hands, holding onto unspoken truths.

Behind her, Zaniya, 65, was framed by a cascade of silver hair. She always exuded serenity and confidence. Her actions were like a sacred dance performed in Gaia's honor. Her constant reverence empowered the girls and instilled a deep sense of belonging.

"The Great Earth Goddess speaks to us," she sang. "Her resilience is the rock beneath life's streams, grounding and guiding, shaping all who cross her path. We must listen to her wisdom and respect her power." Her invocations to Gaia were a rallying cry for strength and spirit that enlightened the commune.

Zaniya touched her heart, attuned to the Earth's subtle vibrations, and sang another epic verse. "Beneath the Goddess's soft exterior lies the strength of granite and the resolve of ages. She is unyielding yet nurturing, fierce yet compassionate. All praise to Gaia. May She remain inside us. Blessed be."

Mary, 61, was a solitary figure absorbed in her journal and thoughts. A woman of few words, she rarely engaged in casual conversation. The Crones and other women respected her privacy and gave her the psychic space she craved. She had a passion for writing and wrote diligently in every spare moment.

Notwithstanding her preference for isolation, she was devoted to other introverts in the cooperative, like Lian. Her partner, Zenobia, was the exact opposite, a social butterfly. Mary treasured solitude, yet she enjoyed the spontaneity of children and often chose their company over adults.

Zenobia, 58, lifted her face skyward to gaze at two vultures rotating overhead. "Relatives, mek we pass thru yuh land wid no trouble," she called. She flapped her hands like wings, mirroring the birds' movements. Her profound admiration for nature inspired others to do the same.

Hehewuti, 74, strode gracefully while counting the wooden beads on her necklace. Every movement was precise and mindful. Her melodious chant weaved through the air, encouraging everyone. "Our Earth Mother is one. She is all. We are Gaia. Blessed be." Occasionally, she spread her palms downward to symbolically embrace the Earth.

Asia was awed by the Crones' devotion, wisdom, and positive demeanor. She was astonished that despite their age, they managed to keep pace with the convoy. "Thanks for doing your best, everyone," she called. Her compassionate leadership motivated the evacuees to push themselves further and fully engage in each task.

In the late afternoon, the exhausted collective dug a trench and made camp on the Eastern side of a dune. As usual, Frida's delicious food boosted everyone's energy and morale. After dinner, the women chatted, brushed their clothes, and cleaned their packs. The girls Pictionary, Charades, and Name That Tune while waiting for Cronetime.

15. Mary's Cronetime

The fiery orb hung low in the Western sky, casting long shadows across the Mohave drylands. It was the women's second night in the desert. The heated dunes slowly lost their fury, and their outlines stretched to greet each other. Earlier, a hostile expanse, the tall mounds appeared hospitable, as if extending an enthusiastic welcome.

It was Cronetime, a sacred hour when the Elders assembled the young ones to pass down knowledge, stories, and wisdom that post-civilized society had long since forgotten. The children sat in a semi-circle on woven mats, glistening with sweat. In the distance, the shrunken trunks of cacti trees stood as a silent reminder of the climate changes they had inherited.

Hehewuti welcomed her audience to Cronetime and offered a tribute to Gaia. She bowed and handed the communal board to Mary, a reserved 61-year-old who rarely spoke.

Mary's gaze swept over the girls' keen faces. They reminded her of the students she taught decades ago. She and Kuan-Yin were the only women in the caravan who attended college prior to their collapse. She taught environmental science at a high school before schooling dissolved, and she missed teaching.

"What would you like to do for Cronetime?" She invited the class to select their own topic.

Lisa, 11, spoke first. "When will this icky heat end?"

"Unfortunately, the heat isn't going anywhere soon," the teacher replied, her tone grave and serious. "In fact, it will only intensify." Her words carried the weight of the urgent situation, making the students realize the severity of the issue.

"Big yikes," Sasha, 15, groaned. "Why?"

Mary's eyes drifted to the horizon where the late evening Sun blazed. "It's complicated," she admitted. "But let's start with why it got hot in the first place." Her finger traced an invisible arc in the sky. "Climate change is caused by greenhouse gases, GHGs for short. They rise into the atmosphere and act like a warm blanket covering the Earth."

Cha'Kwaina, 14, tilted her head into the atmosphere. "Why can't we see the gasses?"

"They're colorless and odorless," Mary explained. "The main GHGs are carbon dioxide, or CO_2; methane, or CH_4; and nitrous oxide, or N_2O. They trap the Earth's warmth in the atmosphere."

"Why it's getting hotter?" Greta, 13, asked uneasily.

The teacher heaved a sigh. "Global warming results from greenhouse gasses," she repeated solemnly. "The more GHGs there are, the thicker the blanket covering the Earth gets, so it becomes hotter."

Phoolan, 16, pointed to the sky. "But where are the gasses coming from?"

"Good question," Mary acknowledged. "Before our societies collapsed, humans were the main emitters. We polluted the air for three centuries by burning fossil fuels like coal, oil, and methane in energy production, agriculture, and transportation."

Greta raised her hand nervously. "Why didn't people stop making the gasses? Didn't they know it would become too hot?"

"They knew," the Elder admitted. "But it made a few extremely wealthy and powerful. The others were occupied by survival, work, entertainment, pleasure, sports, food, religion, identity... There was a need for immediate action, and many young people tried to make a difference. But the leaders did not listen, and the situation worsened."

"That's not right." Cha'Kwaina frowned. "So sus."

Mary nodded gravely. "For a million years, carbon dioxide levels in the air were around 250 parts per million, ppm. They never went beyond 300 ppm. But in the 21st century, CO_2 shot up to 800 ppm."

"Is that too high?" Ma'at, 12, appeared anxious.

The Crone nodded. "Yes. That's more than double the previous limit in a million years. And the increase happened in only three hundred years."

"Earth is wearing two gas blankets now?" Phoolan wrapped her jacket around herself for emphasis.

"Three blankets." The teacher sighed.

"What's a normal temperature?" Sasha wondered.

Mary's gaze softened. She saw some girls were anxious and did not want to alarm them. Yet, she had to describe climate science honestly and not downplay the negative aspects.

"Three hundred years ago, Earth's average temp was around 14 to 16 degrees Celsius," she explained. "That's 57 to 61 degrees Fahrenheit, or what it feels like now. Isn't this cozy?"

"Gosh, I wish it was like this all day," Cha'Kwaina cried out. The girls signaled agreement.

The Crone nodded and resumed, "60°F was the average for the entire Globe. But it was hotter in the thicker middle and cooler at the thinner top, near the poles. The average now is 78°F, or eighteen degrees more." She paused for her students to absorb the difference.

"At the start of the 21st century," Mary continued, "it reached a scorching 57°C in Death Valley, just 250 miles from here. That's a blistering 134°F. But now, it soars above a searing 170°F or 76°C."

"Wow, that's burning hot," Lisa exclaimed. "It would totally fry me."

"We can cook food in the Sun over there," Ma'at suggested.

"But how can I eat if I'm melting?" Lisa worried.

"You'll have to eat at night," Sasha answered. The girls laughed.

Ma'at shook her head. "Why don't the bad gasses just float off into space?"

"Good question," Mary beamed, enjoying the lesson. "Earth has a thin atmosphere, but it stops the GHGs, oxygen, and other gases from escaping into space. In contrast, Mars is much colder without an atmosphere, averaging minus 65°C (-85°F)."

The girls were quiet. They learned why Mars was so cold and Earth too hot. They appreciated the information, but it was upsetting.

Sasha was still baffled. "I don't understand why it got hot so quickly?"

Mary nodded. "Well, in 2050, CO_2 levels passed 500 ppm, and average temp rose above 2°C. By 2080, CO_2 passed 600 ppm and was 3°C higher, a 5.4°F rise."

"And what's it now?" Shasha followed up.

The teacher sighed. "CO_2 is close to 900 ppm. The average temp is 20°C, or 6°C higher. That's an 11°F rise from the last million years of stable climate."

"Six doesn't sound like much," Greta remarked. "So why does it feel so hot?"

Mary held a finger up. "One degree means a lot. In 2000, the average summer temp here in Central Valley was 90°F, but it exceeded 100°F on some days. Now, the average is 115°F and gets to 140°F occasionally."

"That's 25 degrees more for us, double the average." Sasha shook her head sadly. "I get it now."

The students grew silent, processing the facts.

"What happened after it got hotter?" Lisa quizzed.

"A world of trouble," the Crone answered. "Drought caused crop failures and less food supplies. It sparked wildfires, bigger deserts, and water loss. Wildfires burned homes, forests, and habitats. Warming seas created stronger coastal storms and hurricanes."

She took a long breath and resumed. "The bad effects multiplied. Drought made wildfires worse. More fires and wind produced toxic smoke that spread further. Hotter oceans and warmer air caused flooding and tornadoes further inland. Melting ice increased sea levels, flooding cities and Coastal areas."

"That's very bad," Cha'Kwaina interjected.

"Yes, but that's not all," Mary grimaced. "Higher temperatures created electricity shortages and blackouts. Insect-borne diseases spread from the Tropics. More freshwater reduced ocean circulation. All this led to widespread famine, mass casualties, vast migrations, and the collapse of societies."

The girls sat in silence. They had heard snippets of the climate crisis in the 21st century, but the Crone explained how the breakdown occurred step by step.

"Why didn't it get cooler after the collapse?" Cha'Kwaina wondered.

"Another good question." Mary was pleased with the girls' understanding. They were learning and asking the right questions. "Civilization crumpled at the turn of the 22nd century," she explained. "After that, humans did not pollute the air as much. But..." Her voice broke, and she paused to regain composure.

Mary's shoulders sagged under the weight of the knowledge she was about to share. "GHGs last a long time. CO_2 will remain in the air for thousands of years, trapping heat and raising temps."

Cha'Kwaina was stunned. "How hot will it get then?" She was almost afraid to hear the answer.

The Crone's gaze grew distant as if she were looking into a future she could barely comprehend. "It's already 3.5°C greater than before. It could climb to 7°C higher this century, or 13°F above a stable climate."

Greta stared at the Elder apprehensively. "When will the heat come down?"

Mary placed her palms together. "Not until CO_2 decline back to 300 ppm," she said softly. "That will take thousands of years, which means that warming is irreversible for us. Humans will never experience a cooler Earth."

The children and adults fell silent. Mary's words settled over them like a heavy boulder. Her lesson was too painful to digest, and they sat dumbfounded. The wind rushed across the dunes, echoing a mournful prayer. It reminded them of the fragile life they were struggling to preserve.

16. Desert Heat

It was high noon in the Western Mojave desert. The thermometer registered at 125°F (52°C). Ten days into their trek, the forty wayfarers squared off against the hostile terrain with a steely drive. They had covered 30 miles along Route 33 North and were motivated to win the day by crossing another 10 miles or forcing a draw with five.

Asia trudged on against the scorching air, tenacity etched on her face. It was their third day in the Badlands, and they were three weeks and 165 miles away from the Safehouse in Cantua Creek. The scenery grew more desert-like and bleak with each passing day. Dry brush stretched for miles in the shining expanse of sand, like moldy spots on a dirty mirror.

The Star blazed relentlessly, but the procession lumbered along, fueled by their resilience. They took a break under some cacti, hiding from the blinding light.

Lisa, 11, sat beside her younger brother, Elon, searching his face for understanding. "Why don't you boys play with us?" Her eyes pleaded for inclusion.

The nine-year-old glanced at his sister with an uncertain smile and said nothing. The trio of males - two teenagers, Stephen, 15, and Miller, 16, and Elon - usually played together, separate from the girls.

Miller laughed and pushed Stephen out of the shade. Elon left Lisa's side and ran after the teens. Lisa stared jealously at the boys. She longed to join their fun but knew she was unwelcome. "Why don't they like me?" she wondered aloud, her voice tinged with hurt.

Lian overheard and commented, "It's not you, sweetie. They don't like any girl."

"But why?" Lisa sulked.

"Boys think they're better than us," Lian snapped.

"Are they better?" Lisa was puzzled.

"No way," Lian retorted. "Never think you're less. They're bullies which makes them worse."

"I wish they played with us," Lian exclaimed.

The guard was incensed but said nothing.

The survivors resumed their march. Lian led the way, keeping a vigilant watch on her surroundings and companions. She waved at Xóchitl in the rear, and they exchanged warm smiles, a silent reassurance of their shared journey.

Despite her cheer, Lian knew the cooperative was in trouble. The weather was agonizing, the water supply was low, and morale was deteriorating. 'We need a day or two of rest,' she thought.

The line proceeded at a snail's pace along the side of a vast dune. The Mothers carried minors on their hips, and their load felt heavier with each stride. Their steady gait turned into a grueling slog through the sand, with frequent stops. Every tread felt like a victory against quitting or collapsing. The Badlands was winning the standoff.

Ahead of the pack, Asia and Nzinga staggered side by side. Their silence was thick with unspoken worries and the shared exhaustion of their trip. A blast of hot, dry air stung their faces as they crested a dune.

Nzinga broke the reticence. "I didn't think it could get this hot." She squinted against the blinding glare. "The air is choking me."

Asia dabbed at her forehead and grimaced. "It's the kind of heat that seeps into your bones," she confided.

Nzinga adjusted her hat. "It's like walking along a volcano. I feel my shoes melting. Every tread pulls me down, dragging my feet into the molten Earth."

Asia's stare reflected the harsh light and emptiness. "You ain't lying. That ball of fire hangs there all day, burning away everything, our energy, desires, memories of loved ones, even the desire to live."

Nzinga shuddered, shaking off dirt. "The dry dust clings to my face like a second, suffocating layer. Each footfall stirs up more dust. It coats my throat and stings my eyes."

Asia faced the Sun. "The rays penetrate my skin and get inside me, burning away my precious fluids and cells." She pressed her chest, trying to squeeze out the discomfort. "It's scorching my internals like the dryness of a wildfire."

Nzinga shook her head in agreement. "It's relentless, and there's no escape. Every step feels like launching headlong into a smokeless cooker. I dream of rain, waterfalls, the Pacific Ocean." She stared at the Western skyline with deep longing. "A shower to wash off this dirt and quench my bottomless thirst."

Asia took shallow breaths. "We can't let it break us. But I won't lie. It's wearing me down bit by bit."

Nzinga was relieved to express her vulnerability without judgment. "Every day feels closer to being consumed by this infinite furnace." She clenched her fists, trying to channel her frustration into courage. "Buried in the sand and lost forever."

"We can't keep going like this," Asia admitted. She straightened her spine and took a few long breaths. "But we're not giving up. Not until we reach the Safehouse." She peered at her companions in the rear. "We'll make it. We must. For the kids' sake."

Nzinga remained unconvinced, and they tramped silently for a few minutes.

Asia's forehead was etched with fatigue. "This desert in Spring is a preview of what the Coasts will be like this Summer. But Winter will come." The thought of the cold season improved her disposition.

Nzinga clenched her teeth. "The Safehouse better be there. It's the only thing that keeps us going." She wondered if the promised refuge was one of Asia's little deceptions to keep them moving.

Asia did not reply, and the pair paced in silence. The arid desert stretched to the horizon indefinitely.

Asia contemplated logistics. The Safehouse was a great distance away. Perhaps it was too far and out of reach for their deteriorating bodies. The blistering route seemed daunting, nearly impossible. 'Would they lose the deadly standoff against the Badlands?' she wondered.

She cleared her mind and stomped ahead. She had to keep pushing, leading the way. Her community's existence depended on her perseverance. Her training kicked in. She would not succumb to doubt and let the desert win. 'The best solution to despair is to encourage others.'

Asia took another stride and waved the others on. "You're doing great," she called. "We're closing in on the Safehouse. And we'll take a break soon." The promise of shelter, the center of faith in their arduous passage, kept the female company moving.

17. Stranger

At 1 PM, it was even hotter and drier. The Central Valley simmered with low humidity at 130°F (54°C). The climate drifters staggered onward in the sand on the eleventh day of their voyage. The Star on the Orion Arm of the Milky Way bore down on the seared terrain, turning every breath into a scorching intake.

The cooperative was burnt to a crisp like a horribly cooked dish served to an out-to-lunch billionaire in Hades. They listlessly approached the crest of a dune, and Lian paused at the top.

Below her stretched a vast, bone-dry plain with no sign of the promised river on the map. Instead, the land was a desolate expanse, stretching like a canvas of despair. It was dotted with the skeletal remains of charred cacti, their branches twisted and gnarled like mangled bodies on a battlefield.

A sparkle caught Lian's attention beyond the blast zone, a glimmer of something, perhaps water or a relic. Her mind galloped, searching for a plan. They could not survive much longer without water, and the flicker ahead was a possibility, flimsy as it was.

'We've got to keep moving,' she thought. She beckoned, encouraging the others to follow her down the dune. She wanted to get closer to whatever lay ahead but was reluctant to disclose what she saw. It was probably a mirage.

The column slowly descended into the ashen plain. The air was thick with dust and reeked of scorched dirt. They pressed on lethargically as the heat sapped the last of their energy. The celestial lamp painfully irritated their blistered and broken skin.

Some of the younger children began to stumble. Their tiny bodies suffered from exhaustion and dehydration. Their eyes were sunken, and their cracked lips throbbed.

Asia called a rest stop. The drifters sat under whatever shade they could find under the scorched oak trunks. The women, faces etched with worry, helped the children settle.

Lian took in the weary figures and recognized that the weakest members may not last much longer. She had to do something. She climbed a stump and surveyed the distance. Then, she saw movement, a faint figure in the distance.

Her heart raced with a mix of chance and fear. Was it a survivor? Or a threat? She motioned for the collective to stay put and edged toward the indistinct form, her heart pounding.

When she drew closer, the grey outline came into focus. It was a tall woman with tattered clothes whipping in the slight breeze. She strolled with the gait of someone accustomed to the land. She carried a digging stick, and slung over her back was a large, weathered pack bulging with the promise of supplies.

Lian waved, and the woman approached her. She paused, assessing the guard and the haggard group in the rear. Her body stiffened when she saw Lian's weapon. "Who are you?" The woman's words carved through the air, clear and powerful.

"Refugees," Lian motioned disarmingly. "We can trade food for some water."

The woman studied the guard momentarily, then arrived at a conclusion with a decisive head toss. "I'm Hypatia. You don't have to trade. I know where you can find water." She pointed to the East.

Lian's body trembled with relief, but she remained skeptical. "Why should we trust you?"

The stranger frowned. "Because you don't have a choice." Without waiting for a response, Hypatia turned and strolled to her left.

Lian's pupils trailed the retreating figure with apprehension. 'Is she leading us to pedos?' she wondered. She gazed anxiously at the girls clustered in the center of the line. She refixed her attention to the woman, and her intuition signaled it was time to act.

"This way," Lian called. She pointed firmly to the retreating figure. "We follow her to water."

The caravan followed the lead guard hesitantly. They could not discern any moisture in the burnt landscape and were unsure where the lone stranger was leading them. Maybe she was crazy.

Asia caught up to Lian. "Can we trust her? What if this is a dead end? We've got no energy to waste."

Lian focused on the woman ahead and shrugged. "We're out of options." She continued after the stranger, her doggedness shining through her fatigue. "If it's a trap, we fight until the end."

The weather remained extremely oppressive. The unknown woman led them past dune after dune, her stride sure and confident. The convoy staggered and lagged. They were exhausted and needed a break, but Hypatia kept moving. They tried to keep up.

Lian eagerly motioned the line forward. She knew positiveness in the Badlands was vital, like the oxygen they breathed. For the first time in days, she had a fragile promise to cling to. Her pace quickened, and her mood improved in anticipation of beating the odds and quenching her parched throat. The group lurched after her into the unknown.

18. Hypatia

It was nearly 2 PM in the California drylands, and the weather remained unbearably hot at 134°F (57°C). For an hour, the climate wanderers doggedly followed a stranger who promised to lead them to water. They were at the end of a rope, hanging by a thread. It seemed like they were going in circles with no clear purpose. They lost hope in her and were about to quit.

The stranger stopped at the edge of a dry riverbed and dropped her backpack. The survivors caught up to her and looked around, confused. The area was parched and cracked, with no sign of moisture.

"Where's the water?" Lian stared at the stranger crossly. 'Is this woman nuts?' she wondered.

Hypatia pointed her gnarled finger toward a cluster of rocks. "There. An underground spring, down a few feet." She leaned onto her digging stick for support.

Lian smirked. "How do you know?"

The woman spread her arm wide. "This area may seem barren, but it's a library of hidden resources. I've learned to read these dunes like a book."

'A reading room in the Badlands?' Lian thought. 'She must be mad.'

Hypatia took in her secret collection and added, "Don't worry. I've found water here many times." She lifted her chin, firm and confident. The wilderness seemed like a loyal companion to her claim.

Despite their doubts, the dehydrated women set to work, using whatever tools they had to excavate the dry bed. At first, the task was hopeless. The soil was utterly compact, hard like stone. But they took turns burrowing.

After fifteen minutes, a shout arose. "It's damp," Nzinga hollered. "There's moisture below." She kept tunneling, and the caravan cheered when a spurt seeped from the ground.

The women shoveled deeper until the water trickled and grew into a tiny flow. Relief washed over the collective as they wetted their lips and sipped from the ground. After half an hour of excavation, a two-foot hole pooled with water. The women filtered the precious liquid and filled their canteens. Relief was evident in their broad smiles and laughter.

Zaniya lifted her arms gracefully, sparkling with veneration. "Praise Gaia. The Goddess does not chase the winds or bend to storms. She lets them pass, knowing She is constant, steadfast, and unbroken. She is the guardian of the sky, Mother of rivers, and keeper of secrets carved in stone. To honor the Goddess is to prize the soul's endurance, wisdom, and the beauty of untamed nature. Blessed be."

The girls' energy returned, and they sprung to life. Asia watched them splash with awe. Their joy was infectious, proof of the resilience and possibilities of the next generation. The women's emotions lifted, and they laughed harder than they had in weeks.

Lian and Xóchitl circled the improvised water park, grinning. "Es muy bueno. How about Master and Flower, Bhikkhuni?"

"Is it about water?" Lian knew Xóchitl always found a way to relate her Zen tales to their current situation.

The Latina smiled at the thrilled children. "Kinda," she responded. "A young nun was walking with her Bhikkhuni, and they came upon a beautiful flower. The student bent down and said, 'Teacher, look at this perfect flower. How long do you think it will last?'"

Xóchitl paused, and Lian shrugged. "A few days?"

Xóchitl pointed. "That pool is the flower."

Lian grinned. "So are you. And I hope my flower lasts forever."

Xóchitl beamed and continued, "The Bhikkhuni said nothing. 'How long will the flower last?' the student repeated. 'For long as you are looking at it,' the female Monk replied."

Lian laughed. "That splash zone will disappear after we leave." The pair circled the perimeter.

Asia sat next to Hypatia and smiled appreciatively. "We're all indebted to you. Thank you so much."

The stranger bowed and remained silent.

"Why are you out here alone?" Asia searched the woman's face for answers.

Hypatia lowered her head, weighed down by invisible burdens. "I wasn't always alone," she began sorrowfully. Her trembling hands fidgeted with the edge of her blouse. "I once had a family and a community like yours."

The desert librarian paused, and her attention drifted to the skyline. Her face was a synthesis of nostalgia and grief. "We lived in a village by a river, hidden away from the chaos of the cities. We thought we were safe." She clutched her staff, seeking comfort from its presence.

"Many of us lived in small towns," Asia noted. She did not want to intrude but could not hold back her curiosity. "What was it like there?"

Hypatia took a moment to consider how much she wanted to recall. She sighed as memories rose unbidden to the surface of her mind.

"It was beautiful," she said. "Our village had six dozen families. The valley was fertile and green. We grew vegetables and had plenty to eat."

Asia imagined a picturesque place, like her farm.

"My husband, Homan, was a builder," Hypatia continued, gaining strength. "He made several cabins in the village, including ours. The kids were the light of our lives." She stared at the children playing in the waterhole with longing.

"How many did you have?" Asia wondered.

"Two." Hypatia's voice tinged with melancholy. "Tomas and Patti. Their laughter echoed through the valley. It was the sound of happiness, of a normal life despite everything."

The stranger paused and became withdrawn. Sorrow was etched into every line of her face. Inside her was an immense pain that shaped who she was.

"What happened?" Asia dreaded the answer.

Hypatia tightened her grip on the staff until her knuckles turned white. "The river dried up," she shuddered. "The rain stopped. Year after year, there was only drought. It shrunk to a trickle and then vanished entirely. The soil dried out, and the crops failed. Even the wells we dug ran dry."

"Even our lake dried up," Asia said sympathetically.

Hypatia nodded and continued. "Disease came next. Our children were sick, and there was nothing we could do. Homan felt helpless and became angry." She shook her head slowly. "He blamed immigrants and minorities for everything. He claimed they were having too many babies and that overpopulation was causing climate change."

The stranger's breathing faltered, and she was quiet. Her memories were almost too much to bear.

Asia sighed. "My town became an ethnic civil war, 'whites' versus Latinos. Even the kids got involved."

Hypatia shook her head in understanding. "Homan joined a band of 'whites' who thought of themselves as defenders of the color-line. They ambushed dark-colored individuals and families." Reliving the painful memories took a toll on her. She was clearly disturbed by the information she shared.

"It didn't matter if they were citizens," the woman continued in a hollow voice. "Homan and his militia targeted all four Asian families in our settlement. They captured men, women, and children alike, chained and treated them like animals, and peddled them off to Southern slave traders for bits of gold."

Hypatia became silent, and her eyes grew distant as if she had seen too much.

Asia nodded, breathing slowly to calm herself. "I know how you feel. The 'white' men in Laughlin were the same, banding together, enslaving and trading minorities. It was horrible. They killed my parents because they resisted."

Hypatia shuddered, imagining Homan and his gang on their rampage in thousands of communities. She gazed at the fun in the tiny pool. "Homan and his buddies abused the girls and pushed them into the sex trade. It was disgusting." Her eyes were hazy, fixed on her memories. She was silent for a long time, still shocked by what she had experienced.

After a minute, she composed herself and resumed, "I moved to a neighbor's house with my two children. Mothers banded together for the kids. Many got measles, flu, and diarrhea. My two got sicker. Homan neglected them, and soon they were gone."

Asia's chest sank. "I'm so sorry." Her heart ached for the unimaginable loss Hypatia endured.

The stranger stared at the happy kids playing. "I buried my babies. In the same riverbed they loved. I couldn't stay there anymore, surrounded by their memories. Homan and his buddies were wild and out of control. I took what I could and fled."

Asia touched Hypatia's shoulders. "You've lost so much. Yet you've survived. And here you are, helping others like us. That's a kind of power most people can't imagine." She bowed to her companion.

Hypatia let out a weary sigh. "I just keep going. I didn't want to at first. But this desert is alive. It helps me to forget. It's challenging, but I manage to live simply and peacefully. I've learned to find water, food, rest, whatever I need."

Asia glanced at Nzinga standing nearby. They were discovering how to stay alive in the wilderness as well. "We're extremely grateful for your aid." She held the woman's stare. "We almost didn't make it. Thank you."

"It's nothing," Hypatia said. "It's easier when you stay in one place. The Badlands isn't kind to strangers or the unprepared."

Asia knew the stranger's encyclopedic knowledge of the Badlands would make their lives easier and queried, "Can you travel with us?"

Hypatia shook her head deliberately. "This is my home. I cannot leave."

"Why here?" Asia was curious. "It's so desolate."

The woman gazed at the panorama. "I'm alone and away from it all." After a while, she added, "I can't take another loss."

Asia nodded. She understood why Hypatia was wary of attachment.

The stranger pointed to the waterhole and warned, "Don't stay too long. Others know this place."

"We'll depart soon," Asia promised.

Hypatia rose and shouldered her backpack. She gave a final bow and returned the way they came. Gradually, she disappeared into the afternoon Sun.

The children waved at the retreating figure and returned to playing in their precious waterpark. The Mothers and Crones joined the fun, cheerfully sponging off dust from their bodies and clothes. Asia and Nzinga sat observing the collective for a long time.

19. Night Sky

It was 7 PM in Central California. The scorching weather that plagued the day retreated, replaced by a coolness that seeped into the sand and stones. The forty Santa Barbara evacuees started the day with dehydration and fear of dying but ended on a high note, thanks to Lian and Hypatia.

The children reluctantly vacated their splash zone and dried off. After changing clothes, they joined the group to eat Frida's wonderful dinner. Everyone blissfully lounged in the trench and around the camp, a united community in the face of adversity.

Consumed by her thoughts, Asia sat apart from the circle of women around the hearth. Her mind was a whirlwind of memories and doubts. Hypatia's loss and isolated existence disturbed her, and she needed time to process the encounter. One part of her felt empathy for the woman, while another yearned for her solitude, prompting a deeply personal reflection.

Asia's gaze lingered on her lively community, wrapped in warm blankets. The victory of finding water in the desert was cause for celebration, and the women enthusiastically made plans to wash clothes the next day. Asia was proud of them, yet something held her back from fully embracing their collective joy.

She stared at the dunes for comfort. The faint light of the rising crescent Moon outlined their smooth, flowing curves. Earth's daughter hung low in the sky, a slender silver sliver bathing the austere scene in a pale, ethereal glow.

The night's chill seeped into her bones. The warm ground offered a comforting embrace, but it could not dispel the coldness within her. She sat in silence and gradually realized the source of her discomfort. Hypatia's agony over her dead children had stirred up memories of her own loss. The woman was mourning in solitude, taking time to process her pain.

'Did I allow myself enough time to cry for my family?' Asia wondered. 'Or did I bury the pain, afraid of taking the necessary steps to heal?' She had no answers and was frustrated by the uncertainty.

The muteness of the desert night was profound. It was like a solid blanket of soundlessness that pressed in from all sides. It was a quietness that carried a weight of its own, filled with the absence of life. There were no rustling leaves or calls from animals, only the occasional swirl of shifting sand.

Nature was an unfathomable loss as well. 'Why don't I ever weep over life's demise?' she mused. 'For the extinction of countless species?' Hundreds of animals, plants, and entire ecosystems are gone forever. Was it too traumatic to keep track of, or was she too cold to notice and care?

To the East, jagged silhouettes of rocky outcrops stood stark against the night sky. The ground seemed to stretch forever, an empty expanse where time slowed, and the path felt impossibly heavy and unnavigable. In the past, the constellations guided travelers and dreamers alike. She wished they could show her how to grieve.

Watching her parents burn was an indescribable agony. Their death was extremely disturbing, and it threatened to overwhelm her. She was helpless, guilty, and spiraling towards a nervous breakdown. Yet, her Sisters remained, and she quickly submerged the pain to be their caregiver. 'Was burying my sorrows the right thing to do?'

Hypatia's lament revived Asia's survivor guilt. She lost both parents and her two Sisters. Why was she the only survivor of her entire family? 'Am I strong enough to hold space for guilt and sadness?' she pondered. 'Or would I start to spiral again?'

The sky was studded with countless Stars that stretched East to West, North to South. They were so bright and close that it felt like she could reach out and pluck them from the sky. The Milky Way unfurled in a shimmering river of light, hinting at infinite mysteries, of realities beyond life and death on Earth.

The Star-strewn heavens offered peace, a reprieve from life's relentless challenges. With its timeless beauty and solemnity, nighttime reflected Earth's harmony with the Cosmos and the insignificance of humans' place within it. Asia felt incredibly small.

She understood that grief was a personal journey, but how long was she going to stay in denial? 'Am I heartless, or is my refusal to mourn part of self-preservation and recovery from my traumatic past?' She had decided never to wallow in self-pity, but did it lead her to become selfish and indifferent?

Asia sat immersed in troubled thoughts. The harsh realities the collective faced were never far from her mind. The twelve girls were highly prized in a society dominated by opportunistic men. Their toxic masculinity, aggression, and exploitation were a constant threat to the group's safety and well-being. If caught, male warlords would exploit the girls mercilessly. How long could their luck last?

The journey entailed overcoming her past, existing in a hostile landscape, and resisting predatory men. Every mile they traveled, every day they survived, was a struggle against the grim patriarchal dystopia. 'What are our chances of making it to safety?' She shuddered at the low odds.

Asia wanted to stand up and walk around but was immobilized by distressing thoughts. She was nauseous, and her head spun in confusion. She felt like passing out. Then she heard a chant. It was a Crone invoking the spirits for guidance and strength in the trying times.

"The Goddess is great," Zaniya purred. "The mountains do not apologize for their height, and She does not apologize for her power." The Crone's healing words flowed like a lullaby. "She carries the weight of her struggles like a mountain carries the Earth: silent, resilient, and enduring."

Zaniya paused to gaze at Asia and resumed. "Rise from the shadows, Daughters, and embrace your light. Stand with courage, for you are both the darkness that grounds and the light that leads. Like the Sun-kissed peaks, shine with courage, confidence, and inner light. With the Goddess's guidance, stand tall and rooted in your purpose."

The Crone opened her hands slowly, palms outward, offering her benediction to Asia and the commune. "She is merciful to those who honor her and the Earth. Blessed be, Gaias. Blessed be."

Asia's eyes lingered on Zaniya's beatitude. The Elder's beauty and calmness took her breath away. She inhaled deeply and turned to greet the Moon. Even in the darkest hour, Luna promised a new dawn. With each passing day, the caravan grew closer to the Safehouse. She composed herself and felt much better. Once again, Zaniya's invocation saved her from bottomless misery.

20. Zaniya

Zaniya, 65, stood five feet six inches tall and weighed 120 pounds. Her lean frame was shaped by decades of hiking, climbing, and surviving in the wilderness. Her arms and legs, though lacking the fullness of youth, were wiry and firm, reflecting her inner strength and determination. Her deep, Earthy brown pupils seemed to hold the secrets of Gaia, framed by long, silver-tipped lashes, symbolizing her deep connection to the Earth and its mysteries.

Like her verses, Zaniya's appearance exuded tranquility and wisdom. Her profound interest in Goddess culture led her on a spiritual quest after civilization's decline, rooted in deep reverence for natural ecosystems and the female spirit. More than any other aspect of her life, this journey defined her as an individual woman.

She was born in Baja California, Mexico, into an Indigenous Nahuatl community that viewed the Earth as a relative. Her name, Zaniya, meaning 'forever and always' in Aztec culture, reflected her parents' belief that the land was not merely a resource but a living entity with which they had a symbiotic relationship.

Her Mother was immersed in Nahuatl songs, dances, traditions, and culture. As a child, Zaniya learned to forage for wild plants and make delicious foods. Her father explained Aztec beliefs, including the story of the main deity, Huitzilopochtli, the god of war.

According to legend, the male patron of the Aztecs guided the people on a long journey to Tenochtitlan, which became their capital city. At the sacred site, the migrants found an eagle perched on a cactus with a writhing serpent in its beak.

The eagle conveyed the spirit of Huitzilopochtli, the Sun and father. The serpent represented the soul of the Earth and the Mother. The eagle's capture of the snake embodied the struggle of the male celestial figure to conquer the female underworld or Earth.

The serpent's symbolic sacrifice to the eagle elevated masculine power among the Aztecs and implied that the patriarchal order had defeated the previous matriarchal way of life. When she grew older, Zaniya wondered what existed before the female capitulation in Mexico.

In the origin myth, Huitzilopochtli constantly fought the darkness, or female energy. To be victorious, he required nourishment in the form of human sacrifices. His success ensured the Sun would survive the 52-year cycle, the foundation of Aztec folklore. During the Toxcatl festival held for Huitzilopochtli, Aztec captives and slaves were slain ceremoniously.

Zaniya was deeply disturbed by the violent creation story and the machismo aspect of her culture. This discomfort and her desire for a more balanced and respectful worldview led her to explore other Indigenous traditions in Baja California.

One Spring, she encountered Goddess worship in a remote Indigenous community. She was delighted that the matriarchal culture centered females, Mothers, and children in their clan. Her discovery completely changed her outlook and gave her a new spiritual path.

The Native anthropologist realized that female spiritual figures sustained clans before the arrival of Aztecs and devoted herself to preserving stories of the Earth Goddesses. She traveled the Southwest, visiting Native groups and sacred sites, learning from Elders and shamans, and participating in numerous rituals. Her tireless efforts were a testament to her appreciation of female deities and her ancestors.

The Latina learned to worship Goddesses like Xochiquetzal, Atira, Unelanuhi, the Spider Grand Mother, and the White Bead Woman. Xochiquetzal was the Aztec Goddess of love, beauty, sexual affairs, household arts, plants, and flowers. Atira was the Pawnee Earth Mother, and Unelanuhi was the Cherokee Sun Goddess.

Zaniya channeled the female spirits to endure the expanding chaos. When cities and towns were overrun by male traffickers and enslavers, it reinforced her conviction in matriarchal principles. She understood that social and environmental collapse resulted from men's disconnection from nature.

The Nahuatl woman believed that surviving the rapidly changing climate required returning to ancient practices that honored Earth Goddesses and female agency. She educated women in Goddess culture to improve their self-esteem, energy, and resistance to the female dystopia.

The Native historian joined the other women in the Santa Barbara collective and rose to become their main spiritual leader. Her wisdom and sacred strength became vital to the commune's existence. She regularly led Cronetime and eagerly shared her encyclopedic knowledge of the Goddess.

Zaniya's enduring presence was a source of comfort and inspiration. Her daily devotion to the Goddess gave the women and girls essential spiritual guidance, a sense of purpose, and an education about female agency, strength, and power.

She frequently performed rituals that honored the Earth. Through her leadership, the female evacuees navigated the challenges of their migration with grace and wisdom drawn from the Indigenous matriarchal traditions she held dear.

21. Farmhouse

The Badlands registered 129°F (54°C) at 2 PM. The afternoon Sun blazed relentlessly overhead, casting an unforgiving light on the forty frames trudging wearily in a thin line. The dusty, undulating landscape stretched endlessly, with no shade in sight.

On the 14th day of their exodus, they were 100 miles Northeast of the Santa Barbara shelter, alongside Route 33. They covered 70 miles going North from Meiners Oaks and were 125 miles away from the Safehouse. Their last water discovery was three days ago, and supplies were low.

Asia stopped and examined the arid vista. Lian and the scouts had pulled too far ahead. Beside her, Aisha, 26, panted, "Break."

"We'll stop soon," Asia promised. "After we signal Lian." She gripped Aisha's shoulder to encourage the Mother.

Aisha's face knotted in agony. "Please, we're dying from this heat."

"Alright." Asia faced the line. "We'll break here," She announced. "Not for long. No snacks." She gazed tenderly at Aisha's baby, Ida. "Except for children."

The grateful caravan crumbled into the parched sand. Emily glanced at Marge, who worriedly held a droopy child in her lap. She checked Elon's pulse. "He's dehydrated," she deduced. "But not too bad. Give him a drink of my water."

Marge placed the bottle on the drowsy child's lips. "Sip on this slowly." She stroked his damp hair, willing him to stay awake. "Stay strong, son. You and Lisa are all I have left."

Emily squeezed Marge's arm. "We'll get through this," she assured.

Lian's shout pierced the quiet atmosphere from the front. "Sisters. Something's up ahead." She climbed to the top of a dune and pointed East.

Asia hurried after Lian, followed by Nzinga and Xóchitl. They crawled to the ridge and squinted. Far ahead, partially obscured by the haze, was the silhouette of a structure.

"Looks like a farmhouse," Nzinga said.

"Could be a gang hideout," Lian warned.

"Or a mirage," Xóchitl countered.

"We'll check it out," Asia decided. "It may help us."

The caravan advanced with renewed faith. The geometric formation was the first sign of human development they had seen in days. They approached a shabby wooden farmhouse with a small metal chimney. A tattered windmill stood in the rear, three of its four blades missing.

The dwelling was painted with gang symbols from the roof downward. The walls were riddled with bullet holes, and the house appeared abandoned. The graffiti tags included SBM (Santa Barbara Militia), WCWP (West Coast White Power), TC (Tijuana Cartel), BB (Bandidos de Bakersfield), and SCB (Sindicato de Cuchillos Brutales).

Lian cautiously pushed open the creaky front door. Inside the one-room house, dust motes danced in the Sunlight filtering through broken windows. Cobwebs lined the shelves stacked with broken jars and rusty tools. Its owners abandoned it a long time ago.

"Clear," Lian announced outside.

Asia pointed to the back of the property. "Check for a well or a storage tank." The guards searched while the refugees sat in the shade outside. Lian spotted a decrepit well in the backyard. She and Xóchitl cleared the top and discovered it was dry.

Nzinga entered the house and searched it carefully. There was a locked door in the rear. She pried it open to reveal a closet. Inside were four crates of canned food and two large plastic containers filled with water.

"Score," Nzinga yelled. "Food and water."

"How much?" Asia rushed to the porch.

"Four days of food and water," Nzinga answered, showing her some cans.

Asia grinned and addressed the collective outside. "This is a gang hideout. Staying here is dangerous. They could return at any moment." The Crones and women nodded in agreement.

Asia pointed inside, "Let's grab supplies and leave quickly. Nzinga will disperse water." The girls cheered and lined up on the porch to refill their containers.

Gloria, 35, grabbed the leader's hand and pleaded. "Let's stay here tonight, please. It's so nice being out of the wild. The children need to feel human again."

Asia stared at the girls' gaunt features, and her heart crumbled. She outlined a plan: "We'll rest here tonight, double the guards, and leave at daylight." The children squealed, and the women sighed in relief. They were done walking for the day, and resting inside a threadbare cottage instead of a trench was like taking a vacation.

Xóchitl and Lian patrolled the property outside.

"Un hermosa día mi amor. How about Moon Cannot Be Stolen, Bhikkhuni?" Xóchitl's face was full of expectation.

"Too hot for tall tales, X," Lian grumbled.

"You liked the last one," the Latina pleaded. "Master and Flower, remember?" Her companion unwillingly consented.

"After a lifetime spent in the monastery, an elder Bhikkhuni left the Sangha to live alone," Xóchitl began. "The female monk led a simple life in a tiny hut at the foot of a mountain."

"Ah," Lian exclaimed. "Your story is related to this farmhouse."

The Chicana smiled and picked up where she left off. "One Winter evening, a thief visited the Bhikkhuni's empty hut. He was disappointed as there was nothing in the spartan abode to steal. The teacher returned from a walk and caught him."

"So, we're the thieves?" Lian interrupted, faking outrage. "We're stealing from a gang, my lady, probably WCWP or TC. Is that a crime or simply justice?" She surveyed outside the perimeter. "They'd better not be returning."

Xóchitl snickered and resumed. "The Elder felt sorry for the thief. 'You may have come a long way to visit me,' she said. 'And you should not return empty-handed. Please take my drape.' The thief was bewildered but took her only cover and fled. The Bhikkhuni sat bare in the cold, gazing at the large Moonrise. 'Poor fellow,' she muttered, 'I wish I could have given him this beautiful Moon.'"

"The Moon, what?" Lian was puzzled.

The storyteller explained. "This tale is a koan. It's a paradoxical story, meaning it cannot be answered logically. It is used to help students achieve insight."

Lian raised one eyebrow. "Well, I gained confusion. Where do you get all these stories from?"

"None other than our own Kuan-Yin." Xóchitl beamed. "She's a Zen Master, you know." The pair continued walking, debating the meaning of the tale.

They sat for a break, and Xóchitl brushed dirt from her clothing. "This sand is everywhere," she remarked. "It's commonplace but still amazing." She rubbed the teeny particles. "It's clear, like a tiny crystal."

Lian brushed her short hair with her fingers. "It's polished by the wind. Every grain is smooth and almost translucent."

"Like Smoky Quartz," the Latina added. "It anchors you to the present moment, dispels negative energies, and promotes stability and emotional resilience."

Lian laughed. "By blinding my eyes? Nah, that's too New Age-gy."

Xóchitl grabbed a fistful and trickled it through her fingers. "Each grain is hard, yet a handful is delicate and moldable. See how it sparkles in the light. The whole Central Valley is dusted in tiny shards of glass."

Lian stared at the desert. "It's like a wave. It shifts easily and changes constantly. Even a slight breeze can rearrange the whole ground and pile it into mounds." She paused, then added, "And like the ocean, it hums when it moves."

The Chicana nodded. "A dry ocean of glass that clings to everything like a wet magnet." She brushed grains from her shoes. "These fine shards get into everything, the smallest crevice like a fingernail."

She browsed for signs of peril, then continued. "We're drowning in a sea of crystals. Usually, it's like feathers or quicksand. Occasionally, it's tough, like a rock. Regardless of soft or hard, everything feels gritty, like grabbing the jagged edges of microscopic knives."

Lian chuckled. "The surface can change with every step. Most times, it holds me back, like a strong current. Other times, it's a slippery slope pushing me down, like surfing on a board with tiny wheels."

Xóchitl scrutinized the endless stretch of bronze crystals. Her dark pupils reflected their radiant hues. "The way it ripples in the wind is mesmerizing." Her fingertips brushed gently against the ground. "Like waves in a pond, but much more subtle."

Lian stared at the undulating sandhills. "Dunes are beautiful and eerie, almost living things. Mountains that are constantly on the move. You can never really predict where they'll go next."

Xóchitl inhaled deeply. "How long has this crystal ocean been here? How many years did it take for rock to become this fine and perfect?"

Lian shrugged. "Millions. Nature keeps adapting and evolving." She caressed the ground in awe. "Gaia remains resilient even as human achievements and efforts fall apart." The two women fell silent, lost in their thoughts. The only sound was their soft breathing. The Badlands continued to shimmer in hushed beauty.

Inside the farmhouse, the temperature was 10°F cooler. The women stretched out on the wood floor, conversing while the girls played games.

Asia took a moment to reflect on their exodus. Each day was a tremendous struggle, but the collective persevered. With every mile, they grew closer to finding a new beginning, a chance to rebuild and thrive in a more hospitable climate.

The night passed in fidgety sleep. The survivors worried that a vicious gang might return to their hideout and disturb their peace. Asia slept on the porch while the others snoozed inside. When dawn broke, she roused the camp, and the group set out North. They had gambled enough and left with their winnings.

22. Dogs

It was near midnight in the Central Valley desert. The air grew cold and silent. The climate refugees were at the halfway point of their first destination. The Safehouse was 125 miles away. It was their fifteenth day away from the shelter, and they took every precaution to avoid hostiles.

They slept in a shallow trench dug into the side of a hill. The ditch kept them hidden and provided a good defensive position for attacks emanating from the ridge or valley. At its North end, the campfire flickered shadows on the walls. An occasional wind rustled through the sparse brush and broke the peace.

The women and children dozed soundly in the center of the trench. Lisa, 11, and Greta, 13, nestled like birds in a nest. They were recovering from a recent illness and the stress of the trek. The 14-year-olds, Cha'Kwaina, Sasha, Selina, and Karol, were tucked under two blankets. The Crones were spread out, sleeping near the younger children.

Xóchitl stood guard at the perimeter. She missed Lian, who was sleeping. Out of the quiet, she heard distant growls. It sounded like a pack of wolves was heading their way. She rushed to the dugout and shook the leader.

Asia stirred from her tranquil sleep. Her eyelids snapped open, and she stared intently into the blackness. She heard yelps from far down the valley. She nudged Nzinga, lying next to her. "Get up, Z. Wolves are near."

Nzinga sat up and listened. She heard a dozen paws scrabbling in the distance. She rose in a flash, grabbed her knife, and prepared for the worst. Asia swept through the furrow, shaking her companions awake. "Wake up. Wild animals below. Guard the valley side."

The survivors roused and blinked into the darkness. The children were half asleep and sat up, terrified. It seemed that they were experiencing a nightmare. The sharp yaps grew closer, and they huddled in the middle of the ditch. The Mothers and Crones circled them. Their unity was a powerful force calming the girls against the impending danger.

A pack of wild dogs surged up from the valley and approached the dugout. The camp stared at the wild creatures in horror as Xóchitl stood guard at the Southern rim of the den. The women were opposed to the killing of animals, and no one brandished a gun. They waved walking sticks and umbrellas to fend off the impending attack.

The eleven feral canines were determined to get a meal. Twenty-two eyes glowed ferociously in the darkness as razor-sharp jaws snapped desperately at the humans cowering below. They were trying to find a way into the three-foot-deep dugout.

Xóchitl used a blast of pepper spray to force the invaders back from the South end. At her back, the scouts pelted the dogs with slingshots. "Collect stones," Riri, 19, called out.

"Protect the center," Simone, 40, shouted. With one arm, she aimed her flashlight at the dogs to blind them while the other clenched her daughter, Ma'at.

Asia swiveled a walking stick back and forth to thwart entry. "Stay low," she yelled at the girls. "Lie down."

Onawa, 41, stabbed her hiking pole at the canines, and Mary, 61, waved her umbrella to shield the minor children trembling behind them. Gloria, 35, grabbed a stick from the fire and stabbed the flame at the dogs to back them off.

The scouts bombarded the assailants with pebbles while the women gathered more stones. The defenders' togetherness was evident, strengthening their resolve. The starving ferals kept up their assault, determined to enter the trench.

Nzinga's mind raced to devise a plan. She grabbed two long ropes from her backpack and ran to the North end. She whipped the dogs with one line, and they backed off a few feet.

She pushed a digging stick into the top of the gutter and attached one rope. She jammed another stick into the valley side and bound the rope to create a boundary. She placed two more sticks three feet away and tied the line to create an X-shape barrier.

She called Lian, who crouched nearby. "Help me wrap the cord. Form a barricade."

"Got it." Lian swiftly stretched the cable across the top of the four poles, and Nzinga yanked the line taut. Nzinga wrapped her line around two more sticks and continued the zig-zag barrier before the rope ended. She handed her second cord to Lian.

"Double the line so they can't get through," Nzinga instructed. The pair worked backward with the second string until they reached the first stick.

The predators were confused by the thick barrier. They growled and snapped at the bands, but the barricade held. Nzinga watched the frustrated animals and cheered. "Cover under here, everyone." The group scurried under the obstacle, and Asia, Nzinga, and Lian guarded the open end.

The wild dogs could not breach the Northern blockade and stalked the Southern half of the ditch, looking for a way in. Asia looked at Lian and pointed South. "Help Xóchitl."

Xóchitl and Lian coordinated their defense. The Latina belted the dogs on her left while Lian swung a buckle from the right. Lian noticed the animals were starting to get tired. She turned to the scouts and announced, "Now we drive them away."

Lian body coiled, and she readied her slingshot for action. Xóchitl, Riri, Daria, and Phoolan stood behind her, and she gave the thumbs-up for the counterattack. They rapidly jumped out of the ditch and assailed the hungry pack with stones.

In the pitched battle, many hounds were struck and wailed painfully. They started to back off, and the squad pursued them with precise catapult strikes. Abruptly, the creatures gave up. They scampered from the women's organized resistance and vanished into the darkness.

It grew quiet, but the barking reverberated in everyone's psyche in the blackness. Emily checked on the shaken children and found no one was physically hurt. The guards and the scouts returned covered in sweat and dirt. Nzinga acknowledged Lian's and Xóchitl's help, and the pair shrugged modestly.

Asia skimmed the children's anxious faces. "You were brave tonight," she beamed. "You faced danger and protected each other. We're proud of you."

The Firekeeper assembled the Crones for a protective incantation to clear and calm their minds. The Elders' voices harmonized, creating a sound bath that soothed the company. The trench grew quiet as the chanting dimmed.

Zaniya's eyes glistened with unyielding spirit. She pushed herself off the ground to bless the camp. "Gaia is both the gentle stream that nourishes and the roaring storm that cleanses. She does not hide from Her shadows. She walks beside them, letting them teach, protect, and strengthen Her spirit."

Zaniya looked outward, filled with gratitude, and resumed. "Each element on Earth is a testimony to Her divine creations. She is powerful and generous to Her formations. Thank you for our safety, Gaia. Blessed be." Her words echoed in the dugout as the women and children whispered, "Blessed be." The ritual affirmation strengthened their trust and confidence.

After the successful defense, the evacuees crept back into their blankets, and the camp became still. Nzinga guarded her sleeping companions. Her cheerful disposition lasted long into the night.

23. Nzinga

Nzinga, 40, was an outstanding figure. At five feet ten inches tall and 140 pounds, she had a commanding presence that drew attention and respect. Her sinewy form reflected years of military training and survival. Her arms and legs were toned, with well-defined muscles that rippled when she stirred.

Her skin was rich brown, with a smooth texture marred only by faint scars. Her face was angular, with high cheekbones that made her look like a 21st century model. Her pupils were dark black with a sharp glow that missed nothing. Her eyebrows were naturally arched, adding to her fashionable expression. Her hair was a crown of tightly coiled 4C curls that fell below her neck when fully extended. She usually kept it under a hat.

She wore camouflage pants with multiple pockets for storing tools and essentials. Her tops were tanks or short-sleeved shirts. Her well-worn combat boots had seen countless miles of rough terrain. They were scuffed and faded but very reliable. She carried a large, weathered pack made from heavy-duty hessian. It was bleached white from use and covered with pouches.

Her appearance reflected someone always ready for action. She exhumed a combination of practicality, power, and an understated style that reflected her personality. Her ingenuity was a constant source of confidence for the travelers.

She grew up on the outskirts of New Orleans during the collapse, a period marked by social upheaval and racial prejudice. She was an anti-racist fighter who suffered from the psychological toll of her battles. Yet, her courage and resilience shone through.

She was proud of her royal name, which her Mother chose. Nzinga comes from the Kimbundu word *kujinga*, which means to twist. The name was given to Queen Nzinga of Ndongo and Matamba in Africa, a renowned anti-colonial leader. She was born with an umbilical cord around her neck, a sign of her hardships and destined leadership.

Queen Nzinga led a thirty-year war against the Portuguese, starting in 1627, to stop them from enslaving Africans. She allied with rival states and the Dutch to defeat the Portuguese. Her life of resistance inspired the New Orleans native to do the same.

As a child, Nzinga experienced the remnants of jazz, Creole cuisine, and freedom in her city. She witnessed the vestiges of the vibrant African culture and life of New Orleans, Louisiana (NOLA) before the racist enslavement of dark-colored people was re-established by europeans in the state. When she was a teen, enslavers overtook large swaths of the crumbling metropolis to create food plantations.

Nzinga was radicalized and joined the local branch of the African militia at fourteen. The armed network of abolitionists worked to keep european militias and gangs out of minority areas and protect the lives and property of dark-colored people.

Her intelligence, discipline, and leadership led to a rapid rise through the ranks. She formed alliances with Latino, Indigenous, Caribbean, Asian, and other minority groups to strengthen her paramilitary forces. By 21, she was a Battalion Commander in charge of hundreds of fighters. Her collaborative leadership and strict discipline instilled confidence in her troops.

She deployed soldiers and reservists throughout Louisiana to protect African farms, Latino communities, Indigenous territories, and Asian businesses. Through her ten years of service, she led numerous battles against the racist state army and european private militias. Her forces repelled dozens of scorched-Earth raids on minority areas.

During one battle, dozens of minority fighters were slain and captured by a powerful state militia, Louisiana White Power (LWP). Her soldiers' bodies were dismembered, and their heads mounted on the walls of the LWP barracks. The female commander retaliated by ambushing the governor and torching the military base. Her forces retrieved their soldiers' bodies and buried them with honor.

Similar to Harriet Tubman during the previous enslavement period, Nzinga undertook dozens of private missions to recover dark-colored people in european enslavement camps. She guided them to the underground freedom network that led to Canada. Her rescues demonstrated her unwavering commitment to community, justice, and liberation, inspiring others who crossed her path.

However, the unity of the African militia did not last. The men became increasingly misogynistic and started to reject female leadership. Despite her distinguished service, at 24, she was stripped of command and demoted to Platoon Leader in charge of 30 female soldiers. Men refused to be led by women.

Moreover, the African militia began to exploit, capture, and trade females of all ethnicities. Enraged and disgusted, vast numbers of women quit the force. Those who remained were discharged, and females were subsequently barred from service.

Returning home, Nzinga was met with the devastating news of her parents' passing and the displacement of most people she knew. The once friendly community had transformed into a misogynist's paradise, leaving her feeling appalled and angry. Despite these personal losses and upheavals, Nzinga's resolve to protect others remained unwavering.

The militia fell apart a few years later due to infighting between leaders and factions. Minority communities were left vulnerable and unprotected.

Thousands of marginalized individuals and families fled the South in massive caravans. Most traveled West to enslavement-free states like New Mexico, Arizona, and California.

The NOLA native joined a caravan headed North and gained a reputation as someone who could be relied upon in a crisis. The column made it to Arkansas with much difficulty, a significant milestone in their passage. They rested for a month and continued the arduous trek West.

Nzinga was tormented by her violent past and the many lost lives. She became more tolerant of racist and sexist men. While enroute, she partnered with an Indigenous man and gave birth to a daughter, Maya. She traveled to Oklahoma and stayed with the Cherokee Nation to raise her child, instilling the same values of resistance and loyalty she practiced.

When her daughter was sixteen, they voyaged West to New Mexico. Maya found a partner in Taos and settled. Nzinga stayed with her offspring for a year, then roamed to Arizona and California. There, she met the cluster of women at the shelter. She shared their toughness, purpose, and love, and her background made her a formidable presence in the group.

After they departed the shelter, Nzinga fiercely protected her fellow nomads, often putting their needs above hers. She was a woman forged by adversity, driven by a fierce sense of duty, and sustained by the possibility that, against all odds, the collective would find a place where they could rebuild and thrive.

24. Desert Plants

The pitiless 10 AM Sun hurled its blistering stare over the flat topography. The thermometer hovered at 111°F (44°C), and horizontal waves radiated across the dry ocean. On the 16th day of their trek North, the hardened survivors struggled to maintain a sluggish pace. Yet, the caravan inched forward tenaciously. The canine provocation from the previous night lingered, but it did not deter their spirits.

Lian and Xóchitl walked at the back of the line while Asia and Nzinga led up front. "Last night was super scary, right love?" The lead guard was eager to discuss the incident with her friend.

"No son buenas mascotas." Xóchitl grinned. "Bad doggies. No treats for a week."

"They were vicious." Lian shook her head. "Probably had rabies."

"They're just hungry mutts." Xóchitl shrugged. "You don't like dogs or something?"

Lian shuddered and remained quiet.

"Es un nuevo día. Wanna hear a classic Zen tale?" Xóchitl tried to change the subject.

"Is it about pooches?" Lian was still thinking about the midnight attack.

"Woof, woof." Xóchitl howled in jest. "No, it's Carrying the Girl, Bhikkhuni. Two male monks were traveling on the road, like us, see. They came to a shallow river and saw a young woman on the bank. She was hesitant to cross over and get her clothes wet. The senior monk offered to carry her, and the woman gratefully accepted."

Xóchitl paused. Her companion seemed disinterested. "You heard this one before?"

Lian shook her head. "I didn't understand the last one about the Moon."

"This one is easy," Xóchitl promised and resumed. "The senior monk carried the woman across the river, and the two men continued their pilgrimage. The junior monk was angry but said nothing." The Latina grabbed her friend's shoulder and added, "Here's where it gets interesting."

"Maybe for you," Lian gazed at the line, bored.

"You're so ironic," Xóchitl smirked and carried on. "After walking for several miles, the junior monk could no longer hold back his emotions. 'How could you carry that woman?' he shouted. 'We're monks. We're not supposed to touch females.'"

The Latina paused for effect.

"Ah, it's about sexism," Lian exclaimed. "Why didn't you say so. Go on."

Xóchitl grinned. "The senior monk replied, 'I put that woman down at the riverbank an hour ago. Why are you still carrying her?'"

"Ok, not sexism, but about me," Lian swore. "This is about moving on from last night, isn't it?" Xóchitl chuckled, and they continued walking in the rear.

In the center of the convoy, Marielle, 7, trudged alongside the eldest Crone. "It's too hot," she cried.

Regardless of her age, the Crone's resilience was unmatched. "I'm here, daughter," Hehewuti rasped. Marielle's half-closed pupils signaled her fatigue, and the Elder supported the girl's shoulder. Her free hand reached into her bag and retrieved a broad cactus pad. "Use this nopal." She cut and placed the fresh leaf against the child's forehead.

Marielle felt the cool pad on her brow, and Hehewuti squeezed the leaf's juice over her head. The viscous gel trickled down her face, and relief washed over her. "Thank you, Elder," she uttered.

Hehewuti smiled. "Lookout for cactus."

Despite the punitive conditions, the Badlands harbored several valuable plants, including cactus, manzanita, agave, mesquite, pinyon, almond, hazelnut, and yucca. Finding them was crucial for the company's survival.

The prickly pear cacti were one of the desert's most essential and versatile vegetation. The thick, paddle-shaped leaves were covered in spines, but beneath the tough exterior was a wealth of resources. The women harvested the pads, or nopales, and removed the spines. Once cleaned, they were eaten raw or cooked, providing a source of hydration and nutrients.

The cacti bore vibrant red or purple fruits called tunas, which were sweet and juicy. The peak season was late Summer through early Winter, but they were abundant in Spring. Rich in vitamins and antioxidants, tunas were edible raw and offered a rare and welcomed sugary treat. After removing the skin, the evacuees ate the flesh. The edible pits were chewed, spit out, or swallowed.

Manzanita was an evergreen shrub or small tree common in California's chaparral. They can live in poor soil with little water. Flowers and berries bloom from Winter to Spring, and the women harvested them to make flour, sweetener, jelly, and cider. Chewing the leaves relieved nausea and upset stomachs, and the tea helped with diarrhea. They soaked the leaves and used them for poultices to soothe poison oak and heat rash. Stems were utilized for toothbrushes, and the wood was valuable for burning.

The agave or *mezcal* was another beneficial plant. During its flowering, a tall stem grew up to forty feet high. It extended from the center of the rosette and bore many short, tubular flowers.

The group consumed agave flowers, leaves, stalks, basal rosettes, and sap. The heart, or piña, was roasted or boiled to extract its sweet, nutritious core. They stripped the leaves' tough outer layer and chewed them to release moisture. They fermented the sap to create a drink that provided energy and hydration. Agave fibers were used to make ropes and nets.

Mesquite trees were a lifeline in the desert. The pods hung like long, yellow-brown beans. The women ground the pods into flour to make bread. They combined them with water to create a paste rich in protein and fiber. The edible seeds were roasted or boiled to add a nutty flavor to meals.

The cook roasted Mesquite blossoms over a pit of hot stones, formed them into balls, and served them as an appetizer. Frida also used blossoms to make tea. The sap was applied directly on wounds or boiled and gargled like a mouthwash.

Pinyon pines provided a valuable food source, though they were more commonly found in higher desert elevations. The pine nuts were tiny but packed with protein and healthy fats. Although they were labor-intensive to extract from the cones, the kernels were highly nutritious. They were eaten raw, roasted, or ground into a paste.

Desert almonds were harvested in late Spring and early Summer. The deciduous shrub grew to six feet high with many horizontal branches. The outer fuzzy covering of the ripe fruit usually splits when the seed is ready. The seeds were eaten in small quantities and roasted or leached with water to consume in larger quantities.

California hazelnut was a shrub with velvety leaves. The nuts were eaten raw or cooked. Frida ground them to make nut butter, flour, and plant-based milk. She also extracted the oil for cooking and salad dressings. The women crushed the bark to make medicinal poultices and used milk to cure coughs and colds, heal cuts, and as an astringent.

Yucca or cassava was a starchy root vegetable that offered ample sustenance. The young shoots and flowers were eaten, though they required boiling to make them more palatable. The root, or 'yucca potato,' was dug up and cooked to provide a starchy, filling meal. It was boiled, fried, mashed, added to stews, and used to make various foods like chips, bread, and flour.

Though not abundant, these native trees, shrubs, and roots offered crucial nourishment in a terrain where food and water were scarce. Finding edible plants took much care and effort. But even in the sparse desert, life found a way to persist and provided the means for the collective to survive.

While they hiked, the women and children foraged for plants to consume and store for later. Sometimes, they got lucky and found several edible shrubs in one area. When they did, Frida and her helpers prepared delicious three-course meals with appetizers and desserts. Her feasts confirmed the group's power of community and shared effort.

25. Settlement

It was 11:30 AM in the Western Mohave desert, with a reading of 128°F (53°C). Forty drifters wandered along the narrow shade of a dune. They were covered in light clothing and Sun protection, but their faces and arms were sunburnt. It was 16 days since the group left the shelter, and they had completed over 110 miles on blistering feet. They were almost out of water and on the verge of collapse.

Lian led the convoy, searching for signs of moisture in the parched wilderness. The only patch of greenery, a hardy shrub, seemed to mock their struggle to live. 'Humans are not cut out for these Badlands,' it seemed to whisper. It was a cruel reminder of the harsh environment they were trying to survive in.

She rounded the dune and stared hard into the distance. In the shimmering haze, she saw faint outlines that appeared like flags. 'Was it a mirage?' she wondered. She waited for Asia to catch up.

"Do you see that?" Lian was anxious. "Is that a gang headed toward us?"

Asia's breath caught in her throat. She tracked Lian's stare and scrutinized the remote shapes. "They're not moving. It could be a settlement."

"Let me check it out." Lian wanted to go alone.

"No," Asia shrugged. "We'll approach carefully."

The line drew closer, and an outpost with two dozen structures emerged from the dust shroud. Asia was struck by the colorful patchwork of flag poles, tattered tents, and ramshackle sheds in the middle of nowhere. The hamlet was surrounded by a wire fence topped with barbed wire.

The tents were made of torn fabrics unevenly draped. They were supported by wooden poles and barely held up against the elements. The shacks appeared even less sturdy, constructed with salvaged debris: rusted metal sheets, smashed wood doors, broken planks, damaged shutters, car doors, plastic panels, and odd pieces of junk. The improvised roofs were covered with tarp and plastic, creating a colorful patchwork against the blue sky.

Each structure in the settlement looked like it might collapse at any moment. In the center, a fire pit was rung by a circle of stones like seats in a theater. Near the fireplace, four poles hoisted frayed political flags: USA, Confederate, WCWP (West Coast White Power), and a red flag used to signal auctions of enslaved people.

On the right of the hearth, a long wood table stood empty. In the rear were raised solar panels, a windmill, a water well, and two broken wagons. A horse stood inside a dilapidated barn while chickens, dogs, and a couple of goats milled around the compound.

Asia was wary of the display of racist emblems. "Stay low and staggered," she cautioned, positioning herself protectively in front of the line. "We don't want to make easy targets."

"Hello." She approached the gate and waved at the people inside. "We'd like to trade for water." Her group desperately needed water, and they waited anxiously, hoping for relief.

Ten light-colored females in the colony stood staring at the caravan, and four children peered out from behind them. Their sunburnt skin and tattered clothing revealed abject poverty and harsh living conditions. They gaped at the migrants like they were ghosts, momentarily forgetting their work.

Four women were tending a garden, two were repairing clothes, one was weaving a basket, and another drew water from the well in the rear. The women's suspicious attitudes added to the tension of the encounter.

'Where are the men?' Lian wondered. She browsed the colony for men and weapons but saw none. 'Are they waiting in ambush?' She gripped her weapon, ready to respond.

"We're here to trade for water," Asia repeated.

A light-colored, shirtless man with deep-set eyes staggered out of the front hut, pointing a rifle at Asia. He appeared drunk.

"Who're you?" He asked gruffly, glaring at the woman at the gate with obvious irritation. Asia noticed the middle-aged man had a WCWP tattoo on his left arm, a Crusader cross etched on his right hand, and 'Deus Vult,' or god wills it, written on his chest.

The Laughlin native raised her hands in a gesture of peace, palms outward. "I'm Asia. We're refugees looking to trade."

"We don't trade with niggers, wetbacks, and gooks." The man spat into the ground. "Are those escaped slaves you got there?"

"No sir, we're all California-born." Asia waved at her companions. "It's still a slave-free state, right?"

The man spat again. "What y'all doing here?"

"We're out of water." Asia pointed to her backpack. "We've got food to trade."

The man scrutinized her, aiming his weapon at the caravan. "You're hanging with the wrong company, lady. Can't help ya."

"Please, sir," Asia folded her palms in prayer. "We're not asking for free."

The man was unmoved. "Where y'all headed?"

"North." Asia searched his face for any sign of sympathy. "Escaping from pedos, gangs, and the heat."

The man shrugged and pointed to the line. "We ain't helping them stinking bugs you've got there."

"Okay, sir. I'm not asking you to." Asia kept her hands clasped, holding on to a sliver of chance. "But half of us here are like you, right? At least give us 'whites' a drink."

He shook his head and backed up. A light-colored, gray-haired woman rolled out of the shanty in a wheelchair. She placed her hands on his back and stared at Asia. "We don't have enough for ourselves. Nothing comes easy in the Badlands."

Asia stayed optimistic. "I know, Madam. We've got cans of beans, corn, prickly pear fruits, and pine nuts. It's a good treat for your kids."

The woman appeared interested, but the man shook his head, still unsympathetic. The settlers returned to their chores and ignored the desperate escapees outside the fence.

Asia refused to give up. She pointed to her collective. "Madam, half of us are 'white.' And we're dying. I see you have a well in the back. Please trade two buckets for our food."

The pair of settlers glanced at each other and remained quiet. The four racist flags sagged, mirroring their reluctance to negotiate.

26. Trade

It was near noon in Central California. Sand swirled into the migrants' faces as they sat under the scorching Sun. They were beside a rickety hamlet, staring longingly at the shade inside. They hoped Asia would get access for them, but she stood exasperated outside the gate. She was getting nowhere in negotiating for water.

The man in the Confederate compound sneered at the lifeless Goddess collective beyond his fence. "Those black freeloaders ain't getting nothing from us." He kept his rifle pointed at the caravan.

Mary stepped forward and placed a supply bag at Asia's feet. The gray-haired woman's disposition eased when she saw Mary. The Crone was paler and about the same age as her.

Mary looked at the disabled female settler and bowed. "We have fresh cactus tunas and pine nuts. They'll make great jam and nut butter sandwiches for the kids. It looks like they could use some food."

The wheelchair-bound woman stared at the man, and he gave a curt nod. "All right," he waved. "Let's see what you got there." He opened the gate and blocked the entrance half-war. The woman introduced herself as Lysistrata and the man as Tate.

Asia and Mary huddled with Lysistrata. Asia filled two cloth sacks with food: four cans of preserved vegetables, a half-dozen aloe vera leaves, one pound of cactus fruit, four mesquite pods, three ounces of amaranth, and a tiny bag of pine nuts. Her fingers lingered on the last sack before letting it go.

Lysistrata was happy with Asia's offer. "You can refill your containers from the well," she smiled. "But only 'whites' are allowed in here." She looked anxiously at the two women. Asia and Mary nodded.

Tate pointed at the rear. "Lucky for you, the well has water today." He glared at the convoy like they were thieves. "Remember, 'whites' only."

Asia and Mary returned to the cooperative, and the leader explained the plan. She was impressed by the Crone's powerful presence. Somehow, she got the unwilling settlers to trade.

The light-colored members entered the encampment to refill their containers. The boys ran ahead, shouting, "Me first." The darker-colored women and children remained outside. Nzinga, Lian, Xóchitl, and others were incensed but remained quiet.

Asia returned to speak with Lysistrata. "How old is this colony?"

"A few decades," the woman answered. "We're a miners' base camp. Our boys are out prospecting. They return every two weeks."

Asia noticed that the solar panels at the back looked new. "How do you get supplies?"

Lysistrata pointed East. "We send a wagon to Bakersfield every month to trade."

The light-colored migrants filled their water bottles from the well. Mary, Marge, Emily, Daria, Greta, Lisa, and others restocked the water containers from their barred members. The teens, Stephen and Miller, refused to get water for their dark-colored companions and milled around the hamlet instead.

After Emily restocked the medical emergency bottles, she heard a child's persistent coughing. She approached a tent and saw a Mother and daughter on the floor. The child's pupils were glassy, and her breathing was shallow.

"How long had she been like this?" The medic glanced at the Mother.

The bleary woman heaved. "On and off three weeks now. We don't have any medicine."

Emily reached into her pack for a tiny vial of cough syrup, and she gave it to the woman. "This will help. Give her a little every four hours." The Mother's eyelids filled with tears. "Thank you so much." Emily was demure. "It's nothing. Feel better, child." She bade goodbye and left.

Asia glanced at Lysistrata. The handicapped woman was much more amiable than the man. "Are there other settlements near?"

Lysistrata shook her head. "There were a few others around. But they're gone now." She rubbed the back of her neck to ease the weight of her thoughts. "I don't know how long we can hold on. Things have gotten wild." Her eyeballs flared, indicating the word 'wild' carried a heavy burden.

Asia's body tightened. "Wild? What do you mean?" She searched her face for answers.

"Wild dogs raid at night," Lysistrata replied. "It's not safe to be outside the fence."

Asia nodded. "We were attacked a few nights ago."

Tate stepped forward. "People are crazy. Black devils roam the land scavenging for human flesh."

"Scavengers are 'whites,'" Asia corrected. "The men blacken their faces on purpose. You know that, right?"

The man scoffed, and the conversation ended.

Children's laughter erupted from the colony. Elon, his earlier fatigue forgotten, darted between the other kids. "I'll get you," he squealed, chasing another boy.

Marge watched from a distance. She covered her mouth, shielding herself from the emotions swelling within her. Her eyeballs shimmered with unshed tears.

"He hasn't played like that in weeks," Marge whispered, holding Emily's arm for support. It seemed speaking louder might shatter the precious moment.

"He needs other boys to play with." Emily gleamed. "It's what we're struggling for."

At 12:30 PM, the caravan prepared to travel into the afternoon Sun. Lysistrata waved at Asia. "You're good people. Hide those girls. If a gang like sees them, they're done for."

Asia bowed. "Thank you."

Tate gave Asia one final piece of advice. "You'll be much safer traveling with other 'whites.' You can never trust those black devils."

Stephen and Miller lingered in the settlement as if wanting to stay. They spoke to Tate, and the man shook his head. The boys reluctantly left the outpost.

As they assembled to continue their trek, Zaniya touched the ground in gratitude.

"The Goddess does not crumble," she began. "She rebuilds. She does not weaken. She transforms, using every hardship as a stepping-stone toward greater heights. The mountains taught Her that the journey is not about avoiding obstacles but finding the strength to rise above them. Each scar is a story of endurance, each step a demonstration of Her will. She moves through life as a mountain shapes the sky, unyielding and eternal. Blessed be."

The group marched briskly into the Badlands. After rehydration, their emotions were lifted, and they had a new lease on life. The adults were serenaded by the children, who sang a lovely tune about toys they had learned in the colony.

They sang the words over and over again: "Old toy trains, little toy tracks. Little boy toys comin' from a sack. Carried by a man dressed in white and red. Little boy, don't you think it's time you were in bed? Close your eyes. Listen to the skies. All is calm, all is well. Soon, you'll hear Kris Kringle and the jingle bells."

Nzinga walked beside Asia in front. She was angry and felt betrayed by her friend. "You were too nice to those racists," she accused Asia.

"I'm sorry." Asia exhaled loudly. "I had no choice." She was not happy with the hamlet's racial intolerance, but she knew the settlers were part of a trend of raising bigotry in the state. She did what she had to do for everyone's survival.

The minority women were disturbed by the skin-color discrimination they faced and realized they would encounter other racists along the way. However, they drew comfort in knowing their collective was not prejudiced and their leader truly believed in equality.

Lian turned back and warned, "Stay alert. The settlers may tip off pedos." The racist flags in the miners' colony faded into the haze, and the evacuees pressed on North.

27. Asia's Leadership

Asia was not a natural leader. She took the role because she felt she was needed and wanted to help other women. The Santa Barbara shelter was split into ethnic camps: latino, european, african, asian, Indigenous, pacific islander, and so on. There was intense competition for scarce resources, and women were divided into male-dominated groups.

Asia was recognized by europeans at the shelter as one of their own. Nevertheless, she collaborated with different ethnicities to protect children from groomers, pedos, and gangs. The farmer's daughter avoided euros who were extremely sexist and racist.

She maintained close relationships with women from different cultures and had a powerful presence among them. Nonetheless, the Laughlin native stayed in the background, allowing others to take charge. With the influx of additional refugees, the shelter became more crowded, combative, and violent.

Aisa's painful memories of ethnic war in Laughlin prompted her to take a more active role. In early

March 2121, she spoke to dozens of women and started organizing them to form a group. One evening, she invited the Crones, a few Mothers, and other women to a meeting at the front of the shelter. About 15 women showed up.

The farmer's daughter was delighted with the turnout. Her eyes filled with compassion as she paced before the female assembly, sweeping over their worried faces. The waxing Moon cast a dim glow over her gaunt frame.

"I've discussed with many of you a plan to form a women's group and leave this shelter," she started calmly. The Mothers were skeptical of her plan. She could see the uncertainty in their eyes and their fear of the unknown. They felt safer within ethnic clans, with men available to protect them. Most doubted a group of females could last long. She had a high bar to scale to persuade them to leave.

"Some of us are wary of this crowded place," she continued. "But leaving is risky. It's scary either way."

She wanted to impress upon the ladies the weight of her experience and unshakable resolve to protect them. But she had to earn their trust before they could be convinced to leave their co-ethnics and the shelter behind.

The former Buddhist nun took a long breath and resumed. "Let's look at the pros and cons of leaving, okay? There are many disadvantages here. Staying exposes our girls to groomers, pedos, and gangs. Girls are high-valued targets for every pimp, madam, and their goons within a fifty-mile radius."

A few women nodded.

Asia's eyes reflected the vulnerability the women felt. "In addition, minority females of all ages are targeted by european men, including those at this shelter. Girls who are not pale could be trafficked into brothels and slave plantations. It's terrifying."

Her expression hardened. "Last month, we lost six girls. I knew two of them very well: Shireen and

Fatima. They were only 9 and 12 years old." She clenched her fists and swore.

The Mothers moaned in lament.

"You're sad over their loss, I know," the speaker admitted. "Each abduction takes a toll. I miss the girls deeply. I feel helpless. We're just piling on regret and fear with each missing child."

Some of the women cried.

The farmer's daughter grimaced. "We're stuck within ethnic clans and losing girls every week. This strategy isn't working. The racial factions cannot protect girls because safeguarding women isn't a priority for men. They're focused on raising boys, and some even cooperate with the gangs."

The Crones nodded.

Asia shrugged. "We're stuck here with these callous men. Besides, how long can we stay here? It's just a matter of time before the shelter becomes too crowded and unmanageable. Then we'll be forced to leave."

She paused, giving her audience time to process. Then her expression brightened. "Why wait for the inevitable? There's another way. What if we combine as women and children to form a large group and say goodbye to this trap. We'd be a tougher target, and it'd be safer for the girls."

"The men will not let us take our sons," one woman blurted. "We can't leave them behind."

The Laughlin native groaned. "Yes, leaving means living without men, in a tent, and with less food. And we'd still face attacks. Nowhere is safe for women in this racist manscape. We're trapped between the post-apocalypse and men's terror."

The Mothers glanced at each other. They were starting to understand the speaker's reasoning.

Asia was encouraged. "Now, what are the advantages of exiting this hostile place? Well, it gives us more control over security. We can hide, set traps, and see the pedos coming. We'll be free from the racism, sexism, and constant ethnic battles here. And we could try to go someplace safer, like Northern California."

The women groaned.

"That's too far," Marge complained.

"We'll never make it," Gloria chimed in.

Asia shrugged. "I know it's a long way. But others have made it. Many go as far as Canada. With increasing heat, it's the safest choice."

The women exchanged opinions, most in disagreement. After five minutes, Asia held up her hand to speak, and they grew quiet.

"I'm not trying to impose my will," she said calmly. "I'm here to listen, guide, and ensure that every woman, regardless of color or creed, has a say." She placed her hand over her core in a sincere gesture. "Discuss and decide. Some of us are leaving soon."

She left the assembly to examine her proposal. The Mothers, Crones, and other women debated for hours. The next day, they spoke to others in their groups, especially single women. Three days later, over twenty women, many with girl children, decided to leave.

28. Exodus

The Pacific Coast's temperature was comfortable at 87°F (31°C). On the humid and overcast day of March 18th, 2121, a significant decision was made. Forty residents gathered outside the shelter, including twenty adults and twenty children.

The women, empowered by their collective resolve, had chosen to depart the overcrowded asylum, despite their apprehensions about the journey ahead. It was a decision not made lightly, but one that spoke volumes about their collective resolve.

Asia, the beacon of promise, scanned their faces, seeking connections. Her role as a unifying figure was clear as she addressed the group. "Congratulations to all of you. You've made a collective decision to protect our girls. Let's celebrate this unity with a hug, a symbol of our shared strength."

The women and children embraced, some for the first time. The group hug was a powerful symbol of their unity, and the women felt a surge of purpose and determination they had not experienced before. Their initial apprehension about embarking on a journey with strangers was replaced by a shared sense of mission, a feeling of being part of something greater than themselves.

Asia was relieved. "We'll leave in two days, on the first day of Spring." She paused to let the impending deadline sink in. "And remember, we're doing this together. All of us, adults and children." She opened her arms to include everyone. The ladies agreed.

"Next, I will share my vision of the group's charter." The leader raised her right index. "As a female alliance, our primary goal is supporting Mothers and children. We have ten Mothers and seventeen girls. They're the heart of our collective." The women nodded in agreement, their unity strengthening.

The organizer raised two fingers. "Our second priority is ensuring racism and discrimination do not exist in our commune. There is zero tolerance for prejudice and bias. This includes subtle forms of micro aggression." The females concurred.

She held up three digits. "Our third goal is equality. Everyone has the same status, including children. For instance, leadership is a position. The leader is not more significant. Anyone can lead. And we all must be leaders." The adults nodded.

Asia took a deep breath and continued. "I ask each one of you for your trust. In return, I offer my unwavering devotion to your survival." She locked her fingers to emphasize her commitment. The women, reassured by her words, nodded in agreement, feeling secure in her governance.

Zenobia mirrored Asia's wisdom. "We womin be all equals," she exclaimed. "We stronger togetha. We shouldn't be caught up in dis color or age thing. That's just anothr ah da man's trap." Hehewuti clapped, and the other Crones agreed.

Nzinga shifted to the center and pointed to the leader. "She's worked hard to connect us. Before she came, we were all separated into every hue and creed, stuck in a little corner. We were vulnerable and easier to pick off. But now, we're twenty women, armed and united. We're a more powerful force."

The Mothers and women murmured in agreement. Asia's gift of listening and acting compassionately made joining her easier. And they trusted her instincts for survival, feeling a growing sense of confidence in her management.

Even Lian, who had an earlier conflict with the leader, consented. She knew it took guidance to unite the diverse band of women: young, elder, childless, with children, from different ethnic and cultural backgrounds, each with their own fears and dreams. She desperately wanted to be with other women, and the female alliance offered her that chance.

Asia's glow lingered on the women's faces. "I gratefully accept this responsibility," she stated, "knowing fully that leadership is not about power but service." She bowed humbly, affirming her pledge to the women. Her composed presence reassured everyone.

Hehewuti gave her leader a reassuring hug. "You'll always be our guiding Star," she gushed, "It's time you took the Matriarch position seriously."

Zaniya raised her hands to her chest in devotion. "All is Gaia," she summoned. "Like mountains that shape the sky, She inspires by simply being, unchanged, undeniable, and endlessly profound. May the Goddess be with you and with us. Blessed be."

Asia's leadership marked a turning point for the women in the shelter. She gave them a way to act and a sense of direction, which they desperately lacked. She ensured that they were all mentally and physically prepared for the trip.

She organized the women into committees: guards, scouts, camp, supplies, and nutrition. She gave training sessions on defensive skills such as weapons training, loading and unloading backpacks, moving into shielding positions, and signaling for help.

Her commitment to their survival was unwavering. Under her guidance, the susceptible Mothers and children felt ready to escape the horrors of the shelter and the constant threat of kidnapping. Even Marge, struggling with two children, felt comforted.

March 21st, the first day of Spring, was cool and sunny. After a meager breakfast, forty women and children collected their belongings and assembled outside the dysfunctional asylum. They were wary of the unknown and challenges ahead, but eager to leave.

"May the Earth Goddess be with us," Zaniya beckoned. "She is the ancient hymn in the wind and the fierce protection in the storms. May we feel Her sacred power and beauty. Blessed be." Her fingers brushed lightly against the breeze to bestow her bliss on everyone.

With a firm wave of her left hand, Asia led the way out of the shelter grounds with a bounce in her stride. The female caravan trailed closely, trekking toward a brighter future.

29. Bread

It was 2 PM on day 17 of the climate seekers' trek North. The weather was a searing 131°F (55°C) with 15% humidity. The Solar storm's unyielding rays hammered them mercilessly.

The caravan trudged on in the uninhabited Mohave desert, a testament to human resilience. The warmth pressed them like a physical weight, punching them into the soft sand. The dry air slashed at their nostrils like a sharp blade, making each breath a struggle. The group paused for a mid-afternoon break.

Lian and Xóchitl sat with their backs against each other in the sand. The younger guard faced the Sun, providing shade for her leader.

"I still can't get over those settlers yesterday," Lian fumed. "They were pathetically racist to the core. WTF. This is California, not Florida."

"Es Mexico mi amiga," Xóchitl smiled. "Why are you still Carrying the Girl? Don't you remember the last Zen tale?"

"Cuz it was so humiliating," Lian exclaimed. "They made me feel subhuman for being slightly more tan. WTF. You want me to just ignore their mistreatment?"

The Latina shook her head. "You can't kill them all, Sweetie. You don't have enough bullets. Let me tell you another tale, Bhikkhuni, The Oak Tree and the Bamboo. It's really short."

"No." Lian was not in the mood.

Xóchitl began anyway. She knew the Zen tale would be healing for her friend. "In a dark forest, a giant oak tree and a tall bamboo stalk stood side by side. One day, a harsh storm swept through the forest, bending the bamboo and snapping the oak in half."

"I'm not listening," Lian lied.

"The giant tree grieved bitterly," Xóchitl continued. "'I stood strong for decades in this land. But suddenly, I broke and was done for. You're much younger and weaker, yet you did not shatter. How?' The bamboo rustled a reply, 'Flexibility allowed me to yield, ancient one. I adjusted to survive.'"

Lian snorted. "You're saying I'm the broken oak?"

"Adapting helps us acclimatize to this horrid weather," Xóchitl noted. "And to racist storms. May you learn to bend like bamboo."

The lead guard remained quiet. She knew her companion was right.

Marge and Zenobia sat conversing. The children's enjoyment drifted over from where they played.

"They don't realize how bad things are," Marge sighed, referring to the children's innocence amidst their hardships.

"Dey flexible an tough," the Firekeeper replied. "An, we gonna keep em' strong an alive," she promised.

Full of life and irrepressible spirit, the girls played a guessing game in the shade. Cha'Kwaina held a piece of bread, laughing. "Guess what I'm thinking of?" She wiggled her food.

Sitting away from the girls, the two teenage boys, Stephen and Miller, exchanged mischievous grins. "I'm thinking about that Rez nigger's bread," Stephen leered, nudging his partner to grab it.

"I got this, bro," Miller smirked. The boys lunged toward Cha'Kwaina's meager nourishment. "Give it here, you ugly squaw," Stephen demanded.

Startled, Cha'Kwaina ran from under the shade, and the boys chased after her. They caught up and tried to snatch her bread. She turned swiftly and doubled back towards the girls.

The boys tried to grab her shirt to slow her down, but four girls rushed forward, their protective instincts kicking in. Sasha, Lisa, and the twins Karol and Selina, formed a barrier around Cha'Kwaina, who was panting out of breath. Their unity was a powerful shield against the boys' aggression.

"Leave her alone," Sasha's pupils flashed in anger, and she shoved Stephen hard.

Karol seized Miller's arm. "You have your own food." she snapped. "This is hers."

The girls stood shoulder to shoulder, glaring defiantly at the teens. Their courage inspired the women witnessing the scene. The boys were caught off guard by the intensity of their resistance and slinked away in defeat.

However, the sudden confrontation overwhelmed Cha'Kwaina. Her legs buckled, and she collapsed onto the hot sand. The bread slipped from her fingers.

"Cha-Cha," Sasha screamed, and the other girls panicked.

Onawa looked over and saw her daughter in the sand. Her heart seized in her chest, and she sprinted toward Cha'Kwaina.

"No, Cha-Cha." Onawa broke down beside her daughter. "Baby, wake up." She stroked the teen's damp face.

Emily placed her fingers on Cha'Kwaina's wrist to check her pulse. "She's fainted from heat exhaustion," she announced. "Get her into the shade at once."

Emily, Xóchitl, and Lian lifted the teen and placed her into the shade. The children gathered in confusion, and Lian waved them back, ensuring a sense of order. "Don't crowd her."

Lisa lingered for a moment, eyeballs brimming with tears. "Is she dead?"

Xóchitl's expression softened. "No, she's not dead."

Lisa nervously gripped Xóchitl's shirt. "Please don't let anything happen to her."

"She'll be fine," Emily said, fanning Cha'Kwaina's face. Lian stripped off her top, and Zenobia covered her with a damp towel.

Cha'Kwaina lay motionless. She was five feet three inches tall and 105 pounds. She was named after a *Kachina* or doll. In Hopi culture, *Kachinas* were used to communicate with the Great Spirits. Dancers embodied *Kachinas* in ceremonies, and small carved figures were given to young girls.

The teen's face looked pale, and her breathing was shallow and erratic. Emily placed her stethoscope against the child's chest. "Her heart is steady. But she needs to stay in the shade. This heat is deadly."

"We'll stay here," Asia announced. "Until the worst of the heat is over."

The afternoon wore on, and the evacuees sat in an uneasy quiet. The children returned to their circle solemnly, keeping a watchful eye on their friend. Onawa fanned her daughter's face and mumbled her name, willing her to wake up.

Onawa was an Indigenous name that meant 'awake.' It was associated with the lunar cycle. The Moon was a powerful Hopi symbol, personified as a vigilant woman who stayed awake all night. The name reminded the people to be fully awake, aware, and present in the world. It was also an inspiration to live with purpose and intention.

Onawa stared at her daughter as dapple light played across Cha'Kwaina's face. Her eyelids fluttered open, and Onawa shuddered in relief.

"Cha-Cha, you're awake." Onawa's eyelids brimmed with tears, and her body slumped in relief.

Cha'Kwaina focused on her Mother. "Mama, what happened?" She was hoarse from dehydration.

Onawa wiped away her tears with trembling fingers. "You fainted for an hour," she stammered. "But you're okay now, my love. We're here for you."

The group's fears eased when they saw Cha'Kwaina sit up. Her quick recovery was a tiny victory amid their harrowing expedition, filling them with a shared sense of optimism.

Zaniya's knees sank to the ground. She scooped a handful of dirt and tenderly caressed the loose sand. She closed her eyelids and slowly raised the dirt to her forehead. "May the Goddess be praised," she purred. "Her soul is the soil of the land. Every step we take is a pulse of Gaia's heart. Claim your strength and ground yourself like a mountain. Stand unshaken and let the world see your unwavering spirit."

Her mantra carried a note of solemn devotion. She pressed the soil against her lips lightly, feeling its warmth. "Let each challenge be a call to rise higher, Daughters. Do not fear the ascent. Find the courage to climb, and you will discover the view meant only for the bold. Blessed be." Her eyelids opened to reveal a deep, tranquil peace. She lowered her hand, letting the sand slip gently back into the Earth.

30. Eat It Well

The next day, the Crones, the paragons of wisdom who had steered the cooperative since its inception, gathered morning dew and bestowed it upon the children during breakfast. At 8 AM, the temperature soared to 105°F (41°C) as the climate evacuees readied to depart from the camp.

Onawa spotted Stephen and Miller lingering at the perimeter. The memory of the previous day's incident surged through her, filling her veins with adrenaline. The boys' reckless pursuit of Cha-Cha had nearly cost her dearly. The shock it left Cha-Cha in, and the aftermath Onawa was grappling with, were still fresh.

Her heart ached with the memory of the boys' Mothers. She had known them before they perished in the violent shelter, a place they sought refuge in but found only terror. Their deaths still haunted her dreams, and she had solemnly pledged to look after their sons. Yet, their reckless behavior made her promise increasingly difficult, a fact that weighed heavily on her conscience.

"You two, come here." Onawa's command was like a whip slicing through skin. The boys' faces turned from haughty to sheepish when they realized they were in trouble. They lumbered towards her with heads hanging low in embarrassment.

The Mother clenched her fists to keep her fury in check. "Get Cha-Cha's bread from over there," she ordered. "Eat it well. It may be our last."

The boys exchanged furtive glances, and Stephen retrieved the bread. He ate it and denied any blame for Cha'Kwaina's fainting. "She was the one who ran," he insisted, his lack of remorse a bitter pill for Onawa to swallow. She was incensed by his stubbornness, and she told the pair to stay at the back of the line. They sullenly made their way to the rear of the convoy.

Zenobia watched the exchange with concern. She knew Onawa was struggling with her daughter and the boys. The three teens did not get along due to jealousy, and the Mother was stuck in the middle, trying to balance her responsibilities towards them. She walked next to her friend and gently touched her back. "Dey only hungry. Like all ah we."

"I know," Onawa grumbled. Her head slumped, and her anger melted into a deep weariness. "I'm failing to keep their Mothers' promise," she confessed, her voice heavy with the weight of her responsibilities.

Zenobia understood her friend's conflict and felt heartbroken. But she had to lift Onawa's spirit. "Yuh don keep dem alive an safe till now." She beamed. "Dat's doin' way mo' than plenty ah folks woulda."

Onawa watched Stephen and Miller strolling in the rear. Their lack of empathy for others was disturbing. Chasing Cha-Cha was dangerous and careless, and it caused the collective to lose half a day's travel, a fact that eluded them.

The teens' callous actions had to be punished, but she was unsure what consequences they should face. The boys were playful, and their pranks occasionally crossed the line. She feared alienating them further and decided to get to know them better.

The Sun rose higher, and Lian found a low, hidden resting point. The adults dropped their packs and collapsed into the shade. The children curled up close to their Mothers, grateful for the break. Asia surveyed the setting for any sign of danger.

The Badlands was quiet except for the slight wind rustling through the dry brush. Yet, the stillness offered no comfort, only a warning of how alone they were in the forbidding terrain.

Aisha tilted her head to watch a circling committee of vultures. She squinted at the scavengers with foreboding. "Is there danger close by?" she pondered aloud. "Or are they waiting on us?"

Marge gave Aisha a reassuring touch. "Scavenging for dead animals. And we aren't dead yet."

The convoy continued their journey in reticence. The softness was punctured by the rustling of clothing and the thud of boots against the pliant sand. The monotonous landscape made it seem like they were going nowhere, circling endlessly. But their optimism remained like a trickling stream in the dry wilderness.

The sparse life that once lived in the Badlands had long perished. Gone were dozens of species of mammals, reptiles, birds, and insects. Their absence marked the eerie quiet that remained. The children knew no difference, but the Crones were deeply aware of the changes and grieved their absence.

It was dinner time, and the Crones told the children stories about the various creatures that once occupied the land. It was Hehewuti's turn.

"When the people came to the desert," she began, "the animals were the caretakers of the land. Among them was Suma, the desert fox. Suma was small, with fur the color of sand and ears like leaves catching every whisper of the wind."

The girls listened intently, their curiosity piqued, as they ate. Their eyes reflected a mix of wonder and sadness at the thought of the creatures that once roamed the land.

"One year, the rain stopped falling," the Elder continued. "The Sun beat down harder than before, and even the cacti began drooping. Rivers dried up, and the animals grew weak from thirst. The council of animals gathered under the shadow of the last standing mesquite tree. 'We must ask the Rain Spirit for mercy,' Grandmother Tortoise said. 'But the path to her cave is long and dangerous.' Many animals volunteered, but none returned."

The Crone paused for effect, then resumed. "Finally, Suma stepped forward. 'You are too small,' Coyote said. 'The Sun will eat you before you even reach the mountains.' Suma smiled. 'I may be small, but I know the desert better than anyone. I know where the shadows live and how the wind speaks.'"

"Yea, Suma," Lisa interjected. "Foxes are the best."

"So, Suma set off," the storyteller described. "She traveled only at dusk and dawn, resting in burrows and under rocks during the heat of day. She followed the stars and listened to the song of dry grasses whispering secrets. When she reached the mountains, the Rain Spirit was hidden behind a curtain of clouds, silent and sleeping. Suma stood at the edge of the cave and began to dance, not loudly, but softly, so the stones could hear, so the dust could remember."

"I can dance like Suma," Cha'Kwaina added.

The Crone smiled and resumed, "Suma danced stories of parched Earth and thirsty roots, of animals with cracked tongues and fractured dreams. She danced until her paws were sore and her tail heavy with dust. The Rain Spirit stirred. 'Who dances so gently in this time of pain?' she asked. 'I am Suma,' said the fox. 'And my people are dying.'"

"We need to dance for rain," Shasha suggested.

Hehewuti nodded. "The Rain Spirit wept, and where her tears fell, rivers bloomed. She followed Suma back to the desert, walking behind her in a trail of rain. Since then, it is said that the desert fox brings the rains. And when you see the clouds gather low and soft over the mesa, know that Suma is dancing again, whispering to the Rain Spirit on behalf of her kin."

"We really need Suma now," Lisa exclaimed. The girls agreed, even though they had never seen a fox.

Xóchitl and Lian ate together as usual. The Latina loved a red clay bowl she used daily to eat her lentils and rice. After eating, she rinsed it with her spoon and accidentally dropped the bowl. It fell on a rock and shattered into fragments.

"Oh, no." Lian made a sad face.

Looking at the broken pieces on the ground, Xóchitl smiled and said, "Well, it's finally broken."

"Aren't you upset?" Lian looked puzzled.

"¿Quién yo? Why should I be sad or regretful, Bhikkhuni? I knew that one day this would happen." Xóchitl collected the fragments calmly. "Everything in life changes, and nothing lasts forever."

"But it's your favorite bowl." Lian was taken aback by her friend's cavalier response.

The Latina smiled. "If we learn to accept change, let go of attachment to things, people, and circumstances, our mind will be at peace, and we will no longer suffer."

"You're kidding me, right?" Lian was unconvinced.

Xóchitl shook her head. "No, Bhikkhuni. Once we understand that everything is impermanent, we learn to appreciate the present and face events more calmly." She buried her bowl in the sand and tossed her head back. "Time for a Zen tale, Bhikkhuni?"

Lian stared at her companion in awe. Her words carried profound wisdom that always left her in deep contemplation. The Latina was really the most amazing person she had ever known.

31. Reservoir

It was nearly noon, and the Badlands was smothered in a blistering 128°F (53°C) heat wave. The climate nomads kept their bodies fully covered, from head to toe. Their clothing was soaked in sweat, and they had painful burns and welts. Everyone was dehydrated and thirsty, but water supplies were low.

"You're doing great," Asia rasped. "Keep it up." Her words broke the group's unnatural quiet. They were conserving energy and hardly even breathed. But they kept up their spirits and advanced one step at a time.

"We may end up like Donner," Marge complained.

"Donner?" Aisha adjusted the strap for her baby, Ida. "Who're they?"

"Ancient Cali history," Marge mumbled. "I'm frail, depleted, and dirty. My clothes are torn, and my skin is burnt. Must have been what they experienced."

"What's it about?" Aisha looked puzzled.

"The Donner Party was around 90 europeans from Springfield, Illinois," Marge commenced. "In the Spring of 1846, their wagons departed Missouri on the Oregon Trail headed West, towards California."

"That's the period when European settlers were killing Indigenous peoples and taking their lands." Aisha was irritated. "California was then part of Mexico, so their migration was unlawful."

"Yes, but that didn't stop them," Marge confirmed. "They were warned to expect opposition from Mexican authorities in California. And they were advised to move only in large groups." She paused to check on Elon and Lisa. They were fine.

"Those bigoted colonizers were inspired by manifest destiny," Aisha remarked. "They believed the land between the Atlantic and Pacific Oceans belonged to europeans, and god intended them to settle here. It was a racist justification for illegal occupation. More like manifest genocide."

"Yes, and ongoing." Marge shrugged. "Slavery may even be coming here, to California. I'm sorry for you and the other minorities here. Europeans are awfully racist. Makes me ashamed for being lighter in color."

Aisha swore under her breath. "So, what happened to Donner?"

"Well, it usually took four and six months to make it to California, traveling about 15 miles a day," Marge explained. "But the Donner Party took much longer. They reached the most difficult part of the trail in November. They had to travel the last 100 miles across the Sierra Nevada mountain range."

"Scaling the mountains in Winter?" Aisha was startled. "Were they that stupid?"

"Apparently." Marge shook her head. "The wagon train was hemmed in by an early, heavy snowfall near Truckee Lake, high in the mountains."

"Trapped after being in the wilderness for eight months?" Aisha sneered. "Serves them right."

Marge sighed. "They lost many cattle and wagons. Food supplies ran low, and they became divided. Some set out on foot in mid-December to obtain help."

"Stuck for over a month?" Aisha was astonished.

"Longer." Marge surveyed the empty Badlands, wondering if they were similarly stumped. "Rescuers from California attempted to reach them. However, the first relief did not arrive until the middle of February 1847."

"Three months in the High Sierras?" Aisha shook her head in disbelief. "How did they stay alive?"

"Many didn't," Marge disclosed. "Out of 87 original migrants, only 48 survived."

"Nearly half perished." Aisha raised her brow. "But most survived. How?"

"That's the interesting part." Marge paused and stared at her daughter anxiously. "Some of them resorted to cannibalism. They ate those who succumbed to starvation, sickness, and the cold. Two Indigenous guides were murdered and eaten."

"What the hell?" Aisha was shocked. "I knew that europeans scalped Natives, and the government paid them for each scalp. But eating them, that's inhuman."

"Yes, it was," Marge agreed.

Aisha was uneasy. "I hope we don't end up like those damn racist colonizers."

Marge laughed nervously. "Well, they were mostly men. We're women, with equality and unity." The pair was unsettled and continued strolling in silence.

Asia squinted at the shimmering, heat-blurred landscape. She raised her hand and addressed the women. "We're close to a water reservoir. It's been abandoned for decades, but there might be some runoff or a storage tank."

Marge stared at the leader with concern. "And what if there's nothing there?"

Asia gave her a once-over. "We keep moving."

Marge sulked. She was convinced that they were becoming trapped like Donner. But she dared not say anything.

Basked high in the sky, the Sun cast almost no shadow. The arid scenery stretched endlessly in every direction. The only sounds were the rhythmic thud of footsteps and the sporadic sigh of weariness.

The caravan approached the location on Asia's map that indicated a reservoir. In the distance, the dry, fissured ground gave way to a vast, concrete structure reaching tall into the sky. The site was partially hidden by a forest of overgrown trees, bushes, and debris. Although the dam was bare, the vegetation underneath seemed like an oasis.

Asia pointed toward the barrier in triumph. "That's it. Let's check it out." The women's pace increased with the potential for finding water, their hope shining brighter than the harsh orb above.

The grand concrete edifice was built to retain a long-vanished river. Its Sun-bleached walls were a scrap of its former self, like a ruined amphitheater.

Lian had a quick vision and smiled faintly. The broken pieces of stone on the bottom appeared like a cast of actors staging a forgotten Greek tragicomedy for an audience of disinterested plants. It was funny and sad at the same time.

She climbed to the rim of the structure and peered down. A dry riverbed stretched for miles with no sign of water. She led the way lower, carefully navigating through debris and broken material.

At the bottom, the voyagers found a large, rusted storage tank. It was empty, and their mutual distress was unmistakable.

Marge let out a long groan while peering into the hollow chamber. "What now?" Her disappointment echoed like a massive bell.

Asia took a long breath and fought to keep her frustration at bay. She scrutinized the green overgrowth with steely determination. "We need to search the area carefully. There might be another tank or hidden supply somewhere."

The group separated and searched the bottom of the reservoir. The dam shaded the area, which felt cool and humid. Near the end of the right wall, Xóchitl discovered a partially buried cistern.

Xóchitl's features flushed with effort while clearing the brush. She crouched next to the tank and squinted into the bottom. "There's water in this pit," she squealed, glancing at Lian with delight.

Lian peered into the cistern. "We have to filter and boil it. But there's enough to use and carry."

The group was overwhelmed with relief. Zenobia took charge of cleaning the precious liquid, using a makeshift filter with layers of cloth. The women mobilized to help and were grateful for a drink.

Zaniya gave a blessing, "The Goddess knows that the darkest depths hold the richest soil. And it is from these shadows that her roots grow deep, and her soul grows strong. Stand as she stands, Daughters, strong, unyielding, and rooted in purpose."

She took a deep breath and continued, "Rise to face each day as a mountain meets the Sun, unafraid and unwavering. Take that first step toward the heights you dream of. Climb boldly, embrace each challenge, and let no obstacle hold you back. Blessed be."

Hehewuti, the children, and two scouts went foraging around the reservoir for an hour and returned with four baskets full of edible plants: dandelions, miner's lettuce, stinging nettle, saguaro fruit, cholla buds, manzanita berries, and piñon nuts. Frida was delighted to have fresh stock to cook with.

Later, the women circled the campfire, swapping stories with mirth while awaiting dinner. Marge glinted at Asia with affection. "Thank you for not giving up on us." She swallowed hard, and her body shivered. "We were getting close to cannibalism."

"What?" Asia looked puzzled.

"Never mind." Marge waved at Aisha and smiled.

"We'll get to the Safehouse," Asia promised. "It's about one hundred miles away, but we'll make it by taking one step at a time."

32. Desert Night

It was 7:30 PM at the reservoir, and the air was cooling. After a rare dinner feast, the refugees, united by their shared journey, felt full and replenished. They stretched out around the campfire, bodies and minds gradually recovering from the day's rough hike, their spirits intertwined in the dance of survival.

Each person felt a sense of relief and deliverance. The vultures had long since disappeared, and tired sighs were replaced by cheerfulness and mirth.

Lian and Xóchitl stood at the outskirts of the camp, checking the surroundings for any potential threat.

"Que lindo querido. Also lovely is Perfect Disciple, Bhikkhuni." Xóchitl grinned. "Wanna hear it?"

"That's you and Kuan-Yin." Lian chuckled.

"Ha." The Latina laughed. "The ideal Samanerika is not you, that's for sure."

"Maybe one day," Lian teased. "But I'd need a better teacher."

"Or become a better student," Xóchitl sneered.

"Hey, I'm starting to bend like bamboo," Lian protested. "See." She pliantly waved her upper body.

The Chicana grinned. "One day, a student asked her Bhikkhuni, 'How do I become your best disciple?' The female Monk replied, 'Follow me closely, learn all my teachings, and in time you'll be just like me.' The Samanerika grew excited and quickly enquired, 'And what happens after that?' The Bhikkhuni smiled. 'Why, then I'll become your disciple.'"

"Are you copying me?" Lian giggled. "Is that why you keep calling me Bhikkhuni?"

Xóchitl's joyous laughter echoed off the dam.

The evening air grew cooler. The Badlands, which seemed lifeless during the day, began to stir with subtle movements of nocturnal life. Lian and Xóchitl listened intently to every sound.

Small creatures emerged from the crevices of rocks and the shade of sparse shrubs, adapted to survive the arid region. A rhythmic rustling in the sand signaled the presence of a sidewinder rattlesnake. Its body slithered in graceful, looping curves over the dunes. The snake's scales shimmered under the Moonlight, but its cautious, deliberate movements ensured it went unnoticed by potential predators or prey.

Overhead, the distant cry of a barn owl echoed through the stillness. The owl's wings beat noiselessly, gliding over the mounds. Its sharp optics searched the ground for any sign of movement. With its ghostly white plumage almost blending into the night sky, it was a soundless hunter, swooping down to catch unsuspecting rodents or insects.

Out of sight, a pair of desert foxes traveled with practiced stealth. Their fur was a blend of sandy browns and grays that melted into the darkness. Their large ears twitched, picking up the slightest sounds as they hunted for insects, small mammals, and birds. They used soft yips, barely louder than the wind, to maintain contact while exploring their territory.

Below the soil, a myriad of insects and arachnids, each a marvel of adaptation, went about their nightly activities. Unseen by the two guards, a scorpion scuttled across the sand, its translucent body glowing faintly under the Moonlight. Its pincers stood poised, and its tail arched, ready to strike at any threat or prey.

Nearby, a beetle's carapace glistened like polished obsidian on the ground. It burrowed into the sand, seeking moisture and food hidden beneath the surface. Its precarious survival was a reminder of the beauty and fragility of life in the Badlands.

The Badlands' nocturnal inhabitants were survival experts. Each was successfully adapted to the environment in their own way. Bats flitted through the air in rapid, erratic flight patterns. They pursued moths and insects drawn to the warmth radiating from the ground. In the distance, the subtle trill of a nightjar bird added to the symphony of delicate sounds that lined the night.

Despite the impression of barrenness, the wilderness at night was humming with activity. Each creature, from the smallest insect to the largest owl, played its role in the ecosystem's fragile balance. For the two guards sitting under the Stars, the knowledge that life persisted, even in the harshest places, offered some measure of comfort.

It was Cronetime. Zaniya stood tall above the campfire, her shine fixed on the twinkling Stars. Her posture was steady, drawing strength from the celestial bodies above. A moderate breeze lifted the edges of her gown, revealing intricate beadwork that glimmered in the Moonlight.

She stared at the moon and offered a benediction, "Like mountains that shape the sky, Gaia inspires by simply being. She is unchanged, undeniable, and endlessly profound. She does not retreat in the face of hardship. She stands firm, knowing that like a mountain, Her strength lies in persistence."

The Crone looked at her audience and continued, "Do not wait for permission to shine, Daughters. You are your own dawn, your own horizon. Stand as tall as you dare, for this World is yours to shape. Blessed be."

Zaniya extended her arm toward the Stars, locking onto an exceptionally bright one in the Western sky. "There's Venus," she began evocatively. "Do you see the Evening Star low on the horizon?" She pointed to the brilliant light that sparkled with a steady glow. "Venus is the dearest Sister of our Mother Earth. She's a beacon of love, beauty, and connection."

The wise Crone paused to let her viewers find the second inner Planet. Her fingers curled, holding the Planet's light between them. "When the Goddess Venus is close, she blesses Gaia with her warmth. The nights are filled with dreams of love and new beginnings. And our spirits feel more connected, more alive." Her aura expanded, carrying a note of possibility. "It's a time when the Earth Goddess herself listens closely to our hearts, urging us to act on our values, to nurture the bonds we hold dear."

The Elder raised her hand, tracing Venus's path across the sky. "And when Earth's Sister moves away from us, we feel her absence profoundly. The nights grow colder, and our dreams more distant. It's a time of reflection, of understanding what we truly value."

Zaniya hugged her body for a few seconds. "When our Sister Goddess is away, Gaia encourages us to look inward, to find our strength in solitude. And, to prepare for the moment when Goddess Venus returns, bringing her light and love back to us."

She gazed at the children serenely. "Venus's movement reminds us that personal relationships and connections are not constant. They ebb and flow like the tides. We have to cherish others when they are near. And we must find peace within ourselves when our loved ones are far away. It's the dance of life, the rhythm of the Goddesses."

The Crone bowed low to her audience, and her face glowed with inner light. "Let's be mindful of this cosmic dance, Daughters. By being in tune with Goddess Venus's path, we come to understand the movements of our own nature. Blessed be." She sat quietly in meditation, signaling the end of Cronetime.

After twilight passed, the last remnants of color disappeared, giving way to the deep blue of night. Once tinged with fading light, the skyline became a shadowy outline against the blackening heaven. Stars emerge, faint at first, then gradually multiplying.

Stillness settled over the purple landscape. The darkness deepened, and the subtle shades of evening were replaced by the blurred glow of Moonlight casting silvery patches over the dunes. Night arrived fully, and its calmness wrapped the Badlands in a peaceful embrace. The collective crawled into their soft blankets, and the interminable day felt like a distant memory.

33. Two Weeks

It was 10 AM in Central California on the 20th day of the climate nomads' trek to the Safehouse in Cantua Creek. They trudged across the golden sand in a thin line and entered the shadows of a rocky outcrop.

They were grateful for a brief respite from the Star's unremitting glare. The intense 131°F (55°C) heat was punishing enough without the scorching rays searing their flesh. The dry air bit at their nostrils, a precursor of more hardships as the Celestial orb climbed higher. They exited the shade and slowed to a crawl.

Asia saw her fellow travelers' heads and bodies wilting under the powerful Sunbeams. "We'll stop soon," she promised, her skin glistening with sweat. She herself could barely stand. Her slurred speech and slumped shoulders, her once vibrant eyes now dulled, indicated the toll the morning passage was taking.

Nzinga glanced sideways at the leader, noticing the tight lines of exhaustion etched into her face. "You're pushing yourself too hard, Asia. You were night guard, and you skipped breakfast to conserve supplies. But you're our most important resource. We need you to be healthy. You've got to eat and slow down."

Feeling the weight of Nzinga's words, Asia's pace slackened. However, her friend's concern only strengthened her resolve. "Eleven more days to go," she stammered. Her voice wavered, but she sounded determined, a beacon of hope in the face of their daunting journey.

She turned around to check the drooping figures in the line. Sasha and Greta were trailing behind, with arms clutched over their midsections. The girls' steps faltered. Then, Greta crumbled into the ground and stopped moving. Sasha sat beside her in pain as well.

Asia rushed to the girls. "Sasha, Greta, are you okay?"

Greta clutched her stomach. "Cramps." She squeezed her eyelids to shut out the pain. "It hurts."

Sasha bobbed her head. "Mine too. I feel like throwing up." She hunched over in discomfort.

Asia spotted Emily in the line and beckoned her over. "We need help." She used her umbrella to shade the girls.

The caravan stopped. The group's unity was evident in their shared effort and immediate concern for their fallen comrades. Marge sank to the ground to comfort Elon, who was crying. Everyone was stressed and exhausted.

The medic hurried to the teens and checked their vital signs. "It's the heat," she proclaimed.

Asia became alarmed. "Heat stroke?"

"No. They're dehydrated." Emily removed Greta's backpack and helped her to lie flat.

"Are you sure?" Asia was worried.

"Heat stroke is a severe medical emergency," Emily clarified. "You feel confused, delirious, and combative. You can faint or lose consciousness."

"I am confused," Greta groaned.

"You're not." The nurse checked Sasha's forehead. "Your temperature is 98°F, which is normal. You know what's going on, and your speech is clear."

She looked at the leader. "Above 104°F (40°C) is heat stroke." She held Sasha's arms. "We look for hot, red, dry, or damp skin. And a rapid and strong pulse. Heat stroke requires immediate medical attention."

"That's a relief." Asia exhaled.

Emily stared at her nervously. "They need water, and we're almost out."

Asia's face darkened. "How much left?"

Emily muttered, "Less than five gallons."

"Only twenty liters?" Asia clenched her fist. "Give them a drink. We'll find some soon."

Emily took out the medical flask and placed it on Greta's lips. "Drink slowly to avoid shocking your throat," she cautioned.

"Why does water shock?" Sasha asked weakly.

"It feels like a sharp pain deep in the throat," Emily explained. She was the biology teacher for the clan and loved describing health to the children. "It's usually caused by a small blood vessel that presses on the nerves when it exits the area."

Emily tipped the bottle gently so Greta could sip. "You feel a jabbing pain if the muscle in your throat contracts too much. They hurt, but only temporarily, and are usually harmless."

The nurse gave Sasha a turn at the canteen. "Be careful you don't choke from it going down the wrong pipe. Take small sips. Let the liquid sit in your mouth before you swallow."

The girls' mood improved after a few mouthfuls of water. However, they remained seated and resisted moving. In addition to painful cramps, they believed they were close to getting heat stroke.

Two of the group's wise elders stumbled to the back of the line toward Asia and the girls.

Zenobia's face was etched with concern. "Dis heat be killin' us. We ain't gonna survive too long unless we drink plenty."

Thoroughly drained, Hehewuti hunched beside Zenobia. "Let's take cover and wait out the worst of it," she rasped.

Asia rubbed her temple, feeling the weight of the decision pressing down on her. "It's morning. If we stop, we'll lose the whole day."

"The days are longer," Hehewuti rasped. "That gives us more time in the afternoon."

"We ain't gonna last two days like dis." Zenobia worried. "Dem kids be strugglin' fuh real." She gestured toward the girls.

"Some women are sick," Emily reported. "They've got nausea, vomiting, diarrhea, all signs of heat exhaustion. It's too hot. They need rest."

Asia considered Emily and the Crones' counsel. "Alright, we'll rest for a while." She motioned to Lian. "Please find us some shade."

Greta gazed at the medic, puzzled. "What's the difference between heat stroke and heat exhaustion?"

Emily held Greta's hand. "They can be similar. Exhaustion means having a throbbing headache, nausea, vomiting, dizziness, and slurred speech. It results from the body overheating, often due to physical exertion in high temperatures."

She paused and looked at the group. "Our bodies' temperature is below 104 degrees, and no one is being aggressive or behaving strangely."

Sasha nodded. "So, one comes before the other."

"Right," Emily confirmed. "Heat stroke is more serious, with convulsions, seizures, or even coma."

"Then, we only have exhaustion," Greta was satisfied with Emily's medical discussion.

Lian returned to the convoy and pointed West. "There's a cluster of rocks a half mile away. They have Eastern shade."

Asia waved her consent. "It'll do. Help the children get there." She picked up Greta and carried her on her hip while Nzinga assisted Sasha. The caravan began slowly trekking toward the outlying Sun shield.

34. Shade

It was high noon in the Mohave desert, and nature had won the standoff with the climate caravan. The female migrants were nearly out of water and energy after 20 days of trekking in 100-degree weather. They sat in the shadow of a few large boulders, recovering from the morning hike.

When they left the Coastal shelter, the forty Californians did not have robust bodies. The journey's harsh conditions had reduced them to malnourished skin and bones. The children huddled with their Mothers for comfort. Their bodies were drained of life, and their faces were pale and withdrawn.

Asia's eyes darted to Nzinga. "We're running out of time. There's only three gallons left." Nzinga's gaze fell on her water bottle. It was almost empty.

Lian understood the urgency and stepped forward with a plan. "Why don't we send out a couple of search parties to look for water?"

Asia gazed at the guard appreciatively. "That's a good idea. We can wait here for a couple of hours." She turned to Nzinga for support.

Nzinga nodded. "At this moment, shade and water are more important than time."

Lian pointed South. "I'll take Phoolan. Xóchitl and Daria can go West. We'll cover six miles in two hours."

Asia felt comfortable with the plan and addressed the seated women. "We'll recover here and wait for the guards and scouts to return."

The group was relieved to rest and hydrate, but not everyone was pleased. Marge glanced up from fanning Elon and glared at the leader. "We Mothers are barely holding on," she declared. She looked forlornly at her son. "I don't know how much more we can take."

Asia straightened her back and met Marge's distressed stare. She knew the Mother felt guilty and concerned about the health of her two children. Lisa was agreeable, but the boy was a lot more to handle.

Asia closed her eyelids and counted to ten. She was crumbling inside, but she could not let that show. She had to be ironclad for them.

"You're a terrific Mother to your kids," Asia affirmed. Marge sighed deeply. She was pleased to be acknowledged and needed to hear those words. "With both Lisa and Elon."

Marge glanced at Lisa, who was chatting with her friends, Cha'Kwaina, Ma'at, and Sasha. She was glad her daughter had numerous peers and shared a close relationship with them. She felt that Lisa was growing up normally under the circumstances.

She peeked at her son, who was tossing restlessly in her lap. Marge understood why he was always irritable. Elon had no boys to play with, and he was at a stage where he hankered after male peers. The teenagers were too mature to be his friends, and worse, they enjoyed teasing him.

Yet, Elon was intensely attached to Stephen and Miller and constantly tried to appease them. The teens treated her son like an infant and usually chased him away. Elon was frustrated over the poisonous relationship but still tried to be closer to the pair.

Asia focused her attention on the boy. "Elon, you're a valuable part of our team. And you're doing a good job taking care of Momma."

The boy stopped fussing and grinned with pride. He sat by himself and started drawing stick figures in the sand. Marge gave him a miniature astronaut, and he role-played fighting with the toy.

Time dragged by, and the convoy anxiously awaited the guards' return. Their thirst grew intensely, and two vultures circled overhead, seeming to taunt them. The scavengers were a grim warning of what could happen if the scouts did not find water.

Asia checked in with the Crones. The wise and experienced women played a crucial role in her decision-making and guided the entire community. They convened unobtrusively in a corner while Mary scribbled in her notebook.

Asia sat next to Zenobia and started to pick lint from her locks. She was anxious, and it gave her something to do. The Elder smiled appreciatively. Next, she combed and braided Zaniya's long hair. After that, she was tired and fell asleep in Kuan-Yin's lap.

Two hours passed, and Phoolan returned from the South. Her face was streaked with dirt, but she was elated. She leaned on Nzinga for support, catching her breath. "Lian found water," she blurted. The news was a starting rainstorm for the dehydrated collective, a sudden downpour of optimism in their parched world.

Phoolan passed her flask and continued, "We found a small ravine. One spot was damp. We dug until we got a trickle. Lian's expanding the hole now." She spoke rapidly with a mix of exhaustion and joy.

When Asia heard Phoolan's news, she breathed a sigh of relief. "How far?"

"A mile Southwest," Phoolan replied. "Maybe 45 minutes at a steady pace."

Asia stood up and addressed the convoy. "Lian has water. Get ready to leave." She hugged Phoolan, "Thank you. Please show them the way."

The prospect of a drink lifted the group's spirits, and they quickly collected their belongings in anticipation of the life-saving liquid.

"Thank you, Gaia." Zaniya offered a blessing. "Her presence is the dawn breaking over peaks, illuminating the World with quiet strength and boundless compassion. With a gaze as deep as the valley and a heart as vast as the horizon, She stands in unity with nature, embodying balance and grace."

She pointed to the scout. "Daughters, the Goddess is a reminder that perseverance is not the absence of struggle, but the ability to keep going, to grow, and to stand firm despite it. Blessed be, Phoolan."

The women repeated the refrain and bowed to the Crone in appreciation, their determination to keep going shining through their tired but resolute faces. The leader glanced at Nzinga. "Go ahead with them. I'll wait for Xóchitl and Daria and follow your tracks. They'll be back soon."

Phoolan headed back toward Lian, and the relieved caravan trailed. The promise of water propelled everyone forward.

Asia gestured goodbye. 'Lian saved us again,' she thought, her heart swelling with gratitude and relief. After the convoy disappeared, she sat serenely and waited for the second search party to return. She was happy. She felt a strong sense of support and purpose with the collective. She was doing exactly what she wanted to do with her life, giving back to a community of women.

35. Puddle

It was mid-afternoon in the Central Valley. The Sun beat down ruthlessly on the desolate landscape, and the air was thick with dust. Lian, a strong-minded figure, worked tirelessly to expand the hollow in the dry riverbed. The land was motionless, soundless, and breezeless, as if holding its breath in the scorching heat. For Lian, it was like watching the death of a colossal ecosystem in slow motion.

She lit up when her companions approached the ravine and pointed excitedly at the shiny pit at her feet. The glistening pool was an oasis in the lifeless landscape. The group rushed toward the puddle, their hearts lifted by the precious discovery.

Lian scooped some liquid and splashed it on her face. "Water," she yelled.

The children raced to the watering hole. Sabra, 10, scooped a handful and exclaimed, "Wow, this is dope."

Greta, 13, knelt by the edge and dipped her finger. "This is so fire." Her face was lit in wonder, and the painful cramps, a constant companion for a few days, melted away. Sasha, who had collapsed earlier from stomach pain, also found relief after hydrating. And she no longer worried about getting heatstroke.

The Crones arrived last. Zaniya knelt beside the orphan Greta. "This is a gift from our Mother Earth," she declared. "She's showing her love for us."

The dehydrated figures circled the hole and took turns filling their cupped hands with precious liquid. Each drop was savored like a rare treasure. Everyone quenched their thirst and refilled their bottles. Despite the suffocating heat, the children quickly recovered and found bliss in the simple act of splashing.

Asia, Xóchitl, and Daria arrived an hour later. They thanked Lian and replenished their bodies.

The modest upwelling turned into a wet zone. The kids ran joyfully in endless circles, stomping and yelling in pure delight. They dove splat into the mud and slid for a few yards, body surfing. It was fun times.

The adults were infected by the girls' joy and undertook mud baths. The swarm of brown faces frolicking about the wet stage was like a wild kabuki theater without the conflict. The mad playhouse of ecstasy amid hardship demonstrated the power of shared experiences in fostering collective resilience and enjoyment.

The only drama emanated from Stephen and Miller. The teens playfully began to wrestle in the mud, and after one of them got hurt, they started fighting. They punched, kicked, bit, and pulled each other's hair before Asia and Nzinga managed to separate them. Both women were struck in their struggle to maintain the peace. The boys sulked, licked their wounds, patched up their spat, and began sparing again. The girls were shocked by the violence as they had conflicts but never came to blows.

The migrants calmed down, and the splash zone was busy again. Aisha cradled her baby against her chest and surveyed the other Mothers. "Who wants to help me give baby a bath?" The women all volunteered and took turns washing Ida. Each time they took her out of the wash basin, the infant sputtered, and the girls squealed in delight.

It was nearing Sunset, and the temperature dropped. The women dug a trench into the dry riverbed for camp. Lian and Xóchitl unwound on a blanket and carefully cleaned their equipment.

"¿Me gustas o no?" Xóchitl was in a playful mood. "No matter, I like you. That's why I'm gonna tell you Monkey's Wisdom, Bhikkhuni."

"Calling me an ape, Missy?" Lian faked being angry.

"Well, you do act the part." The Latina laughed and started her tale. "A monkey in a forest was known for its clever tricks. One day, a Bhikkhuni entered the forest to meditate. The primate approached her and said, 'I've learned many things from observing humans. For example, when they're angry, they make faces and shout. But when they're happy, they eat cactus bread.'"

"Cactus bread in a forest, X?" Lian interrupted.

"Only checking to see if you're listening." Xóchitl sneered. "The female Monk smiled and said, 'Ah, dear friend. You've learned the secret of enlightenment, simple pleasures.'"

"The kids are happy like monkeys in a water barrel," Lian observed.

"Si. Cuz your puddle is Nirvana, mi amor." Xóchitl beamed. "Simple, beautiful, and perfect."

Asia approached the pair and touched Lian's arm. "You gave us another lease on life today. Thank you."

Lian shrugged. "We're in this together, Sister."

"Thanks to you, we've got a real chance of reaching the Safehouse now," Asia said, her voice tinged with hope. The distant refuge was a powerful motivation for everyone. But the journey was fraught with dangers, and she knew they could not let their guard down.

Lian gleamed. "We will, Sister. We will."

Asia stared at the empty ravine. "No pedos yet. We've been lucky. But they can be anywhere."

Lian's expression turned steely. "Worrying won't change what's coming. We've got to be prepared and act proactively. That can make all the difference." Her words echoed her and Xóchitl's unwavering commitment to the group's survival, a determination that was palpable in the air.

Asia took a long breath. "Yes. You and Xóchitl are a rock for us. Even in the bleakest of times, you never give up. Thank you both."

Lian touched her heart. "We're a collective, Sister. Together, we'll find a way."

The three women sat in repose. Their faces reflected a shared fortitude to overcome whatever challenges lay ahead. Their bond, forged in the crucible of survival, seemed unbreakable. They beamed as Zaniya gave her evening blessing.

"The Goddess does not fear the darkness," the Crone invoked. "Instead, She wears it like a cloak, drawing strength from its depths and clarity from its silence. She embraces the shadows as part of Her journey, knowing that true strength is born from the ability to see beauty even in the dark. Her wisdom is woven from light and shadow, for She understands that the night reveals what the day may hide."

Her melodic voice was imbued with gratitude and humility. "Daughters, you weren't made to remain in the shadows. Ascend like the mountain that touches the heavens. Like eternal peaks, your power is rooted in the Earth yet soars to the sky. You are as timeless as the peaks, as fierce as the winds, and as radiant as the dawn. Embrace your divinity. Blessed be."

The Earth began descending into the evening sky, a canvas of bright purples and fiery oranges blending into darkness. High wisps of clouds glowed with pinks and golds, highlighted by the fading light.

The Moon, a wide silver disc, hovered above the top of the ravine, a serene presence in the gathering dusk. Higher up, the deepening blue crept in, a notice of the night to come, while the last rays of sunlight stretched out like golden fingers, reaching to hold onto the day a little longer. It was a breathtaking sight, a reminder of the beauty that still existed amid their struggles.

36. Lian

Lian, 26, stood five feet six inches tall and weighed 120 pounds. She exuded a lean, athletic strength. Her toned body had muscles that rippled under her skin, reflecting years of martial arts training.

Her face, with its sturdy jawline, bore the marks of toughness. Numerous marks scarred her tan skin. Her deep-set pupils, a piercing shade of dark brown, gave her an intense, almost predatory glare.

She had short, thick, black hair. She occasionally shaved it and usually kept it in a buzz cut. A birthmark rested on the nape of her neck, hidden beneath her hair, known only to those closest to her.

Her attire was practical and durable, echoing her readiness for any challenge. Every detail was a tribute to her preparedness, from a hidden knife in her boot to a quick-release clasp on her backpack and extra straps for cartridges.

Lian was a Chinese word that referred to a lotus, waterlily, willow tree, or waterfall. It symbolized rebirth, purity, elegance, and spiritual transcendence. She was all these things and more. Her name was a constant reminder of the beauty and strength she was meant to embody, a guiding principle in her life.

Her parents were environmental scientists who studied manmade pollution that was driving the world to ruin. Their three daughters were born into a right-wing, anti-intellectual society teetering on the brink of collapse. Climate scientists were viewed as alarmists, and their research was dismissed or even suppressed.

The eldest child, Lian, was curious and adventurous with formidable optimism for change. She often accompanied her parents to climate protests, rallies, and community outreach events. She grew up with people who were fervent about saving the Planet, which shaped her compassionate worldview.

Her parents were ecological stewards who instilled a deep sense of accountability in their daughters. They worked tirelessly and struggled to get others to take their research seriously before it was too late. Because of their advocacy, they were fired from their jobs and barred from the research center they helped to build.

Afterward, they continued to be harassed by conservative european activists and groups who were funded by the fossil fuel lobby. When Lian was 14, her home in Santa Clara was attacked and firebombed, and her parents and two siblings were slaughtered by european christian nationalists.

Lian attended a private boarding school when the raid occurred and was the only surviving family member. She was adopted by relatives but became severely depressed. Her parents' murder and the worsening climate crisis turned her idealism into bitter realism.

Alone and grieving, the fourteen-year-old was forced to grow up quickly, learning how to survive in a world falling apart at the seams. She faced hunger, violence, and exploitation but refused to succumb to the despair and chaos around her.

In spite of her overwhelming loss, the Santa Clara native did not give up, a clue to the strength of her character. She honed martial arts skills and became radicalized, driven by her desire to protect girls and women subjected to masculinist despotic control. Her resilience in the face of overwhelming loss inspired many other women, including Xóchitl.

Her favorite quote was from a 21st century actor, Michael J. Fox: "Man is the most dangerous, destructive, selfish, and unethical animal on Earth. The missing link between animals and a truly humane mankind is man himself, who does not yet see himself as a part of the world, claiming it instead for himself."

She eventually encountered other female survivors at the Santa Barbara shelter and was inspired by their resolve to endure and rebuild. Her tactical skills and natural leadership abilities made her a natural fit for the group's security team. She instilled confidence in her ability to protect the collective.

The climate activist instantly formed a close bond with Xóchitl, and together, they took on the responsibility of protecting the collective. After the group left the shelter, she and Xóchitl used their defensive expertise to repulse several attacks. The assaults tested their coordination, communication, and resourcefulness.

The partnership between her and the Latina guard was balanced. Her fierce force of mind and straightforward attitude were reinforced by Xóchitl's loyalty and calm execution. Their harmony made them a force to reckon with and a valuable part of the female community. The unity and stability in their partnership were proof of their love for each other.

While Lian appeared harsh and impatient, Xóchitl understood and could communicate with her when others could not. Her partner realized that Lian was still traumatized by her family's murder, which shaped her radical feminist perspective. Consequently, the Chicana was able to translate her security concerns into actionable plans the group could follow.

Unlike Asia, the Crones, and Mothers' meticulous, nurturing approach, the couple embodied a more pragmatic, proactive leadership style. Their guidance was essential to surviving the dangerous and unpredictable social and natural environments the cooperative experienced.

Though shaped by different histories, the duo knew each other's emotional and existential struggles. Their partnership was built on mutual respect and dedication to protecting the commune that transcended the overwhelming odds against them. Lian's commitment to the female cause was unwavering, and she inspired Xóchitl and the collective to act courageously.

37. Lian's Cronetime

Evening came to the Western drylands like a soothing balm on a blistering sore. The forty climate wanderers were elated after spending the day at Lian's water park and enjoying Frida's delicious dinner.

It was Cronetime, and Hehewuti called on Lian to take the board. Lian stood upright and surveyed the female congregation with steely resolve.

"My dear Sisters," she opened, "the road toward freedom and equality for women and girls is not easy." Her audience listened with rapt attention. They loved her, and she rarely talked.

"The hazards we face from mediocre men are almost too much to bear." Her harsh tone conveyed the gravity of their situation. "Sexism, misogyny, and toxic manhood are everywhere and deadly." She spread her arms to illustrate its pervasiveness.

"There's a war on females." Lian's expression was troubled but firm. "From relatives to strangers, despicable males of all colors and creeds enrich their lives by capturing and selling us. To these deficient human beings, we're nothing but sexual objects and tradeable assets." The Santa Clara native spoke intentionally as if each word imparted a golden nugget.

She shifted to a more reflective stance. "But despite men's disdainful war on us, women are committed to non-violence." A frown tugged at the corners of her lips. "We want peaceful change, but that's not always possible with these pathetic men. Sometimes, we have to do the unthinkable to survive."

She raised her chin, and her voice rose in aggravation. "Sisters, change is unsettling. To reform this chauvinistic world, we have to first name the oppressor and accept the reality of their battle against us. Daily, they're exploiting girls. The situation is dire and urgent, and no one is coming to save us." Her serious demeanor signaled the weight of her truths.

She paused, focusing on the dark vista and the arduous struggle ahead. "Know this, Comrades, there's still potential for a brighter future in these turbulent times. To claim and achieve for ourselves the rights we now petition from these contemptible losers."

She circled her arms. "Sisters, we're a global force. We see no national boundaries, vast gulfs, or high walls dividing female from female." Her fingers intertwined, mirroring the unity of women, and her words struck the center of the women's hearts.

She took a long breath and resumed. "Nature does not separate the Sisterhood. Female division is completely men's doing. The madams, Jezebels, and pedo co-conspirators all work for the manosphere and its reprehensible dude bros." She stared at her viewers, imploring them to understand men's strategy of separating females. "So, let's not ever blame the victims of the patriarchy, women."

"The lack of female responsibility also applies to racism," Lian continued passionately. "The 'race' thing is entirely men's doing. Insecure males apply 'race' to us by restricting and controlling our sexuality, for their own benefit. They determine which cultural group we're part of, not us. And they punish females who don't comply with their racial rules."

The lead guard gestured at the girls, drawing a positive vision from their youth. "My fellow travelers, the future is in our hands. The task of women everywhere is to strip the ancient, cruel belief of sexism from this Globe. It's not going to be easy, but we have no other choice." Her hands waved emphatically, with fingers splayed to underline the depth of their struggle.

She leaned toward the flock as the weight of her words hung in their hearts. "The cruelties of our rapidly devolving species, and the devastation of this beautiful Planet, will not yield to men's obsolete battles, dogmas, and outworn beliefs. We must stop these self-seeking, macho idiots. Why? Cuz women will not be spared from the sixth mass extinction currently underway." Her eyebrows contracted, accenting the gravity of her message.

Lian glanced over the crowd, ensuring they felt the weight of her words. "We have nothing to lose, my dear companions, and literally everything is at stake." She paused briefly, then added, "Our species cannot be saved by those who cling to a dying way of life. Or by those who prefer the illusion of security to the enthusiasm that comes from the smallest progress."

Her hands opened wide, inviting the female audience into a shared vision. "Sisters, this dying sphere demands the courage, values, and actions of revolutionary girls and women. We are our only hope." She pumped her fist into the air in defiance and concluded her talk. Cronetime was over, and the women glowed with pride. The girls cheered the lead guard for a long time.

Zaniya opened her palms, glowing with pride. She gazed at Lian evocatively. "May the Goddess be praised. Her beauty is not bound by form, but by the life She breathes into the land and the fire She holds within. She is the horizon, where dreams touch reality, where the Earth meets the sky in an endless embrace."

The Crone clasped her hands. "Do not be swayed by fear or doubt, Daughters. Let your roots sink deep, and your spirit rise tall. This is your journey. Step into it with purpose and power. Stand firm, for you are meant to rise. Blessed be, Li, blessed be."

Lian beamed and stepped closer to the Crone. "Blessed be to you, Elder Sister." Her smile transmitted her innate appreciation. "Your trust in Gaia has been our brightest light."

The night was soundless when the survivors crawled into their cozy blankets. Cronetime was immensely inspirational. Each syllable sparked a positive change in the females' attitude. They rested comfortably and imagined better days ahead, knowing their outstanding guard stood close by, watching over her beloved Sisters.

38. Signal

The next day, the Badlands were engulfed in a brutal heat wave. The caravan, struggling to make progress, had to rest frequently and managed to cover only five miles before the Sun dipped below the horizon. The exhausted women dug a trench midway up a hill and settled in for the night. As the clock struck 7:30 PM, the air, which had been oppressively hot, turned light and cool.

Suddenly, a night bird tooted in the distance: three hoots, a five-second pause, then three toots again. An owl's screech was usually benign, but the three-five-three pattern was a dire warning, and the camp froze.

"It's the signal," Nzinga rasped.

Asia's sight trained toward the sound. The two guards were higher up the hill but invisible. She lowered her hand, signaling the others in the trench. "It's the warning," she shushed. "Be quiet and pay close attention."

The group felt the weight of Asia's words and fell silent. Fear gripped them, their breaths quickening, as they strained to hear any sign of danger. The absence of sound only heightened their anxiety, with adrenaline coursing through their veins. The same question echoed in everyone's mind: Why did the guards signal? Are pedos near?

Alone on the ridge, Xóchitl inspected the panorama of gray dunes. The Moon cast a diffuse glow over the scene. She peered into the distance, and her sharp optics spotted two flashlights and several dark silhouettes slowing cresting the hill in the far South, several dunes away. Her pulse raced. The group was moving North, towards the camp. She looked down at the dugout and gave the signal.

Lian was on watch near the camp when she heard the call. She crawled to the ridge, and Xóchitl pointed to the lights. "Maybe a half-dozen people or more, about three miles away," she guessed.

Lian turned towards the camp and waved her flashlight downward, signaling the women to hide. "Those lights are an hour way." Her face tightened, and she gripped her weapon in a vice. "I'll act as a decoy. Tell Asia know my plan."

Xóchitl shook her head and argued with Lian over who should go on the mission.

Marge's face twisted in panic when she heard the signal. She had taken her daughter about one hundred feet from the dugout to relieve herself. They were now stuck outside, as returning could reveal the camp's location. She dashed towards Lisa, her heart pounding in her chest.

"Are you finished?" Marge surveyed the area for danger.

Lisa nodded, appearing confused.

Marge reached out and smothered her daughter. "We have to be quiet," she warned. "And we need to hide, now."

She skimmed the dim hillside for a place to disappear. Dropping to a crouch, she whispered, "Let's go down there." She pointed to two shrubs twenty feet away. She grabbed Lisa's hand, and they crept toward the bushes and stayed flat.

"Freeze and don't make a sound." Marge combed the background, breathing heavily, listening to the stillness. She focused on the ravine below, and her mind raced about what might come next.

Asia glanced at the Mothers in the ditch. Their anxiety was unmistakable. "Form a semi-circle around the children," she advised. The women took up their positions with practiced precision and sat shoulder to shoulder, protecting the girls.

Asia crouched and peered over the trough. Her pupils dashed from side to side, studying the shadows for movement. She softly loaded her weapon, wary of making the slightest sound.

They all sat and waited for an all-clear signal. But none came, and the tension mounted. The women glared into the darkness in confusion. Shadows seemed to shift and dance, playing tricks on their strained senses. Every swirl of wind, every shift of sand sent jolts of fear through the spooked migrants.

After ten minutes, Asia could no longer take the suspense. She decided to send a messenger up one hundred yards to Lian. She called Riri and Phoolan and pointed to the ridge. "Find out what's going on with Lian and come back."

Stephen overheard her plan and announced, "We'll go," He and Miller already had their gear packed, ready to leave. Everyone was astonished. The boys never volunteered for any task before. They were reluctant travelers who stuck to themselves and refused to be friends with the girls.

"Thank you both." Asia shook Stephen's hand. "Find out what's going on and come right back."

The teens slipped out of the trench and dashed up the hill. Onawa stared at them, pleasantly surprised. They were starting to act responsibly and that was a good sign. Marge saw them leave, and she and Lisa quickly rejoined the others in the trench.

The boys met Lian, and she briefed them on the figures they saw in the distance. They offered to join her decoy mission. Xóchitl scampered down and informed the community about the strangers.

"They're probably pedos or a gang," the Latina alerted, pointing South.

The collective was alarmed. They had not faced an attack by kidnappers in weeks. Still, they knew their luck could not last forever.

"Lian wants to create a diversion and lure them away," Xóchitl reported. "The boys offered to help. We'll head West for an hour and double back."

"Be careful." Asia touched Xóchitl's shoulder. The Latina scampered up the hill, and the four silhouettes disappeared into the night.

Asia turned to the group and focused on the girls. She could feel their nervousness. A collective dread hung over them like a dark cloud. She pumped her right fist into the air. "Be brave, my kittens. If we're discovered, we'll fight and defend each of you." Her words were a ray of light amid darkness, inspiring the girls to be fearless.

The evacuees huddled, breathing softly. Selina and Karol crouched beside Zenobia in fight mode. They were fearful but were survivors, like the others.

Gloria's features hardened. She tightened her grip on her weapon and vowed, "We won't let them take you, my children. We'll protect you now and always." Her determination was a source of reassurance for the girls, instilling confidence in their safety.

Fierce and driven, the Mothers echoed her sentiment. They had been through too much and lost too many people to let anyone take more away from them. They were mentally prepared to protect their daughters with their lives but hoped it would not come to that. Their steely resistance was evidence of their maternal will and strength, encouraging self-reliance in facing danger.

Onawa glanced at Cha'Kwaina. Her daughter clutched a weapon and stared defiantly. Her heart rose in pride. "Stay beside me, Cha-Cha," she uttered. "No matter what."

The teen nodded. Marielle, 7, crouched beside her with a stick, whimpering. Cha'Kwaina hugged the child tight. "It's okay. I'm here. I'll protect you."

The girls' chests pounded, and they held each other's hands for support. They were minors forced to become child warriors, a stark reminder of the dangerous circumstances the young inherited in the post-apocalypse.

Time dragged by at a snail's pace, and each second seemed like minutes. The women kept yearning for Lian's plan to succeed. It had to work. The thought of being detected by pedos was harrowing. They waited quietly and tried to remain invisible.

After two hours that felt like an eternity, they heard another signal. The 'all clear' sign indicated the immediate threat had passed.

"The guards are returning." Nzinga's words carried an enormous sense of release.

Asia let out a long breath she did not realize she had been holding. 'Lian's trick worked.' She stared at the others in relief. "Thankfully, the guards and boys led the strangers away. Whoever they were."

The tension in the camp eased, replaced by cautious optimism. The signal meant they were safe. They began chatting, and Asia hushed them. "Stay vigilant and quiet. Until Lian returns." The commune ceased talking and waited for the guards to arrive.

39. Missing

It was 9:30 PM in the Central California wilderness. Asia, perched above the trench, spotted the silhouettes of the two guards approaching from below. Her heart raced. Their return was a relief, but their demeanor hinted at trouble. And where were Stephen and Miller? A cloud of uncertainty suspended over the refugees like a hammer.

The defensive traps, strategically placed to protect the base, were well hidden, and Nzinga guided the guards through. Despite their fatigue, Lian and Xóchitl entered the encampment with a determined stride, ready to defend it at all costs.

"Did you lead the strangers away?" Asia's brows creased in concern.

Lian wiped sweat from her face and willed herself to stand upright. "Xóchitl saw lights three miles away and gave the signal." She pointed to the ridge. "The boys came up, and we left to create a diversion." She went silent.

"Then what happened?" Asia twisted the edge of her jacket impatiently.

Lian tossed her head. "We went right and made some noise. They took the bait and followed. Half an hour later, we turned South to double back." Her voice trailed off.

"Then what?" Asia pushed the guard to answer.

"The teens were gone," Lian said calmly, looking down at her hands.

Asia stiffened when the realization hit her. "You lost them?" She glared at the guard.

Lian shrugged and peeked at Xóchitl, who said nothing. There was a moment of strained silence. The women were filled with anticipation and dread and scoured the dark ravine for the missing youths.

Asia struggled to contain her emotions. Hormones coursed through her veins, and she suppressed a scream. "You lost them in the dark, didn't you?" Her voice trembled with unease.

Asia felt deeply disappointed. "You lost them in the dark, right?" She glowered at Lian, seeking confirmation.

"I don't know?" Lian shrugged. "We searched for a while but saw nothing."

Asia was astonished. "How could you two just abandon them? Tomorrow, we'll break camp at first light and head North. That means they'll be stuck out here alone." She gaped at the pair.

Xóchitl shook her head and remained silent.

Lian sighed. "We had to return for defense."

Asia stepped close to Lian. "Go and find them, now," she demanded. "We can't just ditch our boys."

"No," Lian answered firmly. "We could be in danger tonight." She clenched her fists and stood still.

Nzinga stepped between the opposing women and touched Asia's back reassuringly. She glanced at Lian. "What do you suggest?"

"What if our diversion didn't work?" Lian's wary expression reflected the gravity of their situation. "There could be pedos nearby. We need to prepare for the worst. The girls are the priority, not the boys."

Asia grimaced. "Unacceptable. Please find them tonight. We'll keep the camp secure."

"Leaving camp is too risky," Lian snapped and stepped away from Asia.

"The teens can't be far away," Asia pleaded. "You want us to just sit here and wait? You're the only two that know where they last were." She skimmed the women, seeking support. Most concurred.

Lian crossed her arms. Her frustration increased with each second. "Irrelevant," she fumed. "We need sharpshooters protecting the perimeter."

Asia took a deep breath and tried hard to remain calm. "We'll double the night watch," she promised. "Please get the boys so we can all leave in the morning." She pleaded with clasped palms.

Lian stood rigid and unyielding. The women glared at her, and she scowled. After a minute of intense scrutiny, she uncrossed her arms and recognized the majority's decision.

"Fine, we'll search for them." Lian huffed and raised her chin defiantly at Asia. "But if those strangers find you here, you'd better be ready."

Lian and Xóchitl left unenthusiastically in search of the teens. Nzinga and the scouts secured the perimeter with more traps, and the women prepared weapons to defend the dugout. The night progressed at a snail's pace as they waited nervously for the boys' return. They were tired but too worried to sleep.

Zaniya unfurled her body reverently. She felt the warmth of the Moon on her face as she bestowed her blessing. "The Goddess whispers to those who listen, guiding them to strength, wisdom, and serenity. She stands as a pillar of eternity, teaching patience, endurance, and the beauty of stillness. Gaia's presence is a reminder that true strength is quiet, like the mountains. That true wisdom is patient, like the Earth. All praises to the Goddess. Blessed be."

The commune bowed in respect, following her lead. Their movements were synchronized in a solemn, practiced rhythm. Some closed their eyelids and tried to be calm, while others stared at the sky for courage.

The night sky stretched vast and endless, a velvety expanse of infinity. Stars glittered like tiny diamond grains in a dark desert, most flickering faintly while a few burned brightly. The group shared a moment of solidarity in the uncertain Badlands, their unity a source of courage in difficult times.

Asia and Nzinga guarded the South, searching the darkness for trouble. "Stephen and Miller must be terrified." Asia shook her head, and her shoulders slumped. The weight of their predicament pressed down on her. "I hope they're all okay." She said weakly. "We're not leaving anyone behind."

The guards will find them," Nzinga reassured her friend, her smile radiating hope and confidence. "We'll make it to the Safehouse. All of us, like you promised."

At 10:30 PM, the temperature lowered to 89°F (32°C). The ravine darkened after Moonset, casting an ominous gloom over the landscape. The stars became more numerous, endless, and remote.

Asia and Nzinga knelt inside the ditch, scrutinizing the darkness for movement. They saw and heard nothing. The night's events were taxing, and a brief whiff of smoke added to Asia's unease.

The female collective was exhausted. Soon after the guards left in search of their two missing members, they drifted off to sleep. A camouflage tarp spread over the ditch, and four women on night watch provided a measure of security, and they slept soundly.

Suddenly, a far-away crunch drifted through the night air. It drew Asia's attention immediately. Her head snapped toward the sound, and she strained to pierce the blackness. Blood pounded in her ears, and a shiver rippled through her body.

"Is that the boys returning?" Asia looked at Nzinga in a silent plea for reassurance.

Nzinga also heard the slight sound. She tilted her head, trying to catch any further noises. Every muscle was primed for action. She strained to hear but could not discern anything amiss.

Asia sighed. "Should we wake them up?"

Nzinga shook her head. "That could have been anything. If it repeats, we'll raise them from rest." The pair continued to monitor the silent night.

40. Zenobia's Dream

Zenobia stirred in her sleep. She heard a subtle crunch in the distance and became half-awake. She yawned, and her vivid dreams of a female utopia eased. 'What wuz dat?" She sat up and squinted against the dim light. She saw and heard nothing. 'Me dreamin' or imaginin' things?'

She listened intently to the quiet for a moment. Her eyelids fluttered, heavy with the residue of sleep. Her heart longed for the utopia she had visualized. She slinked into her blanket, and fantasy enveloped her once more like a soothing cocoon.

In her dream, she walked through a lush, vivid landscape bathed in bright Sunlight and comfortable weather. The air was thick with the scent of pine trees, blooming flowers, and moist dirt. The whole place was bursting with water, bright colors, and diversity.

Birds sang from the treetops, and a symphony of melodies echoed through the forest. A cool breeze rubbed against her skin, brushing all worries away. She felt a deep sense of serenity and contentment, which had become elusive since society collapsed.

She proceeded through the dreamscape and came upon a bustling municipality at the edge of the forest. The enchanted metropolis was shaped like a pyramid temple to the mountain in the background. Its development was obviously shaped by gentle and thoughtful hands. The design included numerous parks and stands of the original forest.

The buildings and residences were layered with plants and topped by roof gardens. Natural springs and streams flowed throughout the city, making the urban center appear more like a natural environment than a conquered forest.

On the outskirts, Zenobia was met by a dark-colored young woman in a white frock with long locks. She beamed and gave her guest a cool hibiscus drink.

"Wat's this place?" Zenobia inquired.

"Welcome to Palmyra." The greeter bowed. "I'm Jasmine. Let me show you our beautiful home."

Her escort casually strolled through the streets and used public transportation to show her the nine districts. She pointed out the main social and natural attractions in each area. The residents she saw were healthy and cheerful. Females of all ages and colors moved about the green-covered wards, confident, serene, and radiant.

"Y'all looks happy ova here," the Firekeeper noted.

"Well, we have access to social benefits like health care, housing, and food assistance," the host replied. "We act collectively to preserve our biodiversity, institutions, communities, and families. We make great efforts and sacrifices to maintain equality and diversity in our socialist democracy."

"Da women heh look like dem fear nothing," Zenobia observed. "In me world, dem face abuse on da daily. Only kno' hunger an struggle fuh survive."

"I've heard," Jasmine sighed. "Here, females and males lived harmoniously. We are a gift-giving society with few personal possessions. Female bodies are sacred and are never violated. Crones are our most respected members, revered for their wisdom. Peace reigns, and there's little need for security or prisons."

"We ah de total opposite," the Firekeeper moaned.

Her guide nodded. "Our society is female-centered. Still, it's not defined by sex, but by social responsibility. We place high value on empathy and cooperation and focus on sustainability. To curb our ecological impact, we don't raise livestock. And to promote peace and morality, we don't eat or harm animals."

"Dem value nah exis' in we man hellscape," Zenobia reflected sadly.

Jasmine shook her head in sympathy and pointed to a building. "Our structures are limited in height to blend in with the greenery. Exterior walls are covered in gardens and cared for by city workers. Sidewalks and streets generate renewable energy, and each ward is self-sufficient in food and power. The entire city emits zero greenhouse gas pollution."

"Y'all modern an natural." The guest glanced about, clearly impressed with the architecture.

"Yes," Jasmine agreed. "District planners embrace inclusivity and respect for natural ecosystems. Public areas prioritize safety, comfort, and accessibility. Nearly every block has social activity and creativity centers. Exercise, play, art, fashion, music, and storytelling are vital aspects of our society."

"Whey all de people liv heh?" the visitor wondered.

"We live in spacious social housing apartments with utilities included, a master bedroom, an extra bathroom, a balcony, and other amenities. There're common areas for food gardens, sports, recreation, and socializing. Each 50-unit building includes families of different ages, sizes, and skill sets."

"Y'all get married ova heh?" Zenobia wondered.

Her guide smiled radiantly. "Palmyrans have serial partners and don't marry. Our relationships are mostly with the opposite sex and are built on mutual respect and support. We don't have gender roles or feminine-masculine performance. Individuals are free to do any work, dress however they want, and express their sexuality without restrictions."

"Wat bout Mothers?" the visitor inquired.

"We're female-centered." Jasmine touched her belly. "Mothers have generous maternal leave, free daycare, and domestic help. There's extensive community involvement, which sustains them during pregnancy and birth. Our men are humble and considerate. They act as servitors, assisting their partner with cooking, cleaning, gardening, and other household tasks. Childrearing is a communal effort, and nurturing traits are admired in everyone."

"Who ah de leada heh?" the guest asked.

Her escort shook her head. "We don't have a single leader. Leadership is split into committees composed of female counselors. Committee roles rotate among Elder women from all backgrounds to foster diverse perspectives and prevent consolidation of power. Governance is shared at all levels, and decisions are reached via consensus. Everyone's opinions are valued regardless of position or status."

"Wish we had dat," Zenobia dipped her hands into a cool pool in a public square, feeling the water against her fingertips. The surface settled, reflecting the women around her who had faces full of love and trust.

The sights and behaviors she saw were strange, yet she had never felt more at home. The town gave her the best feeling she had ever had. It was a place she would never want to leave.

While she reveled in Palmyra's pleasantness, a shadow of doubt crept into her mind. The vision was too perfect, too idyllic. Inside her psyche, she knew that Palmyra was unimaginable in real life. For her, survival was an everyday battle, and trust was a rare commodity. She longed for a better way, and the vivid dream hinted at her powerful yearning.

She roused from sleep, and her subconscious began to fade. But the revelation of the womanly paradise clung to her, refusing to let go. She yearned to remain with Jasmine and the women in Palmyra, to believe that such a society existed and was accessible.

The female utopia convinced her that a culture based on ethics, equity, and eco-friendliness was possible. Palmyra was a transformative society where people thrived along with the environment. The unique, woman-conscious civilization could support a quality lifestyle for generations, inspiring the Crone to strive for a better future.

She glided into wakefulness, and the dream dissolved like mist in the morning Sun. Her pupils half-opened, and the treacherous Badlands flooded in. Palmyra's friendly people, hearty laughter, and serenity were replaced by unforgiving darkness and the insecurity of her fragile existence.

The gap between her unconscious and conscious lives could not have been more glaring, but the dream left an indelible mark. As she shook off the last vestiges of sleep, she held onto a potent realization. Almost certainly, her life could never be the paradise she imagined. Nevertheless, she was part of a community headed towards Palmyra.

41. Scream

It was 11 PM in the Mojave Desert. The furrow above the valley floor was quiet and tranquil. Inside, Asia and Nzinga trained their senses on the dark ravine. They had heard something, but then it became quiet. They anxiously awaited the return of four members: Lian, Xóchitl, and the two boys who had disappeared earlier that evening.

A faint mumbling drifted up in the silent night, drawing their attention. "Is that the boys?" Asia whispered. The sound was soft like the dry desert breeze, but it was different as it carried the weight of male voices.

Nzinga grimaced, straining to understand the chatter. "That doesn't sound like them." She leaned forward and trained her weapon on the ravine. She raised her head and made a low-pitched hoot.

The stillness that followed seemed to stretch endlessly, punctuated only by the rustling of the wind. The pressure was nerve-racking. Nzinga repeated the signal, but the response she hoped for remained elusive. The night seemed to press in around them, thick with an unsettling, ominous hush.

Nzinga leaned closer to Asia. "If it's the boys, they would answer." Her two signals echoed off the trench walls, waking the women.

Asia looked grimly at her partner. "Whoever's down there is not part of us."

After a long minute, Phoolan, 16, crawled to Asia and whispered, "Let me check out what's happening. Daria and I will crawl down to the ravine."

Asia's head snapped toward the scout. "No," she shushed. "We need you here." She relaxed and added, "It's too dangerous."

Suddenly, a piercing scream shattered the calm. It was a man in agonizing pain on the right side of the valley. The women and children instantly froze, hearts pounding in terror. Male voices rebounded ominously from below.

"Pedos at three o'clock in the ravine." Asia hissed through gritted teeth, referring to the dangerous men approaching. 'Damn it,' she thought. 'Lian was right. I should have listened to her.'

Zenobia shook her partner, Mary. "Dem traps be workin'. But it's a good an bad sign," she said, referring to the defensive traps along the camp's perimeter.

Mary blinked rapidly, trying to shake off the fog of weariness clouding her mind. "We can't give our position away. I'll try to keep the children calm." She crawled to the center of the trench where the juveniles huddled, terrified.

"We're all here to protect you." The Crone spoke calmly. "But you have to be quiet, okay?" Her words were like a lullaby, wrapping each girl in comfort. "We'll play a game. Try to play dead, okay?"

The girls curled their bodies, closed their eyelids, and faked sleeping. Though petrified, they showed immense bravery by cooperating and playing the pretend game. Their courage made Mary and the other adults proud, and they felt a strong sense of support for the children.

Lisa trembled uncontrollably and could not play the pretend game. "Are they coming for us?" She grabbed Mary, sobbing.

"I wouldn't let that happen, sweetie." The Crone embraced Lisa. "I'm right here with you."

Asia's beams darted back and forth, examining the darkness with hawk-like intensity. Every shadow seemed like a potential threat, and her muscles coiled to react. But she knew they had to remain invisible.

The muffled scream from below clawed at the refugees' minds, sending chills down their spines. But the women were not idle. They quickly prepared weapons and ammunition, their readiness reassuring the girls and instilling confidence in them.

"Another bloody spike," a man yelled. "They're everywhere. Watch out."

The adults in the dugout murmured anxiously.

"We need to stay hidden." Asia was focused, in stark contrast to the tension in the camp. Her breathing was normal, and she steadied herself for the pedos' attack with sheer willpower.

The women mirrored Asia's self-control, becoming the epitome of bravery. Their courage in the face of danger was inspiring, and they were prepared for any eventuality from the males below. The children found comfort in their leaders' strength and resolve, feeling inspired and courageous in their presence.

"May the Goddess be with us," Zaniya invoked softly. "In the face of adversity, She does not bend or break. She digs her roots deeper, letting every obstacle shape her strength. Be unafraid of the climb, Daughters. Each step strengthens you, each struggle shapes you, and every summit reveals the depths of your power. Blessed be."

42. Booby-trap

The California wilderness was pitch black, lit only by Stars. Asia glanced up, trying to relax while contemplating their situation. Wisps of clouds drifted high, barely visible against the darkened backdrop. In the infinite space, constellations blinked, their ancient patterns telling stories lost in time.

"Oh hell." A male howled in pain. "The whole place is booby-trapped. You ugly bitches gonna pay for this." The man's shouting echoed through the ravine.

The migrants huddled in the trench, hiding from the men below. Their chests throbbed frantically. "How many are they?" Onawa wondered aloud. No one answered.

"Wake up, my pretties. Daddy's home." The man's sadistic glee was unnerving.

Asia's skin crawled. She glanced left to right, weighing their limited options. The hill, once a good vantage point, felt like a trap with the men closing in. Every second counted, and she had to act fast.

She felt the pressure in the dugout, the weight of the collective's focus on her, trusting in her to lead them out of danger. She took a moment to focus on her breath. 'We have to leave this spot,' she decided. Off to the left, then up and over the ridge.

But exiting the trench carried the risk of being seen. 'We need a diversion to improve our chances of escaping,' Asia mused. Her attention flicked to the lookouts. "Phoolan, you and the scouts go right. Distract the men while we slip out on the left."

Phoolan's face brightened when she heard Asia's plan. From the first scream, she wanted to act, to see what they were up against. She was accustomed to being ahead of the pack, scouting for opportunities. But Asia refuted her suggestion, and she could not disobey her leader. She felt trapped in the ditch and was glad for the mission.

"We'll lure them away." Phoolan was steady and calm despite the dangerous proposal. She glanced at Riri and Daria. "Let's go." She swiftly loaded her backpack and shouldered her weapon.

"No." Simone, 40, squealed with the raw, primal fear of a Mother protecting her child. "We have to stick together and wait for the others." She instinctively reached out to grab Phoolan.

Asia held back Simone. "If we stay here, they'll find us. We'll search for Lian, Xóchitl, and the boys later."

A loud, painful shriek added to the pressure. "You damn whores. We're gonna beat and sell you all."

Phoolan felt desperate about the delay. They were wasting precious time. She had to convince the camp that they would not become separated.

"We'll circle and meet you North." Phoolan's words were more of a vow than hope, to instill the courage they desperately needed. "Rather than fight, let's escape." She knew the ladies preferred the path of least resistance.

Though dreading parting with the three scouts, the women reasoned that Asia's strategy was the safest. Simone clenched her teeth and shifted closer to Zenobia, a silent gesture of their resolve.

"It gon be aight," the Firekeeper assured.

Asia exhaled slowly, feeling the burden settle on her shoulders. Her fingers lingered on Phoolan for a moment, conveying trust. "Stay close and low. Use the darkness to your advantage. We'll wait for you one hour North. Join us once you're in the clear." Her words were a reassurance of her leadership.

Phoolan gave a gentle, reassuring smile. "We'll reunite soon." The three scouts waved goodbye and slipped silently out of the trench.

Asia faced the escapees with an unbending attitude. "We'll go once the pedos take the bait." With steely determination, the group strapped their packs and prepared to exit the furrow on short notice.

Zaniya watched the departing scouts with pride. Her chest rose gently, and she gathered her emotions in recitation. "In the vast wilderness, Gaia is the heartbeat, grounding each creature, nurturing every life. Her spirit is expansive like the Cosmos. May the Goddess be with you. Blessed be." The scouts disappeared into the shadows above.

43. AWOL

It was 11:15 PM in the Central Valley. The air was thick with tension, and the occasional screams of men, distant but growing closer, disturbed the quiet of the female migrants' encampment. The moon cast an eerie glow over the rugged terrain, adding to the gloomy mood. The women huddled together, their hearts pounding with fear, hoping the young scouts could save them with a diversion.

The escape plan was set. They would sneak out of the dugout, go left, and crawl up to the ridge. The women, their determination to survive unwavering, were ready to face whatever came their way. But the thought of losing contact with Lian, Xóchitl, and the two boys filled them with dread.

Still, the capture of the girls and the group's existence hung in the balance. The collective, bound by a strong sense of camaraderie, hugged each other for support. They had repelled several attacks in the past and were prepared to do so again. As the threat approached, they waited anxiously for Asia's signal to either fight or run.

Earlier, around 9:30 PM, Lian and Xóchitl, best friends and trusted comrades, left the trench on a mission to find the two missing boys. Lian was unwilling to go and was exceedingly upset. After they left, she tried to convince Xóchitl to ignore Asia's plea to find Stephen, 15, and Miller, 16.

"Tonight's way too dark to find their trail," Lian appealed. "We'll have better luck in the morning."

Xóchitl was surprised. "Going AWOL? We can't simply abandon our mission."

"It's pointless to search again," Lian complained. "We didn't miss anything before."

Xóchitl was adamant about following orders. "You agreed to do this, right?"

"Comrade Leader wasn't taking no for an answer," Lian sniped. "She gave us no choice."

"Well, she wasn't alone, was she?" Xóchitl was upset. She prided herself on always completing her assignment, and Lian was making her break her allegiance to Asia and the collective's will.

"It's foolish and dangerous," Lian groaned. "That woman will get us both killed."

"It's our job to take risks." Xóchitl softened her tone. She was anxious about staining their relationship and wished she could de-escalate the conflict.

"I'm not deserting, I'm prioritizing assets. I'm done risking my life for those two bullies," Lian seethed. "All this stress for two spoiled male brats?"

"Whatever you say." Xóchitl decided to stop arguing with her best friend. Lian was stubborn, and she knew she could not change her mind. The pair stood silent for a minute and calmed down.

Lian started to climb up the hill, and Xóchitl followed her to their previous defensive position overlooking the ravine. She sat quietly and watched for danger.

"How about a Zen tale, X?" Lian wanted to appease her friend.

The Latina was delighted by Lian's olive branch. "Sure, what should it be about?"

"I don't care," Lian admitted.

"Alright, Bhikkhuni. This one is called The Sound of a Single Bell." The storyteller adjusted her stance to be more comfortable.

"I like the sound of it," Lian laughed.

"Gotami was a troubled young nun named," Xóchitl began. "Her master, an Elder Bhikkhuni, gave her a simple task: 'Go to the village and bring back the sound of a single bell.'"

"Gotami bowed and set off," the narrator continued. "As she walked through the village, she heard many bells: temple bells, market chimes, the jingling of carts and harnesses. But which one was the 'sound of a single bell?' She was confused."

"Interesting." Lian nodded with approval.

The Chicana smiled and resumed. "Gotami approached the blacksmith and asked, 'Which is the best bell?' He pointed to his hammer and struck the metal. 'This is the purest sound,' he claimed as the loud ring rattled the workshop's walls."

"Next, she asked the vegetable seller," the narrator continued, "and she buzzed her small handbell. 'This is the clearest sound,' the vendor insisted.' The sharp jingle echoed through the marketplace. Then, an ox's bell tinkered behind the nun, and its timeless chime reminded her of the family's cow. She wandered the town, hearing many bells, but could not decide which one had a single clang."

"So hard to choose," Lian commented.

The Latina nodded. "Gotami was confused and returned to the temple empty-handed. She bowed before her Bhikkhuni and admitted, 'I've failed. Every bell I heard was joined by another sound: an echo, a voice, a wind chime. I couldn't find the sound of a single bell.'"

The speaker paused, and Lian grinned. "What happens next?"

"The conclusion," Xóchitl snickered. "The master smiled and pointed to Gotami's heart. 'Close your eyes. Calm down and just listen.' The nun did as she was told. At first, she heard nothing. But then, beyond the wind, beyond the birds, beyond her own breath, there it was. A single, silent chime resonated deep within her. Her eyes widened. 'I hear it.'"

"Hear what?" Lian was puzzled. "Her heart?"

The narrator smiled and resumed, "The Bhikkhuni nodded. 'That chime is the sound of a single bell. It was within you all along.' From that day forward, Gotami no longer sought wisdom from others before listening to herself."

"I kinda get it," Lian nodded. "It's what I do. I trust my own instincts."

The storyteller agreed. "True insight comes not from seeking outward approval but from trusting what is already within us." The guards chatted pleasantly, keeping watch from the ridge.

About an hour later, a sharp crack resonated from below. The two women became alert.

"Did you hear that?" Xóchitl's brows narrowed, and she strained to hear any further noise.

Lian skimmed the darkness below and raised her hand to test the wind's direction. It blew from the West. The noise appeared again, a kind of mushing. Someone was treading carefully through the spongy sand at the bottom of the ravine. The footsteps were faint but unmistakable.

"Is it the teens?" Xóchitl wondered.

Lian shook her head. She heard the low, edgy murmur of several men. She glanced at her partner and mouthed, 'Pedos.' An ominous apprehension passed between them.

Without a word, the two women began crawling across the top of the hill to opposite sides of the ridge. By the time the men entered the area, the pair was in a triangulated position using night vision scopes to aim their weapons at them.

Lian breathed slowly, consciously. She was a bit nervous, but her defensive mind kept her focused. She calculated range, wind, temperature, trajectory, and the target's movement.

The seconds stretched into long, agonizing moments, each heavier than the last. After the men started screaming, the scouts exited the ditch and headed toward them. Their presence complicated the situation. It meant she had to act sooner.

"Wahooo." A man yelled out in agony, "We're gonna beat and sell you all." She saw seven heat signatures staggering up the hill.

In the trench, the Mothers surrounded the juveniles, and the children clung to them in anguish. Greta grabbed Asia's arm. "I'm scared," she cried. Her breath came in shallow, uneven bursts.

"It's going to be alright." Asia hugged the child and focused on the ravine. Shadows were moving at the bottom, and she was ready to meet the challenge. "Hang on," she shushed. "Stay calm." If the diversion failed, she was mentally ready to aggressively defend her clan.

44. Tracer Light

It was 11:15 PM in the Badlands. The air was thick with angry male voices, sharply diverging from the silence that enveloped the desert. The painful screams and violent threats reverberated in the minds of the climate migrants in the shallow trench.

As they huddled, the women's resolve to protect the girls burned like a fierce flame in their hearts. They were firm in the face of danger, determined not to let a single child slip from their grasp.

Rather than confronting the kidnappers or gang, they preferred to take flight and find another place to hide. The scouts left to create a diversion, and the women, with a hastily planned escape route in mind, waited restlessly to execute their getaway.

As the seconds ticked by, the men grew closer and were soon located directly below them in the valley. The campers felt hemmed in and miserable, dreading what could come next. They faced a daunting decision - some wanted to stay and fight, while others preferred to run away.

'If we bolt, we'll lose three scouts." Gloria declared.

"Yes," Onawa retorted. "Plus, the guards and boys."

"We'll be down seven," Marge uttered uneasily.

"Those men may capture some girls," Aisha fretted.

"We'll be totally ruined," Simone opined.

The women conversed in hushed, anxious tones, and the girls mumbled timidly. They were stuck between a rock and a hard place, with no clear path to safety. Panic set in, their breaths coming in gasps as they struggled to find a way out.

And then, in a moment of startling relief, it happened. From the corner of her vision, Asia saw a sudden flash sweeping down the hill from the top right, a red tracer cutting through the darkness with its sharp, striking brilliance.

One of the dark silhouettes below fell, and his yelling stopped. Asia's breath caught in her throat. 'That's a sniper. Who is it?'

Another marker light erupted from the top left of the ridge, its brightness carving through the night like a jagged streak of molten iron. Another man dropped to the ground and became silent.

The attackers shrieked and scrambled to find cover on the bare ground. They started shooting at the ridge, and bullets whizzed over the furrow. The women and children dove onto the floor.

Three more beams rained from above, and three shadows crumpled below. After a few seconds, two more red flashes erupted, and the firing and shouting from the ravine ceased.

The hush that followed was redemptive like a soothing, peaceful bath. The quiet was broken only by the ragged breaths of the stunned survivors. After the chaos, the profound silence that descended cast an eerie calm over the scene. The women strained to hear more male voices, waiting for the other shoe to drop. But there was nothing, just the calm desert night.

"Are there pedos on the ridge?" Asia whispered.

"You mean a rival gang?" Nzinga muttered.

"Yes. Whoever took those men out." Asia stared at the top of the hill. It was too dark to see anything, and it was eerily quiet.

Suddenly, an owl's measured call pierced the night, reassuring everyone they were safe.

"It's the guards," Nzinga observed in surprise.

A wave of relief washed over Asia's body. She closed her eyes, savoring the warm feeling of security that now enveloped them.

Nzinga trembled in relief and disbelief. "The guards saved us?" Her face glistened in the dim light, and she hugged Asia, searching for confirmation.

"It had to be." Asia looked toward the signal and nodded. "They returned just in time."

Gradually, the suspense in the trench eased. The abrupt turn of events left them pleasantly surprised. The women waited eagerly to greet their protectors while Asia checked for signs of movement. The men were all gone, neutralized before they could strike.

"It's over," Marge gushed as tears of joy streamed down her face. "Thank goodness." The tension that had gripped the collective finally dissipated, leaving a profound sense of relief in its wake.

Lian and Xóchitl approached the trench, exhausted. They were followed by Phoolan, Daria, and

Riri. The two guards were tense, weighed down by the gravity of their encounter. Their swift and efficient defense was totally unexpected, and everyone was appreciative, a stark contrast from the tension that had gripped them moments earlier.

The pair sat alone at the camp's perimeter to debrief, and no one bothered them. They respected the guards' need for privacy.

The group enveloped the scouts in a warm embrace, praising their fearless spirit. Zaniya held Phoolan close and spoke with deep devotion. "Gaia's power is not just in her light but in her shadow. She is a quiet reminder that the path to greatness requires embracing all facets of oneself." She paused and gazed at the two guards on the boundary.

"Step into the unknown, Daughters," the Crone continued. "For the path forward is carved through courage. Embrace the journey, and let no storm sway your resolve. Awaken the mountain within. Let your resilience shape your path. Your power lies not in avoiding struggle, but in rising through it. Blessed be."

The group echoed "Blessed be." The children returned to their blankets and chatted excitedly about the night's danger and their bravery.

Asia was relieved but worried. She approached the guards for an update. "What happened out there?"

"We saw the three scouts and brought them back in," Xóchitl said casually. She placed a firm hand on Lian's back. "Thankfully, our lead guard acted bravely. The diversion was not needed."

"Who are those men?" Asia looked at Lian.

Lian shrugged and glanced at Xóchitl.

The Latina tossed her head. "Likely the same pack from the South. Maybe pedos, scavengers, or a gang."

"How did they find us?" Asia wondered.

The Chicana pointed to the right of the ravine. "We took the boys and led them away hours ago. But then, here they were." She appeared puzzled.

Lian glared at Asia. "You were wrong to send us out," she charged. "Those men showed up right on our doorstep, just like I predicted."

Asia shuddered, betraying her anxiety despite her effort to stay calm. She was grateful that the security team returned to protect the camp. She knew that arguing over strategy would antagonize Lian further. She remained silent and stared into the night sky.

45. Lies

It was 11:30 PM in the California wilderness. Beneath an endless expanse of inky blackness, the heavens stretched vast and unyielding. The darkness felt alive, pressing close, pierced by the cold glimmer of countless Stars. The otherworldly glow of the Milky Way arched overhead like a spectral river fleeing from the drylands below.

Three women gathered at the edge of their hillside camp to debrief the night's events. The leader scrutinized Lian and Xóchitl with concern.

"Any news on the boys?" Asia asked nervously, referring to the two teens who had gone missing.

The guards shook their heads in unison. The Latina said nothing and looked at the lead guard. There was uncomfortable reticence between them. Asia stared expectingly, and they took a long time to respond.

"We searched again for them but had no luck." Lian's voice lacked any trace of deception. "Then we heard the men's commotion and rushed back."

Asia's voice carried a note of relief. "Good thing for us that you did."

Lian was still upset, and her voice trembled with suppressed emotion. "But what if we didn't, Sister?" She stepped closer to the leader, clenching her fists. "Seven armed pedos could've easily overcome your defenses. So why did you make us leave?"

"Me?" Asia's irritation was clearly noticeable. "Your mission was everyone's plan."

The two women stared at each other. Each was unwilling to yield yet reluctant to go further in their contest of wills.

Xóchitl interrupted the leaders' disagreement with a thoughtful speculation. "Maybe the pedos found us by accident." The two women calmed down, grateful for the intervention.

Lian's body sagged in exhaustion. She was too tired to debate and offered an olive branch to her leader. "It's dark. Maybe we missed something. I'll look again in the morning." She yawned and took a long stretch.

Asia bowed to the pair. "Thank you for saving us."

"Da nada," Xóchitl beamed.

Lian's expression loosened. "Our strength lies in supporting our weakest members, Sister. Protecting the girls should always be our priority."

Asia sighed. "Yes. This hill isn't safe. We'll leave after your return tomorrow."

Asia and Lian understood the caravan needed them both to survive. They had to cooperate with each other, and their unity reassured everyone.

The group settled down, but sleep was elusive. The memory of the tracers and the threat they narrowly avoided weighed heavily on everyone's minds.

Asia lay awake, staring at the Cosmic ceiling, her thoughts racing. She knew their voyage was far from over, and the challenges ahead would grow more complex. But with women like Lian and Xóchitl by their side, she felt optimistic. The pair was reliable, resourceful, and strong-minded, qualities they needed to see them through the unforgiving post-apocalypse.

Lian was twitchy and alert. Her beams locked on the ravine while her hand rested firmly on her weapon. The dim light of the Stars cast a shadow across her face, making her features appear stern.

Xóchitl sat beside her with a casual air, differing noticeably from Lian's intensity. She met Lian's stare and playfully scolded her. "First, you disobeyed your command, then lied about it. Two sins in one night."

Lian glared. "You defied our orders, too."

"I did it for you, silly." The Latina grinned.

"Thanks, but you mean for us." Lian shook her head. "Anyway, we must sin. Otherwise, Jesús would have died in vain."

Xóchitl laughed. "Think they'll figure out we never left, Bhikkhuni?"

Lian shrugged. "Not unless you tell them, Sister." She appeared a bit troubled.

"¿Qué? Why would I betray my master?" The Chicana smiled at the thought that her friend was so similar. It was uncanny, like they were identical twins. "This reminds me of The Crooked Tree."

"Oh no, here it comes," Lian groaned.

"In a forest of straight, tall pines, one crooked tree stood out," Xóchitl started. "Its trunk curved oddly, and its branches were bent in strange directions. The other trees mocked it. 'You will never be made into a temple beam or a ship mast,' they said. 'You're twisted, ugly, and useless.'"

"I'm not crooked," Lian protested. "Just prudent."

"One day, the woodcutters came," the narrator continued. "They looked at the straight trees and began to chop. One by one, the tall pines fell, and the forest was cleared. The warped tree was the only one left standing."

"So, deviance does have value," Lian noted.

"Years passed," the Latina resumed. "Birds nested within the crooked tree's branches, travelers rested in its shade, and children played around its roots. The winding tree smiled quietly."

"Was its smile also not straight?" Lian wondered.

The storyteller grinned. "You should smile too, Bhikkhuni." She bowed and continued. "The curved tree took a moment to reflect. 'Since I didn't fit the mold, I was spared. Because I am different, I remained.'" Xóchitl folded her hands and grew quiet.

"What does it mean?" Lian queried.

"This tale is about conformity and deviance," Xóchitl replied. "The straight trees represent people or things that adapt perfectly to society's standards.

They're efficient, useful, and predictable. But because of their compliance, they're more easily exploited or discarded. In the story, they are chopped down."

"They're followers, not leaders," Lian observed.

The Latina nodded. "Being different, strange, and nonstandard is often considered a flaw. But from a Zen perspective, it can be a source of strength, authenticity, and unexpected worth. The tree's true value is revealed only because it was left alone to grow into what it naturally was. What society views as 'crooked' may actually be wise."

"Like our Crones." Lian yawned and covered her mouth quickly. "I get it."

"You need to rest, Bhikkhuni. I'll guard this shift."

Lian joined the evacuees huddled in the ditch and fell asleep immediately. The night slowly slipped away. The cooler air clung to their skins, seemingly reluctant to surrender to the inevitable onslaught of heat that would sweep across the Badlands at dawn.

Xóchitl stared into the shadows, arms wrapped around her weapon. She was sleepy and exhausted, but proud of her crooked partner and their service to the female collective.

46. Xóchitl

Xóchitl, 24, was a modest figure with a humble demeanor. She stood five feet five inches tall and weighed 120 pounds. Her toned muscles and sinewy strength were shaped by constant movement and necessity rather than deliberate exercise.

Short, thick, jet-black hair framed her gaunt face and warm brown skin like an impressionist portrait. A few faint scars crossed her cheeks, complementing her aura of resilience and courage.

Xóchitl was a *Nahuatl* word from Mexico. It meant flower or blossom, and it symbolized growth, beauty, and life. The name was often associated with delicacy, elegance, and femininity.

The female guard was anything but delicate. She wore baggy canvas pants that allowed freedom of movement and sturdy dog-eared boots that had served her well. Her shirts were typically sleeveless or short sleeves, made of tough, breathable fabric that dried quickly and protected her from the Sun.

She carried a sturdy, weathered burlap backpack that had seen better days but was durable and reliable like her. She wore a belt with various tools and holsters for her weapons, which were always within reach. Her pants had a metal buckle with an engraving of the Virgin of Guadalupe, the patron saint of Mexico and a central figure in its customs.

She loved the iconic Mother of Jesus and fondly remembered attending her vibrant feast day as a child. For Xóchitl, Our Lady of Guadalupe was a religious symbol of energy, endurance, and culture. The iconic character was deeply ingrained in her values and identity, and the buckle reminded her of her family.

Revered by millions, La Guadalupana is usually portrayed with Indigenous features and attire: darker skin, floral dress, dark ribbon, traditional Aztec mantle, or *tilma*, blue-green cloak, or *serape*, and a white tunic, or *huipil*.

The eagle and cactus, symbols of Aztec culture, are often added to the Virgin's feet. She stood atop a crescent Moon, representing Coyolxauhqui, Mother of Goddesses and Gods, fertility, life, and death. The Moon symbolized female monthly cycles and the nurturing qualities of the Goddess.

Comparable to Coyolxauhqui, the Latina Virgin Mary embodied femininity, Motherhood, and spirituality. She inspired Mexican women with pride, strength, and heritage.

Women worshiped the saint through prayer, offerings, and pilgrimage. They sought protection and guidance and shared personal stories about her intercession. Devotees celebrated La Guadalupana's feast day on December 12 with music, dance, and food.

Xóchitl grew up in a Chicano community in New Mexico that worshiped the saint. They prayed to her when, in her teens, a devastating drought forced her community to abandon their homes. Her family joined a caravan of displaced people, benefiting from the Latino community in the crisis.

However, the Western passage to a habitable zone was long and treacherous, and bandits attacked the convoy multiple times. Xóchitl, at sixteen, found herself fending for her younger brother, Juan, after their parents were killed by Anglo slave traders. A fierce yearning to protect her brother and those she loved became a defining aspect of her personality.

The siblings settled in the forests of Arizona, and she inspired other Chicanas with her unwavering strength and resilience. A few years later, Juan and his friends left the community to become gold miners. She tried to stop the fourteen-year-old from going, but he was stubborn, and she never saw him again.

The loss of her parents and brother left a profound void in Xóchitl's life, which she felt for a long time. She wanted to see the ocean and traveled to the Pacific Coast. Eventually, she found her way to the Santa Barbara shelter and met other female survivors like Asia and Kuan-Yin. The Crone taught her Zen, which helped her to let go and start living in the moment. Her curiosity was insatiable, and she quickly became wise like La Guadalupana. Her fluency in Nahuatl, Spanish, and English made her invaluable to the band.

Her favorite quote was from Frida Kahlo: "I used to think I was the strangest person in the world but then I thought there are so many people in the world, there must be someone just like me who feels bizarre and flawed in the same ways I do. I would imagine her, and imagine that she must be out there thinking of me, too. Well, I hope that if you are out there and read this and know that, yes, it's true I'm here, and I'm just as strange as you."

The Chicana steadfastly supported other women through their many trials at the shelter and in the

Badlands. Her community spirit earned her great respect and trust. She excelled in her security role, relying on her combat skills and resourcefulness to defend the female cooperative, a responsibility she took on with a deep sense of duty and commitment.

Her partnership with Lian was breathtaking and transformative. It gave her family, purpose, and integrity. And the intimate connection restored her formerly positive and irrepressible attitude. After a long period of isolation, the Latina warrior once again felt comfortable in her own skin. Moreover, her selfless actions on behalf of the female collective ensured her family's legacy endured in their native land.

47. Found

The early dawn in the Badlands was a moment of quiet magic where the world slowly stirred from night's embrace. The horizon glowed with a soft, golden hue, blending into lavender, pink, and pale blue. The air was dry and crisp, carrying the faint scent of Earth and distant blooms. The heat started rising, and the thermometer hovered at 96°F (35°C).

It had been 21 days since the female caravan left the Pacific Coast. The women and children slept like logs in the dugout, their bodies and minds utterly depleted from the late-night attack.

At 6 AM, Lian and Nzinga quietly slipped out of the camp. Despite the calm atmosphere, the two guards felt an underlying edginess, an awareness that the relative comfort was temporary. The oppressive heat would soon return to test their endurance.

Slipping down the hill, Lian crouched low to navigate the uneven ground. She moved stealthily, checking the shadowy expanse for signs of movement.

Nzinga stopped, her attention fixed ahead, brows crumpled in concentration. She gestured toward the left of the ravine. "There're bodies down there."

Lian peered into the dim light. "Yes." She extended her hand downward. "Let's get closer."

The two crawled down the slope, careful not to trigger a slide that might betray their presence. The gruesome scene became clearer. Several gray figures lay motionless near the bottom of the valley.

Nzinga discerned seven european men lying lifeless in the dirt. The soil around them was stained dark with blood, and the atmosphere was thick with the metallic scent of violence.

She saw a WCWP and Deus Vult tattoo on the body closest to her. She recognized the racist insignias on the gatekeeper at the settlement. "He's the man at that miners' outpost." She pointed to the body.

"That's Tate." The lead guard could barely conceal the anger bubbling beneath the surface. "We saw him four days ago."

"He tracked us here for our precious girls." Nzinga crossed her arms, trying to shield herself from the gravity of her own words. "Just like the other pedos."

Lian spat in disgust. "Well, that racist bastard found precious lead instead." She stepped over his remains with a flicker of dread, took a few steps down, and recognized something among the scattered bodies. Her face shifted from rage to horror.

Nzinga noticed Lian's sudden change. She leaned in and tracked her line of sight. "What is it?"

The Santa Clara native trembled as she stared at two bodies. "They're wearing the same clothes, blue shirts, jeans, and white sneakers." She shook her head and winced. "It's Stephen and Miller."

Nzinga's face was a mask of confusion. "What?" She got closer and stared at the teens. "The poor boys," she cried, brushing Stephen's arm. His blood-soaked clothes reminded her of her service in the militia. "These damn pedos captured and brutalized them," she swore and pulled her hands away.

Lian stared at the crumpled pair. "There're no signs of bondage or torture. Were they working with Tate?"

"No," Nzinga glared at Lian. "You're wrong."

"Believe your eyes." Lian stared at her companion. "Their hands and legs are free. And they have knives on their belts."

"You never liked the boys," Nzinga agonized.

The lead guard shrugged. "If they're hostages, why didn't they call for our help? I saw them talking to Tate at the settlement. Why? They were planning a strike. They volunteered to go on the diversion, then hastily abandoned me and Xóchitl to meet this nasty bunch."

Nzinga was shocked by Lian's accusations and shook her head doubtfully.

Lian was uncompromising. "They've deceived us all this time. At the first opportunity, they plotted against us with these racist dude bros."

"But they're our family," Nzinga pleaded.

Lian was irritated by Nzinga's denial. "If they felt part of us, wouldn't they have warned us of the raid?"

The NOLA native was speechless, struggling to grasp the gravity of the indictment.

"They have weapons," Lian screeched, clenching her fists. "They joined Tate and his buddies to hunt us like deer last night. And they almost succeeded."

Nzinga's voice strained in disbelief. "You're making things up. Running away and attacking us? Come on."

Lian clenched her teeth and struggled to control her frustration. "Well, how did Tate know exactly where we were? It was dark, and we were hidden."

Nzinga swallowed hard. The bitter truth of Lian's words settled in her throat like a stone. The boys' intentional or coerced presence placed the entire camp at risk. She stood up and brushed the dirt from her hands. "Alright, I've heard enough. Let's bury them."

"Who, these two?" Lian pointed to the teens. "Oh, hell no. I'm not wasting any energy on traitors."

"So, what do we do now?" Nzinga sounded beat.

Lian took a deliberate, calming breath. "We collect the ordnance and report to camp."

The pair hurriedly gathered the men's weapons and ammo and strapped them to their packs. With a last glimpse at the corpses, they began climbing the dune with their heavy load.

48. Betrayal

The Sun rose rapidly over the drylands, and the thermometer climbed alongside. Lian and Nzinga strained under the weight of their loaded packs, and hiking up the hill became a slow slog.

Lian stopped for a break. She searched the sky, seeking answers from the heated atmosphere, but none was forthcoming.

"Face it, Sister. Everything has changed." She tightened her straps and continued climbing. "Women can no longer raise males who are willing to protect them. Their sons, like those two boys, eventually turn into predators. Women are completely on our own."

Nzinga stared at her security associate. "Don't rush to judge. You probably wouldn't have rejected male privilege if you had it."

"They had a choice," Lian snapped. "We all do. They decided to become monsters. We didn't. We could've lived selfishly and collaborated with pedos. But we preferred to be allies to other women."

Nzinga glanced at the bottom of the hill. "The boys were attracted to some of our girls. And they may have wanted to be fair to their Sisters. But it is hazardous work trying to protect girls, with little benefit."

Lian shook her head vehemently. "Those two had no respect for females. In the shelter, they treated their own Mothers like maids. You saw that, didn't you?"

"No, I didn't," Nzinga countered.

"Well, I did." Lian took another step. "And they were mad at Onawa for not acting like their maid. Tate was attacking their adopted Mother, and they helped or did nothing. Why? Cuz she wasn't european?"

Nzinga continued to climb, speaking calmly to persuade her companion. "Look at it from the boys' side. They lived in fear because of the girls. Plus, they preferred living in the city but got stuck with us in this hostile wasteland. They did what was best for them."

Lian fumed. "They abandoned us without warning, then returned to kidnap and murder. What the hell?"

The conversation ended, and the pair hiked in reticence. When they entered the camp at 7 AM, the refugees were delighted to see the cache of arms.

"What did you see down there?" Asia hastily stored some ammo in her backpack. Lian hesitated to answer.

Nzinga glanced down at her load and selected a weapon for herself. "Seven corpses. Tate from the settlement and four other men." She paused and said softly, "Plus Stephen and Miller."

The women were shocked. Asia looked to Lian for confirmation, and she nodded grimly.

Onawa grimaced. The weight of the news struck her physically. "My boys," she cried.

"I'm sorry." Lian clasped her hands.

"Why? They were barely teens." Onawa's tears spilled over. "Were they tortured?"

"No, they had weapons." Lian looked away, dreading the next question.

"What? How did they die then?" Onawa raised a shaky hand to her head in agony.

"By my hands, last night." Lian exhaled loudly.

Onawa gasped, and her anguish melted into anger. "You killed them?"

"They were a bunch of men hunting us last night." Lian shrugged. "I didn't know two were ours."

Onawa stumbled backward at the thought of her sons colluding with the kidnappers. "Right, of course not. How could you have known?"

Lian placed her hand on the Mother's back. "Our discovery is upsetting for everyone. But they're gone, and we must continue to protect the girls."

"Yes." Onawa clutched her chest, shaking in grief.

Lian sighed and stepped back, allowing the Mother space to recover from the painful surprise.

Zaniya felt dread in the women's hearts and extended her wisdom. "Gaia knows that mountains cast shadows. And in those shadows lie mysteries, strength, and a path to deeper understanding. The mountains do not apologize for their height, and She does not apologize for her power. Her spirit is like stone shaped by wind and rain, steadfast, transformed through time and challenge, yet never diminished."

The Crone touched her heart. "Daughters, rise from the shadows and embrace your light. Stand with courage, for you are both the darkness that grounds and the light that leads. Let each trial be fuel for your ascent. Stand tall, climb high, and know that with each step, you draw closer to the summit of your potential. Blessed be." The women bowed gratefully.

Zenobia noticed Onawa's inconsolable grief and approached her. "We heh fuh you, dear." Her forehead raised in concern. "Nah carry dis stone by youself."

Onawa stared into the wilderness in anguish. "I'm so confused." She stared at the ground, ashamed. "Why did my sons betray us?"

Zenobia absorbed the gravity of Onawa's words. "It ain't yuh fault dey turned out bad." She hugged the Mother in sympathy. "Yuh had em fuh under a month."

Onawa nodded and cried.

The news of the boys' treachery was devastating, and the Firekeeper glanced at the children playing with dolls in the trench for relief. The lightness of their tea party differed dramatically from the turbulence she felt in her heart.

The doll play was like watching a timeless ritual that girls invented a million years ago. Zenobia realized that performing with female figures was much more than child play. Dolls were a crucial tool that helped early humans to advance by improving their communication, education, socialization, childcare, healthcare, community, cooking, empathy, fashion, and many other aspects of daily life. She was glad for the revelation. It alleviated the boys' treachery.

49. Nightmares

It was 8 AM in the Western Mohave boondocks. Long shadows stretched across the sand, revealing delicate ripples shaped by the wind. In the distance, the dunes shimmered like glass, their curves bathed in a golden glow. A few hardy shrubs and a lone cactus stood still, awaiting the entry of the climate caravan.

After breakfast, the nomads loaded their packs and headed out of the ravine. They trudged through the bare terrain cautiously, trailing Asia in the lead. The pedos' screams lingered in their memory, and they were glad to leave the besieged camp. It was a chilling reminder of the ever-present danger they faced from predatory men across the region.

Admiration flowed toward Lian and Xóchitl, who leaped into action unexpectedly and saved the group from calamity. The much-loved duo was modest, downplaying their courage with quiet humility.

The day was uneventful, and after a long time on their feet, the collective lounged in camp as Sunset approached. They were three weeks on the journey, and 85 miles away from the Safehouse. They had enough water and food to last them a few days.

The women exchanged painful glances. Their hearts carried the unspoken weight of the boys' loss and betrayal, and the chilling secrecy pervaded the trench. They concealed the discovery to shield the girls from the impact of their brothers' demise.

The memory of the previous night's violence left everyone ill at ease. However, they were reluctant to relive it through discussion. The youngsters slumbered together, trying to find solace, but some were tormented by nightmares.

Lisa, 11, tossed and turned in her sleeping bag. The arduous day, coupled with the recent attack, took a grim toll on her psyche. She puffed rapidly and shook from the intensity of an unpleasant dream. She was caught in a house fire when she was seven and suffered from a recurring nightmare.

She was back in the shelter, surrounded by flames and chaos. She screamed uncontrollably, but her cries for help were swallowed by the roar of devastation. The air in the lodging was thick with smoke, stinging her eyeballs and choking her throat. The walls groaned, and the sounds of splitting timber and shattering glass permeated the chaotic scene.

Lisa searched for a way out as her heart pounded franticly. Flames danced hungrily across the four walls, licking at the fragile wood, curling their fiery fingers over every exposed surface. The heat was unbearable, pressing in from every side, making her skin feel like it was being scorched from the inside.

The refuge she had clung to felt like a prison, its walls closing in with every crack and creak. The inferno was eating her from the inside, and its infinite fury was ravaging everything she had on the outside. The flames reached higher, devouring the ceiling and roof. It was like a living, breathing monster, and she was trapped inside.

Lisa's shrieks were lost amidst the deafening howl of destruction. She screamed harder, but the bonfire raged louder, mocking her desperation. It swallowed her cries like they were nothing more than murmurs in the wind. The shelter vibrated with the terrifying sounds of the firestorm: exploding canisters, the building collapsing, and the floors cracking from the furious blaze.

Her mind reeled in confusion, and her body instinctively pressed deeper into the sanctuary, seeking safety. Every flicker of light felt like a bad omen, and each flareup was like a giant tongue attempting to eat her. The ravenous flames seemed intent on making her their next meal.

Her companions and family were either too frozen in terror to budge or too far gone in fear to notice her predicament. There was no way to get help and no time to escape. The inferno was everywhere, smothering everyone, and it was inescapable. She called out to her

Mother, but her skreels were buried beneath the suffocating rumble.

Lisa went in and out of sleep. She tried focusing on the camp and her friends lying in the trench but could not shake off the nightmare. She sunk deeper into her sleeping bag and wept.

Greta, 13, lay in a corner of the dugout clutching her tattered doll. She got separated from her parents at eight and was haunted by thoughts of being lost. In her dream, she searched the scorching Badlands endlessly for the commune with the flaming Sun, her only companion. The dreadful vision felt real, and she was unbearably hot, like having a high fever.

The hallucination clung to her like the oppressive daytime heat. The same terrifying trance returned every time she drifted off into an uneasy sleep. She was far away from the caravan, lost. Her frantic cries for help were absorbed by the empty wilderness. The landscape stretched infinitely before her, an ocean of cracked soil, dry and crumbling beneath her bare feet. She was confused and terrified of dying alone.

The orange ball hung high in the sky like a scolding giant punishing her for some unknown mistake. The blinding orb scorched her skin and drew every ounce of moisture from her body. It smothered her, pressing down her shoulders like a heavy shroud. It blinded her vision, and she was disoriented. The terrain was utterly soundless except for her labored breathing and the indistinct shuffle of her footsteps.

She stumbled forward, searching desperately for the other girls. But there was no sign of their footprints, no sounds of laughter, no reassurances in the air. It was like she was alone on another Planet, alien and heartless.

Her hands trembled. She clutched her shawl tighter, but the fabric offered no protection from the blistering winds that whipped dust into her face. When her vision cleared, the scenery was a graveyard of desolation. Skeletons of dead trees clawed at the sky, their twisted forms casting ominous shadows that seemed to follow her. Distantly, the ruins of a city shimmered in a genial greeting, but she knew it was only a mirage.

The blinding beams seemed to speak - a low, droning hum soaking her ears with vocabulary she could not understand. It was an ancient, primal language, full of disdain and indifference, mocking her futile attempts to escape and survive. She shouted in defiance, but the light only burned brighter. The rays seared into her exposed skin until she felt like she would burst into flames.

When she woke up, it was always the same. Her body was drenched in sweat, and her heart pounded like a drum. She glanced around frantically, reassuring herself that the others were still there. She saw dozens of huddled forms resting in the dim Moonlight, yet the fear lingered, gnawing at the edges of her mind.

Was it a sign of the future, she wondered, or merely the cruel tricks of her tired mind? The Badlands had a way of seeping into her psyche, blurring the lines between experience and hallucination until she no longer knew what was real. She clutched her doll and sobbed.

50. Therapy

It was 9 PM in the Mohave wilderness. Stars and Galaxies littered the night sky like a vast forest of fireflies. The glow of gas, elements, and metals from billions of years ago was mesmerizing. Still, the Cosmic brilliance was lost on the girls in the trench trapped in nightmares.

Lisa and Greta whimpered, caught in the throes of their scary dreams. Their distress caught the attention of the Crones napping nearby. Though exhausted, Zenobia and Mary got up to comfort the weeping pair.

The Firekeeper approached Lisa and sat beside her. "Wat de matta, daughta?"

Lisa's sight fluttered open, and she gazed at the Elder with tear-streaked cheeks. "The fire is burning, and I can't escape."

"Oh, dat's scary." Zenobia smiled. "But dem flames merely bad dreams, my child. Ain't nothin' fuh bun heh. See, is only sand."

The Crone rubbed Lisa's back and spoke soothingly. "Me gun sleep wid yuh now. Dem dreams only shadows, daughta. Dey can't mess wid da light we gats heh, aight?"

"I'm sorry." Lisa's terror started to ease.

"No need, daughta." Zenobia hugged her charge. "Now, close dem eyeballs an tek ah deep breath. Picha ah place whey yuh feel safe an happy. Like splashin' in ah puddle wid yuh friends, or ah cool breeze blowin' while yuh eat."

Zenobia guided her through several positive visualization exercises. Her words and massage helped steady Lisa's racing mind until her breathing normalized. The Firekeeper described her own dream of Palmyra, and soon, Lisa was fast asleep.

Meanwhile, Mary sat beside Greta. "Why can't you sleep, my daughter?" She stroked the child's hair tenderly.

"I don't know," Greta whimpered. "Bad dreams.'

"I see," the Crone muttered.

Greta wept. "I'm scared of getting lost."

"Being misplaced is a common dream." The Elder nodded. "I get it too, sometimes."

"But it doesn't stop." The teen sobbed. "It comes every time I try to sleep."

"Well, nightmares are not all bad." The Crone paused in contemplation. She understood the cause of the child's fear. "They can be useful."

"How?" Greta was confused.

Mary smiled. "Because they show us what we're terrified of, so we can work on getting over them."

"I'm so scared of being alone," Greta sobbed.

"If we don't understand our fears, they will continue to control us." Mary continued caressing the teen's hair. "You were once an orphan. So, naturally, you're afraid of being abandoned."

The child's sobbing subsided, and she listened attentively to her Elder.

"But you're no longer by yourself, my child." Mary pointed to the women in the trench. "You've got lots of Mothers now. Sisters, Aunts, and Grandmas, see?"

"But what if I fight with the other girls?" Greta remained anxious. "Will they kick me out?"

The Crone smiled. "We're a big family. And you're a valuable daughter in our clan. We'll never leave you behind. I promise."

"I'm scared of getting lost." Greta looked worried.

"If you do get lost, we'll search for you day and night until we find you, okay?" Mary held her hand. The orphan nodded and began to loosen.

Mary smiled and continued, "I'll teach you how to travel by the Stars, so you'll never be lost."

The teen calmed down as her Elder explained how to find Sirus and Polaris. She was curious about the Cosmos and wanted to learn more about navigation. But the Crone decided it was too late.

"Now close your eyes," Mary directed. "Think about a happy place. In this space, you're surrounded by friends. You're playing and having a good time."

The teacher guided Greta to envision the lively scene, a lush, green field where she was encircled by playmates. The air was filled with laughter and the smell of fresh bread. She imagined the fun, and her breathing steadied. Her fear slowly dissipated, and she fell soundly asleep.

In their camp the following evening, the Crones discussed the girls' poor mental health and urged the Mothers to address the problem.

"Encourage the children to share their feelings," Hehewuti counseled. "Let them know it's okay to be afraid and that they're not alone. With patience and understanding, we can help them feel safer and more in control of their thoughts."

Kuan-Yin spread her fingers, wrapping an invisible blanket over the female congregation. "Create safe spaces for them to express their emotions. Develop a consistent bedtime routine, like storytelling, reading a book, singing a lullaby, or offering a back rub."

Mary advised, "Encourage your child to imagine a protective shield around them while they sleep. This could be like a force field, a guardian animal, or any image that makes them feel strong and safe. Teach your child how they can change the nightmare while it's happening. Guide them to imagine a happy ending, like turning the monster into a harmless animal."

Comforted by the Crones' presence and words, the children freely expressed their doubts and fears. Their nightmares became less frequent, and the camp's atmosphere shifted from worry and uncertainty to communal support and healing. The Crones fortified the collective's emotional fortitude, ensuring they remained comforted despite ongoing challenges.

That night, Zaniya made an offering for restful sleep. "Just as valleys need shadows to define the peaks, Gaia honors the darkness within as a source of her grounding and resilience. She understands that the night is not an absence, but a presence holding secrets and strength that only those unafraid of the dark may find. Her beauty lies in the contrast, in the balance between her light and her shadow, each giving depth and dimension to the other."

"Daughters," she continued, "do not let the shadows of doubt hold you back. Embrace your purpose, for within you lie the power to shape your own destiny. Stand firm in who you are. Like the Goddess, draw strength from within and know that your journey is one of both courage and purpose. Blessed be."

51. Owl

It was 8:30 PM in Central California, on day 23 of the climate evacuees' Northern trek. They were 65 miles away from their destination in Cantua Creek. The night sky stretched vast and infinite, an intense, velvety black punctuated by the cold gleam of Stars.

Clusters of Suns and Galaxies shimmered like scattered diamonds. Some were faint and distant, others burned bright, their light traveling across the ages to be seen at that moment.

A thin crescent Moon hung low, casting a dim silver glow over the darkened drylands below. The rolling surface was etched with pale, shadowed dunes and shallow, broad valleys. The air was stagnant, and the sky felt almost too quiet like it was holding its breath.

The camp was quiet except for the sporadic crackle of the fire and the muted breathing of the sleeping women and children. Lian and Xóchitl were on watch on the perimeter.

"¿Está todo bien?" The Latina queried. "Want to hear something nice, Bhikkhuni?"

"Your tales leaves me confused," Lian retorted.

"Not this one, promise." Xóchitl gave her a thumbs up. "It's called The Garden of Love. A young nun approached the Zen Monk and asked, 'Teacher, how can I make someone love me?' The Bhikkhuni smiled and led the disciple to a small garden behind the temple. 'See this flower?' she said, pointing to a delicate blossom. 'If you wish for it to bloom faster, what would you do?'

"That's called grooming." Lian sneered. "It's what men do, the lousy bastards."

The Chicana laughed. 'Well,' the nun answered, 'I would water it and make sure it gets sunlight.' The female Monk nodded. 'And what would happen if you pulled at its petals, trying to make them open sooner?' The disciple frowned, 'That would only harm it.'"

"See, I knew it." Lian smirked. "This story is about female child abuse."

Xóchitl cracked up. "The Bhikkhuni nodded. 'Love is like this flower,' she said. 'You cannot force it to bloom, nor can you demand love from another. All you can do is nourish the other with kindness, patience, and presence. If the flower or love is meant to bloom, it will. If not, then appreciate the other's beauty as it is, without trying to change it.' The nun bowed. She understood that love is not about possession, but about nurturing and letting things unfold naturally."

"What are you getting at?" Lian faked outrage. "Are we not thriving?"

Xóchitl ogled her friend "My name means flower, Bhikkhuni. I'm always blooming." She smiled and concluded, "Many people try to make others love them by demanding affection or trying to change them, but true love flourishes only when given space, care, and patience. Love is not about possession or control, but about appreciation and nurturing. We must love with an open heart, without expectations or pressure, allowing relationships to grow in their own time."

"So true," Lian admitted. The pair reflected on their relationships and monitored the surroundings.

Asia and Zenobia sat by the trench, partially illuminated by the fire's embers. The flawless panorama around them was soothing. Dark silhouettes of cactus trees stood like sentinels safeguarding the camp.

Asia shuffled her feet, the coarse sand sliding under her boots. The cool night air bit her skin, but she ignored it. Her beams flickered over the sleeping forms, ensuring they rested comfortably. Zenobia was lost in thought, her attention fixed on the inky blackness beyond the perimeter.

A sudden movement in the nearby trees caught Asia's attention. She stiffened, and her hand instinctively moved to the hilt of her weapon. The Firekeeper glanced at her, noticing the suspense in her demeanor.

"Did you see that?" Asia was apprehensive.

Zenobia inspected the trees. "Yea, dey is somethin' out dey."

Asia's breathing halted when she caught sight of a massive shadow gliding soundlessly toward them. "Woah, over there." She pointed to a silhouette.

The Crone followed Asia's finger. She spotted movement between the cacti and froze. "Is ah night creature. Ah great horn owl."

A vast shadow swooped in, landing on a cactus near the pair. It had large, glowing orbs, like embers piercing through the dark. Asia loosened her grip on her weapon and leaned forward. "I've never seen a night bird this big before."

The great horned owl was a majestic and imposing creature. Its presence was awe-inspiring in the dim light. Its massive wings, spanning nearly five feet, were covered in dense feathers ranging from mottled brown to deep gray, allowing it to blend seamlessly into the night. The bird's body was robust and muscular, with a thick, rounded chest and a powerful, hooked beak that gleamed in the Moonlight.

"It's as wide as a child is tall," Asia marveled.

Perched silently on the branch, the owl's large, rounded head was crowned with prominent tufts of feathers that resembled horns, giving it an almost mythical appearance. Its piercing oculars, set deep within its face, were a striking yellow-orange. They were steady and unblinking, holding a depth of ancient wisdom and intensity that pierced straight into Asia's heart.

"So beautiful and silent," Asia whispered. The Crone nodded.

The owl's thick, razor-sharp talons gripped the branch with quiet strength. Each movement was deliberate and precise. It exuded an air of calm confidence and mastery of its domain. Its head turned nearly 180 degrees with an uncanny, fluid motion to silently survey the surroundings with a tranquil, watchful presence.

"What's it hunting?" Asia wondered softly.

"Rats an snakes." Zenobia guessed.

The great horned owl had an aura of unyielding power and mystery. It was a creature of the night that carried the weight of untold secrets and a connection to Gaia that felt both protective and ominous.

Asia's attention was locked on the avian visitor. The creature's presence soothed her. "Why is it here, so close to us?"

Zenobia bowed respectfully to the night caller. "Some folks say owls be go-betweens. Ah guide to da othda worlds. Dey says when ah owl come fuh visit yuh, it brin' a message from de spirits." Her words were tinged with reverence.

"Maybe she heh to say we ain't all by we selves." The Elder noiselessly brushed the Earth in a gesture of devotion. "Dat even wid dis vast emptiness about, dey is somethin' out heh keepin' an eye pun we."

The female owl blinked slowly. Its orbs shifted between the two women, acknowledging their presence in her domain.

Asia felt a shiver run down her spine, but it was not from the cold. "Maybe it's telling us to trust our path."

The Crone concurred. "An fuh we to keep up da faith. Da road ahead ain't gonna be easy."

The bird released a low, resonant hoot that echoed through the air. Then, it spread its mighty wings and silently ascended into the sky, slashing through the darkness. Asia and Zenobia exchanged smiles. Their connection deepened by the shared experience, a bond forged in the night's quiet and the exquisite creature's presence. They were united in a moment of shared wonder and reverence.

"We're not alone." Asia beamed, watching the shadow until it disappeared.

Zenobia stood upright, brushing the dirt off her hands. "Me feel like we gats protection."

After the owl disappeared, the night felt different, less hostile, and more alive. A slight wind rustled through the cacti, carrying the faint scent of cucumber and blossoms. The Stars twinkled overhead, acknowledging the sacred encounter.

Asia and Zenobia stood side by side, their breaths visible in the cold air, staring into the open vista. The owl's blissful presence had dramatically changed their perception of the night, and they were entirely at ease. Like the serene bird, they felt like natives of the Badlands.

52. Sick

It appeared suddenly on the 24th day of the climate nomads' flight to safety. Cha'Kwaina, 14, woke up feeling unusually weak and feverish. She brushed it off, attributing her feelings to fatigue, but by noon, her condition worsened.

Onawa, her Mother, and Emily, the nurse, noticed that the teen's symptoms included a persistent cough, fever, chest pain, tiredness, shortness of breath, sweats, muscle aches, and a rash on her upper body that seemed to be spreading.

The situation became alarming when Daria, 17, and Sasha, 15, showed similar signs. By mid-afternoon, the line was filled with coughing, moaning, and worried whispers.

Marielle, 7, leaned against a rock, breathing heavily. Her head sagged, and her eyelids were droopy and painful. Emily tried to give her some medicine. "One more sip. This will help with the fever."

"It's too bitter," Marielle complained. "I don't feel good. I just wanna die." Her words came in gasps.

"Don't talk like that." Emily's expression betrayed her concern. "You're going to get through this. But you have to take this medicine."

She suspected the sickness was Valley Fever. The lung infection was caused by breathing in spores from the fungus Coccidioides, which lived in the desert soil. Most people got better on their own, but some needed antifungal medication.

The medic knew that it could take months to fully recover from the disease, and fatigue and joint aches could last even longer. Supplies for treating fungal infections were limited, and their sparse medical supplies were inadequate for handling a widespread outbreak.

Seven ill members were difficult for Emily to deal with. After night fell, the temperature dropped, and the coolness felt like an ice box for those with high fevers.

Asia's heart ached. She sat by the fire beside Ma'at, 12, clutching her ragged doll. "I feel so sick," the child gasped, her eyes filled with tears. The fire's warmth seemed to be the only thing fighting back against the cold hopelessness that gripped the camp. It was a long, restless night for everyone.

The following morning, Asia, Emily, and the Crones decided on an emergency plan. Lian and Phoolan found a rocky overhang, and underneath, the women created isolation tents in an improvised hospital. They took turns aiding the sick.

Zenobia worked the first shift. "We'll use all we gats to mek yuh comfy," she promised. "Rest up, tek it easy, an drink often."

Emily added, "Let us know if you need water, to vomit, the restroom, whatever."

Drawing from their knowledge of traditional remedies, the Crones created herbal treatments for the patients. They had several dried herbs with antifungal properties, including thyme, cinnamon, oregano, clove, mint, citronella, geranium, lemongrass, eucalyptus, and peppermint. They used these to create soothing oils, balms, and teas.

Frida made soup for the ailing members. Nzinga ensured healthy ones had enough water and food to strengthen their immune systems. Asia assisted in preparing meals and relieving the caregivers, so they were not overwhelmed.

The eleven patients were cheered by the tents and improved healthcare. Still, the Valley fever outbreak significantly damaged the collective's spirits. The fear of becoming ill and witnessing the suffering of their friends and family created a pervasive sense of dread.

The Crones, however, used their wisdom to bolster the group's mental health. Kuan-Yin told a tale about recuperation that inspired everyone. The Crone's name was derived from a revered bodhisattva in Buddhism. A bodhisattva was a person who could reach nirvana but delayed it out of compassion to save suffering beings. The name meant 'One who hears the

World's cries,' and Guanyin embodied peace, kindness, mercy, and love.

"In a small, vibrant town nestled at the edge of rolling green hills," Kuan-Yin began, "there lived a young woman named Savitribai. She was known for her boundless energy and love for the outdoors, often seen tending to her lush garden of roses, sunflowers, and lavender. Savitribai's garden was her pride, and it seemed to bloom in rhythm with her radiant spirit."

The vision of a lush garden brightened the Mothers' and ailing children's moods, and the narrator paused to let the image work its magic.

"One autumn, Savitribai fell gravely ill," the Crone resumed. "A persistent fever drained her strength, leaving her bedridden for weeks. The once-lively gardener grew pale, and sheer exhaustion silenced her laughter. Her garden, too, began to wither like it was mourning her absence."

"Oh no," Cha'Kwaina gasped and coughed.

"Friends and neighbors visited often," Kuan-Yin carried on. "They brought soup, flowers, and warm words of encouragement. Despite their kindness, Savitribai felt trapped in her frailty, longing for the day she could walk among her flowers again."

"She's like us," Lisa commented weakly.

The Crone beamed and resumed her narrative. "One day, an Elderly neighbor named Mrs. Pule knocked on Savitribai's door, carrying a small potted plant. It was an off-color sapling of a lemon tree. 'This is the tree of small steps,' Mrs. Pule indicated. 'Every day you care for it, even a little, it will remind you that recovery is about patience and persistence.'"

"I wish I had one," Marielle pleaded.

"I'll get you a cactus plant tomorrow," Aisha promised.

Kuan-Yin smiled and took up her yarn again. "Savitribai placed the tree by her window. At first, she could only water it while lying in bed. Days turned into weeks, and she began to sit, stand, and shuffle around the house. Each small victory felt epic, and the lemon tree thrived under her care."

"Wow," Sasha remarked. "They healed together."

"Yes," the Elder replied. "By spring, Savitribai's strength had returned. She stepped back into her garden, now overgrown but brimming with potential. Her neighbors came together to help her prune, plant, and revive the space. Inspired by her journey, Savitribai added new plants, ones she'd never grown before, like tomatoes and basil, symbolizing her growth and spirit."

"Oh yeah," Lisa cried. She was pallid and pale but managed to smile.

"The lemon tree found its place in the garden's center," Kuan-Yin continued. "It was a living reminder of the power of persistence. By summer, Savitribai's garden was more vibrant than ever, and so was she. She hosted a garden party to celebrate the revival of her flowers and the strength she had found within herself."

"Can we have a party after we recover?" Cha'Kwaina asked meekly.

"We will," the Crone promised. "From that day forward, Savitribai's story became a symbol of faith in the town, reminding everyone that small steps can lead to extraordinary renewal even in the hardest times."

The Mothers and their sick children were relieved after hearing the heartwarming tale. The Crones persisted in providing positive affirmations to the unwell and healthy.

On the second day in the infirmary, Zaniya offered sage advice to the sick and recovering females. "Gaias, every storm has an end. You're not alone in this struggle. Together with the Goddess, we can weather this storm. The Goddess does not retreat in the face of hardship. She stands firm, knowing that like a mountain, her strength lies in perseverance."

After three days in the clinic, the women's efforts started to pay off. The herbal remedies, combined with rest and proper care, began to slow the spread and severity of the illness. Most ailing survivors recovered, and their improvement boosted the camp's confidence.

A day later, Emily reported to Asia and the Crones, "We're managing to help those who are suffering and no one else has symptoms."

The Valley Fever fungal outbreak subsided, though the emaciated figures were left physically and emotionally drained. However, the experience strengthened their bond and reaffirmed their commitment to thinking positively and supporting one another.

53. Traveler

On the 29th day of the climate migrants' voyage, Sunrise began with a golden glow. Asia was pleased that the sick members were on the mend and could continue their journey through the Badlands. The group covered 180 miles since they left Santa Barbara and were 45 miles Southwest of the Safehouse near Fresno.

Bright rays edged over the land, painting the sky pink and orange and dissolving the remnants of nighttime. The early light filtered through cacti branches, casting delicate shadows on the sand. In haste, daylight climbed higher, bringing an overbearing, harsh clarity to the Badlands.

The women and children hastily packed up camp and exited the temporary hospital. They started walking at 8 AM in the forbidding expanse of emptiness. Nothing but dry scrub and seared sand stretched to the vanishing point, but they pressed on.

Lian took her usual place at the head of the line. She examined the vista for any sign of danger and waved them onward. The four-day recovery period was spent in relative safety. Yet, they all knew the risks of lingering in one place too long.

"Everyone okay?" Lian called back cheerily.

The Mothers murmured their assent, ensuring the minor children were securely strapped to their backs or clinging to their hands. The Sun was climbing, and they could not afford to waste time.

Asia was tired from night watch but in high spirits. "Another seven days to safety," she beamed, trying to will the promise into reality. She skimmed the eager faces and offered a bright smile.

"We can try to do ten miles today," she encouraged. She glanced at a few of the younger members and grinned. "You're doing great."

Lian's gaze was fixed on Elon, the only boy in the commune. He was running ahead of her and the line. His energy was impressive, and her sight never left his tiny, wiry frame. She noticed that he was pretending to stalk the sand like a predator. His vision darted left to right, expecting prey to leap from behind every bush. He was acting like the dominant male of the pride.

'That boy's daring stands out from the girls' cautiousness,' Lian thought. It was an indication of the girls' survival instincts and the complexities of trust in their misogynist environment. Still, he probably sensed that he was not vulnerable to being kidnapped.

The line trekked North, and the rising heat made each step a struggle. The terrain offered an occasionally scraggly bush or cluster of rocks for shelter. The air was thick with dust, stirred up by the steady march of feet. The punch of boots into pliant sand was hypnotically numbing, and the wanderers were lost in their thoughts.

Elon ran further ahead and suddenly stopped. Lian was close behind and was quick to react. "What is it?" The boy pointed ahead. His sharp sight was fixed on something, a slight movement.

Lian tightened her focus and saw what caught his attention. Far off in the distance, there was a lone figure. The outline was too far to make out any details, but it progressed slowly toward them. Seeing another human in the Badlands instantly set her on edge.

Lian turned and yelled, "Company." She straightened her back and vigilantly tightened her fingers on the strap of her weapon. The air was tense, and her caution contrasted sharply with the figure's gradual approach.

Asia scoured the view and approached Lian. She told Elon to rejoin the group, and he returned to his Mother. The two women approached apprehensively, prepared to face whatever the lone figure might bring.

Lian raised her chin and focused on the lone figure. "Could be a lone survivor, like Hypatia." There was a hint of caution beneath her calm exterior. "Or it could be a decoy. Either way, we need to be ready."

The women in the line positioned themselves around the children. Asia signaled for them to keep moving but at a slower pace, keeping her attention on the approaching frame.

They drew closer, and it became clear that it was a lone traveler, a man dressed in ragged clothing. He was hunched over with a large pack on his back and stepped very slowly like he was about to expire.

The stranger noticed the Lian and Asai and raised his arm half-heartedly. "I need water." His voice was gravelly and strained. He had a Southern accent and spoke with a drawl. Lian guessed he was 45 years old, five feet ten inches tall, and 145 pounds.

Lian's brows lined in distrust. "Sorry, but we don't have enough for ourselves."

"For the love of god and country." The man petitioned Asia with clasped hands.

"Where're you headed?" Asia looked puzzled.

"You're the boss, right?" The stranger stared at her. Asia nodded. "Just a miner searching for precious stones." He shifted the weight of his loaded backpack in a battle to stay balanced and avoid tipping over.

Lian pointed to the traveler with a steely scowl. "You best be moving on."

The man was taken aback by Lian's forceful presence but continued disregarding her and focused on Asia. "Name's Jeffery. I can trade some tools and mining advice."

The women exchanged guarded looks. He did not appear successful, and they doubted he had anything useful to share. The Crones sometimes went prospecting and found a few precious stones. They did not need his advice, and Lian signaled Asia to buzz the man off.

Asia rested her hands on her hips and took a deep breath. She figured that having a light-colored man in the rear might deter pedos. "You can follow at 100 feet. But don't come any closer or else." Her pupils locked onto the man, conveying her unspoken threat.

The miner was grateful for the minor mercy. "Thank you," he grinned.

The climate caravan threaded along, with the stranger a hundred feet behind. The sudden encounter with a man disturbed the women. His mere presence was a sign of their vulnerability. Trust was a luxury they could not afford, and even simple decisions carried the weight of survival.

Lian was confused. 'Why did Asia place the caravan at risk?' she wondered. The man was useless and more of a burden and threat. She wanted to say something but could not question Asia's authority in front of the stranger. She sulked and remained quiet, feeling the weight of Asia's risky decision.

The party trudged through the arid geography, looking for shade to rest. Elon was fixated on the man in the rear, trying to make sense of his discovery.

Marge noticed his attention and reached over to squeeze his hand. "Look ahead, son. You'll trip and get sand all over."

Elon bobbed his head, but his attention shifted back to the stranger. "Can he be my friend?"

Marge peeked at Jeffery. He seemed harmless, but that could have been an act. "Maybe, son. We have to wait and see."

The drifters continued their expedition, and the Sun inched ever higher. With each step, they drew closer to the promise of shelter, if only for a while.

54. Jeffery

Under the relentless midday glare, the female travelers pressed on their passage North, fleeing a racist and sexist frontline in search of safety and a better life. The thermometer read 129°F (54°C) with 10 percent humidity. Aisa placed her umbrella higher in the air and peeped at the unforgiving Star. Not a cloud in sight. She rubbed the back of her neck and called for a break.

The miner stopped at a wary distance. The women, particularly Lian, eyed him like a hawk. The girls, on the other hand, were a mix of caution and curiosity. Lian and Asia approached him.

"Shouldn't you be out prospecting?" Lian scowled at him and shook her head in disgust. "Why are you following us?"

Jeffery shrugged and addressed Asia. "I've had no luck recently." A bitter smile tugged at the corners of his mouth.

Lian rested her hands on her hips defiantly. "We're not open to visitors. You need to get back to digging."

"Have any stones to trade?" Asia hoped he could be beneficial in some way.

"Nope. Traded the last one weeks ago." He looked at Asia. "Where y'all headed?"

Asia inspected the man's face, unsure how much to reveal about their plans. "To a Safehouse."

"Where?" The stranger was incredulous.

"A hundred miles." Asia doubled the distance.

"Can I come?" Jeffery pleaded with clasped hands.

Asia considered his request. She could use him to ward off attacks until they got near the Safehouse, then dismiss him. After a long pause, she responded affirmatively, "You can walk behind us. But don't cause any trouble, understand?" The intensity of her look left no room for doubt.

Jeffery met her stare. "You've got nothing to worry about from me."

Lian stared at Asia and shook her head in indignation. After Stephen and Miller's betrayal, she was not thrilled to have a male stranger in their midst. She decided to keep strict surveillance over him and let the scouts take the lead.

With the rest over, the group prepared to make headway again. Elon ambled beside Jeffery, who smiled at him. The boy giggled. Having another man around, even one who was broken, comforted him.

That evening, Lian insisted he slept further away and escorted him to a spot 300 feet from the camp. Jeffery unloaded his pack and turned to face her. "May god have mercy on your dark soul."

"Goddess, you mean," Lian corrected firmly.

Jeffery became angry. "The lord died for your sins, witch. Be respectful."

Lian shrugged. "But your guy didn't stay dead for long, did he? He got up three days later. So, he gave up what, a weekend? Big deal." The stranger was stunned by her response but remained quiet.

Lian left the befuddled man and joined Xóchitl twenty feet away. She stared at the miner, letting him know she was watching him.

"Ola mi amor," Xóchitl greeted her friend. She was cleaning her backpack and felt like sharing.

"A student asked her Bhikkhuni, 'Teacher, what miracles have you performed?'" Xóchitl gazed at her companion.

"Living during dark times?" Lian guessed.

Xóchitl smiled. "The female Monk replied, 'When I am hungry, I eat. When I am thirsty, I drink. When I am tired, I sleep.' The nun was puzzled. 'But isn't that what everyone does?'"

Xóchitl paused for effect, then continued. "The Bhikkhuni beamed and said, 'No. When people eat, they do not focus on eating. When they drink, they do not simply drink. When they sleep, they are restless.'"

Lian had a puzzled look.

"People lack mindfulness," Xóchitl offered.

"I don't like that one." Lian pouted. "Tell me another Zen tale."

"Por supuesto Bhikkhuni. How about Painted Tiger?" The Latina was eager to please. "A young nun wanted to impress her fellow students. She often spoke of her deep understanding of Zen. She recited sutras flawlessly, quoted ancient masters, and carried herself with an air of wisdom. But despite her words, she had never truly experienced enlightenment."

"Okay." Lian glanced at the miner and refocused on her companion.

"One day, the Bhikkhuni called her to the meditation hall," Xóchitl resumed. "The teacher pointed to a wall where a fierce tiger had been painted in striking detail. Its eyes glowed with intensity, and its fangs were bared as if ready to strike. 'Tell me,' the master asked, 'if this tiger was real, would you be afraid?'

"Of course," Lian interjected. "Tigers are nothing to mess with. Like that fellow over there."

The Latina nodded. "The young monk laughed. 'Of course not, Bhikkhuni. It is only a painting.' The master smiled. 'And so is your Zen. It's beautiful and impressive but without life.' The apprentice fell silent. In that moment, she saw through her own false pretense. From that day forward, she stopped speaking of Zen and began truly practicing it."

"Wow, actions are louder than words." Lian beamed. "Thank you, Bhikkhuni."

In the trench, everyone was exhausted. Zaniya stared into her open palms and made a blessing. "The Goddess is both dawn and twilight, light and shadow. She is an embodiment of balance. Her strength is drawn from honoring all parts of Herself. Like the night sky filled with hidden stars, Her darkness holds countless treasures. Each one is a testament to Her beauty and Her courage."

The Crone raised her open palms to the group. "Daughters, be both soft and strong, open and unbreakable. Walk with courage, knowing that your existence is one of transformation and triumph. Honor your manifestation by embracing every part of it. Stand tall like the mountains, resilient and graceful, knowing your purpose is worth every step. Blessed be."

The women and girls graciously bowed to their Elder. They curled into their sleeping bags and slept soundly.

55. Take Off

The early morning light crept over the sand dunes, casting long shadows that stretched across the endless terrain. The women and children rested well during the night, everyone except the guards.

Asia stirred in her blanket and welcomed the dawn. She noticed Lian and Xóchitl were already up and speaking in low tones. She was pleased to see them. The pair was inseparable and good role models of loyalty for the collective.

Asia approached Nzinga, the late-night guard. "Any sign of trouble last night?"

Nzinga shook her head. "No, it was quiet."

Asia gestured to Jeffery, wrapped in his blanket. "What about him?"

Nzinga shrugged. "He slept all night."

Asia noticed the Sun was rapidly burning off the morning mist. "We start off right after breakfast."

The refreshed community congregated near the campfire for a modest meal. Jeffery stood apart near his bed as Lian demanded. His pupils darted nervously around the camp. The lead guard noticed something was off in his demeanor that morning.

Marge, who got to know Jeffery a bit, was helping to serve the children their meal when she noticed the man's hunger and walked over to him. "Why don't you join us?" Marge pointed to the campfire.

Jeffery glanced at her. "Don't eat with niggers." He spat in the direction of the group.

"What?" Marge was taken aback by the man's racism. He reminded her of Tucker, her husband. She noticed that 'white' men in the state were becoming increasingly racist. "They wouldn't bite," she joked.

"How can you stand being with those ugly apes?" Jeffery stared at her in disgust.

Marge frowned but did not press further. She returned to finish breakfast with the children.

The climate evacuees packed up and obstinately continued trekking North. Jeffery followed in the rear. Lian paid close attention to him but did not suspect anything was amiss.

The caravan inched forward under the stern view of the hydrogen Star. Their surroundings remained unforgiving, with vast expanses of dried dirt and sporadic skeletal remains of cacti and shrubs. The heat was intolerable, making every step feel like a trial.

A few hours into their march, Lian noticed Jeffery trailing and mumbling. He seemed distracted by something. 'Something's eating him,' she thought.

Asia called out to the group, "We'll break here. Look for supplies. We need twigs for tonight's fire." The wayfarers huddled for snacks. Afterward, some foraged for edible plants. Lisa and Elon searched for sticks in the rear, away from the others.

Jeffery ambled one hundred feet away from the group. He stooped behind a shrub, reached into his bag, and pulled out a small rope. He crumbled it in his palm and strolled over to Elon. Lisa was nearby.

Suddenly, Jeffery lunged toward Lisa. His face was contorted insanely with desire. He grabbed Lisa and quickly tied the rope around her hands. Like a demon possessed, he started dragging the child away.

Elon saw his sister struggling and froze. Her petite frame turned and twisted, trying to free herself from the large predator. Her breath hitched in her throat, and she shrieked silently in terror. Then, she let out a terrified scream.

"Help. Mommy, help." Lisa's high-pitched screech chiseled through the Badlands like a sonic boom. Her legs kicked frantically, trying to find footing. The man kept dragging her away, but she was much more challenging to manage than he planned.

Marge's heart skipped a beat when she heard her daughter's cries. She spun around, observing the scene with horror. "Stop. Leave my child alone." Her hands clenched into fists, and she charged furiously at the kidnapper with the force of a Mother's protective instinct.

The guards sprang into action. Lian bolted toward the pedo, her heart thudding against her ribs. "Hey, you. Stop, dumbass." Xóchitl raced ahead.

Jeffery kept dragging Lisa away. His breathing was heavy, and a grotesque craving was etched across his face.

Xóchitl lunged forward, focusing on the kidnapper like a laser. She forcefully tackled the pedo and grabbed Lisa away, sending him stumbling backward. The kidnapper's grip on the child slipped, and she darted safely away into her Mother's arms.

Jeffery thrashed about, pinned beneath Xóchitl and Lian. He strained against them, but their pressure held firm. He turned red, and a storm of anger and frustration swirled in his face.

Lian's body drained of color, and her expression hardened into astonishing fury. She clenched the kidnapper's shirt, her body trembling with rage. "You devious devil. You're a freaking pedo." She punched his head hard with her right fist and spat into his face.

She kicked the pedo repeatedly with her steel-tipped boots until Asia and Nzinga dragged her off his bloodied body. "Arrggghhh," she screeched in rage.

Asia shook her head in disbelief. "How could you? We trusted you. Marge was especially nice to you. And you repay her by trying to steal her daughter?"

Jeffery trembled, trying desperately to explain his actions. "I'm a dead man. They're after me." His gaze dropped, unable to meet the woman's piercing glare. "I've got one chance to repay the Bandidos de Bakersfield gang, to get back what I lost."

Lian stood over him with clenched fists. "You monster," she bellowed. "We took you in even though some of us had reservations. You're no miner. You're a predator." She kicked the man's groin and stepped on his chest. Her nostrils flared with barely restrained anger.

Jeffery's body withered, and he shrank back in pain. "I am not," he pleaded. His attention flickered between Asia and the ground. "The Bandidos forced me to be like this."

"Survival doesn't justify kidnapping." Lian kicked and spat at the pedophile again.

56. Punishment

It was nearly noon in the Badlands. The climate wanderers were on edge over the attempted kidnapping of Lisa. They were relieved the guards caught Jeffery quickly and stared at him with revulsion.

Lian took a long breath and searched the women's faces. "We can't have a pedo lurking about." Her tone was sharp and unwavering. "We have to neutralize this threat now."

Asia's lips pressed into a thin line. She stared at Lian in shock. 'Is she suggesting we kill him,' she wondered. She had to intervene. "We'll leave him here with food and water."

Lian snapped, "He gets nothing." She knelt beside Jeffery, tied his hands and legs rigid with his own rope, and laid him face down in the dirt. She rumpled through the man's backpack and confiscated a switchblade and two precious stones.

Asia frowned at Lian. "Untie him, please."

"No." Lian stood over the pedo, clenching her teeth. She leaned in and spat into his face. "We leave this human garbage tied and without anything to attack us with."

Asia was concerned. Leaving the stranger bound in the Sun without water was giving him a death sentence. It was cruel and would set a bad example for the children.

Asia, Lian, and Xóchitl held a private, heated exchange for a minute. It ended when Lian punched her left palm and stormed off to scout the way ahead. Nzinga and Xóchitl dragged the man to a shaded spot, leaving him with water.

The female convoy prepared to depart while Jeffery tugged desperately at his restraints. "Untie me, please." His vocals quivered, rising in pitch with each word. "I'll not trouble you again, promise." His eyeballs, wild and desperate, searched for mercy.

Asia tightened the strap of her pack and stared at the squirming pedo. He breathed rapidly and snaked toward her.

"I'm a 'white' man, for Christ's sake." Jeffery's face was mangled in anger. "We're better than these black bitches." Sweat streamed down his head as he raged. "Why are you listening to that slant-eyed whore? Don't let these baboons do this to me, to us."

Asia sighed and signaled it was time to leave. She started walking, and the caravan followed. A few in the line glanced back at the pathetic figure, but no one tried to help.

Jeffery's screams grew more frantic. He trashed about ferociously, trying to break his restraints. "No, dear god, no." His yells became a haunting wail that echoed into the stillness. He struggled mightily without success, and then his body sagged in defeat. His anger dissipated, and he started sobbing loudly like the terrified child he tried to abduct. However, the irony was lost to him.

The attempted abduction cast a dark shadow over the survivors. Jeffery's pleas gradually faded, leaving a lingering sense of discomfort that settled into the pit of their stomachs. Each step forward became heavier than the last.

The weight of Lian's punishment added to their already crushing burdens. The Sun drummed down mercilessly, but the coldness in their hearts chilled them to the bone. Lian, Xóchitl, and the Crones were the least affected by the man's crime and retribution.

Lisa clung to her Mother. Her wide eyes reflected the terror she had endured. "Th-thank you for saving me," she stammered to Xóchitl.

Xóchitl knelt to Lisa's level. She reached out and gently cupped the child's cheek, her thumb brushing away a tear. "We're a family, hija." A reassuring smile tugged at her lips, and she embraced Lisa warmly. The girl's quivering eased in her arms. "We always look out for each other."

Zaniya held her elbows up in veneration. Her shine, filled with gratitude, locked onto Xóchitl. "May the Goddess be praised," she called out. The women repeated her refrain.

"The Goddess is this entire sphere," the Crone resumed. "She is where dreams touch reality, where the Earth meets Sky in an endless embrace. The Earth speaks through her. With each breath, She renews life, drawing strength from the stones and beauty from the skies. She is both the gentle spring that nourishes and the roaring storm that cleanses. Each element is evidence of her divine presence."

The Elder continued in a lush and musical tone. "Daughters, you are not just a part of the landscape. You are the mountain. Rise boldly, persevere fiercely, and let nothing keep you from your destiny. Step into your own power and carry it with you, unshaken. Let each challenge become the foundation of your unbreakable spirit. Blessed be."

Zanyia towered like the divine being herself, and her voice carried a mystical vibration that resounded through the wilderness. "May the Goddess bless you,

Lisa. And may she bless your Mother, Marge." The Crones bowed in devotion.

57. Marge

At 35, five feet seven inches tall, and 135 pounds, Marge's features were soft and tender. Her deep blue eyes often carried a guarded expression, though they loosened when she was with her children. Her skin was chapped and Sun-kissed, showing signs of exposure to the harsh environment. Her blonde and slightly wavy hair fell to her mid-back.

She had weathered many storms before meeting the asylum seekers. Her previous life was a painful blend of co-dependency, terror, and survival. It shaped her into the fierce protector she was, especially when it came to her kids.

Born in what used to be a bustling suburb of a large city, she grew up between crumbling infrastructure and hostile gangs. She was raised in a Christian community that valued faith and worship. Her purpose in life was to glorify god and enjoy him forever. She dutifully served her church, respected its male leadership, and looked forward to being a traditional wife.

In her mid-twenties, she met Tucker, a charismatic pastor who shared her devotion and dreams of wanting a family. They married, and Marge gave birth to Lisa, then Elon, the two beams of light in her life.

At first, Tucker was a good husband. But his charm masked a darker, conservative side that revealed itself in his choice of work. He and other men in the church started a slave patrol. The 'white' armed militia captured innocent minorities in California and exported them to Southern slave states. He often kept minority children chained in the house, waiting for a sale. When they resisted or tried to escape, he would beat them mercilessly.

She resented Tucker's chauvinistic bigotry and loathed his enslavement of dark-colored people.

However, her european congregation supported Tucker and the militia, and there was little she could do to stop them without risking her own life. She tried to comfort the captured children in her home as best she could.

Tucker's racism soon turned to sexism, and he became increasingly abusive to her. The first time he hit her was after Lisa was born, and she went into shock. His assault came out of nowhere, sparked by a trivial disagreement over dinner. He apologized afterward, blamed his outburst on the stress of work, and promised it would never happen again.

The new Mother was scared and confused, desperately wanting to believe her husband. Her friends warned her to leave, but she had an infant to think about. Splitting her family amid the ongoing ecological and social crises was terrifying.

Tucker's violence became more severe and frightening. He controlled and isolated her from family, friends, and other parishioners. He convinced her she was worthless and no one else would want her.

Her husband's physical abuse was accompanied by daily psychological torment: swearing, hurtful names, gaslighting, manipulation, and relentless criticism. Marge turned into a shadow of her former self, living in constant fear of the man who once claimed to love her. Tucker was sexually abusing the minority girls he caged in her home, and did not try to hide his infidelity.

For the children's sake, Marge tried to keep the family together. She shielded Lisa and Elon from the worst of Tucker's wrath, often taking the brunt of his anger. But it became harder to ignore that he was turning violent toward the children. She realized his racism influenced his sexism, and it was only going to get worse.

One night, after a brutal beating, Marge knew she needed to change her living situation. With her body aching and pulse racing, she soundlessly packed a few belongings, woke Lisa and Elon, and fled into the night.

The Mother of two had no clear plan, only the desperate need to escape. She went from family to friends until she found refuge in a shelter among a group of Mothers. The women helped her with childcare, counseling, and support to rebuild her life. She still felt guilty over her support for Tucker's evil enslavement business.

Conditions inside the shelter deteriorated, and violence escalated. Several Mothers died, leaving orphans and children who were kidnapped. Marge and the other Mothers banded together for protection from the numerous pedo gangs, like the Santa Barbara Militia (SBM), LA Police Warriors, Tijuana Cartel, and others. She saw a glimmer of hope in their alliance, a chance for survival.

However, when the group decided to abandon the shelter, she was unwilling to leave. She worried her children would not survive the arduous passage North to safety. But with nowhere else to turn, she joined Asia's group. She knew their path would be perilous, but she was not alone.

She was fiercely protective of Lisa and Elon and vowed never to let them experience the horrors she endured with their father. The single Mother's journey was about protection, caring, and healing.

She was learning to trust again, to find joy in the little moments, and to reclaim the sense of self that her abusive partner stripped away. Through the support of the other women, Marge was rediscovering her power and the vibrant life she once had. It was a spirit that had never wholly dimmed, regardless of everything.

58. Dispute

It was 2 PM in the Mohave desert. On day 29 of their climate migration, thirty-eight wanderers slowly progressed Northward in a gloomy procession. The memory of the morning kidnapping attempt lingered like a bitter aftertaste.

The afternoon Sun turned the Badlands into a scorching tsunami that seemed to engulf them from all sides. Each step was a battle against the rising heat. Asia kept the caravan moving with constant reminders to take precautions and positive affirmations.

Lian was ahead, scouting for possibilities. She was practical, direct, and often unyielding in her approach to survival. She respected Asia's wisdom but felt her decisions were not aggressive enough to protect the commune from constant danger.

Lian's experiences taught her that survival sometimes required hard decisions and swift action, which usually meant setting emotions aside. She was firmly committed to her security role, and her hard work was proof of her awareness of their dire situation.

She felt that Asia was too cautious and overly concerned with maintaining harmony at the expense of security. She believed that the collective needed someone willing to make the tough calls without hesitation, and this belief placed her at odds with the leader's benevolent approach.

Xóchitl was more balanced than Lian, but she shared her safety concerns. Though she respected Asia, she agreed with Lian that there were times when the group needed to act more decisively. She was torn between her loyalty to Lian and Asia, but there was not much she could do to assuage their brewing enmity.

The asylum seekers continued to face dangers: wild animals, scarcity of resources, and the constant risk of hostile gangs and pedos. However, the divide between the Crones and Mothers who supported Asia's management, and the scouts and others who leaned toward Lian's assertive stance, was a looming threat.

The disagreement came to a head when the wayfarers faced the crucial decision: whether to leave Jeffery free or bound and with or without food. Lian argued that he should be kept tied up without water and food. Asia wanted to leave him free with enough supplies to survive a few days.

Earlier in the day, Lian, Xóchitl, and Asia huddled to decide, and were engaged in a heated debate.

"We'll be sitting ducks with him roaming free, Sister." Lian stepped closer to Asia. "If we untie him, we're risking everything. He'll sell us out to the gangs. He needs to stay bound. You want him trying to kidnap another girl?"

Asia's brow drew in concern. "And what if he dies?" Her body shuddered with the consequences of Lian's plan. "We can't be judge, jury, and executioner." She shook her head and sighed. "We don't want to become like these vile men, do we?"

Lian stared Asia down. "Look, the man is blatantly racist. He'd kill me and the other minorities if he had a chance. You don't have a problem with that?"

"I'm sorry about his behavior toward you." Asia shook her head. "But does that equate to a death sentence?"

Lian scoffed. "He was willing to steal, rape, sell, or kill a girl child. I'll take full responsibility for his punishment. Your conscience is in the clear."

Noticing the standoff between the two leaders, Xóchitl stepped in to intervene. "Lian has a point. We guards are responsible for dealing with hazards. Lian's decision is consistent with her duty. She's only trying to protect us."

Asia remained unconvinced.

Xóchitl stretched her palms out in a gesture of openness. "Maybe we could leave Jeffery tied but in a shady spot with water. He'll survive longer and could free himself, but we'll be days ahead by then."

Asia took a deep breath. She needed an exit ramp from the conflict. Xóchitl's plan was less of a death sentence and provided them with some safety against the pedo. She nodded and looked at the lead guard.

Lian resented having to share their precious resources. And the possibility of having to worry about Jeffery in the future troubled her. But arguing with Asia was tiresome. She stormed off, resigned to Xóchitl's compromise.

Xóchitl was happy her intervention succeeded. Even though she strongly supported Lian, she knew her role was to allow both women to get part of their plan accepted. Her diplomacy worked only because they were willing to give up some of their demands. She knew how far Lian would go and held her red line of keeping the man bound.

She and Lian had a powerful bond. During the refugees' most dangerous moments, Xóchitl always backed Lian. She used her agency to support Lian's assertive actions and defended her decisions against the others. For example, whenever Lian stressed the need to neutralize some danger, Xóchitl swiftly agreed, recognizing the risks involved.

Her partner was the point person in the group's battle over strategy. While Lian pitched the hard truth to Asia and the others, her job was to provide tactical support for her plans. Her loyalty to Lian was unshakable, and Asia and the entire company respected her allegiance.

The decision about what to do with the kidnapper was not the most significant dispute between the two leaders. There were many other splits. Asia recognized the danger of their conflict and willingly agreed to Xóchitl's plan. The resolution temporarily diffused her strained relationship with Lian, but the underlying dispute over tactics was far from resolved.

Lian felt baffled, believing her approach was the safest one. She was becoming more stubborn in her disagreements with Asia.

On the other hand, Asia realized that maintaining unity required carefully navigating their growing differences. She was willing to give Lian the benefit of the doubt. However, she was responsible for the children and behavior of the collective. She was the leader and needed to set a good moral example, which limited her options.

The assembly continued traveling North in unity. However, the ill feeling between Asia and Lian simmered beneath the surface, threatening to erupt at any moment.

This mounting battle over management style inserted a layer of complication into their voyage. It could either bolster the cooperative through resolution or undermine their very existence if the division grew too large to bridge.

That evening, Lian and Xóchitl ate dinner quietly. Lian was upset and avoided eye contact.

The Latina tried to placate her friend. "Look, I know you're mad. You feel no one listens or follows your plans. But I did back you up with Asia. Just not all the way."

Lian sniffed and gave her the silent treatment.

Xóchitl continued trying to reach Lian. "Well, if you're not going to talk, I will. This tale is called The Bamboo Grove's Promise, Bhikkhuni. Please listen." The lead guard said nothing.

"In a quiet village nestled between misty mountains," the Chicana began, "there lived an old Bhikkhuni named Visakha. Her most devoted student, Khema, had followed her for many years, learning the ways of wisdom, patience, and inner peace. One day, war broke out in the land, and the village was in danger. The people, fearful for their lives, fled into the mountains. Khema, however, remained by her teacher's side. 'Bhikkhuni,' she said, 'I will not leave you. I am your student, and I will protect you.'"

Lian pretended not to hear, and Xóchitl continued. "Visakha smiled and pointed to the bamboo grove swaying in the wind. 'Do you see how the bamboo bends with the storm but does not break?' Khema nodded. 'Loyalty is like the bamboo,' the Monk continued. 'It does not resist foolishly, nor does it snap in fear. It flows with the wind but stays rooted in the Earth. True loyalty is not just standing by someone's side. It is knowing when to bend, when to stand firm, and when to let go.'"

Lian glanced at her friend briefly. The Latina smiled and concluded her story. "Khema pondered the

Bhikkhuni's words and realized that loyalty was not mere stubbornness but wisdom in knowing how best to serve and protect. The war passed, the village was rebuilt, and Khema remained beside her master. She did so not out of blind duty, but out of deep understanding and love."

59. Asia's Dilemma

It was nearly dawning the following day. Asia woke up early and sat on a flat rock alone in the dark. Her sleep was disturbed by reflections on the climate nomads' journey in the post-apocalyptic world. The three dozen survivors were her sanctuary and purpose, and she worried their unity might not endure.

Her attention was fixed on the subtle light emerging from the far vista. Dawn crept in sluggishly, casting a delicate glow over the desolate Badlands. The emerging light in the darkness was mesmerizing, but she barely noticed it. Her mind was consumed by the thoughts that had haunted her from the previous day.

Jeffery. The name felt like a stone in her throat. The stranger traveled with the collective for only a few days, but his actions shook them to the core. His quiet, brooding presence made her uneasy, but she placed judgment aside and tried pulling him into the fold.

And then his treachery confirmed Lian's worst fears. He was a racist pedo who tried to steal a child, scaring her possibly for life. But how was leaving him tied up any better than what he attempted with Lisa?

Asia closed her eyelids and took a long breath. She tried to calm the storm of uncertainty raging inside her. Anger, dread, sorrow, and guilt swirled within, but she knew she could not let them take hold. She recognized the damage that unchecked thoughts could have on her psyche: confusion, anxiety, suffering, depression, despair, and more.

Out-of-control thoughts and emotions were the underlying cause that brought civilization to its knees. And the cycle of unrestrained hate and violence, born out of social conditioning and self-interest, was being passed down from one generation to the next like an eternal curse.

'Everything arises from the mind,' she reminded herself, recalling the Zen teachings she learned at the monastery. 'Only the present is real. All else is Maya, an illusion that takes us away from the real.' Her body loosened, and she felt a moment of vulnerability slip through her usual stoic demeanor. She did not try to stop the feeling.

'Hatred does not cease by hatred, but only by love. This is the timeless directive.' The words were like a mantra, a lifeline she had repeatedly returned to in the racist and sexist dystopia she lived in.

But how could she hold onto that truth? How could she love when her heart was heavy with the pain Jeffery, Stephen, and Miller had caused? The boys sold their sisters out, and Jeffery almost took a daughter. The thought of what might have happened had the guards not intervened churned her stomach.

'Stay in the present. We're all fine now.' A wave of release rushed through her psyche, improving her disposition. She paid close attention to her breath and drifted to the teachings she studied so long ago.

'Violence and sorrow are rooted in ignorance, in lack of attention to our thinking.' How could she put this wisdom into practice? 'When we do not understand the nature of suffering, the root of our feelings, we lash out, trying to protect ourselves and control what we fear.'

The men's vile actions became transparent. She realized they were stuck in ignorance. The boys and Jeffery were products of a racist and sexist society that taught them power came from domination. They believed survival was a zero-sum game where you took what you could or were left with nothing.

'Did that mean they're innocent? That they had no choice but to follow their programming?' She became confused again. She and other women in the commune exercised compassion, even in danger. But not all women were. Lysistrata was racist, and Lian was intolerant of men. Why were they different?

'Violence only bred more violence.' Breaking the cycle required awareness and empathy for others. Yet, understanding Jeffery's mindset did not lessen the threat he posed. Kindness did not mean allowing him to endanger others. Why was she so trusting?

Was she ethnocentric? Did she trust the boys and the miner because they were 'white' like her? Would she have acted the same way if they were African or Latino? Was she racist, like the men? Was Lian right not to trust them? Her mind raced in doubt, and she breathed to calm her thoughts.

Lian insisted on leaving the predator tied up. It was unkind, but was it the best option? She had always believed in second chances, but could she continue to believe in male redemption as machismo increased and societal collapse worsened?

In the Badlands, the stakes were high, and even minor decisions could affect survival and result in extinction. Was she too gullible and careless to insist on Jeffery's freedom? She was totally bewildered.

Asia stared at the breathtaking sunrise before her. 'I must protect the girls,' she concluded. It was her primary duty, but the question remained: How could she safeguard them without perpetuating the violence that had already engulfed the Globe?

'What is the right direction?' Maybe it was not about punishing biased boys and men but changing how they viewed minorities and females. Showing them that there was another way, one that did not end in racism, enslavement, and female abuse.

She contemplated this alternative scenario and realized that it would be extremely challenging given the rampant bigotry and misogyny that existed. The seeds of prejudice and superiority were deeply rooted in european and other males, and it would take many lifetimes of re-education to uproot them.

Even so, she refused to give up on manhood entirely. If she did, she would lose the essence of her being and relinquish the core values that kept her going. Her conviction was that, regardless of everything, change was possible. Even after environmental and societal collapse, there was room for recovery, unlearning, and regrowth.

Then she recalled her encounter with Tate. The european miner was a rabid racist who supported enslavement in the South. He was also a vile opportunist who convinced the teens to abandon the group and join him in an assault on their Sisters. Sadly, Tate's racism and sexism was not unique. He was like many other euros she knew back in Laughlin.

'Were all men so evil that they were beyond transformation?' This is what Lian claimed. Was any man voluntarily willing to forego their false privilege, advantage, and power? She had never met a man who was genuinely fair and non-discriminatory. Yet she refused to succumb to Lian's gloomy pessimism.

She took another long breath and composed herself. 'Wisdom and sympathy must go hand in hand. One could not exist without the other.' How could she practice this truth? She would do anything to protect the girls and her fragile community. But she would not let anger or fear dictate her actions. Confronting Jeffery, pedos, and other men was necessary, but not with unrestrained aggression.

She would seek to understand and reach these uncritical, childish men. And if reforming toxic masculinity failed, and racist males continued to threaten her commune, she would take the necessary steps to defend her clan. And she would do so with a clear mind, free from ego, fear, and hatred.

'Hatred never ceases by hatred, only by love.' It was a difficult path, but it was the only course she could take. It was the single means that gave her optimism in an impossible situation that seemed determined to crush every shred of positivity. It was a trail that honored Gaia and being in the moment. It meant being cautious but also accessing each situation, each male, on his own merit.

Asia stood up, resolved and ready to face whatever came next. She had chosen to be choiceless, to let the reality of euro male dominance unfold. She would seek the truth in each man by venturing into the pathless land of direct experience without any expectation, no matter how good they seemed.

60. Scavengers

The thermometer reached 125°F (52°C) in the Central Valley. It was late morning, and the climate nomads had marched three miles since breakfast. On the 30th day of their trek, they were less than a week or around 35 miles away from Cantua Creek but were low on water and food.

By midday, the heat was unendurable. The gravel beneath their feet seemed to radiate flames, and every breath felt like inhaling fire. Asia called for a break under the sparse shade of scraggly bushes. The women and children collapsed in exhaustion.

The Sun-burnt assembly had barely begun to recover when Lian rushed back. "Sisters, there's people up ahead."

Asia's expression shifted from fatigue to alarm. "How many? How far?"

Lian's fingers fidgeted with the handle of her weapon. "Six, two klicks away. I'll show you."

Lian led Asia and Nzinga to the top of a nearby rise. At the summit, Asia's disposition sank at the sight of a blackened emptiness below. The few cacti and shrubs in the landscape were carbonized skeletons, like scars on a battlefield. It was not the devastation that filled Asia with dread but the movement within it, the half-dozen males slogging through the charred vista.

"Probably scavengers." Lian looked grim. "They're headed Northeast, in the same direction we are."

Asia's stomach twisted. Scavengers were a serious hazard in the Badlands. The ruthless bands of men preyed on settlers and travelers alike. They were renowned for their heinous torture, decapitation of victims, and cannibalism.

Lian glowered. Their blackened forms were hideously ugly, almost painful to watch. "We should ambush them. We've got a good position."

Asia considered Lian's plan. The scavengers were relentless in tracking human prey. The guard wanted to fight fire with fire, but that was risky. She shook her head firmly. "No, we'll lose precious ammo confronting them."

Lian shook her head in disagreement. "If they see us, we won't be able to lose them."

Asia remained firm. "If we use the sniper rounds, we'll be down to close engagements."

"They may have some." Lian sounded optimistic.

"Scavengers with .300 Winchester Magnum ammo?" Asia shook her head. "I doubt it." She started crawling back to the group.

Lian turned and pleaded to Nzinga for support. "Let's act before they do." Her fellow guard said nothing and slipped off the rise. Lian stared at the scavengers in frustration. Her security plan was being ignored again.

Asia informed the collective about the danger and laid out her strategy. "We'll back away from the threat. They're heading East, so we'll go West until we find a safe hiding place." She faced Xóchitl and pointed to the way they came. "Lead the way."

"What if they pick up our trail?" Lian was apprehensive.

Asia touched Lian's arm. "I know you'll do a good job erasing our tracks, Li."

Xóchitl led the convoy around the dune and away from the scavengers. The dread of discovery and being hunted drove everyone forward.

An hour passed, and the Sun began its slow descent. The evacuees were exhausted, and their pace slackened. Every rustle of wind, step on a pebble, or break of a twig sent shivers down their spines. Each sound carried a potential for discovery by the scavengers.

The afternoon's dust began swirling, and Asia spotted the shelter she had sought. There was a slight depression between two dunes. The narrow gap offered some protection if they were shadowed.

"Over there." Asia pointed to Xóchitl. "We'll camp there, in the shade."

The survivors entered the shaded ravine, and the Crones chose a rocky outcrop on the right bank to establish camp. The women dug a trench, constantly inspecting the background for any sign of movement.

Asia, Nzinga, and Xóchitl sat in front of the worn assembly in the trench. Asia addressed the collective. "This spot provides some cover, but we must stay vigilant. If the men find us, we leave immediately."

The women concurred, and Asia continued, "Lian and Xóchitl will guard the left side of the ravine, and Nzinga and the scouts will guard the right."

Nzinga tried to calm the group. "We'll lay traps on both ends, so we'll hear them before seeing them."

The evening progressed, and the camp was not attacked. But the frightened convoy remained hidden. The scavengers were unaware of their presence or had lost their trail.

Lian and Xóchitl sat on the ridge on the lookout for scavengers.

"I get no respect," Lian complained. "What's the point of planning our defense if no one listens?"

"E tu Tambien," the Latina replied. "You don't listen to me, Bhikkhuni. Let me tell you a Zen tale."

Lian consented.

"The Moon in the Water," Xóchitl began. "A young nun named Yuri trained under a wise Zen master. One evening, after years of study, Yuri faced a great disappointment. She had failed an important test that would allow her to advance in the monastery. Feeling unworthy, she sat by a still pond, staring at the moon's reflection in the water."

"I share her frustration." Lian commiserated.

The Latina nodded. "Sensing her distress, the Bhikkhuni approached and asked, 'Yuri, why do you look so troubled?' Yuri sighed. 'I have failed, Master. I worked hard, but I was not good enough. My efforts were wasted.' The Monk picked up a small stone and dropped it into the pond. The ripples distorted the moon's reflection, breaking it into scattered fragments."

Xóchitl stared at the moon and continued. "The Bhikkhuni said, 'Look at the moon. Is it broken?' Yuri shook her head. 'No, Master. The moon is still whole in the sky. Only its reflection is disturbed.' The female Monk smiled. 'And so, it is with you. Your failure is only a ripple on the surface. Beneath it, you remain whole, untouched, and full of potential. Let the ripples settle, and you will see yourself clearly again.'

"I should calm down." Lian composed herself.

Her companion smiled. "Yuri bowed deeply. She understood that failure was just a passing disturbance, not a reflection of her true self."

Dawn arose, and the travelers emerged from their hiding spot, hungry but rested.

Zaniya was active and full of energy. "Let us seize the day and live it with fullness," she announced. "May the Goddess guide our way. The shadows do not deter Her. They call Her deeper, showing Her that light is only meaningful when it has darkness to define it. Stand tall like the mountains, Daughters. Face your fears and embrace every part of who you are. Rise to your full power and let the world feel your strength. Blessed be."

The female collective faced the hostile Badlands with renewed vigor. With Lian leading the way, they quickly set off North, eager to put more distance between them and the terrifying scavengers.

61. Acorns

It was 10 AM in the California Drylands. The heat was stifling, pressing down on the climate evacuees like a heavy blanket. It was 119°F (48°C), and the air was bone-dry. The persistent Western drought had long drained humidity and moisture from the land, and the evacuees struggled to breathe.

After a grueling uphill climb, the women and children rested their aching bodies, parched throats, and inflamed nostrils. Little water or food was left, but there was no time for despair. If they could survive, they would be five days away from the Safehouse.

Hehewuti perused the bare panorama with the precision of a native forager. "Girls, let's see what edible plants we can find." She raised her hand, motioning them to follow.

The children, driven by hunger and the faint glimmer of optimism, fell behind her. Lisa, always the quickest, darted ahead with the energy of youth, her tiny feet kicking up clouds of dust in her wake. Her purposeful eyes swept the ground, searching for anything to sustain them. After a few minutes, her face lit up. She spun around, bursting with excitement.

"Over here." Lisa's hand shot up, pointing at a cactus hidden behind a rock. Its thick, green pads were adorned with delicate blossoms and reddish fruit.

Hehewuti reached out to touch the plant. "Well done, Lisa. This will help us." She crouched, pulled out a worn knife, and sliced the cactus pads efficiently. "Keep looking, girls."

She carefully drained the precious liquid over a cloth strainer into a dented container. The girls found a few more cacti, and the Crone worked on each one.

At the last cactus, she held the container with both hands and gently urged the children, "Take a few sips." The girls took turns, and the thick drops soothed their parched throats.

"It's nutritious, daughters," Hehewuti noted. "It has electrolytes that help your cells grow and function properly." She watched closely, willing the small amount of liquid to be enough to sustain them.

The children paired off and continued foraging. One duo found a prickly pear cactus and harvested the fruits. Another discovered chia sage and collected the seeds. One pair saw a date palm loaded with ripe fruit and filled a basket.

Hehewuti handed the desert harvest to Frida, who accompanied the foraging party. The cook smiled in appreciation. "We'll make something good out of this," she assured them. She knew how to stretch the scanty treasures into a meal.

Hehewuti led the girls along a dried-up stream bed, and their feet crunched the splintered Earth. The setting was desolate. Yet, amidst the arid wilderness, life persisted in tiny, hidden pockets. After ten minutes of walking, they approached a fire-scarred area dominated by a massive oak tree. Its branches were gnarled and blackened, but it still stood with leaves.

"Scratch the ground, search under branches," Hehewuti directed. "Look for acorns."

The girls darted under the tree, searching for a spot to dig. Cha'Kwaina, with her keen eye for detail, spotted a shaded area beneath a broken branch that looked promising. She knelt and brushed away layers of ash and debris, uncovering a small cache of acorns, evidence of her growing skills and self-reliance. Her dark orbs shone with the thrill of discovery.

"Hey, Gaias, look what I got," Cha'Kwaina called out, trembling with excitement.

Hehewuti glowed and carefully examined the medium-sized nuts. She let out a breath of relief. "These are good. Look for more. We can make bread with these." She planned to show the girls how to grind the acorns into flour.

The children's faces lit up with the thought of bread, and they rushed to search for more acorns. They worked eagerly, hands moving in a flurry. They dug the soil and stuffed nuts into bags. The laborious task became a game, with laughter filling the air. For a moment, the weight of their migration disappeared.

Hehewuti straightened up and took in the almost comic scene of scampering forms, digging on all fours.

They ran out of places to dig under the oak tree and were exhausted from the exertion.

"Let's head back," Hehewuti gestured. "We've got enough for a few meals."

The girls stored their findings and headed back to the group. They felt assured in their foraging skills, and their contribution was vital to the group's survival.

Hehewuti staggered in the rear, her thoughts already on to the next challenge. But she allowed herself a moment of satisfaction. The girls were getting better at gathering. They found enough food and liquid to sustain the caravan for the night, demonstrating their perseverance and her mentorship. Seeing their progress in the face of such great adversity was a proud moment for her.

During Cronetime, Hehewuti called on Mary to take the board. Mary was reluctant to speak, but the girls insisted, and she decided to tell them Queen Tomiris's story.

"In the wild, wind-swept lands East of the Caspian Sea in Central Asia," Mary began, "the Massagetae clan roamed. They were fierce, nomadic Scythians who lived around 600 BC. They raised horses and herded sheep and goats. The women were skilled riders, expert archers, and fierce warriors. They were the source of Greek legends about the Amazons."

"Amazons?" Phoolan asked. "Who were they?"

"The Amazons were female warriors," Mary revealed. "They were known for their physical agility, strength, archery, riding, and combat skills. Their society was closed to men, and they raised only their daughters. They returned sons to their fathers, with whom they would only socialize briefly to reproduce."

"A female clan like us," Shasha exclaimed.

"Yes," Mary nodded. "They were quite famous. Commanded by their Queen, the Amazons regularly went on expeditions into the far corners of the world. Besides military raids, they built Goddess temples and established numerous ancient cities like Ephesos, Cyme, Smyrna, Sinope, Myrina, and Pygela."

"They were like Sybils with swords," Cha'Kwaina commented. "Warrior prophets."

The teacher smiled. "Now back to our story. The Massagetae tribe was guided by their own laws and ruled by a Queen unlike any other. Tomiris, daughter of warriors, widow of a fallen king, and mother to a young prince. She bore the crown not through inheritance but through courage, governance, and diplomacy. Clad in iron and wisdom, she ruled not from palaces but from horseback. Her authority was unquestioned, and she united the steppe clans."

"Far to the South," the Elder continued, "Cyrus the Great, founder of the Persian Empire, had conquered the mighty kingdoms of Lydia and Babylon. His dominion spanned from the Mediterranean to the Indus Valley. But it was not enough. The steppe region of vast grasslands, untamed and free, called to him. And there, in its heart, stood Queen Tomiris."

Mary paused for a breather.

"Tell us more," Lisa pleaded.

The Crone smiled and picked up the narrative. "Cyrus, king of kings, invited the Queen's husband and son to Babylon and had them killed. Their deaths left the Queen heartbroken. Next, Cyrus sent envoys to the steppe with velvety words: 'Great Queen,' they said, bowing low, 'Cyrus offers you his hand in marriage. United, your people will share in his glory and peace.'"

The narrator took a moment to gaze at her eager students before carrying on. "Queen Tomiris's eyes narrowed. She stood before the envoys, tall and unflinching, a hawk's feather in her hair and an iron sword at her side. 'Cyrus seeks not a wife, but a throne,' Queen Tomiris said. 'Tell your king: I will not be his bride, nor my people his subjects.'"

"Wow. Challenging the mighty king." Riri was impressed. "She was fierce."

The narrator took a drink and resumed. "Spurned, Cyrus turned to war. He crossed the Araxes River and built a camp just within Massagetae lands. Queen Tomiris gathered her Scythian warriors: archers who could strike a target mid-flight, horsemen who rode like the wind, and elders who spoke of omens. Before dawn, they painted their faces with ash and blood and rode into battle with a fury born of loss."

"Were both sides evenly matched?" Phoolan asked.

"No, Cyrus had twice as many soldiers," Mary noted. "Still, the clash was monumental. The sky darkened with arrows, and the Earth trembled beneath thousands of hooves. The Persians, trained and disciplined, were overwhelmed by the nomads' wild, unrelenting assault. Tomiris and other female warriors fought at the front, cleaving through enemy lines as their war cries echoed across the battlefield."

"Women on the front lines?" Riri was amazed.

"By dusk, the combat zone was red with blood," the storyteller explained. "Cyrus the Great lay among the dead, his armor dented, and his crown cast aside. Tomiris stood over his body and addressed the lifeless king: 'You sought to satisfy your thirst for blood with nomads,' she said. 'Now drink your fill.' She dropped his head into a sack of blood."

"Oh no," Ma'at gasped.

"That day, the empire halted at the edge of the steppe," the Elder said. "The story spread of a Scythian Queen who defied the world's greatest conqueror, not with castles or armies alone, but with the unbreakable will of a Mother, and the raw fury of pastoral people who refused to be ruled."

"What happened to the Queen?" Sasha asked.

"Queen Tomiris faded into legend," Mary answered. "But her tale remains, etched into the stones of time, as the woman who stood against a vast empire and triumphed. For the past 2500 years, she was remembered by the common female name, Tamara." She bowed and gave the Cronetime board back to the Eldest Crone.

62. Hehewuti

At 74, Hehewuti bore the weight of her years with a grace that spoke volumes of her wisdom and toughness. Standing at five feet seven inches and weighing 130 pounds, her slender yet robust frame was a testament to her strength.

Though bony, her hands were tough and capable, with veins that stood out prominently against her skin. Her face was a map of experience, etched with deep lines that traced her life's long, winding paths. Her silver hair had streaks of its original dark color, falling to her upper back.

Over her loose garments, she wore a lightweight, hooded cloak made from a patchwork of tan and brown fabrics, ideal for staying hidden in the wilderness. Her attire reflected the thoughtful, deliberate nature of a woman who had spent her life in close communion with the Earth.

Her footwear, sturdy hand-sewn moccasins crafted from the skin of a deceased deer, reflected her resourcefulness. Reinforced with extra padding for long treks, the soles allowed her to move silently, an example of her deep connection to the natural world.

For Native Peoples, moccasins were more than just footwear. They were sacred, often passed down through generations, and symbolized the wearers' life journey, a narrative woven into the very fabric of their soles.

Because Mother Earth (Unci Maka) is sacred, moccasins allowed the People to tread on her with honor and respect. The Crone encouraged the girls to look for dry animal skin and showed them how to cut and thread it to make their own moccasins.

Born in the Hopi Nation on the Colorado Plateau, she grew up before society disintegrated. Hehewuti means warrior Mother spirit. From a young age, Hehewuti was drawn to her People's ancient tradition. Her Grandmother, Zitkála-Šá, was a medicine woman.

She saw a spark in the child and took her under her wing.

Zitkála-Šá taught her granddaughter the sacred knowledge of herbs, the songs that called upon the spirits for guidance, and the stories that held the ancestors' wisdom. She learned to listen to the wind, to read the signs in the clouds, and to understand the language of the animals and plants that shared the land.

As a medicine woman, she became the keeper of traditional knowledge, which brought her great respect and responsibility. Her healing and storytelling skills became known throughout her community. She never married and remained childless.

The Mesa native realized that Hopi's nature-based knowledge and ways of life were being forgotten and felt obligated to preserve her culture. The enormity of the task was a heavy burden she carried with grace and determination, a weight that all who knew her felt. However, the environment was changing rapidly, and teaching about vegetation that no longer existed was pointless.

Hehewuti and other Pueblo females toiled tirelessly to re-matriate the land, a practice of restoring the land to its original state. They dug deep wells, irrigated the land, and cultivated dry-weather crops. However, Puebloan men resented female leadership and did not cooperate with the women folk.

The women's sons and male relations chose assimilation with their pink colonizers over returning to matriarchal practices. Hehewuti watched in sadness while her people fought and became divided. The Hopi Nation fractured, and its people scattered.

During her years of wandering, Hehewuti found other female Elders like Zaniya, Mary, Zenobia, and Kuan-Yin. Together, they formed a bond that would become the foundation of the collective led by Asia. The Crones' profound connection to the Earth and ability to see beyond immediate challenges made them a pillar of support for the women and girls.

Hehewuti was the collective's most revered Crone, and her spirit remained solid and unbroken. She taught the children the traditional songs, the stories of ancient lands, and the ways of survival that had kept her going through the darkest times.

Her life had been an intricate tapestry woven with spirit, wisdom, and an unbreakable connection to Gaia and the Solar cycles. She was a living link to a time of gifting, empathy, and compassion that once was. Her presence was a reminder of the resilience of human will and the enduring power of awareness.

Hehewuti carried a miniature pouch of sacred items such as dried herbs, a carved coyote figure, and a turquoise stone. These tokens connected her to the Pueblo Nation and its traditions. When the nights were long, and the voyage seemed impossible, she took out her sacred items and held them close, drawing courage from her Hopi heritage. She knew that her path and the mission of the female collective were far from over, but she was ready to face whatever came next.

63. Gust

It was only 10 AM in the Central Valley, but the Sun was already merciless as if she had cursed her third daughter, the Earth, for unknown offenses. The air was lifeless, and the humidity hovered at 12 percent, turning each breath into a sharp sting.

The sand blistered beneath the climate nomads' feet, radiating the searing 123°F (50°C) temperature through their soles. Their heads sizzled like grilled corn on a stovetop. Even with the choking heat, the group kept moving. They were 32 days into their Northward trek, and the females remained steadfast in their quest for safety.

If they could endure the brutal solar assault, the Safehouse was 25 miles Northeast or within four days' reach. They were close to Asia's promised reprieve, and the proximity alone created an extra spark in everyone's step. Their unity, shaped by difficulty, represented the female spirit and strength from shared experiences.

Cha'Kwaina, 14, wiped the sweat off her neck and sipped from her flask. Her face was flushed from the relentless glare, and her focus darted towards Sasha and Karol.

"Can you believe it, a real house?" Cha'Kwaina was ready to bask in the refuge that was so close yet seemed so far. "Even if it's only for a few nights, it'd be like a vacation."

Sasha, 15, walked beside Cha'Kwaina. She shifted her pack and crossed her arms to ward off the memories she was about to share. "We used to have a house on a farm." She was on the verge of tears. "We were fortunate until an invisible disease came and killed the animals." Her attention dropped to the ground, and she cried softly.

"I'm so sorry." Karol, 14, held her friend's shoulder in support.

Sasha fidgeted with her hair, trying to pull a painful memory into focus. "Then Dad fell ill. Mom and I fled. We left him to die." She sobbed and looked at Cha'Kwaina. Her face was damp and red.

Sasha tilted her head to the sky, looking for forgiveness. "We survived, but the guilt and misery were overbearing. I was miserable until I found you."

The three girls embraced and wept together. Their group hug symbolized their friendship, which had kept them close and inseparable. At that moment, they were not just three individuals but a collective force against the harshness of their lives. Their bond, forged in hardship, was a ray of hope in their journey.

"Thank you for being my friends." Sasha regained her composure. "You've helped me more than you'll ever know."

"We're together for a reason," Karol whispered. "We've all suffered and seen too much. But we're lucky to have each other."

The girls' mood improved, and the conversation returned to the Safehouse. Their faces lit up with anticipation for the comfort it promised, a longing that resonated with anyone who yearned for a haven.

"I can't wait to wash." Sasha raised her hands, scrubbing them, seemingly feeling the dirt falling away. "Imagine soaking in a tub." Her words triggered a collective gasp.

"A bath may free these knots." Cha'Kwaina tugged her hair dreamily.

"I'm thinking about a feast." Karol held her hands to her mouth. "Roasted corn and vegetables, baked pastries, hearty bean soup, fresh oranges, and fruit-flavored juices." She tilted her head to savor a refreshing beverage. The girls' mouths salivated, and they swallowed Karol's imaginary drink.

The vivid fantasy momentarily helped the trio escape their harsh reality. Visions of comfort and normalcy fueled each step, pushing them onward.

Suddenly, the wind whipped up, howling with an eerie intensity that sent a shiver through Lian's spine. "Windstorm from the East," she roared. "Get down now." Her hands fluttered, trying to catch the attention of the caravan.

The children, lost in chatter, were oblivious to the sudden change in weather. The women felt a surge of fear and vulnerability. The wind, like a cruel master, whipped at their clothes, threatening to tear them from their bodies.

"Lay down" Asia's cry was lost in the deafening roar of the advancing gale. She leaned forward, trying to push against the raging tempest.

The squall shrieked through the line, forcing the migrants to their knees. The children scrambled to their Moms, faces pale with fear. Greta staggered, and her features contorted when the wind nearly knocked her off her feet. Her arms flailed instinctively for balance before a Crone gabbed her.

The gusts intensified, whipping up a wall of dust that engulfed the convoy. The landscape quickly vanished, replaced by a choking haze. A tsunami of dirt pummeled their bodies with startling force. Sand and rubble whipped across their faces, cutting into their skin and blinding their vision.

Panic ensued. The girls screamed and frantically sought cover behind the adults, except there was nowhere to hide. Their cries pierced the tempest, but the anguished Mothers could only hold on and wish the squall would soon pass.

"Stay together," Asia shouted through the cacophony. She lunged at two girls close to her, covering them with her body.

"Cover your eyes." Xóchitl clenched her teeth and squinted against the stinging dust. "Stay together."

The windstorm raced through the line, tearing at their clothes and packs. Marielle, 7, lost her footing and was dragged by the wind until the Firekeeper grabbed her by the ankle. The tattered forms cowered while the gale blasted everything in its path.

Abruptly, the storm's ferocity waned. The wind grew calm, having exhausted its fury.

Asia was relieved. She brushed dirt from her face and body and stared at the line. Dust covered everything like a gray, powered blanket. But the caravan had weathered the storm. Their spiritedness and endurance shone through.

Blinking through the muck, the girls sluggishly rose from their crouched positions and shifted lazily to collect their scattered belongings.

Cha'Kwaina stood upright and scrubbed sand from her clothes. "From a water bath to a dust bath." She exchanged an expression of shared fatigue with Sasha, a look that conveyed the weight of their journey and the toll it had taken on them.

"We can't expect anything." Sasha frowned. "This world has a way of ruining all our dreams."

Bit by bit, the ragged figures cleaned themselves. Their slow motion reflected the anguish of the ordeal. Emily checked for injuries. The survivors were fine, apart from light scratches and bruises. Their weary bodies bore the scars of their flight to safety, a vivid token of their trials and tribulations.

Asia took a moment to survey the scene. She noticed their supplies were in disarray and promptly began retrieving and cleaning each item. Despite the grime and weariness, her expression remained positive and upbeat. She was a formidable role model for her community, and they all drew strength from her perseverance.

Zaniya stood erect, bowed to the decreased tempest, and gave a blessing. "In the vast wilderness, Gaia is the heartbeat, grounding each creature, nurturing every life. Her spirit is as expansive as the heavens. Daughters face the winds that challenge you and the storms that try to bend you. You are stronger than you know. Stand tall, rise high, and keep moving forward. Blessed be."

64. Wagon

Two hours later, it was high noon in Mohave, and the heat intensified. The three dozen climate survivors struggled to keep pace. They planned on covering ten miles but had lost an hour in the morning's dust storm. Their intention was in a brutal standoff with the weather, and the hydrogen Star was winning.

At the head of the line, Lian searched for shade and a much-needed rest stop. She watched for windstorms, wary of being caught off-guard again. She squinted into the distance, and her beams locked onto a rapidly approaching low cloud in the far South.

The swirl was slight but approaching unnervingly fast, stirring up the Badlands like a dust devil. But something was off. The wind was blowing from the North, in the opposite direction of the dirt cloud. Her pulse quickened when the realization hit her. Someone or something was moving fast toward them.

Lian let out a sharp, high-pitched yell that cut through the line. "Pedos. We need to hide now." She grabbed her weapon and pointed it at the threat.

A wave of panic crashed over the drab figures. Xóchitl's pulse soared, and her beams flitted nervously across the uneven ground.

Asia appeared grim. 'Not another crisis,' she thought. She searched the nearby dunes and pointed toward a shadowy recess behind a wide boulder to the left. "Over there."

Lian kept checking the plume and realized there were two tracks. Time was running out.

"Move it." Lian hiked up quickly toward the boulder. "No time to lose."

The climate nomads sprang into action, adrenaline surging. They scrambled up the dune, fleeing from whatever was barreling toward them. Xóchitl grabbed her jacket and swept the ground behind them, erasing their tracks the best she could.

They reached the flat stone and laid flat in its shadow. The girls hugged and cowered. Lian tossed a camouflage tarp over the group, trusting it would conceal them.

The security team took defensive positions on either side of the cover, and Lian explained the chaotic scene unfolding below.

Two trails rapidly advanced from the South, churning up the sand. The first plume revealed an old open wagon rattling over the uneven ground. Two horses strained to pull the heavy carriage.

On the box seat, a dark-colored teenage girl clutched the reins, steering the winding cart. Six terrified minority females sat in the carriage. They were different hues, from dark to light, and appeared to be in their teens and early twenties. The females were shoeless and scantily dressed. Their desperate screams sliced through the air like the crack of a whip. It seemed like the women were escapees.

Trailing close behind, a second dust cloud unfurled to reveal a quartet of male riders. The middle-aged european men looked like four horsemen of an unfolding female apocalypse. They represented conquest, trafficking, abuse, and domestication.

"Come back here, you black bitches." The pursuers taunted. "Daddy wants a kiss." The gap between hunters and hunted narrowed with each stride.

"No. Stop. Please." The women's pleas resonated through the drylands.

Undercover, Zenobia's face was etched with concern. She leaned closer to Mary and mouthed, "Dem ladies be runnin' away from ah brothel."

Mary gasped. She strained mentally, trying to psychically pull the females away from the pedos.

Under the tarp, the horsemen were an unseen, menacing force. Their cruel hollers pierced the survivors' psyche and penetrated to the core of their beings. "Don't run away, my pretty darkies. You're born to be whores."

The horses pulling the wagons gasped for air, slipping. The sound of them straining under the relentless Sun captured the brutal chase.

Phoolan, 16, clenched her fist in anger. Her attention shifted to the Crones huddled behind, looking bleak. "I know it's dangerous, but shouldn't we do something?"

Hehewuti shook her head gravely.

"We can't risk it." Zaniya's deep-set orbs conveyed the weight of unspoken truths.

"Our first priority is protecting our girls," Kuan-Yin's hand rested protectively over her chest to emphasize the importance of their responsibility.

Several women screamed from inside the wagon. "No. Let us be."

The shrieks pierced the girls' hearing, and they covered their ears in horror. The shouts were a haunting reminder of their own vulnerability.

The escapees' cries sent shivers through the frayed women. They agonized over their limited options and the Crones' decision not to intervene. The choice between saving others or saving themselves was not fair. Still, they felt guilty and remorseful.

Lian stared at the pedos with clenched jaws, clutching her weapon. She nudged the shapes cowering undercover. "We can't simply stand by Sisters." Her body was primed for action.

No one said a word. Lian's attention flicked between the approaching wagon and Xóchitl. "We can help them, X. There's only four pedos." Her face was a mask of anger and desperation.

Under the screen, Asia's face reddened. "We need to stay hidden," she beseeched Lian. "We'll find someone who can help."

Lian became infuriated. "Sister, there's no one here but us," she screeched. Her body leaned sideways, trying to bridge the distance between their opposing views. The leader said nothing.

The women's shrieks in the wagon penetrated the soundless wilderness. The horsemen pursued the desperate escapees zealously, clearly enjoying the chase. The dunes were filled with female distressed cries and male frenetic howls.

The emotional scene reminded Lian of the horrible incidents of female abuse she witnessed on the Coast: men chasing women through the streets; vile predators stalking innocent prey; ladies being punched, whipped, and tortured in public; girls and women chained, caged, and sold at trading posts; preadolescent girls offered for sale in redlight districts.

She dressed and passed as a man to evade harm. Her reaction was always to ignore the injustices. Intervention meant being killed by a vicious mob of men in trying to stop one. She hated herself for her inaction. She wanted to make up for the years of closing her eyes and ears.

The odds were finally in her favor in the wilderness. She and Xóchitl could end the chase with two shots each. They had to act. She glared at the Latina, but her fellow guard refused to make eye contact. Lian could not act alone.

The horses stumbled and strained under the stress of the chase. Their breaths came in short, labored gasps. Seconds ticked by, and Lian screamed inside. Her tears flowed, blurring her vision of the chase. She bowed her head and wept.

The pursuit veered Northwest, and the dust rose high into the sky. Lian watched, exasperated. The plume gradually disappeared, swallowed by the vast, remorseless wilderness.

The terrified females stayed under the cover for a long time. They were too startled to stir.

Asia was the first to exit the tarp. She stared at the dust cloud and touched Lian's arm gently. "We know how powerless you feel." She inhaled deeply and exhaled slowly. "Thank you for your restraint. We must play it safe, for everyone's sake."

Lian's face was a storm of sorrow and anger. "Those pedos will pay, I swear." She shrugged off Asia's hand and stomped off down the hill. Her footsteps were fast and heavy. Each tread echoed her intention to be alone with her thoughts.

A comforting hum emerged from undercover as Zaniya summoned Gaia. "With each passing storm, the Earth Goddess grows wiser. With each season, She grows stronger. Her spirit is unbreakable, Her resolve unwavering. In Her silence, She carries the weight of the World. In Her stillness, She finds Her strength."

The Crone chanted softly, then continued, "Meet every shadow with the strength of the mountains, Daughters. Let each trial forge you. She is a reminder that perseverance is not the absence of struggle, but the ability to keep going, to grow, and to stand firm despite it. Blessed be."

65. Meditation

Noon in the Badlands was auspicious. The intense and unrelenting light cast a stark, almost surreal brilliance over the landscape. The Sun sat directly overhead, bathing the arid terrain in a blinding, white-gold glow that eliminated shadows and flattened the contours of the land.

The sky was a deep, vivid blue, cloudless, creating a sharp contrast against the pale, sun-bleached sands and rugged rock formations. The air shimmered with heat waves, distorting distant objects and giving the horizon a mirage-like quality. The harsh, unfiltered light amplified the desert's vastness and emptiness, emphasizing its raw, untamed beauty while conveying a sense of isolation and desolation.

The female collective sat under a tarp on the side of a dune, under its shade. It was as quiet as a graveyard, and the females inside the sheet were also speechless. A few Mothers and Crones emerged cautiously into the blinding light to survey the scene. The horsemen of the apocalypse were gone, and they breathed in relief.

The girls emerged from their hiding place in shock, their bodies trembling with fear. Three remained huddled under the cover, their minds unable to process the reality of the recent events. The echoes of the females' scream in the wagon reverberated in their ears, rendering them speechless and motionless.

Ma'at, Lisa, and Selina cried uncontrollably, and their Mothers, Simone, Marge, and Emily, could not console them. The trio refused to advance any further. Their route went in the general direction of the male terrorists, which made them even more scared.

Asia sat with the three girls under the tarp, her presence a soothing balm amid their turmoil. She held Ma'at's hand and caressed it gently.

"I'm so scared," Ma'at sobbed. Asia nodded.

"We should stay here or go the other way," Selina implored.

"The bad man tried to take me away," Lisa wailed.

Asia held Selina and Lisa's hands. "My dear daughters, I understand your torment. But let's not focus on what's making you anxious." Her voice was soft and healing. "Let's concentrate on the present moment, okay? Breathe slowly, inhale, exhale."

Asia was serene like a statue, contrasting with the apocalyptic whirlwind that had just passed. Despite her weariness, she exuded strength and attention.

"Now, let's focus on what's normal." Asia sat comfortably with her neck straight. "Breathe. Your breath is always in the present moment. By paying attention to it, you can center yourself and calm your restless mind."

She took several lungsful to demonstrate deep breathing and continued. "You're not too hungry, thirsty, tired, or sick. So, physically, you're fine." Asia removed the camo screen and stood erect in the shade. "Girls, look at the beautiful blue sky." The girls stared at the cloudless expanse, unimpressed.

"Are there any storms or dangers brewing?" Asia made a 360-degree spin. "Now, listen carefully. Can you hear the quietness of the Badlands?"

The girls sobbed and listened. The stillness seemed like a blanket, calming their fears.

"You can feel the wetness of your tears on your skin, right?" Asia smiled. "Can you smell the faint scent of cacti in the air? Nature is completely normal, isn't she?" Asia breathed and remained silent.

The three females stopped crying and listened intently to the desert.

"Don't your lips taste like salt? Can you sense the solid ground under you? You feel balanced and not dizzy, right? You can also detect the temperature and humidity, right?" Asia sat unflustered. "All your senses are working. Your bodies are functioning perfectly, and there's no danger. In this moment, you're safe."

She smiled and embraced the trio. Her warmth enveloped Ma'at, Lisa, and Selina, and they grew calm. They thanked their leader for help and were willing to resume the North Passage.

The caravan continued moving, shaken up from the close call with ruthless bandits who capture and trade females, but revived by their brief rest. They paced for several hours and climbed a steep hill to make camp for the evening.

Asia decided to take the board for Cronetime and led the children through a body scan meditation. Hehewuti placed some blankets on the ground for them to lie on.

First, Asia led the girls through several yoga stretches: triangle pose, cow, downward dog, forward fold, tree pose, and child's pose. Next, she showed them a seated position with her legs crossed in a double lotus pose.

"This Buddha pose symbolizes enlightenment, inner wisdom, and emotional stability," Asia explained. "The triangle shape created by the crossed legs is a solid foundation. The triangle formed by the thumb symbolizes the unity of the teacher, teachings, and the learners."

Asia sat quietly, and the girls mirrored her position. "Now, lie down straight, arms by your side." She laid flat and paused for the group to follow. The girls lay on their backs, staring at the evening sky.

"To calm our minds, we need to unwind our bodies," Asia resumed. "So, piece by piece, we'll bring awareness to different parts of our body. Close your eyelids and take a big breath. We'll loosen our muscles from the bottom to the top, starting with our toes and moving upward."

"Pay attention to your breath," she intoned. "Breathe slowly and profoundly. Inhale, exhale. This practice helps you become more aware of how your body feels," she explained. "It grounds you in the present moment, fostering a deep connection between mind and body." The girls were fast asleep by the end of the relaxation yoga.

Lian and Xóchitl were on guard. Lian enjoyed Asia's yoga and meditation exercise and wanted more. "Can you tell me a Zen tale, por favor?" she asked.

"Por supuesto, Bhikkhuni," the Latina replied. "This one is The Shadow in the Cave. A young nun named Sanghamitta was plagued by fear. She feared the dark, failure, and the unknown. One evening, she approached her Zen master and asked, 'Bhikkhuni, how can I overcome my fear?'"

"Oh, I like this one," Lian remarked.

Xóchitl grinned and resumed. "The female Monk handed Sanghamitta a small lantern and led her to the mouth of a deep cave. The entrance yawned like the mouth of a great beast, and its depths were shrouded in darkness. 'Go inside,' the master said. Sanghamitta hesitated. 'But Bhikkhuni, I cannot see what is in there. There could be dangers lurking within.'

"Yup, like a gang of pedos." Lian looked scared.

"Could be," the Chicana admitted and continued. "The Monk nodded. 'Take one step.' With trembling hands, Sanghamitta lifted the lantern and took a step into the cave. The light showed a small patch of rocky ground. 'Now take another step,' the master said. The nun did, and the darkness retreated slightly, revealing more of the path. 'Do you see?' the Bhikkhuni asked. 'Fear is only the darkness before you. But with each step, you bring light to what was unknown.'"

"We conquer fear by facing it," Lian suggested.

"Yes," Xóchitl said. "Sanghamitta stood in silence, understanding filling her heart. From that day on, whenever fear gripped her, she remembered the lesson of the cave: the only way to overcome fear is to step forward, and with each step, the darkness fades."

"Lovely," Lian beamed, and her partner smiled.

66. Barn

It was 3 PM in the California wilderness. The fiery orb hung high, casting a harsh spotlight over the parched Earth. The temperature was startling at 132°F (56°C), approaching its daytime peak. The climate caravan snaked through the flat terrain toward Cantua Creek with Lian in the lead.

The dry desert air was like an endless wave, sharp and unyielding. It rushed into Lian's nose, crisp and biting, pulling every trace of moisture from her nostrils. Each breath felt jagged, like the air itself was searching for relief. She could feel the tickle of dust particles brushing against the inside of her nose and scraping against her eyeballs. She was used to painful discomfort, and it ceased to bother her.

The wanderers gingerly approached the Safehouse. The large, derelict three-story farmhouse loomed tall inside a chain-linked fence. Its paint was peeling, and the wood was weathered by time and neglect. Behind the farmhouse, there was a giant barn in even worse condition. Its roof sagged, and the structure appeared to be barely holding together. There was no farm or garden on the property.

The disappointment on the girls and women's faces was noticeable. The dilapidated homestead was more reminiscent of a haunted house than a sanctuary. Their expressions, etched with exhaustion and a flicker of aspiration, told the story of their month-long, strenuous voyage.

Lian stepped boldly toward the fence. Her face flushed and sweat slicked down from the unrelenting heat. The Goddess' congregation shuffled behind her, their footsteps rumbling over the worn trail.

She reached the gate and pushed. The lock held firm. She glanced at the others and shrugged. She pounced like a cat, gracefully leaped over the fence, and landed inside the yard.

Her boots crunched on the gravel path as she strode towards the farmhouse. Her body stiffened, and she instinctively touched her weapon. 'Let's see if anybody's home,' she mused. Her resolve was unwavering despite the fading promise of shelter.

The farmhouse windows were dark and lifeless. The lead guard bounded up the stairs to the front door and knocked. The lack of response from the inside was crushing. She tried the doorknob, but it was locked.

"Damn it." Lian slammed her fist against the bare wall. "What now?"

Asia scaled the fence and stepped close to the lead guard. Her voice was calm and unwavering. "Check out the barn. It's probably open."

Asia searched under the doormat and found a key. She tried it on the front door, but it did not fit. She returned to the gate, placed the key into the padlock, and it swung open. The relieved party swarmed inside the open yard.

Lian headed toward the gigantic barn. The immense structure was made of wooden planks that had faded, broken, or gone missing. The two massive doors were slightly ajar, and Lian pushed hard against the left one. It swung open on rusty hinges to reveal a cavernous interior.

Light streamed in from holes in the roof and gaps in the walls like spotlights on a dark stage. It was mesmerizing. Dust motes floated lazily in the shafts of Sunlight. A stuffy, defecating smell wafted up her nose, and she saw bird poop marks on the rafters above.

She stepped into the barn. It was packed with an unexpected assortment of items, resembling an agricultural graveyard. Ancient mechanical tillers, harvesters, mowers, rakes, shovels, ladders, and water pipes were strewn about.

The rusty collection included piles of broken furniture: drawers, cabinets, a stove, bookshelves, dinner tables, couches, chairs, coffee tables, and a grand piano. Additionally, bales of hay were stacked randomly from front to back. The packed interior juxtaposed sharply with the barren landscape outside.

Lian inspected the dusty barn with unease. She could almost feel the weight of decades of neglect pressing down on her. The others started to stream into the barn.

"Be careful," Lian warned. "There are sharp, rusted objects everywhere." Her fingers curled into tight fists to keep her nerves in check. 'The Safehouse was an unsafe animal shed,' she thought.

Nzinga quickly organized the women to clear some of the rubble to create a space for them to sit in the shade. They piled some of the debris in a corner, and the children uncovered various treasures, from dusty blankets and stuffed pillows to a few broken mirrors.

Marge glanced at the cobweb-strewn rafters and scattered debris. "This is a horror show." Her face twitched in defeat and anguish.

"But it's got shade," Onawa countered. "It's better than nothing." She gestured, indicating the space they had to work with. Her tenacity to make the best of their situation instilled confidence in the women.

"Me can clean dis place right up, mek it nice an cozy." Zenobia heaved a sigh. "Me been thru spots way wus dan dis."

Nzinga approached the back of the overcrowded structure and discovered a stack of dusty wooden crates. She unsealed one of the boxes, revealing dozens of tin cans, though many of the labels had faded.

She held up a dusty tin container for the others to see. "Food can." Nzinga carefully pried another crate open, and her fingers trembled with anticipation. It was stocked with cans of corn. "These crates are filled with provisions," she announced joyfully. The unexpected discovery of groceries brought a wave of optimism to the group.

Asia stepped closer and inspected the cartons. "Enough food for a month." She nodded approvingly. "This trip was not a waste after all."

The moment of buoyancy was abruptly shattered by a distant holler. "Stop."

The women's heads snapped towards the voice in alarm. The barn fell silent, and Asia reached for her sheathed weapon. The survivors' joy was replaced by a nervous stillness, a tense anticipation for the unknown to reveal itself. They waited breathlessly, their hearts pounding, for the next turn of events.

67. Who's There?

A shadowy individual emerged from the farmhouse's doorway and sauntered onto the porch, casting a long shadow into the hiding place. The survivors reeled. Fear and uncertainty had become their constant companion. It was an unnerving state they could never become accustomed to.

"Who's there?" The female figure's Western accent shattered the silence. She sluggishly descended the creaky porch and aimed her shotgun at the barn. "Come out now." Her voice echoed through the shed.

Lian squinted through a gap in the massive wood door. She discerned a woman in her late fifties walking straight at them. The stranger's pupils darted nervously from side to side, afraid of what she might find. Her weapon was aimed directly at Lian hiding behind the door.

Lian's mind raced. "Someone armed. Get down quickly." The migrants scrambled to hide, seeking refuge in the depths of the shelter.

Lian focused her weapon on the advancing figure.

"Stand down, Li," Asia shushed. "We don't know who it is."

The woman stared into the derelict museum and yelled. "Get out. We have protection." She steadied her aim into the barn.

Dozens of scared bodies held their breath, waiting for the lead guard to act.

Lian was unsure about her next move. She wanted to confront the woman and disarm her immediately, but that would violate Asia's order. She stood frozen in her indecision.

The stillness was broken by the sharp warning from outside, muffled slightly through the wooden walls. "Leave now. Or I'll shoot."

Asia stepped forward and called out, "Don't. We're friendly." She stared at the silhouette in the door frame and raised her hands slowly. "We're refugees looking for a night's shelter. We don't wish any harm."

"Come on out," the woman demanded. "Let me see you." She backed away a few steps but kept her weapon trained on the leader.

Asia braced herself and cautiously strode out the door with her arms held high. "I am Asia." She gestured toward the main building. "I was told this place is a Safehouse."

"Who else is with you?" The light-colored woman took another step back.

"There's a few dozen of us." Asia's lips curved into a sheepish grin. "We came a long way to find this place. We're headed North."

The elderly stranger squinted at the leader and shouldered her weapon. "I'm Katherine Gilman. This used to be a safe house." The words were heavy on her tongue.

"Nice to meet you." Asia offered a handshake.

Katherine shook her hand and leaned to the outside wall, bracing herself against the barn's disrepair. "I know this place isn't exactly in good shape. I'm sorry."

"That's okay," Asia replied. "Nothing is."

Katherine unwound and smiled. "I'll help you. Come on inside. We have food and water." She straightened up and headed toward the main building.

"Let's go," Asia shouted to her companions.

The wanderers were thrilled. The hostess of the long-sought destination offered them aid and sustenance. They exchanged hugs.

Asia led the posse inside the Safehouse, and they sat on the floor of the sparse living room. The friendly dweller hurried past the dining room and entered the kitchen at the rear. She stepped toward a tall cabinet on the right side and opened it to reveal stored foods in glass jars. "Use all you need," she said.

The women ogled the unexpected abundance.

"We've got connections with Northern growers," Katherine explained. "Plenty of last year's harvest. Potatoes, beans, and nuts. They're stored here and in the barn."

The host opened cupboards stacked with cloth bags and clay jars of dried foods. "Fruits, vegetables, and herbs. Bread is in the pantry over there." She pointed to a large closet to the left of the kitchen.

Frida was delighted to find legumes and seasonings. She grabbed her bags and restocked her supply of lentils and spices. "Wow," she gushed. "I haven't seen so many fresh ingredients in a long time." She imagined all the different cuisines she could make.

The bounty was beyond the women's expectations. After their initial impression, they could not believe such largess existed inside the derelict building. "Why do you need all this food?" Marge looked puzzled. "How many people live here?"

"Two of us, but my partner is out," Mary sighed. "We trade food to miners and use their stones to barter with growers."

"So, this stock is temporary." Asia was surprised.

Katherine nodded. "The water barrel at the back door is nearly full. Make yourselves at home." She smiled and sat at the dining table.

The mood in the Safehouse was positively lit. Asia had led the survivors to a place of safety, and they were finally able to unwind. The constant threat of hunger and thirst was gone. It was like having a second life in an alternate Universe.

Cha'Kwaina explored each floor for novelties, and the minor children followed like ducklings. They were overly excited and shouted each discovery to the Mothers below: scented soap, massage oils, cosmetics, hair and toothbrushes, toilet paper, and menstrual pads. The aged dwelling was filled with shrieks of joy and wonder.

The girls marveled at the large tub in the second-floor bathroom and the stack of clean towels in the hall closet. The Mothers made a sign-up list for sponge baths. Though dull and run-down, the Safehouse had most of what the wayfarers expected.

Zaniya rose in reverence and reached for the ceiling. "Like the mountains, Gaia's journey is slow, steady, and powerful. With each step forward, She moves closer to Her intention. Her legacy is not in Her ease, but in Her endurance, Her ability to withstand and rise again with quiet, unshakable strength."

The Crone paused, then resumed. "Rise with purpose, Daughters. Do not fear the heights ahead. You are meant to rise, to grow, to reach new horizons. Step forward and trust in your strength. Let your dreams guide you. Move forward with the strength of the mountains. You are here to climb, to grow, and to thrive. Blessed be."

68. Safehouse

It was nearing Sunset in the Western Mohave desert. Xóchitl sat outside by the gate, searching for any sign of trouble. She glanced briefly at the old dwelling with longing. She could hear the merriment inside and wished to be part of it.

But she was on guard duty and would have to wait until her shift ended. The party inside was noisy, reminding her of a Zen tale, The Loud Nun and the Bhikkhuni.

An apprentice, eager to learn, went to her Zen master and asked, "Bhikkhuni, what is the way to enlightenment?" The female monk regarded her kindly and answered, "Sit quietly and meditate."

The young nun, however, could not contain her energy. She fidgeted and tapped her foot restlessly. She talked about other teachers' wisdom, and the techniques and philosophies she learned. "I already know this, and I understand that," she droned testily. "Why don't you tell me something new?"

The female monk sat serene and silent. Then, she wordlessly motioned the nun to follow her outside. They walked to a nearby stream, and she pointed to the swiftly flowing water. "What do you hear?"

The apprentice responded immediately, "I hear the melody of rushing water."

"Indeed," her teacher noted. "And what if I told you that your words are like this rushing stream, constantly flowing and loud, but utterly empty? You speak a lot of what you know, but you do not listen to the gap between your words, and the space between your thoughts."

The nun appeared puzzled, and the Bhikkhuni explained, "When the water becomes still, it reflects the sky perfectly. Similarly, when your mind becomes quiet, you will see things like they are. But if you continue to speak and change position, the stillness of meditation is lost."

The learner became silent, and together, they sat by the stream, watching and listening to the water flowing. The Bhikkhuni beamed. "True understanding comes not from speaking, but from listening."

The tale reminded Xóchitl that wisdom often arises from introversion and stillness, and that strident reflections sometimes drown out buried, quieter truths. She gazed at the Safehouse serenely and began to appreciate being alone with her thoughts.

The setting Sun cast a warm, golden glow over the dwelling, giving it a dreamy look. The three-story building stood like a fortress. Its walls were worn yet remained upright and sturdy. The boisterous place was a model of resilience in the post-apocalypse.

The air inside the Safehouse was cool and inviting, contrary to the torridness the group had endured earlier. The women lit several oil lamps, and the vivid flickering pushed back the gathering darkness. Frida and her helpers expertly worked on dinner while Zenobia lit the fireplace.

The echoes of water washing, food bubbling, firewood popping, and people chattering floated through the aged premises. The scent of burning logs, mingled with the aroma of food simmering, imbued the bustling residence with comfort and safety.

Stirring two pots, Frida turned to the emaciated females in the living room. "Who wants to eat?" The shouts of "Me" were deafening. They attracted the girls on the second floor, who rushed down to eat.

The Cook and her two helpers piled a feast onto everyone's clay plate: penne pasta, marinara sauce, roasted corn, salsa, and pine nut salad, all topped with a dash of rosemary oil. For dessert, they chose Pueblo bread sandwiches with nut butter or fruit jelly.

The girls sat at a long rectangular table in the dining room. They ate ravenously, drank, and laughed with abandonment. They recalled funny stories from their arduous trip and planned a fashion show. Their energy was infectious. They were playful, loving, and fully immersed in every moment.

The Mothers, Crones, and women sat in a circle in the living room and ate. Asia held her hand up to speak. "We must recognize Frida and her wonderful assistants for this splendid meal." The women clapped, and the Cook took a bow.

"We must also thank our gracious host, Katherine." Asia smiled mischievously. "She wanted to shoot me but thankfully didn't."

Katherine acted out pointing her weapon at Asia, and the women broke out in raucous laughter.

The living room was bursting with warmth and light. Sitting with the Crones on the floor, Kuan-Yin noticed a couple of signboards above the front door.

One was a worn print poster that read, "Destroy the Patriarchy, not the Planet." The Crone wished the world had heeded that vital message. Sadly, they did the opposite – men destroyed fragile ecosystems and boosted male domination.

The other marker was a wooden sign with two words carved into it. The letters were red and faded but still legible. "Separatist Sisters." Kuan-Yin pointed to the placard, crinkling with intrigue. "Who are they, and what are they separating from?"

Lian stared at the poster and carving in wonder. 'Both signage are awesome,' she thought. 'But what does the engraving mean?'

"This place," Katherine commenced reverentially, "belonged to a group of women who called themselves the Separatist Sisters."

69. Separatist Sisters

It was 7:30 PM in the dried-out Central Valley. The women ate in the Safehouse's living room, absorbed in Katherine's tale. They completely tuned out the excited children eating in the dining room. It was like Cronetime for adults, a designated period for communal activities and discussions, with the householder performing.

"This shelter was established by women for women," the host began. "A dozen courageous women organized themselves for the impending collapse of government and society. Their decision to relocate to the desert was not reactionary, but a deliberate withdrawal from an untenable situation."

The Crones' smiles revealed their deep respect for the storyteller and the women of the past.

"The movement dates to the 21st century when a few women mobilized in Fresno for mutual support," Katherine continued. "It was led by Marti Gearhart, an environmental activist. She and other urban women faced mounting sexism, consumerism, environmental degradation, and social unrest."

"And insane racism," Nzinga added. "Minorities throughout California are being captured by euros and traded away to Southern slave states." The women nodded in sympathy.

"Decades before the collapse, Marti and other like-minded women fled the crowded city to this unpopulated spot in the desert." The storyteller swung her arms in a circle, her passion evident in every word. "They were gifted this property thirty miles West of Fresno. The women were from different cultures and ethnic backgrounds. Many were highly educated."

"When they arrived, they were disappointed to find that Cantua Creek no longer sang and had dried up. The land was dry, barren, and infertile." Katherine took a sip of water and resumed. "Marti realized that it would take immense effort to make the place habitable. However, she was undeterred. The land's remoteness was an advantage, and she saw the potential to create a female commune that would be safer than living in the city."

"How did they make it work?" Lian was totally engrossed in the tale.

"First, they dug an artesian well, and the water made agriculture possible." The caretaker spread her arms. "Next, they constructed a building big enough to house everyone. And finally, they made a barn to store their tools and produce. They added hundreds of bales of grass and compost. This improved the soil enough to grow fruits and vegetables."

Hehewuti sighed. "We tried to farm but failed."

"The commune was sustainable and bountiful," the storyteller disclosed. "They cultivated food and used solar and wind energy to power machines. They were self-sufficient and had few ties with the outside world."

The housekeeper pointed to the sign. "Marti coined the name *Separatist Sisters*, and the group was guided by her core beliefs of equality and uncentering men. Her favorite saying was, 'Girl, you've got to remove men from your eyeballs.' She believed that climate change and societal collapse were driven by patriarchy, male greed, and people's disconnect from nature. Their philosophy was rooted in ecofeminism."

The Crones glanced at each other in awe. They felt the same way.

"What is ecofeminism?" Lian looked baffled.

"A feminist theory that the exploitation of women and nature are interconnected," the host explained. "The women felt true liberation required dismantling both patriarchal structures and unsustainable economic practices."

"And economic racism," Asia added. "Enslavement restarted after capitalism failed." The group nodded.

"Whey dey go?" Zenobia frowned.

Katherine sighed. "The Separatist Sisters faced serious challenges. They agreed a segregated, safe space for females was essential. However, some of the younger members, who had never known the outside, began questioning their isolation. Others felt the need to help women suffering in the cities. Marti informed those who wanted to decamp to do so without guilt. And the few who stayed could leave anytime."

"What happened to Marti?" Kuan-Yin was curious.

"She died here in the commune, holding space for future generations of women." The caretaker appeared sad. "One of her final acts was to carve the sign and place it above the door." She glanced at Asia curiously. "How did you know about this place?"

Asia gestured towards Mary with a casual wave. "Our esteemed Elder mentioned a Safehouse when we were staying at the shelter on the Pacific Coast." She acknowledged the Crone with a respectful bow. "Since then, I've only dreamed about coming here."

Mary blushed from the sudden attention. "I used to live here as a child. There were many women's spaces back then. But civilization declined rapidly, and men turned female communes into brothels and traded the girls. This farmhouse is the last one in the area."

Zaniya held her arms up. "What a blessing for us. Thank you, Goddess. Girls need to feel safe, and female-only spaces like this provide that. Blessed be."

After dinner, Lian rushed outside and handed her companion a massive plate of food. Xóchitl grinned and ate hungrily.

"Want to hear about the Separatist Sisters, Bhikkhuni?" Lian beamed with anticipation.

The Latina smirked. "I thought you'd never asked." She had never seen Lian so excited. Her friend was a private person who rarely communicated. Xóchitl held a subtle poise that suggested she was aware of the impact the knowledge would have on her. "Lay it all on me," she encouraged with a mouthful of food.

70. Zaniya's Cronetime

It was 8 PM in the Central Valley. The full Moon bathed the Safehouse in silvery light, and a gentle breeze swirled through the open windows. Inside, the living room was framed by flickering candles and the fireplace. The vibrant illumination created long dancing shadows on the walls that appeared like a fast-paced puppet show.

Hehewuti held her head high and twinkled. "Let's get ready for our nightly ritual. Girls, come downstairs. It's Cronetime." The women and children gathered in a tight circle in the center of the living room. The Crone stood calmly by the kitchen door and rang a small bell.

Zaniya emerged from the dark kitchen and entered the living room in a flowing white gown. Her face and hands were covered in vivid white, giving her an almost otherworldly presence. Three glass bead necklaces adorned her neck, reflecting the candlelight like a spiral Galaxy.

She wore bracelets on her hands and feet that jingled with every gesture, adding a rhythmic accompaniment to her movements. A jewel crown rested on her head, sparkling like Stars. Zaniya strode elegantly into the room, her gown swishing like a rippling pool. Her audience, struck with awe, could not take their eyes off her.

Hehewuti accompanied her, carrying a basin of water. With a graceful bow, she gestured for Hehewuti to leave the bowl near the window. She tilted the basin, aligning it perfectly to capture the full Moon. The water rippled, creating a mesmerizing light. She used a circular mirror to catch the Moonbeam and reflected it around the room. The lunar lighting was so enchanting that it held the audience spellbound.

The Crone was lit by candlelight, resonances off the water's surface, and the gleaming mirror. With a high-pitched wail, Zaniya launched into her performance. Her ululation rose and fell and became chants that blended seamlessly into each other. Each chant was punctuated by the lively jingle of bracelets, creating a hypnotic rhythm that echoed through the Safehouse.

She flounced with fluidity and purpose, miming a story about the early Earth, Theia, and their daughter, Luna. Her motions flowed into each other, appearing to have no beginning or end. She frolicked with the mirror, using intricate poses and hand gestures to tell an eternal tale of birth, life, and death.

Shadows on the walls swayed as she spun and chanted. The Moonlight's reflections off the water and mirror added a mystical vibe to the scene. The lunar ballet was a silent play of loss and renewal, and the girls sat spellbound, engrossed in the magic of jingles, dance, pulsing beads, and enchanting light. Their eyes sparkled with wonder, and their hearts beat in rhythm with the hypnotic performance.

The metaphorical Moon dance continued, and Zaniya whirled and twirled until she collapsed onto the floor with a flourish. The girls cheered wildly.

The Crone sat with poise and twinkled. She carefully chalked a word on the floor, and the girls squinted at the unfamiliar term.

"What does it say?" Lisa bubbled with curiosity, her eyes wide with anticipation.

"Take a guess." Zaniya grinned mischievously, her eyes twinkling in the candlelight.

Cha'Kwaina leaned closer, touched the letters, and sounded them out. "A-P-S-A-R-A," she pronounced. "Apsara." The word lingered in the air.

"She was a Goddess," Ma'at declared.

Zaniya chuckled. "Not quite. An Apsara isn't a Goddess, but a spirit from the clouds and waters, capable of changing shape whenever she wishes."

"Bet." Phoolan was impressed. "Wish I could."

Sasha's imagination ignited. "Like a mermaid?"

"Yes." Zaniya rattled her bangles for emphasis. "But not only water. Apsaras were ethereal beings who floated through the skies, like angels."

"Mermaid angels." Lisa's face lit up.

Cha'Kwaina pieced it together. "So, they're like petite Goddesses of the water and sky?"

"Yes." Zaniya stood up. "Apsaras were youthful dancing divas." She whirled elegantly, mimicking the nature spirits she described.

She adjusted the water bowl, letting it catch the Moonlight, and swirled the liquid. "They waltz like the Earth and Moon, spinning like this." The water circled and sparkled in the Moonlight. "Come and join me. Let's party like Apsaras."

The children jumped up with excitement. They began orbiting in pairs, mimicking the Moon revolving around the Earth. They spun and circled until they dropped from vertigo.

Laughter and merriment filled the Safehouse, echoing off the walls. Zaniya, swaying with approval, glowed at the joyous atmosphere.

"See, I'm an Apsara?" Lisa rotated vigorously.

Elon smirked, "Girls can't be angels."

"Why not?" Sasha struck a dramatic pose mid-twirl. "We don't have powers, but we can dance."

"Can Elon be an Apsara?" Lisa wondered.

Zaniya winked at the boy and twisted. "Anyone can learn to curl like an Apsara. We may not turn into one, but the joy and magic of trying is real enough."

Cha'Kwaina laughed and made a grand gesture. "Then let's dance." The living room vibrated in an energetic rave, with Zaniya's bangles keeping a fast beat. The women looked at each other in amusement. Zaniya's Cronetime was always good times.

71. Breakfast

It was the 38th day of the survivors' move to the North and their second morning at the Safehouse. Simone, 41, the Mother of Ma'at, and Gloria, 35, the Mother of Sasha, were the Sunup guards. It was 6 AM, and the pair gazed East in anticipation.

A mellow light brushed the serene atmosphere above the Badlands. They watched in amazement as dawn beautifully transitioned from dark indigo to lighter shades of lavender and pink. An intense orb of golden warmth arose from the edge, casting a vibrant orange over the gray scenery. Shadows quickly receded, giving way to a brilliant shine that painted the tops of dunes with promise. The landscape seemed to exhale a tranquil breath. Daylight began anew.

"The cycle of life continues." Gloria smiled.

"It's so amazing." Simone nodded. "Birth, death, and rebirth."

Beams of radiance filtered through the windows of the dim Safehouse. The dwelling was alive with the children's commotion. The kitchen, a calm harbor amid the storm of activity, was alive with Frida and Marge's nurturing presence. They hovered over the stove, preparing breakfast.

The heavenly scent of lightly fried nopal tamales wafted through the house, mingling with the aroma of boiling oats and the fresh bouquet of cut fruit. The spacious galley was a comforting reminder of the weeks of shared meals and the bond it fostered.

Breakfast was served. The children's faces were bright and fresh, like the food. They eagerly ate at the large wooden table in the dining room, their chatter filled with plans and excitement for the day ahead.

Cha'Kwaina, wearing a clean dress, tasted her hot oats. "This cereal is highkey." She beamed at Sasha and quickly scooped another spoonful.

Sasha spread jam on two slices of bread and took a bite. "This breakfast is slay."

"This place is da GOAT." Cha'Kwaina's lips parted in a wide smile. "So glad we made it."

Sasha gave a thumbs up. "I feel like we could get the farm up and running again." Her friend nodded and scarfed another spoon of oats.

Asia and Nzinga sat in muted conversation in a crook near the front door. The leader looked up and clapped to get the women's attention. "Let's make the most of our time here. Organize your activities for the day and use it fully." The women agreed.

The Mothers helped Frida clean the kitchen and created a laundry schedule. Some of the Crones left to forage for cacti to make wine. Kuan-Yin scheduled a self-defense class for the girls in the living room. And

Lian planned weapons training for the young women in the barn.

The drifters' spirits were renewed in the rare refuge from their harsh reality of violence, disease, and famine. The living room vibrated with activity.

The first activity was morning yoga with Onawa in the living room. The Mother sat in the morning light and led the girls through a forward fold, pyramid pose, bridge, cat-cow, triangle, tree pose, and reclined twists. At the end of the stretching exercise, Onawa shared an Indigenous tradition, sparking a sense of wonder in the girls.

"The Diné instill in their children the belief that every morning brings a completely new Sun," she began. "Each day, the Sun is born, shines for only one day, and then sets in the evening, never to rise again." The girls were amazed at the Navajo's wisdom.

The Hopi teacher continued, "Once the children reach an age where they can understand the concept of temporary existence, the adults take them outside at dawn, saying, 'The Sun has only this day. You must make the most of it, ensuring the Sun doesn't waste its precious time.' Realizing the value of each day is a great way to live and reconnect with our innate joy."

Next, Onawa asked Kuan-Yin to enlighten the class with a Zen tale. The martial arts instructor grinned. "Two female nuns at the Buddhist sangha were arguing about a flag fluttering in the wind." Kuan-Yin waved her hands. "One student insisted, 'The flag is moving.' The other countered, 'No, the wind is moving.' Both students felt they were right." The storyteller paused and asked, "What do you think?"

The class erupted in disagreements. Opinions were equally divided between flag and wind. The children, eager to win, vigorously argued for their views, and a shouting match ensued. Eventually, they grew quiet and turned to the Crone, begging for the answer.

Kuan-Yin smiled and continued her tale. "A female monk, or Bhikkhuni, overheard the two nuns in conflict and decided to intervene. 'The flag is fluttering in the wind. But neither the flag nor the wind is moving. It is your mind that is moving.'"

Kuan-Yin's answer did not please anyone.

"What does it mean?" Cha'Kwaina was puzzled.

The Crone took a deep breath and gazed gently at the girls, "What does this story mean to you?"

"It's the wind," Ma'at answered confidently.

Kuan-Yin touched the teen's hand and responded soothingly, "Both answers could be right or wrong. We don't know. And our views may vary from one day to the next. This clever tale is about movement, both inside of us and the outside. And it suggests that what is real is beyond our understanding."

"Just tell us who's right." Lisa was frustrated, her emotional investment in the story evident.

The Crone smiled. "The nuns' argument represents being caught up in appearances. Maybe Earth's passage around the Sun moves both wind and flag." She paused for her point to sink in.

"Sick." Sasha was amazed. "The Earth is moving."

"Things may not be what they appear to be," Kuan-Yin continued. "The Bhikkhuni's position is that both nuns were trapped in opposite thinking. They were focusing on objects, instead of realizing that their perception or mind is what's truly moving."

The children looked baffled, and Kuan-Yin explained further, "Your perception of the desert changes in the day and night, right?" The girls agreed. "This shows that our minds interpret and give meaning to the world, rather than the external objects themselves being the ultimate truth." She stood silent while her audience reflected on her Zen tale.

"That's like how the heat affects me," Sasha exclaimed suddenly. "It all depends on my mood. Wow, I get it now." The children exchanged other examples of how their opinions of reality shifted.

Kuan-Yin shined. "Alright, girls, let's get ready for self-defense class."

72. Wine

It was morning in the Badlands. Simone and Gloria stood vigilant at the gate as the landscape slowly surrendered to the advancing daylight. The barn, a proof of the farm's former prosperity, stood tall at the back of the property. Its weather-beaten wood, a witness to the slow passage of time, echoed the spirit of the women who used it four decades ago.

Outside the West side of the barn, four Crones sat at a table in the shade, diligently making wine near a firepit. Hehewuti, Zaniya, Mary, and Zenobia chatted while a pot of water boiled above the fire. Laughter and banter filled the air, indicating their deep friendship.

Hehewuti moved with a speed that defied her age. Her dedication to the craft of winemaking was evident. She carefully selected and prepared the prickly pear cacti fruits, ensuring that only the best would be used.

She peeled the skin and removed the fruit's seeds. Leaving the pits would make the liquor bitter. She saved the seeds to juice and make oil later. She sliced the thick, spiny skins into small squares and placed them into a jar to make jam. She handed the peeled fruits to Zaniya, who chopped them into tiny pieces and placed them into the boiling pot over the fire.

Mary, the tallest of the squad, stirred the fruit in the pot. She was a woman of few words, and when she spoke, her voice was like the low rumble of distant thunder, directing attention. After simmering for twenty minutes, she ladled the pears into a clay mixing bowl on the table. "Here you go," she announced.

Zenobia, the youngest Crone, mashed the boiled fruit in the mixing bowl. "Dis grain is gonna be good," she remarked while humming a lovely tune. Her wild and untamed curly hair framed her face, much like her personality. She added lemon juice, raisins, and cane sugar and stirred the mixture. She covered the bowl with a thin cloth and left it to ferment for an hour.

After the first fermentation, the Firekeeper squeezed the cooled juice through a cloth strainer into a wine bottle. She added sugar and yeast, corked the bottle, and left the mixture to ferment again. She handled the liquor like it was a precious gift.

The Crones worked quickly. Hehewuti took the filled bottle and placed it in the shade. "We have to watch the temperature during storage," she cautioned. "Cooler temperatures can cause the fermentation to be slower and may even stop it altogether. Higher temperatures can result in off-flavors."

The other Crones nodded. They had less experience in the process and trusted the Elder's judgment.

Hehewuti beamed and continued, "The wine will be dry when it's done fermenting. We can add more sugar if you prefer a sweeter taste."

Zaniya shrugged. "I don't care either way."

"I like it dry." Hehewuti smiled. "Dryer gets you higher." She grinned.

They worked quietly to finish another bottle.

"Think it's 'nough to trade?" Zenobia wondered.

Hehewuti pondered how much they could transport. "It'll have to do." She glanced at the filled container. "We're making a dozen bottles. That's more than we can carry."

The Firekeeper pointed to a fermenting bottle. "Each wan is precious. Da passage ahead ain't gonna be easy, so we gon need every last drop fuh trade." She stared at the ten empty receptacles. "We makin' it strong, means we aimin' fuh ah bigger trade." She corked the third bottle.

Hehewuti looked at her companions, sensing the unspoken thought that lingered between them. She set down her knife and reached out, touching Zaniya's back. "Elders, let's take a bottle for ourselves. There's no need to feel guilty."

Zaniya smiled. "After all that walking, we deserve to treat ourselves gently." She pointed to the house. "It'll be a good reward for everyone."

The Firekeeper did a cheerful dance. "Y'all, leh we raise we glasses tonight 'fore Cronetime." Her sight met Mary's, who beamed in silent understanding.

"Oh, what a good time it'll be." Hehewuti chuckled.

"I'll be toasting with tea." Mary frowned. "I like alcohol, but alcohol doesn't like me. I woke up with a hangover so bad, I thought I was allergic to fun."

Hehewuti snorted. "Last night, I thought I was the life of the party. This morning, I realized I was the cautionary tale." The Crones cracked up. "So, I finally decided to quit drinking for good. Now I drink for evil." There were more giggles, and she continued telling jokes. "What do you call a drunk cactus?" They looked at her expectantly. "A spiked drink."

Hehewuti banged the table hard. "My doctor told me to watch my drinking, so now I drink in front of a mirror." She got more laughs. "A bartender broke up with her girlfriend, but she kept asking for another shot. But you know, we have to take life with a grain of salt. Plus, a slice of lime and a shot of tequila."

"Oh, me gats wan," Zenobia blurted. "Me told meself long ago dat me must stop drinkin'. But me ain't 'bout to listen to some drunk who talk to sheself."

"You're right to ignore her." Zaniya slapped her thighs. "As for me, I only drink on days that start with 'T' - Tuesday, Thursday, today, and tomorrow. And since I started this liquor diet, I've lost three days already." Her audience rolled in laughter.

Zaniya grinned at Mary. "Hangovers are just your body's reminder that you had too much fun. You should drink wine because it's not good to keep things bottled up. I'm not saying alcohol is the answer, but it helped me to forget the question."

"Okay, last one," Mary squealed. "What did the bartender say after a book walked into the bar?" She glanced at the baffled faces. "Please, no stories."

The Crones laughed heartily and continued their brewing. Though aged and battered, like the Safehouse, they were tough and cheerful. And reminiscent of the liquor, their camaraderie was a source of warmth and comfort.

Zaniya opened her palms in reverence. "Like the mountains at Sunset, Gaia allows the shadows to stretch over Her form, knowing they do not diminish Her but make her more profound. The mountain's shadow stretches with the Sun. The Earth Goddess understands that to rise high is to cast a shadow. Embracing the Sun makes Her whole. Blessed be." The Elders bowed to Zaniya, expressing thanks.

While they worked, the Crones mentally prepared themselves for whatever lay ahead. They knew that their bond, like the wine they fermented, would become stronger and sustain them in the future.

73. Water Mission

Bright light filtered through the shuttered windows of the Separatist Sisters' refuge. After breakfast, the girls did yoga with Onawa in the living room. Asia and Nzinga sat by the front door, staring at a tattered map.

The leader searched for a route to a local spring. She was relieved that the collective was recovering and adding calories. They could remain at the refuge for a week or more. However, the water barrel at the door was nearly empty, a cause for concern.

To address the situation, Xóchitl, Riri, and Daria dug the bottom of the dry well behind the barn. Despite a day of effort with no sign of moisture, they persevered. The task was arduous, but their unity and camaraderie made it bearable.

Asia's finger hovered over a location marked with a faded cross. "Katherine says this is the spring."

Nzinga leaned to examine the chart. "That's a hard five miles." Her face was a storm of emotions. "On the return, carrying two full cans will slow you down. It's too risky going alone."

"I need you here." Asia wanted the Nzinga to stay and guard the group. "It's my inkling and no one else. You should help them dig the well."

Nzinga shrugged. "That's a lost cause. The water table is probably hundreds of feet below."

"You don't know that." Asia was moody. "And there's no harm in trying."

Nzinga touched her friend's back. "There's enough hands on deck." She sighed. "Let me go with you." She was deeply concerned about her partner's safety.

Asia shook her head. "We can't afford to lose two people. You need to lead if I get lost or killed."

"Two of us stand a better chance." Nzinga smiled. "We wouldn't get popped, I promise."

Asia met Nzinga's stare and realized she could not dissuade her. "We need to be hasty and discreet." She adjusted the straps on her pack. "We can't lead any pedos back here."

"Discreet is my middle name." Nzinga grinned.

The pair informed Lian of their excursion and left the Safehouse. The route required strenuous climbing over steep dunes and hills. They had to avoid trails and use natural cover to hide from potential threats.

Nzinga led, and they navigated the jagged topography with a steady rhythm. Each step was carefully placed, avoiding loose rocks and hidden dips that might twist an ankle and slow their progress. The late morning Sun pummeled downward mercilessly, casting almost no shadow.

The two seasoned hikers were accustomed to the dance of survival in the desert. Nzinga checked the surroundings with strict vigilance. She raised her hand, signaling for Asia to halt. They breathed heavily, assessing the background.

Asia listened intently for any unnatural sounds. The stillness differed utterly from the excited buzz they left at the Safehouse. She smiled, thinking about all the fun the girls were having, and became more tenacious about extending their stay.

They pushed onward through a dense patch of scrub. A bird call pierced the mysterious territory, indicating that an enduring ecosystem existed beyond their struggle. Asia considered each call a good omen.

They navigated the undulating terrain with skill and grit. Even with their strength and experience, the expedition was taxing. And after a while, the landscape shifted. Sand and rock gave way to cacti, silverbush, shrubs, and a glimpse of distant mountains.

"What is that highland?" Nzinga pointed East.

"The Western Sierra Nevada mountains, 150 miles away." Asia was surprised that the Sierras were visible, but she stood on a high ridge. "The Sequoia Forest."

"The Giant Sequoia trees?" Nzinga gushed.

Asia nodded. "Our California natives were the most massive individual trees in the world. A hundred years ago, about 60,000 remained. They grew to over 200 feet with a trunk of 20 feet. Some dated to over 3,000 years, older than the Buddha."

"Wow. I always wanted to see them." Nzinga peered into the distance with her binoculars, imagining she could see one.

"They're long gone." Asia sighed. "Logging, fires, drought, and disease. They didn't stand a chance."

"No way." Nzinga was devastated. "A single tree lived through the Bronze Age and countless empires: Sumer, Indus, Kush, Egypt, Xia, Greek, Shang, Persia, Zhou, Roman, Inca, Maya, Qin, Han, Aztec, Aksum, Arab, Tang, Mali, Songhai, Ghana, Swahili, Nok, Moor, Song, Ming, Qing, Mongol, Ottoman, Spanish, British, Iroquois, and American. After existing for all that time, that Sequoia is now gone? What chance do we have?" Asia did not have an answer.

The pair continued pacing soundlessly, remaining cautious. After twenty minutes, they paused for a break from the unremitting glare, their breaths coming in heavy puffs.

Asia unfolded the scrunched map and studied it. "We're on track. The water source should be below that far ridge on the left."

Nzinga looked towards the spring's direction. "We'll have to approach with caution. There may be others at the water hole." Her voice carried the tension of the situation, and they both remained on high alert, ready to face any potential threats.

"I hope not." Asia sagged. She glanced at the ridge, and the stress of the danger pressed down on her like a ton of bricks. Still, she was mentally prepared to fight for the spring if necessary.

They climbed and became lost in thought. Asia reflected on the fragile collective and their precarious flight to safety. The responsibility of keeping the group together weighed heavily on her shoulders.

Out in the wilderness, every decision she made felt like a matter of life or death. The pressure of making the wrong turn was nerve-racking, but second-guessing herself was unhelpful. She needed to be more reflective, but she also had to be wary of uncertainty.

Yet, she could not stop worrying that dissent would tear the collective apart. How would the comfort of the Safehouse affect them after they leave? Would they become more ill-tempered and feistier? Aisha, Marge, and other Mothers were already rebellious.

Could she manage to contain all their competing interests and keep everyone united? She did not know, but she had to keep trying. If they stayed together, they would have a better chance of protecting the fifteen girls. On the other hand, they could perish quickly if they separated into individual or small groups.

Unlike Asia's worrisome thoughts, Nzinga swaggered ahead with serene confidence. She pondered the Safehouse and was glad that her companions were comfortable. She focused on the steep hill and looked forward to rejoining the party at the sanctuary.

74. Diamondback

It was early afternoon in the parched Central Valley. Asia and Nzinga pressed on with their mission to secure water from a local spring. The uphill trek under the blistering Sun was grueling.

Suddenly, a faint rustling shattered the silence, causing the duo to freeze. Asia pointed in the direction of the sound. "Pedos?" Her heart raced with the possibility of danger. "Let's take cover."

They crouched behind some dense brush with their backs pressed against the rough leaves.

"How many?" Nzinga clutched her weapon.

"Can't tell." Asia's expression darkened. "Possibly wildlife. Stay low and ready."

Nzinga shifted her stance, preparing for whatever might emerge through the bushes.

They waited in edgy silence, their pulse racing. After a few minutes, no one approached, and Asia got up to investigate. The couple slowly advanced toward a narrow pass between two large rocks.

"Hisssss." A loud vibration disrupted the stillness. Asia's heart skipped a beat when she spotted the source, a giant rattlesnake coiled in the middle of their path. The snake's oculars locked onto her, its rattle shaking menacingly.

Nzinga's mouth gaped when she saw the massive snake. "Damn it, I hate snakes." Her face contorted, and a shiver ran down her spine. "Let's get out of here."

Asia swallowed the lump in her throat. "We're not turning back. This is the route."

"We've got to." Nzinga was freaking out.

Asia took a long breath. 'I must center myself,' she thought. 'Be in the moment.' She focused on breathing. Her body loosened, her breath became even, and she made peace with the animal. "We'll wait it out," she insisted. "If we give it space, it'll leave."

"Huh?" Nzinga's pupils darted nervously. Her body was in fight or flight mode. She shivered and aimed her weapon at the creature.

"Don't shoot," Asia warned. "It may tip off others, and then we'll have bigger problems."

"But what if it attacks?" Nzinga wanted to scream.

"It will not." Asia's body remained immobile. "Snakes usually won't strike unless they feel threatened. We must be patient."

"For how long?" Nzinga's tone betrayed the panic she struggled to suppress.

Minutes passed, though it seemed like hours. It felt like the Sun was baking a pie, and Asia and Nzinga were the filling. The snake lay stubbornly in place, and its occasional rattle was the only sound.

Nzinga's mind raced. Every muscle wanted to flee, and she fought mightily not to run.

"Be still," Asia shushed. "If not, it'll take longer."

Nzinga shook. She held her friend's shoulder for support and took deep breaths.

"That's right, just breathe," Asia urged. "Snakes are mostly harmless. They represent the underground and female energy. Your fear of them is part of male demonizing of nature and the womb."

Nzinga calmed down. "I've got a lot of male energy, I know. I've had to become hard like them so I could deal with all the racism down South."

Asia looked sad. "I'm sorry. I shouldn't have judged you. You've got fewer options than I do. So, you have to be less trustful to survive."

Nzinga shook her head. "Everywhere I go, I face multiple forms of male oppression. Sexism, racism, ecocide, micro aggression, cultural imperialism... It's never-ending. And it's left me with many traumas."

Asia remained quiet, sensing her friend needed space to reflect.

Nzinga sighed. "It's not like one tyranny is better than another. They're all horrible. Being female and getting trafficked by men for sex is terrible. Becoming enslaved by racists for being a minority leaves you completely brutalized. Drinking polluted water can kill you. You're on guard all the time. It's too much."

Nzinga was on the verge of tears, and Asia held her hand in support.

"Down South, they don't usually hang females. Women are valued as prostitutes." Nzinga sniffed. "But Africans and Latinos are completely despised. European men form hunting parties and kill us for fun and sport." Tears rolled down her face. "Racists could hang me just for a science experiment, to see how long my body takes to die."

"I'm so sorry." Asia wept with her partner. "Things will be different up North, I promise."

The duo sat in silence. It seemed like the diamondback was listening to their conversation and felt sad for them. It uncoiled, slithered off the path, and disappeared into the brush.

Nzinga exhaled in relief. "Thank you, Goddess." A comforting smile touched her lips.

Asia's mood improved. "Patience is bitter, but its fruit is sweet."

The pair continued their expedition and reached the water source without further incident. It was a small, trickling stream shielded by dense vegetation. The sight of the water brought overwhelming relief, and they took a moment to bask in their success. Nzinga scouted ahead and confirmed they were alone.

Asia set up the first water sack. "It'll take twenty minutes to fill these up." She pointed to her backpack. "After this, let's eat."

She straightened her back, radiating a quiet strength. "This journey has been difficult. But despite the heat, thirst, starvation, attacks by wild dogs, pedos, and Jeffery, we've lost no one."

Nzinga's mouth crinkled at the corners. "You're not counting the boys."

Asia's forehead gathered in contemplation. "We didn't lose them. They left on their own free will."

Nzinga sighed and said nothing.

With containers filled, the couple headed back toward the Safehouse, remaining cautious and alert.

"Luck and cooperation," Asia concluded her point. "No matter what happened, we faced it together."

"Thanks to your leadership." Nzinga smiled.

Asia beamed. "And your bravery."

"Except for snakes," Nzinga whined. They laughed.

The shared experience with the diamondback and finding the spring reinforced their spirit. They were more than survivalist friends. They were partners, united by their shared objective to ensure the safety of their female collective.

75. Training Day

It was the morning after the climate refugees arrived at the Safehouse in California's Badlands. Simone and Gloria were on watch duty. They stood by the gate of the Safehouse, a former sanctuary for those seeking refuge and empowerment, on the lookout for any looming threat.

After breakfast, the spacious living room was abuzz with activity. The freshly swept wooden floor became a tai chi dojo for the girls, a united wall lined up in front of Kuan-Yin. The exercise was intended to hone the girls' skills, build their confidence, and foster a sense of solidarity. The windows were open, and cross-ventilation cooled the makeshift practice area.

Kuan-Yin, 60, stood with her arms resting. Her calm demeanor was in sharp contrast to the energetic girls'. Her long, silver hair was tied back in a neat braid, and she wore a simple tunic that allowed ease of movement. For the second time, she demonstrated an inward block with fluid precision.

"Self-defense is not only about combat." The Crone announced. From the guard position, she turned her left arm inward to the right, leaving her closed fist turned towards her face. "It's about protecting yourself and others while being aware of your surroundings." The Sensei repeated the block in slow motion. "Situational awareness is critical. The mind is calmer when it understands the environment."

"What if someone attacks you from behind?" Greta, 13, grabbed her neck.

"Good question." Kuan-Yin nodded approvingly. "Remain calm, then try to break free using your elbows. Twist your body like this and aim for their midsection. Let's practice this defense."

The children paired up and mimicked their Sensei.

Kayla, 8, elbowed Lisa. "Sorry," she apologized.

"I'm okay." Lisa, 11, brushed off the sting.

Kuan-Yin walked over and adjusted Kayla's stance. "Make sure you're not too rigid. Move with the flow of the attack, not against it."

Ma'at, 12, spoke up. "Elder Kuan-Yin, how do we stay calm when we're scared?" The girls stared at her.

"Fear is normal," the Sensei said. "Training helps you to manage fear. Do these moves until they become second nature. That way, when you're scared, your body responds naturally since it knows what to do."

The children took Kuan-Yin's words to heart and continued exercising. They practiced five basic blocks: rising head level, inside hooking, outside, downward, and groin sweep. With each repetition, they grew more confident in their self-defense skills.

In the barn, the teens were engaged in kick training with Lian, dressed in practical, battle-worn gear. Phoolan, 16, was her assistant. The dusty air was filled with grunts and the occasional instruction from Lian, urging the girls to kick, withdraw, and stay grounded.

"Keep your weight balanced and your guard up, Cha-Cha," Lian called out, correcting her form.

Cha'Kwaina, 14, dripping with sweat, adjusted her position. "It's harder than it looks."

"We need to be prepared for any situation, Sisters." Lian demonstrated a front kick. "The five tenets of karate are courtesy, integrity, perseverance, self-control, and stubborn spirit."

Sasha, 15, glanced over at the Sensi. "How do you stay so focused? Doesn't it get tiring?"

Lian chuckled. "It does, but we're not only training our bodies. We're training our minds to be durable." Her emphasis on mental strength highlighted her holistic approach to training.

Encouraged by Lian's words, the teen girls pushed themselves, and their kicks became more precise and fluid. They practiced front, round, side, and back kicks.

The Sun neared its midday intensity, but few of the students noticed. The barn and living room were filled with the sounds of combat until the training sessions ended for lunch.

Revived, the two groups of students sat at the dining table sharing stories from their training. Their determination and focus inspired each other. After lunch, the teens gathered outside in a circle around Lian and Phoolan. The two Sensei stood under the shade, holding sturdy wooden poles.

Lian tapped her rod on the ground. "Sisters, we're going to learn stick fighting. A stick is a powerful tool if you know how to use it."

She stepped forward, probing the eager faces before her. "The first thing you need to understand is balance." The Sensei demonstrated a low, grounded stance. "Keep your feet apart, knees slightly bent, like an oval. You need to be ready to step in any direction."

Cha'Kwaina mimicked Lian's stance. "Like this?"

The Sensei smiled. "Exactly. Stay light on your feet but rooted to the ground. You want to be able to react quickly while remaining stable."

Lian adjusted Sasha's grip on her pole. "Hold the rod firmly, but not too tight. You need to swing with speed and control." She sliced the air with her stick. "Remember, the key is to strike with precision, not brute force. Guide the shaft so it does the work."

The training session progressed, and the courtyard buzzed with striking lumber. The teens practiced deflection, blocking, and striking from their left shoulder, right shoulder, and left hip. The Sensei went among the students, offering tips and corrections.

"Remember to strike and withdraw," Lian said. "Now that you've got the basics, let's practice putting down an attacker." A hush fell over the teens.

Phoolan formed a mock, aggressive stance, rushed towards Lian, and swung her rod at her. "First, block the attacker." The Sensei deflected the blow with a swift motion. "Then counter." She simulated a hit on Phoolan's side, stopping short of contact.

"Aim for vulnerable spots like ribs, knees, groin, and head," Lian instructed. "You don't have to overpower them. You only need to be quick and precise enough to incapacitate them briefly to get away."

Ma'at raised her hand. "What if they're stronger than us?"

"Good question." Lian signaled Phoolan to attack. "If they're bigger, use their motion against them." She shifted her weight, evaded the attacker, and kicked her forward. "Leverage is your friend. The key is to stay calm, think on your feet, and use their momentum."

Lisa grappled with the idea of actual combat. "What if we really hurt them?"

Lian's features slackened. "It's never easy. But if it's your life or theirs, you must do what it takes to protect yourself. We fight to survive, not to harm."

The training session continued with more drills and guidance, and the girls grew more confident in their abilities. Around 3 PM, the Sensei assembled her students for a final word.

Lian held her fist up. "When we fight as a unit, we survive together. Trust in your skills and rely on each other." The Sensei bowed. "We practice again tomorrow."

The young women exchanged strong-willed glances. They knew the way ahead would be fraught with danger, but they had taken a crucial step towards being ready for whatever came their way. Their camaraderie and mutual support were evident. They ran to the Safehouse for snacks but allowed the minor children to enter first.

At 6:30 PM, Asia and Nakeisha returned from the well, flushed with exertion. Their shoulders hunched, laden with eight sacks of water, but their spirits were high. They carefully refilled the barrel in the kitchen to the brim and kicked back, pleased with the day's effort.

Frida, the Mothers, Crones, and other women were amazed. Asia did not disclose the purpose of her trip when she left in the morning, and they were overjoyed by the resupply of precious liquid. Xóchitl, Riri, Daria, and the other diggers were also ecstatic when they found out they no longer had to dig the dry well. The women, guards, and scouts rallied around their leader and toasted with sweet-tasting spring water.

Zaniya beamed at Asia and rose in prayer. "All praises to Gaia. Her power is the kind that moves unseen, like roots spreading deep in the Earth or rivers that flow beneath the surface. In Her heart, She carries both dawn and dusk, each blending into the other, each necessary to fully see Her power and purpose."

The Crone held her arms wide. "Daughters, like a mountain, ground yourself in who you are. Seek the mountain within you, a power so rooted, so grounded, that no storm can shift it. Stand tall in your truth and let nothing break your spirit. Let the world adjust to the heights of your spirit. Blessed be."

76. Extortion

The afternoon Sun dipped at a snail's pace in the barren wilderness, casting long shadows across the yard of the Safehouse. The dry atmosphere was profusely saturated with heat and dust as the thermometer held steadily at its daily high of 135°F (57°C). The worn refuge for women in the post-apocalyptic Central Valley glistened in the haze.

It had been 40 days since the group left the shelter and four days at the Safehouse. Each day, the washed-out abode felt more like a proper home. The girls started referring to it as Barbie's House.

Xóchitl was the lone guard outside. She crouched behind a thick bush about twenty feet from the fence, wondering what Lian was up to in the three-story dwelling. She wished she had her company.

Suddenly, Xóchitl stiffened. The dry wind carried a faint noise to her ears. It sounded like two male Spanish voices from the path outside. She cleared her mind and stared past the perimeter.

Two forms emerged from the haze, moving with a rush that set her instincts on high alert. She gave the owl threat signal but was unsure if anyone heard it inside the boisterous residence. She did not have time to run to the front door and provide a warning. She called out repeatedly, "We've got company."

Two Latinos in their twenties hastily approached the property and stopped outside the fence. One was tall and lanky with torn and dusty clothes. The other man was medium height and wore a wide-brimmed hat that shaded his face. It did little to hide the uncertainty in his movements.

The men's grim faces were etched with the hardships and brutality of their lives. The tall man reached for the gate and pushed against it frantically. The metal chain and padlock rattled but held firm.

"Stop. Or I'll shoot." Xóchitl's command vibrated through the fence like a buzz saw. She remained hidden behind the bush. "Who are you?"

"Nosotros somos SCB," the tall man answered. He ogled through the fence to find the speaker. "Abrir y pagar." His tone was laced with angst.

Xóchitl's pulse sped up. Sindicato de Cuchillos Brutales, the Brutal Knives Syndicate, was a gang known for its ruthless tactics and so-called protection services that amounted to extortion. 'Open up and pay.' What were they demanding?

"Entrégalo a nosotros," the man with the hat demanded harshly. "Comida ahora, cerda." He glanced over his shoulder nervously.

'Were there others on the path behind them?' Xóchitl wondered. She translated their words as she sized them up. 'Give it to us. Food now, pig.' The Latinos did not have any guns displayed, but they were still dangerous. She had to prevent them from entering the premises. The best option was to get them to leave.

"Nosotras no tenemos comida ahora," she asserted. "We don't have any food now."

The tall man exchanged a quick glance with his companion. "Esta es Latina." He leaned against the gate. "Ahora, o te arrepentirás," he yelled.

'Now, or you'll regret it.' Xóchitl wondered what the two could do. They seemed reluctant to jump the fence. She stuck her rifle out of the bush, and it sparkled in the golden evening light.

"¿Cuánto cuesta?" Xóchitl shouted. "How much?" She had to keep them talking to buy time for Lian, Asia, and the others inside to prepare for whatever came next.

The tall man banged his fist on the fence and barked. "Dos cestas de comida, ahora." He rattled the chain on the gate for emphasis.

'Two baskets of food, now.' Xóchitl let out a short, humorless laugh. "¿Dos cestas? Nosotras no tenemos tanta comida." She repeated herself in English. "We don't have that much food. By no means. De ninguna manera."

"Escucha puta," the man with the hat shouted. "No hablamos de términos."

Xóchitl's face hardened. 'Listen, bitch. We're not talking about terms.' That was uncalled for. She did not trust these men. Their sudden appearance reeked of a trap.

Her mind raced. What should she do? The potential danger to the girls loomed like a dark cloud. Either she eliminated the threat or gave them a small concession.

"Está bien, bueno." She needed to stall them some more. "Okay, good." They expected two baskets of food, but enough was inside to easily fulfill that demand. Was that why Katherine kept so many supplies, to pay for protection? And where was Lian? Did she know what was happening?

"Yo iré a buscar la comida," Xóchitl promised. "I'll get the food." She remained behind the shrub, her weapon pointing at the pair. "Mantente fuera de la valla. Wait outside."

The tall man's face eased slightly. "Está bien. Rápido."

The front door slammed, and footsteps approached from the house. Xóchitl's pulse slowed when she recognized Asia's steady stride. The leader pointed a rifle at the gate and stopped beside her.

"What's going on here?" Asia spoke calmly, but there was an unmistakable undertone of authority.

Xóchitl glanced at Asia. "SCB men demanding two food baskets for protection. They look unarmed."

"Extortion." Asia aimed her weapon at the tall man. "And who are you protecting us from?"

"¿De quién nos estás protegiendo?" The Latina translated to the men.

"Otros pandillas," the man with the hat responded. "Bakersfield Bandidos y Reyes de Fresno."

"Hombres muy malos," the tall man added.

Asia stepped closer to Xóchitl, pointing her weapon at the man. "Tell them we'll give two baskets. But if they return soon, their boss will hear about it."

Xóchitl conveyed her leader's message. The men's bravado faltered against two armed adversaries. The tall young man stared nervously toward the path. "Bien," he spat in anger. A vein throbbed in his temple, and he glared at Asia resentfully. "Apurarse."

Asia mirrored his scowl unflinchingly. "I think we understand each other."

"Creo que nos entendemos," Xóchitl clarified.

Suddenly, the two men started backing away from the gate in terror. Asia and Xóchitl exchanged glances. What was scaring the gang members off?

77. Ultimatum

It was 4 PM in Cantua Creek. The sandy trail leading to the Safehouse radiated an almost tangible force, while distant mirages danced teasingly between the dunes. Sweat evaporated before it could bead, leaving only a parched, thirsty sensation in its wake.

Even the breeze, when it stirred, brought no relief. It was a blast of furnace-like air that sapped the energy from everything in its path. The world felt slow and sluggish, weighed down by the sheer intensity of the Sun's unyielding glare.

Outside the Safehouse. Asia and Xóchitl stared anxiously at two Latinos standing outside the gate. In the distance, they heard hooves pounding in the dirt. Two horses appeared, growing louder with each stride.

Dust swirled in their wake, a gritty curtain that signaled their aggressive approach.

The SCB men at the fence exchanged panicked looks. Their hands twitched with switchblades, which appeared to be their only weapons. Their attention was focused on the approaching horses, and they completely ignored the women.

The horsemen closed the distance rapidly, their faces shadowed under wide-brimmed hats. A burly man with a jagged scar slicing through his cheek yanked back on his reins, bringing his horse to a skidding halt before the fence. He slid off his saddle and drew a handgun. The other thinner man followed suit, dismounting in a fluid motion.

Without hesitation, the burly man pointed his handgun at the SCB men. He sneered at his adversaries, tilting his head upward. His gun barrel glinted ominously in the harsh sunlight, and a single shot cracked the quietude, sharp and merciless.

The tall man's precious life was punched right out of his body, and he crumpled to the ground. His accomplice barely had time to react before another shot rang out. His expression was frozen in mid-air, a combination of surprise and despair. He joined his companion in the dirt.

The peace that followed was punctuated by neighs and snorts. The gunman tottered leisurely and went through the dead men's pockets. He found an old-fashioned watch and dangled it mockingly before kicking the lifeless body. The dull thud of boot against flesh carried a chilling finality.

Satisfied, he turned around with his cold stare fixed on the gate. He aimed his pistol at the rusted chain. The shot shattered the hush, and the thick chain exploded in a spray of metal fragments.

With a grunt, he pushed the gate open. Its hinges groaned and swung wide. He gestured to his associate, who followed him without a word inside the fence.

"Stop right there." Asia hurled her command at the gunmen, sharp and forceful. She squatted behind a boulder near the gate opposite Xóchitl, who hid behind a bush. Asia's shotgun protruded from her cover, pointing at the killer.

The brawny man halted, and his lips curled in disdain. "Which woman dares give a man an order?" His Southern accent dripped with arrogance, each word dawdling, savoring his perceived superiority.

Asia's chest heaved with controlled breaths, and she tightened her grip on her weapon. "What's your business here?" Her body shook in anger and defiance.

The man threw his head back and laughed, a harsh, guttural sound that echoed through the empty yard. He took a step closer, glinting with malice. "Fresno Kings owns this turf now. If you're hiding more spic scum... Look, you're white like us. Don't be a traitor."

His attention skimmed to the outside, where the two bodies lay motionless. His grin widened, proud of the carnage.

Asia's heartbeat accelerated. "I'm alone," she rejoined firmly. "The men are outside the fence, as you can see. I prevented them from entering."

"What these beaners doing here?" the killer fumed.

"Demanding protection," Asia answered quickly. "Two baskets of food. Said they owned the territory."

"No, Kings do." The killer pointed to the two lifeless forms. "These dead wetbacks is your warning." A smirk played on his lips. "Now you'll give us double. Four baskets a week. I'll be back to collect, sweetie, with more Kings. We've got military hardware. Don't think that shotgun will save you."

The gunman turned sharply on his heel and walked off the property with his companion in tow. They mounted their animals and rode off, leaving a cloud of dust in their wake.

Asia's chest tightened, and her blood pounded in her ears. "Xóchitl, stay alert." She sprinted to the house and threw open the door in haste. "Everyone, pack now. The gang is coming back. We leave in fifteen minutes." She gazed at the cowering women while she struggled to contain her dread.

Elon's lips quivered, and tears poured from his face. "No, no, I don't wanna go." He banged his fist against the wall and screamed.

Marge hugged her son and stroked his hair. "It's not safe here. We must leave, okay?" She forced a reassuring smile, and a tear slipped down her cheek.

The group packed hurriedly and rushed out of the Safehouse. They hiked rapidly away from Cantua Creek, heading North for an hour. Asia paced at the back of the line. She examined the vista behind for horsemen. Nzinga carefully erased their tracks and there were no signs of pursuit.

She wondered if she had made the right choice to leave the Safehouse. She called for a break and consulted the Crones. They approved of her decision-making. It was getting dark, and they decided to camp. The night passed without incident.

The following morning, Asia addressed the climate refugees before they departed camp. She stood tall, shoulders squared, hands clasped firmly before her.

"Thanks for your cooperation yesterday," she began. "I know you wanted to remain at the Safehouse, but that meant clashing with gangs. Our goal is North, not staying there." She sparkled with purpose and explained plans for their next steps.

"We'll find another safe place to rest again soon," she reassured. "We've made it here, near Fresno, 250 miles from Santa Barbara. But we have to keep moving." Her gaze was unwavering, and her attitude exuded confidence.

"Our final destination is Humbolt, Northern California," she continued. "It's double the distance we've covered so far. But we can do it. We've already hiked a third of the way there. If we keep pushing, we'll get there by summer." The Crones and Mothers clapped softly to show their agreement.

"Being positive is critical for staying alive," Asia continued. Her hands moved in small, encouraging gestures like she was physically pulling them together.

"If we act like one, we'll survive this passage together."
She glanced at Zaniya. "Please give us a blessing."

The Crone stood tall and blissfully recited her offering to Gaia. "The Earth Goddess does not shout, She whispers. She reminds us that every stone in our path is a step toward our destiny. The Goddess does not fear the fall, for She knows She will rise again, and so will you."

"Daughters," Zaniya continued, "you're a force of nature. Be unyielding like the cliffs, fierce like the wind, and timeless like the sky-kissed peaks. Do not fear the climb, for the Goddess walks beside you. Step forward in faith. Every challenge is a step toward greatness. Keep climbing. Blessed be."

78. What Matters

The midday radiance hung in the cloudless atmosphere, punishing and uncompromising. The thermometer hovered at an unbearable 131°F (55°C), and the air shimmered in waves, distorting the horizon. Warmth pressed against the skin like a heavy, suffocating blanket, and each breath seared the lungs with dry intensity.

The foothills of the Sierra Nevada mountains stood still, lifeless. The heat had drained the hill's energy and life, leaving behind only the oppressive, all-consuming glare of the medium-sized Star.

The Safehouse, a sanctuary for four days, was a three-day memory. They had invited Katherine to join them on their Northern trek, but she had to wait for her partner. The infant Ida was sick overnight, and they stopped for a day to help her recover.

They started walking on the morning of their 44th day away from the Santa Barbara shelter. They were 15 miles North of Cantua Creek, tracking parallel to Route 33 again. Asia's preferred route restarted after it stopped on Route 5, ten miles South. It continued off Highway 5, going Northwest past Yosemite and Modesto to end near Stockton, 125 miles away.

Lisa's face flushed red as she stared at the cloudless sky. "It's like the Sun is trying to burn us alive," she muttered. Her thoughts drifted back to the Safehouse, a place where she felt normal and safe. The brief visit was like a dream, snatched away too soon, leaving her and the others with a sense of loss and longing. Everyone felt defeated and miserable.

The caravan moved sluggishly across the endless expanse of dusty ground. Nzinga wiped the sweat from her cheek and glanced at Asia. "How much farther until we rest?" She was trying to conserve energy. She and Asia were at the back of the line, while Lian and Xóchitl led up front.

"We can't stop now," Asia insisted, shaking her head tiredly. "The heat will only intensify later. We must keep moving, no matter what."

Nzinga felt a pang of frustration gnawing at her resolve. She was used to being in control, but in the stark wilderness, there was no map, no guide, only survival. "I hope there's something out there worth finding," she muttered, more to herself than to Asia.

Asia caught the doubt in Nzinga's words. "There must be. If not, we'll make it ourselves." Her dogged optimism resulted from her family's tragic history and honor of their sacrifice.

The pair trudged in secrecy, their shadows short and flat across the broken plain. Around them, the scenery was a bleak tableau of despair. Jagged rocks jutted out of the ground like the bones of some ancient, long-dead beast. The twisted remains of cactus trees, stripped of life and limb, stood like creepy sentinels guarding a graveyard of extinct species.

Nzinga felt frustrated and depressed. The trek in the endless desert seemed pointless, like a road to nowhere. "I can't stop thinking about the past," she muttered. "We've lost so much. Some had everything, husbands, children, relatives, homes, and possessions. All that matters."

"Think positively," Asia counseled. "About what you gained. This female collective, for example."

Nzinga sighed. "What happened to the girls in the shelter we left behind?"

Asia kept her focus forward. "Who knows? Most likely, they haven't done well. The root of suffering is attachment. Worrying about them is pointless. All that matters is surviving this moment."

Nzinga adjusted her backpack. "I worry about what's in store for us in the weeks ahead."

Asia's gaze remained transfixed on the skyline, and her jaw was set. "Do not dwell on the past or dream of the future. Remain in the here and now."

"What if this desert never ends?" Nzinga grunted.

Asia breathed deeply. "The Badlands starts in the South, in Mexico. Maybe it extends all the way down to the bottom of the tropics. That's why we're heading North, away from the hottest part of the Planet." She motioned ahead. "It has to end somewhere."

"Yes, but where?" Nzinga was not persuaded. "This desert stretches East for thousands of miles. It includes California, Arizona, New Mexico, and Texas. Even Louisiana is drying up."

Asia shook her head. "Those States are all South. We're heading deeper into the temperate, cooler, and wetter zone."

Her words did little to ease the ache in Nzinga's heart. "The natural ecosystem may improve, but the social environment is not. It's becoming worse. Stephen, Miller, Jeffery, the dead men at the Safehouse. Our path is littered with bodies." She slumped and groaned with heavy thoughts.

Asia understood her friend's despair and her fears of finding racism in Humboldt. Yet, worrying about the future was a danger to Nzinga's psyche. She had to cheer her up somehow.

She straightened up and said hoarsely, "Men run the Globe. They've ruined nature and civilization, and all women now suffer the consequences." She breathed deeply. "But we're adapting. We're resisting, trying to make the best of a bad situation. That's what matters."

Nzinga was quiet. She knew Asia was right, but her memories of better times were a constant companion, haunting her every step. It all seemed like a science fiction fantasy on another Planet.

"What's the alternative?" Asia stared toward the distant dunes. "Torture by necrophiliac scavengers, enslavement by racist militias, trafficked by gangs and pedos, and a quicker death if we're lucky?" Her eyes met Nzinga's, offering a glimmer of possibility amidst the man-made devastation.

Up front, Lian listened half-heartedly to Xóchitl's Zen tale. "This one is called The Heavy Rock and the Flowing River, Bhikkhuni," the Latina started. "There was once a young woman named Raicho who lived in a quiet village surrounded by mountains. For years, she carried a deep sadness within her, a weight so heavy that it felt like a great stone pressing on her chest. No matter what she did, she could not lift it."

Lian became attentive. She felt like Raicho.

"One day, an Elder Bhikkhuni was passing through the village," Xóchitl continued. "She noticed Raicho sitting by the river with a troubled face. The monk sat beside her and asked, 'Young woman, why do you look so burdened?' Raicho moaned and said, 'I carry a sadness that will not leave me. It follows me wherever I go, and I do not know how to escape it.'"

"I get her." Lian sighed. "We're Sisters in sorrow."

The storyteller continued, "The monk picked up a large rock and handed it to Raicho. 'Hold this,' she said. Raicho took the rock and frowned. 'It's heavy.' The Bhikkhuni nodded. 'Now, walk into the river and let go of it.' Confused, Raicho waded into the cool water and released the rock. It sank quickly to the riverbed, disappearing beneath the flowing current."

Xóchitl paused, and her companion grew impatient. "What happens next?" Lian nudged her.

The Chicana grinned. She liked it when the lead guard became absorbed in her tales. "The Bhikkhuni asked the woman, 'Is the river burdened by the rock?' Raicho watched the water swirl and dance around where the stone had vanished. 'No,' she said. 'The river keeps flowing as if nothing had happened.'"

"The monk smiled," Xóchitl resumed. "She said, 'Your sadness is like that rock. You have been carrying it for so long you have forgotten you can set it down. Let your heart be like a river, flowing, embracing, but never holding on too tightly.' Raicho stood in the river for a long time, feeling the water rush around her. Her heart felt a little lighter for the first time in years."

"That sounds too simple." Lian grimaced. "My rock is stuck inside me. I can't simply drop it."

The Latina concluded, "And from that day forward, whenever she felt the weight returning, Raicho would go to the river, let the water flow around her hands, and remember that she could always let go."

"What does it mean?" Lian appeared confused.

"Many things," Xóchitl shrugged. "The flowing river symbolizes life, change, and impermanence. Just as the river continues to flow regardless of what falls in, life moves forward, and joyful and painful emotions come and go. Letting go of the rock signifies the act of acceptance and release. It doesn't mean forgetting or denying pain but rather recognizing that we don't have to be controlled by it."

The pair walked silently. Lian contemplated her sorrows and was inspired to let them go.

79. Trinket

It was late afternoon on their 44th day of travel, and the 37 female nomads dug a trench on the side of a hill. The air was filled with the pleasant aroma of spring, but the ambiance in camp was strained. They were still shaken by the encounter with gangs at the Safehouse and intensely missed the female refuge.

Onawa and Gloria were sitting away from the others, trying to console their daughters, Cha'Kwaina and Sasha. The two friends were visibly shaken, their young hearts torn between desire and fairness. Their emotions were a turbulent sea, with waves of distress and hope crashing against each other.

While walking, they found a trinket, a small gold chain with a cross. Each girl claimed the trinket and their spat escalated into a full-blown quarrel.

Cha'Kwaina clutched the pendant. "It's mine. It was lying in the dirt, and I picked it up."

Sasha glared at her friend. "I saw it first, then showed it to you. So, it's rightfully mine."

Cha'Kwaina was unmoved. "You didn't want it. And I really like it because it reminds me of home."

Sasha was unhappy. "I don't understand why everything is always taken from me."

The girls' argument distressed their Mothers. Onawa and Gloria had always been close, but the stress of their excursion and the trinket dispute tested their relationship.

Onawa recognized her daughter's attachment to the trinket was a longing for connection to the past and a sense of normalcy amidst the turmoil. Still, she advised submission, "Cha-Cha, why don't you let Sasha have it? She's your best friend."

Cha'Kwaina grew more distressed. "But Mom, it's not fair. She's always taking things from me."

Gloria knew her daughter's frustration was driven by feeling overshadowed by the other girls. She wanted to be respected and was distraught over her perception of unfairness. "Cha-Cha, please give it to Sasha."

The Mothers' involvement in the conflict made the girls even more upset.

Onawa placed a comforting hand on her daughter's shoulder. "I know it's hard. I'm here for you." She looked at Gloria. "Cha-Cha's been through a lot today. She needs this small win."

Gloria was equally defensive. "Sasha's feelings matter too. We need to teach fairness. Otherwise, our alliance will not last long." She sat next to her child and gently rubbed her back. "I know it feels unfair. We will find a way to make this right."

Onawa offered a compromise. "How about Cha-Cha keeps the chain, and Sasha takes the cross?"

Gloria was desperate for the conflict to end. "That sounds fair." She looked at Sasha. "We'll make a nice lace for the cross, so you'll also have a necklace."

The teary-eyed girls agreed to the compromise. A sense of relief washed over them, like a gentle breeze after a storm, as they realized their friendship was more precious than any trinket.

Sasha smiled weakly. "I guess that's fair, Cha."

Cha'Kwaina relaxed. "We can exchange chains."

The antagonism dissipated, and the Mothers worked to fashion a multicolored string for Sasha's cross. The creative process soothed their frayed nerves and the rift that had opened between them.

After the friction subsided, Zenobia approached the squad and spoke delicately. "Sometime, da stuff we be arguin' bout seem big, right there an then. But dey only shadows of de bigger cruise we on. We gotta remember dat de strength of we togetherness is way mo' vital than any lil' trinket or belongin'."

The foursome was relieved by the Crone's presence. She continued, "In me kulcha, dey's ah good tale 'bout dis. Wan long time ago, in ah village by da sea, dey was ah weaver named Anika. Everybody know she fuh she cloths. Dey wasn't only pretty, but dey told stories too. Chiefs an merchants always be hittin' she up, offerin' gold, jewels, an all kinds ah treasure fuh she wuk."

The girls and their Mothers listened intently to the Firekeeper. "Even wid all dat fame, Anika she life simple, livin' inna small hut. She didn't have much, only she loom, she tools, an wan colorful cloth dat hung ova she bed. Dat wuz wan real masterpiece dat she mek when she wuz young."

"Wish I could see it." Sasha sighed.

The Crone paused for a drink, then continued. "One day, wan rich merchant rolled up pun she wid ah big deal. He wants de cloth ova she bed real bad, an wuz willin' to pay she wan whole chest ah gold fuh it. But Anika, she only smile an seh, 'No, thank yuh.' De man wuz pushy. 'But why not?' he asked she. 'Yuh can buy wan big house wid alla dat gold. Yuh can live easy for da rest ah yuh life.'"

The foursome was fully captivated by the tale. The storyteller carried on, "Anika point to da ocean out she window. 'Yuh see dem waves? Dey crash an dey pull back all day, neva holdin' onto dey shore. Life only like dat. Stuff come an go, just like da tide.' Da merchant walk away, confuse."

"She refused?" Cha'Kwaina gasped. "Not good."

"Den wan night, wan nasty storm hit da village," Zenobia resumed. "Anika hut gat battered down by da wind, an by da mornin, everythin' she own wuz gone, she loom, tools, even she beloved cloth. Da village wuz sorry fuh she, an offered she wan place to stay, an food. But Anika only smile an say, 'Da storm ain't tek nothin' from me dat wasn't already slippin' thru me fingers.'"

"Wow, that's some storm," Sasha remarked.

The Crone nodded and kept going, "Anika borro wan loom an she gat back to wuk. Day by day, thread by thread, she makin' wan new cloth even betta dan da wan she loss: brighter, wid mo colors, scenes from da sea, da storm, an da calm afta. When she done, alla da village come fuh check it out. Dey couldna believe how well she art show da ups an downs of life."

"Would she sell or keep it?" Cha'Kwaina wondered.

Zenobia shrugged and kept on, "'How yuh can weave somethin' so beautiful afta losin' everythin'?' one man ask she. Anika smiled, 'Da wind may tek what wuz mine, but it can't tek me mind, what me create. Me art, me spirit, dey ain't merely stuff. Dey ah wan part ah me, like da wind is part ah da sky.'"

The storyteller spread her arms wide to indicate the wind and sky. "Suh, Anika keep on weavin', unbothered by alla dat she loss, showin' everywan dat da real treasure in dis life is da things we can't hold on to, only we can share, like love an joy. Dis story remine me dat material stuff are only passin', an da true wealth lies inna creativity, toughness, an spirit dat can't be taken away from we."

"Wish I'd that kind of spirit," Sasha sighed.

The Firekeeper concluded. "Yuh chain an cross, is kinda like dat cloth. It ain't gats no real power by its lonesome self. It is wha yuh do wid it, how yuh let it shape yuh friendship, that fill it wid meanin'. By sharin' dat piece ah jewelry, it turn into wan sign of yuh care an connection, not somethin' dat split yuh apart."

The foursome exchanged thoughtful glances. The weight of the Crone's words sunk in, and their frustrations over the trinket faded. The two girls hugged, and their Mothers held hands. With the dispute over, the necklaces became shared possessions that symbolized their collective spirit, creativity, and harmony.

80. Tumbleweed

It was 1 PM in the Sierra foothills on day 45 of the climate migrants' evacuation from Santa Barbara. The nuclear fusion Star blazed mercilessly overhead, heating the atmosphere to 129°F (54°C). It turned the dry forest into a vast, sizzling rotisserie with thirty-eight asylum seekers on the skewers. The entire sky seemed to descend, pressing down upon the heads and bodies of the survivors like a waffle iron.

The caravan was 35 miles West of Fresno, traveling parallel to Route 33, slowly progressing North, five days after leaving Cantua Creek. Waves of warmth emanated from the parched landscape, distorting the perspective and making the hills flutter like sheets on a clothesline. The women marched through the parched scenery apprehensively.

Their footsteps reverberated in the stillness like a discordant shuffle in a grave requiem for themselves. Their solemn procession was utterly unappreciated and unacknowledged by the somber audience of sand, stone, and dry brush. Nonetheless, the line staggered on in the Sun-baked oven with unwavering fortitude. Each member drew courage from mutual will to survive.

Out of nowhere, a gust blew in from the East, cutting through the oppressive quiet. The scorching blast carried the scent of dry dust and seared sand. In the distance, the wind sent dead tumbleweeds rolling across the powered valley floor.

Lian trotted closer to Asia and Nzinga. She squinted into the expanse, struggling to make sense of the unusual movement. The clumps congregated in the distance and coalesced into massive spheres of thorns. "Are those balls getting closer?" She was trying to convince herself that she was not imagining things.

Asia strained to see against the harsh sunlight, seeking to grasp what was happening. She stopped in her tracks, and her hand reached instinctively for her scarf to wrap her nose from the forceful wind. Her expression darkened.

A few tumbleweeds carted frontward, kicking up dust in their wake. The wind intensified, whipping up the dried, four-foot plant clusters into dozens of bouncing thorny globes that hurtled toward them. It was mesmerizing and terrifying.

"They're coming right at us." Asia's voice cut through the air. "Circle to protect the children." The women looked up and saw a wall of brambles racing toward them, threatening to tear through anything in their path.

Nzinga scrutinized the landscape for any sign of cover, but there was none.

Marge grew pale. She staggered, clutching for Lisa's arm. "Circling wouldn't help much." She shuddered in terror. "What do we do?"

Asia switched between the incoming threat and the line. She stared at the children desperately. "Lie on the ground." She waved her hand downward.

The girls dropped flat onto the scorching ground and pressed their bodies into the dust.

Asia pulled a few girls under her, crouching to protect them with her body. Regardless of her own peril, she wanted to shield the children. It was part of her duty and care.

Sweat-drenched and grimacing, Lian scrambled on her belly across the scorching sand to the middle of the line. The searing pain of heat was less tormenting than the agony she imagined from the thorns. Every instinct screamed at her to proceed faster, to help the stragglers to get down.

She stared at the disorganized women. She needed to inspire them to form a barrier, an idea she got from Asia's actions. "Form a wall. Stay on all fours. Tighten your packs and use them to deflect the blows."

Nzinga helped the women tighten their packs. Lian and Xóchitl took positions on the Eastern edge of the line, bracing themselves for the onslaught. They gripped each other, hunched under their packs.

A wall of women covered the vulnerable center of the line. They united quickly whenever facing danger. The harsh wind whipped around them, causing their clothes to flap wildly.

"Here they come," Asia shouted. "Cover your face and hold tight." The women covered their eyes and heard a deafening roar of howling sand and snapping twigs.

The wooden projectiles raced like buffaloes in a stampede. One of the giant balls slammed into the ground near the line, exploding into a spray of sharp brambles. The pyrotechnic was thick with dust and debris, making it almost impossible to see.

Each blow from the weeds sent shivers through their bodies. Their knees buckled, and they constantly readjusted their stances to maintain balance.

Cha'Kwaina's heart pounded. Her pupils burned from the gale's stinging abrasives. A bramble shattered, and a sharp piece grazed her arm. She bit back a cry, focusing instead on the safety of the other girls. "Hold on," she called with all her strength.

The fierce gust drove the hazardous tumbleweeds onward. Most bundles zipped by, but a few landed perilously close, scattering sharp thorns that sliced through the women's backpacks.

Lisa trembled with fear, clinging to Marge's arm. "I'm scared, Momma." Marge squeezed her daughter's hand. "It'll pass soon," she promised. "Hold on."

The windstorm lasted ten minutes, but it seemed much longer. The survivors held their ground, and the balls bounced off their backpacks without cutting them. The minutes dragged by, and abruptly, the gale decreased. The thorny onslaught slowed to a crawl and stopped. The air became still again.

The line was littered with debris. The flat terrain seemed like a battlefield of bramble warriors defeated by the Wind Goddess. The women rose to their feet and stared at the vanishing balls. A loud cheer arose from the line as the girls celebrated. They all felt a sense of good fortune in surviving the onslaught.

Asia shook her body and pack. "Is everyone okay?"

The women and girls checked themselves and each other for injuries and damage. There were a few cuts and scrapes, and some backpacks were ripped, but nothing severe.

They all felt immense relief and allowed themselves a moment of celebration amidst the devastation. Surviving the treacherous windstorm allowed them to drop the rock, to shake off the deep malaise they suffered after fleeing the Safehouse.

The girls laughed in delight and chanted, "Thank you, Apsara. All praise to the Goddess." Their voices swelled, and they reached for the sky in a spontaneous dance of gratitude.

The women caught the teens' infectious spirit. They joined in the dance and synchronized. Their voices blended with the girls' chants, and the harmonious chorus echoed through the Badlands. The Crones danced and shared knowing smiles.

Zaniya's features sparked. "Good work, everyone. We're learning to work with Gaia." The Crone beamed and touched her chest. "The Goddess does not descend for fear of heights. She rises, knowing the World is Hers to embrace. She is the keeper of ancient secrets, woven in the roots of every tree, echoed in every valley. Her knowledge is as timeless as the hills She guards."

The Crone bowed to gently touch the ground and continued her benediction. "Daughters, with each passing storm, we grow wiser. With each day, we grow more seasoned. May our spirit remain unbreakable, and may our resolve remain unwavering. Blessed be." Her gleam swept over the dancing female forms with an expression of profound satisfaction and joy.

81. Trench

It was a quiet twilight in Central California. The climate nomads gathered in camp after the tumultuous attack by rogue weeds. The atmosphere clung to an agonizing 108°F (42°C), and the ground was still uncomfortably warm. The low humidity offered a bit of reprieve in the windless atmosphere.

The girls sat waiting for Cronetime. The trench was bathed in greyish shadows under the moonless sky. A small fire and the glimmer of distant Stars broke the approaching darkness. The flight from the Safehouse had stretched to five days, and their faces were etched with fatigue. But even with the heat and weariness from the long trek, they had a remarkable spirit.

Zenobia sat beside the fire, deftly stitching a torn pocket in a child's backpack. "We gettin' close to da Sierras," she murmured.

"Can't wait." Onawa sat beside her, carefully mending a hole in one of the girls' jackets. Her gaze flickered to the distant hills Northeast of the camp.

Lian and Xóchitl sat at the camp's perimeter, gazing at Venus emerging from the darkening sky.

"Es muy bueno. Is it time for a Zen tale, Bhikkhuni?" Xóchitl raised an eyebrow. Her companion consented. She came to appreciate the transformative power of storytelling in lifting her spirit and fostering a positive outlook.

"This one is called The Woman Who Built a Bridge," Xóchitl started. "In a quiet mountain village, a young woman named Keiko sought the wisdom of an Elder monk with a simple question: 'Why are women considered less than men? Apparently, we're rivers meant only to flow under the bridges built by others.'"

Lian grinned. She was loving Xóchitl's tale already.

"The Bhikkhuni smiled and led Keiko to a narrow gorge," the Latina carried on. "A stream wound its way through the rocks below. 'Here.' The female Monk handed Keiko a bundle of wood and rope, 'Build your bridge.' The woman hesitated. 'But I came for wisdom, not labor,' she said. 'Labor is wisdom,' the Bhikkhuni replied and walked away."

"Interesting so far," Lian smiled encouragingly.

"For days, Keiko labored under the Sun and Stars," Xóchitl kept on. "She cut the wood, tied the ropes, and carefully tested each piece. Villagers passed by, offering advice and sometimes ridicule. 'Why waste your time?' a man laughed. 'No one will use your stupid bridge to nowhere.'"

"Men." Lian spat. "So entirely predictable and ridiculous."

"But Keiko continued on for weeks," Xóchitl resumed. "With every knot and beam, she felt her doubts unravel. A month later, the bridge was finished. It stood strong and steady. The villagers gathered, curious about her work. Some crossed the bridge, laughing in delight. Others still doubted its purpose. The Bhikkhuni returned and sat at the crossing. 'Now, what have you learned?' she asked Keiko."

Lian held her breath in suspense, but her friend remained quiet. "I know," Lian offered. "She realized that men are utterly selfish and clueless. And women should always ignore them."

Xóchitl laughed. "Keiko gushed. 'I learned I am not a river meant to flow beneath anyone's bridge. I am the architect of my path, and others may cross if they choose.' The Bhikkhuni bowed deeply. 'Wisdom flows from action. And now, your bridge inspires others to build their own.'"

"Same thing," Lian blurted. "She just said it nicer."

"From that day on," Xóchitl resumed, "Keiko taught anyone who asked how to build a bridge of wood, stone, and spirit. The village grew richer not in wealth, but in shared strength and self-reliance. Her bridge boosted female pride and confidence."

The two guards stared at Venus, contemplating the relevance of the tale to the female collective.

"The power to change perceptions and realities lies in our hands," Xóchitl reflected.

Lian agreed. "And in the structures we choose to build for ourselves and others to follow."

She glanced at the girls nestled in the trench. She was grateful they were becoming adjusted to the rhythm of their nomadic way of living. Like a bird's melody in the wilderness, their giggles and excited chats permeated the camp. It was a comforting counterpoint to the harsh repose of the desert.

The girls sat and waved their arms in a dance, moving like one. Their bonds were forged through shared travails and triumphs, and the silent realization that friendships were all they had in their dangerous social domain.

Cha'Kwaina's face lit up as she recounted an Apsara tale she had heard during Cronetime. She leaned forward, sparkling with the memory. "And then the Apsara got up to dance," she said dramatically. "It was so beautiful that the entire village gathered to watch." Her arms arched dynamically through the air, mimicking the fluid motions of a ballerina.

"I am an Apsara," Ma'at said, waving her arms.

Sitting by the fire, the Crones, the respected elders and leaders of the community, peered at the girls with pride. "They're so resilient," Mary marveled. Her eyelids glistened with unshed tears. "They've seen more than children should, but they still find joy."

"Dey de reason we fightin' fuh." Zenobia's shine lingered on the children. "Fuh dey tomorrow."

The other Crones concurred. They were glad to be guardians of the girls, the keepers of their health and spirits. In the quiet moments under the blanket of

Stars, they found solace in simple acts, like watching their wards play and act out female-centered stories.

Venus continued her migration down to Earth, patiently waiting for the Moon to rise. The Crones sat watching the cosmic dance while the Mothers and women exchanged experiences from the day.

The mood in the camp was tranquil. In the dark warmth of the dugout, the community of climate evacuees found a fleeting peace, a moment of joy from the harsh realities of their exodus. Their bond and shared experiences brought them comfort and warmth amid immense challenges.

82. Kuan-Yin's Cronetime

The daytime heat was gone from the Sierra foothills, followed by cooler temperatures at dusk. A slight breeze carried the scent of pine blossoms. It was Cronetime, a sacred part of the climate refugees' daily routine. The flames snapped faintly, casting dancing ghosts on the narrow walls of the trench.

The girls' faces alighted in anticipation. Hehewuti held the board that signified the storyteller's turn and gave it to Kuan-Yin. The Crone was dressed in a loose fitting *Hanfu* made up of a thin-cuffed, knee-length tunic with a sash, and a small, ankle-length skirt. She loved the Chinese traditional outfit which was created around 1600 BC during the Shang Dynasty.

"Each of you is part of the Earth Goddess," Kuan-Yin opened. "And you're protected by Her."

She paused, letting her words sink in, before raising her arms to the Milky Way. The beads on her gown caught the light, making her seem almost otherworldly. "Think about the Planets," she invited, pointing to positions of each World in the night sky.

The children trailed her fingers, although some Planets were not visible. In their minds, they see the magnificent celestial bodies glowing from the energy of the Sun.

"You learned about Venus from our esteemed Elder Zaniya." Kuan-Yin gleamed at her students. "Venus is Earth's Sister Goddess. Now, we'll discuss the Outer Planets that serve as Gaia's protectors, the Triple Goddesses."

"The Earth's guardians," Lisa shouted.

The Crone nodded. "The three guardians are Mars, Jupiter, and Saturn. Mars, with her fierce strength and unwavering courage. Jupiter, with her wisdom and guiding light. And Saturn, the keeper of time and the protector of life's cycles."

Kuan-Yin spread her arms wide. "Jupiter and Saturn are giants. Over 1,000 Earths can fit into Jupiter, and more than 700 in Saturn. Massive comets that could destroy Earth become moons of Jupiter and Saturn. Jupiter has 95 Moons. Saturn has her rings and an amazing 274 Moons. These objects are trapped in the outer Solar System and cannot hurt us."

The Crone did a tight Cosmic dance. Her two arms represented Jupiter and Saturn. She spun them around, shielding her body like the Earth. "This pair are Gaia's greatest protectors, celestial guardians for all time." She stopped and pointed to a reddish spot in the sky. "And Mars protects us from a belt of smaller rocks between Earth and Jupiter."

"The Asteroid Belt." Sasha beamed.

"The Triple Goddesses keep us safe," Cha'Kwaina added, then chanted, "Thank you, Apsaras, all praise to the three Goddesses." The girls joined the chant and celebrated for a minute.

Kuan-Yin held up her hands and picked up her lesson. "The Sun is the Mother Goddess of all eight planets. She welcomes the Earth Goddess in a cycle each day - dawn, dusk, and dawn again."

Ma'at was puzzled. "What does triple mean?"

"Birth, death, and rebirth." Kuan-Yin spread her arms wide. "This endless cycle is the way of the Sun Goddess and the entire Universe. The ancients used the Triple Goddesses to show that life is eternal, and the human body is merely one stage."

The children were reflective. They gazed at the Stars in honor, like they were protectors.

Kuan-Yin shook her head. "Men have forsaken the Triple Goddesses. So, they fear death. And out of fear and envy, they destroy life." She paused and continued, "But those who honor the Goddess do not dwell on death. Our focus is birth, life, and rebirth."

Karol was awed. "Are they watching over us now?"

Kuan-Yin's eyes twinkled. "Yes, always. The Triple Goddesses guard the Earth like we protect each other. Every night, they remind us that we are never alone, even in the darkest times."

"How?" Elon shrugged. "We can't see them?"

Kuan-Yin waved her arms. "Protection isn't always something we see. It's in the air we breathe, the ground beneath our feet, and the water that cools our thirst. It's in the strength of community, the wisdom passed down by Elders, and the courage you show daily."

The fire popped several times, punctuating her words. The children were thoughtful, absorbing the profound meaning of the Crone's message.

Cha'Kwaina, ever the romantic, spoke up. "How can we honor the Triple Goddesses?"

Kuan-Yin glanced over the group. "We honor them by simply loving ourselves. Each of you has their spirits within. When you show kindness, you reflect Jupiter's wisdom. When you stand up for what's right, you channel Mars' strength. And when you care for each other, you honor Saturn's protection."

Lisa held up her hand. "So, we're all connected to the Triple Goddesses?"

Kuan-Yin nodded. "We're connected to the Stars above and the Earth below through the love we share. The Goddesses live through us. We worship them by doing our best, fulfilling ourselves."

The girls felt grounded and empowered. They started the evening with playful dancing, which developed into a deep connection between Apsara stories, the Outer Planets, and each other.

"It all makes sense now," Sasha beamed.

Kuan-Yin shined. "You're the guardians of this World, but you're not alone." She swept over the circle, ensuring her message was reaching everyone. "The Goddesses are in you. Gaia knows that even the tallest mountains were once mere dust. They became shaped over time by pressure, persistence, and the tranquil power of endurance."

The trench was silent. The weight of Kuan-Yin's words hung in the air. Then, on cue, the children began to sing a song honoring the Triple Goddesses. Their faces glowed with awe and resolve.

The Crones watched with quiet pride. Kuan-Yin's Cronetime was profound and enduring. It left a lasting impression that would carry the female collective forward through the challenges ahead.

83. Night Watch

After an all-day trek with a tumbleweed attack, the female evacuees succumbed to exhaustion at 8 PM. They lay burrowed in the trench, bodies tangled in sleep. The night was tranquil, and a cloudless sky granted the Moon to cast its silvery glow over the rolling panorama. The subdued light bathed the trench and its occupants in an ethereal silhouette.

Lian circled the top of the dugout soundlessly, observing the sleeping forms, ensuring everyone was settled and secure. Their breathing was rhythmic and calm in the cool air, quite distinct from the exertion of flaming breaths earlier.

She was sleepy and tried to stay awake by focusing on motivational thoughts. 'I must stay alert. It's a few more hours until Xóchitl's watch.' Her friend was curled up in her blanket, snoring and hugging her weapon like a pillow.

Above the dugout, shadows danced and shifted with the gentle movement of the night breeze. Lian knew the peaceful scene masked potential dangers lurking in the darkness. She had to stay alert. Her mind raced with thoughts about the previous attacks and possible future threats. She peered into the blackened monotony and mused, 'It's so quiet, almost too quiet.'

She sat at the edge of the camp and took stock of the dim vista. The vast Badlands stretched vaguely before her, punctuated by the occasional distant outline of a jagged rock or a sparse, twisted tree. Her pupils flickered back and forth, surveying for any sign of menace. There was no movement.

Notwithstanding the stillness, she felt the weight of accountability heavily on her shoulders. The safety of the fragile commune depended on her vigilance. She thought about the bond she shared with them, their trust in her, and the strength they drew from each other. The sense of female self-reliance, community, and empowerment was strong and growing. And after a month and a half on the road, the girls were safe.

She shifted her position, trying to find a way to sit that would keep her awake and alert. Her muscles ached from the day's exertions, and her eyeballs felt swollen and painful. Her body was depleted, but she pushed it aside and focused on surveillance. 'My determination is shining through my weariness.'

It was a constant battle, the need for rest versus the burden to defend. She had to win the internal struggle between her body's need for rest and her mind's stubbornness to persevere and stay up. Being alert was not just a duty but a part of her commitment to the safety of the female cooperative. She had to stay awake, no matter what the cost.

She took a deep breath and scanned the visible perimeter. 'I will not fail my Sisters. Not after all they've endured.' She saw nothing. Her determination to protect her Sisters was unwavering, and she was grateful for the Moon's company in her solitary vigil. She noticed the Milky Way's magnificence extending across the night sky. It was acutely different from the bleak wilderness inside and outside her thoughts.

A faint noise, like the crunching of dry leaves, interrupted the stillness. The rhythmic sound was barely audible, but it was enough to set her on high alert. 'What was that? It sounded unnatural.' Her hand instinctively reached for her weapon. Her senses sharpened, and she searched the shadows for any movement. Nothing.

The resonance emanated upwind from the North. Her pulse raced as she leaned toward the source of the noise. 'Could it be scavengers?' Not likely, since they rarely hunted at night.

'Pedos?' She took a short breath. They can attack anytime. She held her breath and strained to hear any additional noise. Nothing.

'Miners and migrants rarely wander in the dark,' she considered. Gangs do attack during nighttime, but they usually travel on horses. The disturbance was not loud like hooves.

Minutes passed, and it remained quiet. 'Probably a night fox digging for insects,' she mused. The wide range of potential sources and implications added to her tension.

The Moon continued its steady climb, casting serene light over the stationary hills. The moonshine's stable, magical lighting differed strikingly from her unsteady suspense.

'I must stay focused.' She stretched her arms and legs and resumed her watch. In the eerie quietude, she knew the night's calm was deceptive. 'I am the spear, the head of the formation.' Her features hardened.

The night stretched on, and she stayed alert but heard nothing. The Earth's satellite continued its slow, leisurely passing over the Stars. Her nocturnal friend was both comforting and troubling. The Moon indicated the fragility of her solitary situation and the courage she required to endure.

84. Tantrum

It was 11 PM in the Sierra foothills. The Moon was near its zenith, a fuzzy ball in the misty sky. Lian was half-asleep on watch and struggled to stay awake. She had another hour to go before being relieved by Xóchitl. The three dozen females slept soundly in the trench. Her bloodshot eyes stared blearily into the hills. All was quiet.

The tranquility of the night was shattered in an instant by a desperate plea. Elon's urgent wail rattled everyone's nerves, jolting them awake.

The boy's scream alarmed Lian and jolted her into action. The racket revealed their position, and she prepared her team to defend the trench. "I got right," she hissed to Xóchitl, training her weapon to the North. Her fellow guard jumped out of her sleeping bag and waved, 'Okay.'

Mary stirred from her sleep with half-opened eyelids. Zenobia sat up beside her, agitated. "What he hollerin' 'bout dis time?" She scowled at the disruption to her deep sleep.

"I wanna snack," Elon's urgent cry reverberated off the trench's walls and traveled far into the silent hills.

His Mother, Marge, was visibly distressed and appeased him with a promise. "Please calm down. If you stop screaming, I'll get you something."

"No, get it now." Elon refused to give up his immediate demand.

Marge's face was a blend of exhaustion and apprehension. The constant battle with her son was wearing her down, and the potential danger of alerting nearby gangs amplified her anxiety.

She tried to remain calm. "Stop it, son, please." Her lips quivered in fear. She tried to reach him through the haze of his tantrum. "The bad men will hear you and come after us. You need to be quiet."

"I'm hungry." Elon was inconsolable. "I don't care." He sobbed and pounded his fists into the trench floor.

The women wanted to support Marge, but there was a delicate balance between offering help and respecting a Mother's authority. The nuanced dance of support and deference added a layer of complexity to their interactions regarding her son.

Zenobia was less reluctant to intervene and crawled over. "My son," she said tenderly. "If yuh keep it down, I'ma hook yuh up wid some sweets, aight?"

The promise of a sweet snack and the Firekeeper's calming presence broke through the child's emotional storm. His sobbing lessened, and his pleas became softer. "My belly. It hurts."

Marge rubbed his belly. "It's okay." She retrieved a couple of desert almonds from her backpack and handed them to him. Zenobia gave him a cactus fruit.

"That's a good boy." Marge's words calmed her son. The boy whimpered and munched hungrily. The camp became quiet, and the women relaxed.

However, the security team was nervous. Asia, Xóchitl, and Nzinga met Lian at the edge of the camp to discuss options. Lian reported hearing noises earlier, which alarmed Asia and Nzinga. The possibility of exposure pressed heavily on their shoulders. The team's responses differed, creating more tension.

Asia's face lined in unease. "We have to leave," she concluded. "If we don't leave, we may see a repeat of the gangs at the Safehouse."

Nzinga concurred. "We're sitting ducks now. We need to find someplace else to hide." She usually aligned with the leader's plan.

Xóchitl recalled the gang encounter with a shudder but remained silent.

"What do you think?" Asia queried Lian.

Lian shook her head. "We've got good defensive position, and visibility is low. We stay put and hide."

"Fleeing is safer," Asia said adamantly.

Lian fumed. Why did the leader ask her opinion if she planned to ignore it? "Well, if we move, we've got to do so ASAP."

Asia raised her thump. "I'll tell the others." She returned to the trench and clasped her hands. "Everyone, gather your things. We leave immediately."

The women gathered their belongings and prepared the children. They were remarkably adaptable, quickly adjusting to the changing circumstances and becoming accustomed to their situation's unpredictability.

Lian paced back and forth, studying the darkness. 'We should be preparing more defenses,' she seethed. She and Xóchitl exchanged a grim glance. Neither thought it was safer to leave.

Lian paced near the trench, apprehension radiating with every step. "Let's go," she hissed. "We can't afford to waste another minute," Xóchitl saw that her friend was extra nervous and more irritable than ever.

The group put their packs on and lined up to leave. Marge tried apologizing to Lian for Elon's behavior, but the guard refused to listen. She turned her back and walked ahead.

Asia followed Lian and grabbed her arm. "What's up with you? Why are you mad at Marge?"

Lian's beams locked onto Asia's. "That boy has to go," she declared, her frustration evident in her tone. "He'll get us all killed."

Asia released Lian's arm. "What are you saying?" She was shocked by the guard's suggestion. "We're Marge's support group. We're her village. If he goes, she goes." She paused, letting her words sink in.

Lian remained unconvinced, and her aggravation increased. "It's either him or all of us," she snapped. "Like the other two, he's pampered, privileged, and out of control. We're just enabling and spoiling him."

The abrasion between the two leaders, Lian and Asia, was tangible. Their conflict was an ongoing bruising battle of wills between Asia's loyalty and Lian's feminist values. Their conflict reverberated through the group, leaving everyone feeling the strain of their opposing beliefs.

Asia's body sunk under Lian's accusation. "We can't kick a Sister out." There was a firmness in her words, a line she refused to cross. "You know that."

Lian's face twisted in anger. Without another word, she turned and headed down the hill. Her silhouette was quickly swallowed by the darkness.

Asia watched the lead guard leave with concern. The choice Lian wanted her to make was too much to handle. The collective was at a crossroads, and how she handled the crisis would determine their future.

She returned to the group and spoke urgently. "We have to leave now." Her attention lingered on Marge and her child. "But we can't make a sound, you understand? Let's go."

Zaniya made a quiet blessing as they prepared to depart. "A mountain does not fear the storm, nor does Gaia, who watches over it. She who walks with the Goddess carries Her wisdom, strength, and unshakable presence. Stand fearless, my Daughters. Blessed be."

The women and children scurried after Asia into the dark, misty night in a daze. They were sleepy and upset but trusted their leader enough to abide by her plans. Xóchitl guarded the rear, and they rushed downhill, following Lian into the eerie darkness.

85. Night Move

It was 11:30 PM and chilly in the Sierra foothills. The climate evacuees stumbled after Lian in the encroaching blackness, exhaustion evident in their slow, faltering steps. It was eerily quiet. The night move unsettled the minor children, and the need to rush strained everyone.

The Moonlight cast a creepy glow across the strange environment of hills and valleys. Lian led the way, squinting into the shadows. She was annoyed and uneasy. Evacuating the camp at night created an unpredictable vulnerability she could not solve.

The misty shadows made it difficult to gauge depth and distance, and she strained to see what lay ahead. 'Are we far enough from the trench yet?' she pondered. 'We need to make it to the next hill and climb. That means twenty more minutes in the dark.' She increased her pace. "Keep moving," she urged the line.

The drowsy women and girls staggered after her. She could hear Elon's whimpering trailing through the uncertain night. He had a snack, but the discomfort of their hasty departure and the difficulty of the night trek left him unsettled.

A coyote's howl broke the stillness. It reminded the group of the night they faced a vicious canine attack. The girls in the middle of the line lurched, and Ma'at lost her balance.

"I got you," Cha'Kwaina said, helping the child. Lisa and Sasha stopped to assist, and the line moved forward.

Xóchitl's heart fluttered. "Slow down ahead," she called. "The line is separating." Her instincts were on high alert for any danger in the vegetation.

The weary band proceeded through the shadows, the weight of their drowsiness pulling at them with every step. Suddenly, an oppressive layer of fog began to roll in, shrouding everything in a dense mist.

In the rear, Marielle, 7, stumbled and fell, clutching her ankle. "My ankle broke," she cried. Xóchitl knelt beside her and examined her leg.

"Ouch, it hurts," Marielle complained.

"It got twisted," Xóchitl said. "It'll feel better in a minute." She helped Marielle to a seated position. The line stretched onward.

The air grew denser, enveloping the collective in a haze. They separated further, with some members far ahead. The visibility dropped again, and the once-clear outlines of women became ghostly shapes.

"Wait up," Xóchitl called. The invading fog turned the unfamiliar landscape into a surreal, shifting panorama of shadows.

"I can't see anyone." Lisa grabbed Cha'Kwaina, terrified.

"We need to catch up," Cha'Kwaina comforted the child. "But don't rush, or you'll trip." She looked to the front, trying to make out movement through the thick cloud. She saw no one. The line was swallowed by an impenetrable curtain of fog.

In the rear, Xóchitl helped Marielle to stand. The child limped on one leg. The guard's beams swept over the flat terrain, but she could hardly see anything. As the dense vapor increased, she became apprehensive.

'This fog is strange,' Xóchitl thought. 'There's not enough vegetation to make it so thick.' She looked up to see if there were clouds in the sky, but it was too dark to discern anything. She began to feel anxious and briefly recalled the Zen tale, The Shadow and the Moon.

One evening, a young nun named Kisagotami sat trembling under the vast sky. The wind whispered through the trees, but all she could hear was the pounding of her own heart. Sensing her distress, a female Monk approached. 'What troubles you, Kisagotami?' she asked gently.

'Bhikkhuni,' Kisagotami confessed, 'I'm scared. Afraid of failure, the unknown, and the darkness that follows me wherever I go.' The Monk pointed to the full Moon above. 'Come, let's take a walk. As they walked, the Moon cast their long shadows onto the ground. The teacher suddenly stopped. 'Try to run from your shadow, Kisagotami.'

Puzzled but obedient, Kisagotami took a few steps forward, then ran. Yet, no matter how fast she moved, her shadow remained. Breathless, she returned to the Bhikkhuni. 'It follows me no matter what I do. The Monk smiled. "Now, turn and face the Moon.'

Kisagotami turned, and in doing so, she saw her shadow shrink behind her, fading from view. 'Fear is like that shadow,' the Monk said. 'When you run, it follows. But when you turn and face the light, it loses its grip on you.

Xóchitl looked up, searching for the Moon. She could not find it. The Moon was hidden behind a wall of thick mist. She held Marielle's hand, and they inched forward.

Just up ahead, from the line's left side, screams suddenly pierced the gloom. The cries were desperate, almost primal, sending tremors down the travelers' spines.

"Help, Mom. They're taking us," a girl's shrill cry reverberated in the darkness.

Panic ensued. One of the Mothers shot her weapon, alarming the guards. "Don't shoot," Xóchitl bellowed. "You'll hit one of us."

"No. Help. Mom." a teen's squeal rang out from the left. "Pedos. Mom." Her holler sent a shiver through the line, amplifying their terror.

Asia's blood pounded in her ears. She turned toward the scream, her breath coming in short, sharp bursts. "Grab each other," she shouted. Her words were swallowed by the miasma. She ran back, grasped three children, and hugged them close.

"Help. Stop. Mom." The penetrating shrieks continued from the left.

"Form a circle," Asia roared, searching the enveloping haze for the screaming girls. A low cloud pressed in from all sides, creating a cocoon of uncertainty and horror. The children in the line bawled in fear, drowning out the retreating yells from the left.

86. Fog

It was 11:30 PM in Central California. The climate caravan was under attack by unknown assailants, but the guards could not respond. It was dark, and the group was enveloped by thick fog. Visibility was almost zero, and Asia had no idea what was happening beyond her reach. Her mind raced, dreading the loss of group members.

Children's screams emanated from the left. "Mom. Help. Stop. No." As the seconds ticked by, the urgency of the situation became more intense. Each passing moment heightened the migrants' fear and desperation. The calls for help shifted from left to right, heading East.

Simone's face turned ashen. "That sounded like Ma'at." The Mother shuddered, her chest pounded, and each beat echoed her terror. The line was filled with confusion and panic.

Greta clung to Asia, shaking uncontrollably. "Please don't let them take me," she bawled.

Asia swallowed hard. She stared into the swirling fog and strained to listen to the retreating shrieks. "Stay together and stop shouting," she shushed. "We need to hear what's happening."

The terrified survivors clustered, and the women tried to calm the girls. The screaming subsided from the line, and they heard distant calls for help. "Stop. Mom. Pedos."

The desperate pleas gradually subsided, leaving an unsettling silence. Asia peered nervously into the haze. Every sound was magnified in the oppressive stillness.

The fog gradually dissipated, and the women regrouped in the center of the line. The waning Moon hung high over the horizon, casting a cold, silver light over the distraught company.

Lian returned from the front, and Asia did a head count. She checked again and discovered four missing girls - Lisa, 11, Ma'at, 12, Cha'Kwaina, 14, and Sasha, 15. A shroud of gloom fell over the line.

The panic-stricken Mothers of the absent children ran after their daughters. They could not go far in the darkness and rejoined the group, frantically seeking their help. Asia stood frozen, and no one knew what to do. The upset children sobbed uncontrollably for their missing friends.

Onawa whimpered in disbelief. Her only child, Cha'Kwaina, was gone. Marge hugged Elon and wept for her daughter, Lisa. Simone was inconsolable over her daughter Ma'at's disappearance. Gloria stared into the sky, speechless and numb from her daughter Sasha's absence.

The loss of four members threatened to devour the hearts and minds of the female survivors. The depth of their loss was unfathomable, and each Mother's heart shattered into a million pieces.

Gloria's soul ached. She felt faint and powerless. She stared at the Moon as though the glowing orb held the answers to her plight. Each breath was a reminder of her missing child. She clenched her fists, and her knuckles were white from straining.

"I'll find you, Sasha," she swore. Her words were more than a vow. They were a lifeline, a beacon of light in her infinite misery.

Asia's face, lit by the Moon's pale light, was streaked with agony. She wiped her tears away and uttered, "We'll find her, Gloria." Her vocal cords wavered like they might shatter. "We wouldn't rest until we get our daughters back." Her promise was a small comfort against the encroaching despair.

The women gathered with the grieving Mothers and hugged. They clung to each other, drawn tighter by their pain. A loud wail revealed the depth of their collective sorrow. Hehewuti spoke through tears, "Finding our daughters is our only priority. Nothing else matters."

As the women embraced, their shared loss seemed a bit lighter. The expanse of indifferent hills encircled them, holding them together. The air was heavy with the scent of the Spring, mingled with a trace of tears shed under the pale Moon. The outline of a lone pine tree stood on the left, a hushed witness to their anguish. Its long arms reached out, offering assurance.

Standing together, sobbing, each woman solemnly promised to traverse any distance and endure any hardship until they reunited with their abducted daughters. Their pledge was a powerful balm against overwhelming gloom. It was a sign of possibility amid immense uncertainty.

Zaniya held her palms open and offered a benediction for the collective and the missing girls. "Dear Gaia, please keep our Daughters safe." She glanced at the grieving Mothers and continued. "Mountains rise through fire and force. So too does the

Goddess, and so too shall you. The path may be steep, but the Goddess is with you. Keep going, for your soul was made for this purpose."

The Crone gazed into the Eastern night. "You're not lost, Daughters. You are merely ascending, just as the mountains have done for eternity. Rise like the hills, weathering storms. Stand tall against the winds of uncertainty, and never let despair sway your indomitable spirit. We're coming for you. Blessed be."

87. Canister

It was 11:45 PM. The Sierra Nevada foothills were serene and soundless, a sharp contrast to the anguish felt by the climate escapees in their midst. The guards circled the area, searching for attackers. The pedos were all gone.

Lian found a warm canister and showed it to the collective. "This is a fog spray. The pedos used this to blind us." The tin can shone brightly under the Moon's glow.

Asia wiped her tears and took the cylinder from Lian. Her fingers traced the warm metal surface. It was labeled "Military-Style Maximum Smoke Grenade."

"The pedos used this camouflage tool to attack us?" Asia was stunned.

Nzinga took the can from Asia and sighed. "I've seen these before. It's a slow-burning, high volume, continuous discharge smoke grenade. It's used in attacks, extraction, and crowd management situations. They emit grey-white smoke for around two minutes."

She felt defeated but continued, "There was over ten minutes of fog. The pedos used several of these, one after another. The smoke hid their movements and confused us while they grabbed the girls."

Lian swore under her breath. "They must have heard Elon shouting. Then tracked us here."

Asia shook her head in disgust. "This fog can is extremely dangerous." It was a cruel tactic, using fog to disorient and blind victims, she thought. The canister was a tool of their oppression, symbolizing what they had to struggle against.

Lian's face tightened, and she paced nervously. "We're wasting time," she snapped. She clenched her fists. "The girls can't be far. We have to go after them now." Her unwavering commitment was a light in the darkness for the suffering Mothers.

Asia shook her head sharply. "No. We need to keep everyone here safe. There could be other pedos lurking." Touching the head of a sobbing girl, Asia took a deep breath. "Besides, we can't go after the pedos, dragging the children with us. What if they have more smoke grenades?"

The pair faced off in the dark. The air was thick with friction, agony, and despair.

Asia glanced at the huddled figures. The aftermath of the attack left a chilling sense of loss and dread. The grieving Mothers were willing to pursue the attacker, but the children were too crushed to move.

Asia glared at Lian. "We've no idea where they're going. Running after pedos in the dead of night is out of the question."

"We know where they're taking the girls," Lian exclaimed. Her expression was an amalgam of single-mindedness and alarm. "They're headed East, probably to Fresno, where they'll get the most for them. If we leave now, we can catch up before they reach the city."

Asia sighed. "I'm sorry, but we're incapable of doing that." Her face was set stubbornly. "Let's sleep on it and devise a plan in the morning."

Lian flashed red in anger, but she focused her mind on the immediate crisis. She had to come up with another plan. "Alright then, we'll split up." Her tone was urgent, and she gripped the straps of her backpack like they were a lifeline. "I'll take Riri and Phoolan and head East. We'll look for traces of the girls."

Asia considered Lian's plan. They had to do something to regain their lost members, and the sooner they acted, the better. A search party would provide a much-needed confidence boost to the severely demoralized collective. And Xóchitl and Nzinga were available in case of further attacks.

Nevertheless, Lian's plan was risky. She would be accompanied by two inexperienced scouts. The trio was not enough to take on pedos or gangs. Yet, she knew that Lian was determined to leave. There was not much she could do to stop her. It was a battle of wills, and she was too devastated to win over the guard. The potential danger of the plan hung heavy in the air, a stark reminder of the high stakes of their mission.

Asia relented to Lian's request, although she remained worried. "Fine. We'll camp up on the right side of that hill." She took a step forward, her face tensing with the weight of her decision. Her beams bore into Lian, and she spoke in a brighter tone. "We'll wait, and you can meet us here."

Her shine lingered on Lian, silently pleading for their safe return. She turned away and started organizing the move to camp.

The Firekeeper leaned close to Lian. Her forehead was crumpled with concern. "Be careful now, Sista. If dey catches yuh, we down by three mo'. We can't handle dat kinna loss." Her fingers gripped the edge of Lian's cloak, her silent plea for their safe return echoing the weight of the potential loss.

Lian nodded. "I'll not lose two more," she promised.

As the three women prepared to head East, Xóchitl grabbed Lian's arm and squeezed gently. "Give a signal if you need our help." She offered a gritty smile and stepped back. "Good luck."

88. Grieving

When the female climate nomads separated, it was close to midnight. Despite the darkness and the vast Sierra foothills, they were determined. The Moon's dim light did little to dispel the foreboding and grief everyone felt, but their spirits remained intact.

Under Lian's leadership, Riri and Phoolan went East, rummaging for their kidnapped Sisters, Lisa, Ma'at, Sasha, and Cha'Kwaina. These girls were not just fellow travelers, but their closest friends and companions. The spirited caravan headed Southwest to set up camp on a nearby hill.

Riri, 19, was five feet seven inches tall and weighed 125 pounds. Phoolan, 16, was five feet three inches tall and weighed 115 pounds. She was close to Sasha and Cha'Kwaina and determined to find them. Lian had trained the two scouts to use various weapons. They were both armed, however, only the lead guard carried a sniper rifle.

The trio scoured the darkness, inspecting the ground and bushes for any sign of their captive Sisters.

Lian stopped and listened but heard nothing. "Look for any sign, footprints, broken branches, ripped clothing, anything. Stay alert for pedos." She pushed on, and her team tailed close.

"Cha-Cha is courageous and clever," Lian whispered. "Sasha is brave and bold. They might leave signs to where they're going." She moved ahead. "They'll put up a struggle, which will slow the pedos down. If we hurry, we'll catch up with the kidnappers."

"How far away is Fresno?" Riri wondered.

"Three days," Lian answered. "We've got plenty of time. But to rescue the girls, we must first track down the pedos' trail."

The trio picked up their pace and walked for half an hour. There were no signs of the missing girls.

Then, Phoolan spotted a glimmer in the grass. She crouched and picked up a gold chain lying on the ground. "I found something." Lian and Riri hurried over, and she held up the chain. "This is Cha-Cha's."

Lian stared at the jewelry. "Good job, Phoolan. You've found their trail." She examined the ground for footprints. "They went this way." The trio continued East with renewed optimism.

The main group trudged along a narrow path toward a hill. They reached the bottom and climbed to the ridge. Asia selected a hidden spot, and the group started preparing their second campsite for the night.

Asia and Nzinga, the group's pillars, organized supplies, while Xóchitl and Daria set traps and alarms. The Crones collected wood for the campfire, and the Mothers worked on the trench. Each member, young and old, had a specific task, fostering a sense of unity and distracting everyone from their shared misery. Despite individual grief, each member felt like an integral part of a larger whole.

When the group settled into the trench, it was close to 2:00 AM. The atmosphere in the camp was strained as the collective could not rest. They kept thinking about the four missing girls.

Asia addressed the heartbroken assembly. "You're all worried about the girls, I know, but we mustn't despair. We have to trust them and Lian. Maybe they'll escape or be rescued. They're tough and will survive the pedos. We must be patient."

The Crones nodded in agreement. The Mothers looked up at their leader with a glimmer of optimism. The children were pale but mustered faint smiles.

Asia straightened her posture and continued, "This is a good lookout spot. We can monitor the area in all directions. We'll see if the search party sends a distress signal, and we'll keep an eye out for pedos."

Her gaze swept over the caravan, sympathizing with the worn-out faces. "Even though we haven't slept much, we need to stay alert and look for signs. Xóchitl, organize a watch schedule and take the first shift. We can't afford to be caught off guard again. Everyone, get some rest."

Asia's words injected trust in her leadership. It reassured the group and instilled confidence in the missing girls' ability to endure captivity.

The sky above was a deep indigo, speckled with distant Stars. The occasional howl of a wild animal or rustle of leaves in the wind reminded the women of the forest's ever-present dangers.

Zaniya opened her arms, beseeching the land for courage. "Gaia's spirit is like stone shaped by wind and rain. She is the breath of the highlands, the soul of the cliffs, and the heart of the ancient stones. The Goddess teaches us resilience. No matter how strong the storm, She remains rooted in Her power. She is steadfast, transformed through time and challenge, yet never diminished."

She gazed at the group warmly. "Like these sacred mountains, Daughters, you are carved by time, yet unbreakable in spirit. Like the towering peaks, you've risen with grace and resilience above all obstacles. Our strength comes from being together. We've faced dangers before, and we'll face this one too. Listen to our leader, and we'll be safe. May the Goddess be with us. Blessed be."

Everyone in the trench was physically and emotionally exhausted. They cuddled each other and fell asleep.

89. Guilt

It was 2:15 AM in the foothills of Sierra Nevada. It was quiet and peaceful. The air was chilly, with a slight Easterly breeze. The climate evacuees napped in the dugout while Asia and Xóchitl guarded the camp.

Nzinga could not sleep. She was too sad and tormented to rest. Since the kidnapping, she had been unusually quiet. She took a moment to speak to Asia alone. "What do you think will happen to the four girls?" She frowned, and her voice broke.

Asia was pragmatic. "Likely, they'll be treated well until they're traded. The better their condition, the more the pedos will gain from the trade."

"I see," Nzinga nodded slowly. She was tearful and on the verge of breaking down. She felt responsible for the girls' capture. She was distressed but thought she could not reveal her feelings to anyone. Asia and the other women needed her to be strong, and she did not want them to know how devastated she was.

She kept thinking that the assault and kidnapping was her fault. She had spent years in the militia and knew fog grenades were commonplace. She blamed herself for not realizing they would eventually be used to attack the collective.

She had used the devices many times and criticized herself for not informing Asia and the guards about the danger. And during the pedos' assault, she regretted not warning everyone that the fog was unnatural. From the first moment she saw the sudden thick mist, she should have known it was a smoke attack.

She experienced overwhelming guilt. The psychological burden was unbearable, and she even considered running away from the others to punish herself. Her body shook in grief. "I should've known it was smoke grenades, not a mist." She sobbed and held on to her friend's arm for support.

Asia squeezed her hand and said nothing. She, too, felt guilty and wanted to cry. But emotion was a luxury she could not spare. She was tired and had to focus her mind on the task at hand. "We're here now," she said gently. "We play the cards we have. It's all we can do."

Nzinga sobbed. She tried to slow her racing thoughts and regain self-control. She knew Asia was right. Kidnapping was a reality of their daily lives. There was no use in second-guessing the past. Or was there a point in doing so? "What can we learn from this mistake?" she wondered aloud.

Asia shrugged. She had already considered this question. "They caught us off guard because we were moving at night. Next time, we will stay and fight. Like we did in the first attack."

Nzinga heaved heavily. "I should've warned you about fog cans long time ago."

Asia shook her head. "We can't think of everything, dear. Somethings will slip through the cracks." She hugged her friend and counseled, "It's not your mistake, Z. The men are at fault. No one blames you for anything. So don't beat yourself up over this."

Nzinga sobbed quietly, and Asia reassured her. "Even if you did warn me beforehand, I might have forgotten, or it would not have made a difference. The pedos' attack was lightning fast."

"It was," Nzinga agreed.

Asia smiled weakly. "My dear Z. Tomorrow's a new day with new challenges. We need you. I need you. Now more than ever."

"I'm sorry." Nzinga nodded. Once again, her friend was thinking correctly. She had to recover and become strong again for Asia and everyone.

"You're fine," Asia assured. "You'll feel better in the morning after some rest."

Nzinga was utterly drained. "I'll get some sleep." She headed into the trench to nap.

Asia sighed. She wished she could cuddle with her partner. It would do them both some good. But too much was going on, and she had to stay alert. She approached Xóchitl at the perimeter of the camp.

The guard announced, "Aisha and Daria will relieve us in three hours."

"Thank you for staying up." Asia looked at the guard with concern. "I know you're worried about Lian." She paused momentarily, then added, "She and the scouts will be fine."

Xóchitl's lips pressed into a thin smile. "She's a warrior. It's them pedos who should be worried." Her answer filled the leader with pride and confidence.

Asia touched the Latina's shoulder. "You'll be a great lead guard until she returns."

Xóchitl met Asia's beams. "As you are," she said humbly.

"Thank you." Asia hugged Xóchitl, and they sat watching over the surroundings. It was calm and quiet. The suspense remained, but she felt renewed purpose and unity. She would keep the collective safe and wait for Lian's return. One way or another, she was going to get her daughters back.

The female survivors dozed in the trench. The firelight flickered across their faces and cast long shadows on the walls. They dreamed that Lian, Riri, and Phoolan would return soon with the missing girls, Cha'Kwaina, Sasha, Lisa, and Ma'at.

End of Part I